Cleaning Out A Snake Pit

Before the Wheels Fall Off

Earl Snort

Barlow Adams Series Book VI

TotalRecall Publications, Inc.
1103 Middlecreek
Friendswood, Texas 77546
281-992-3131 Tel
www.totalrecallpress.com

ISBN: 978-1-64883-2772
UPC: 6-43977-62772-8

Library of Congress Control Number:

FIRST EDITION
1   2   3   4   5   6   7   8   9   10

Not a speck of this is true. It's all a pack of lies.

DEDICATION

This book is dedicated to the stunning teenage girl in the red dress with blond hair, green eyes, and creamy smooth skin. She was the most captivating female I had ever seen. I first saw her from across the room. I became mesmerized at once. She looked at me, so now that I had been caught staring, I walked over to her. Some of the rest is a blur, but I got a date for that night. The odyssey began. That was 54 years ago. We've been married for 52 years and are still going strong.

Muchas Gracias

To JFW, a military compadre for 55 years, for proofing the draft of this book and making corrections on my American and Mexican grammar. Any mistakes belong solely to me.

Also Dedicated

To the heroes encapsulated in this brief vignette by LTC David Grossman, U.S. Army (Retired). The complete essay is lengthy, but well worth reading. You know who you are. He wrote:

"If you have no capacity for violence then you are a healthy productive citizen: a sheep. If you have a capacity for violence and no empathy for your fellow citizens, then you have defined an aggressive sociopath - a wolf. But what if you have a capacity for violence, and a deep love for your fellow citizens? Then you are a sheepdog, a warrior, someone who is walking the hero's path."

Worth Remembering

"Veni. Vidi. Vici." - Julius Caesar's after-action report written to the Senate in Rome, after he won the Battle of Zela against Pharnaces II of Pontus, in 47 BC in modern day Turkey. The Roman army was greatly outnumbered.

Smugglers Blues

"There's trouble on the street tonight. I can feel it in my bones . . . . I'm sorry it went down like this, and someone had to lose. It's the nature of the business. It's the smuggler's blues." Written by Glenn Frey and Jack Tempchin and performed by Glenn Frey.

About the Book

It's 1974. Deputy Barlow Adams is on patrol in Quayle County, Texas, late at night. He initiates a traffic stop on a speeding truck. It screeches to a halt, and both occupants bail out, flourishing firearms. A gunfight ensues. One is killed and the other is wounded. A search of the truck reveals 60 kilograms of high-quality marijuana known as Oaxacan Highland Gold, or OHG for short. This leads to Deputies Slick Oldman and Barlow Adams being temporarily assigned to a DEA Task Force in El Paso. The stakes are high and the drug smugglers are deadly.

LIST OF MAJOR CHARACTERS

MAJOR CHARACTERS - QUAYLE COUNTY
Sheriff Solomon "Sheriff Sol" Pratt
Chief Deputy Sheriff Alexander "Chief Alex" Snodgrass
Deputy Sheriff Clarence "Slick" Oldman
Deputy Sheriff Barlow Adams - Protagonist
Sarah Mae Baker Adams - Barlow's wife

VAL VERDE COUNTY, TEXAS
Sheriff Will Shive

EL PASO COUNTY, TEXAS
Sheriff Adrian Brady
Captain Stan Howard
Lieutenant Fred Wendell
Sergeant Julio Elias

DRUG ENFORCEMENT ADMINISTRATION
Special Agent in Charge Ralph Eaton
Special Agent Carmine Valenzuela

PRIMARY VILLAINS
Pedro Ibarra
Raphael "Chico" Salazar
Pepe Aguilar
Igor Sampson
Geraldo Flores
Bruno Cruz
Conrad Turnipseed

PROLOGUE

Spring Buck Up In Arlo, Texas

Monday, March 22, 1965

It was 6:45 on a cold, dark, and windy evening in the Texas panhandle. Grandma Bea had just finished washing the supper dishes. Barlow was drying and putting them away. Grandma asked, "Barlow, did you forget something today?"

"I can't think of anything."

"How was school?"

"It was fine."

"Hmmm. According to the school calendar, today is report card day. What did you do with yours?"

"Oh, that. It's in my English book. I plum forgot all about it."

"Guess it's a good thing I didn't. Dishes are done. Why don't you go fetch it and bring it to me?"

Barlow sighed. He walked slowly back to his room and pulled his report card out of his English book. He took it to the parlor, where Grandma had already taken her seat for the evening in her favorite rocker. He waited for her to put on her spectacles before he reluctantly handed it to her. Then he sat on the couch and waited for the axe to fall.

"Hmmm. Let me see. What have we got here? First period - Biology - B. Second period - English II - A. Third period - Latin II - B. Fourth period - Study Hall - A in Deportment. Fifth period - Civics - A. Sixth period - Geometry - D.

"Hmmm. Let's look at Geometry a little bit closer. First term - D. Second term - C. Third term - D. Fourth term - C. Fifth term - D.

"That only leaves one more term, Sweetie, 'til end of the year and final grades. Nothing changes, and you'll receive As in English and Civics. B in Latin. Got a chance for an A in Biology if you make an A sixth term. Then we have Geometry. Geometry's looking real bad. Even if you make a C this term, you could still wind up with a D for the year. Supposing you did manage to pull your grade up to a B, still the best you can hope for is a C for the year. Is that what you want?"

"No ma'am."

"What are you going to do about it then?"

"Grandma, Geometry's really hard. I don't get it. I understood Algebra but I don't understand this. Besides, Mr. Whitman grades hard. Never has a curve. Several kids are flunking for the year. Not kidding. I'm lucky to have what I got. Only one person has an A in his class and that's Sheila Gooch, and she makes straight As. Never had a B since the sixth grade."

"So that's it, huh? Gonna give up. Roll over. Take a D like it's *The Red Badge of Courage* and you're Stephen Crane."

"I don't want to but I may have to."

"Barlow, this world is full of quitters, but Adamses are not a part of them. Tomorrow, you stay after class and talk to Mr. Whitman. Ask him what you can do to pull up your grade, and then do it! Apply yourself like you never have before, just like it's deer hunting or baseball. I mean it! I'm gonna ask you what he said when you come home. If I don't like your answer, then I'll drive over to the school and ask him myself. You've never, ever had a D on a final grade report, and you won't like what's coming your way if you get one this year. Understand?"

"Yes, ma'am."

"Barlow, anything in this world worth having takes hard work, effort, perseverance. You have to earn it yourself. There are no free lunches. Nobody gives it to you, not even for your good looks. You stand on your own two feet. Then you can be proud of yourself and what you've accomplished, even if it's just a C in Geometry. You're the finest grandson an old woman could ever have. Your momma and daddy would be proud of you and what you've accomplished since they passed away. Make them proud.

Make me proud. Most importantly, make yourself proud. Will you do that?"

"Yes, ma'am."

"Good. I know you can do better. She pulled out a fountain pen from her apron pocket. She wrote *Beatrice Mae Adams* and the date on the line below her last four signatures. Here, I signed your report card. Now study hard. Give it your best effort. Do not let Mr. Euclid get the better of you. Mr. Whitman, either!"

"Yes, ma'am."

Chapter 1

RAFAEL "CHICO" SALAZAR

1938 - To Present (1974)

Rafael "Chico" Salazar was born in 1938 in El Paso to Juan and María Salazar (née Ruiz). Both were immigrants from Ciudad Juárez, Mexico, back in the day when nobody was paying much attention to illegal immigration. All you had to do was catch a ride or walk across the border. In their case, they hitched a ride on a produce truck. They helped the farmer offload his wares. When he left for home, they stayed, carrying everything they owned in four pillowcases.

They rented a small, two-bedroom, adobe house on Hope Street in a working-class Mexican barrio. Juan found work right away as a pump jockey, and later as a mechanic at the Sinclair service station a block from their home. It was a one-man operation, owned by an older, portly, bald-headed Anglo named Otis Stevenson. Juan was his only employee.

The station had two pumps - one for regular and the other for hi-test, otherwise known as ethyl - back in the day when the pumps were activated manually (pump jockey muscle-power) and regular gas sold for 19.4 cents per gallon. Most of Mr. Stevenson's income was generated by fixing flats, changing the oil, replacing points, spark plugs, and blown fuses, selling or recharging batteries, changing bulbs, headlamps, and taillights, replacing fan belts, as well as performing any other necessary repair. They did it all except for bodywork. Mr. Stevenson was a kind man and a compassionate employer.

Juan and María had three children - Angel, Rafael, and

Isabella, all of whom were born in El Paso. Angel was born in 1930, and Isabella was born in 1940.

Angel hated school. He loved helping out (for free or maybe for a 6-1/2 ounce, cold bottle of Coca-Cola) at the gas station. He learned basic auto mechanics at his father's knee. He quit school upon completion of the eighth grade at age 16. He convinced his papa to sign for him when he turned 17 to enlist in the Army. World War II was over, and America was still the Land of the Free and Home of the Brave. If you had any doubts, all you had to do was ask Juan or María Salazar or any of their kids. They'd set you straight in their broken English. However, unbeknownst to nearly everyone in America, the Korean War was just around the corner.

Angel completed an 18-week basic training course [BCT] at Ford Ord, Washington. The Army hadn't instituted advanced individual training [AIT] in those days. Angel was so proud, and so were his mama and his papa. His first posting was at Fort Hood, Texas, near Killeen, halfway across the state from El Paso. He was assigned to the Transportation Corps, where he was a deuce-and-a-half [2-1/2 ton] truck driver. He did a tour in Korea and one in Vietnam. By 1970, with 23 years of unblemished service, he was a platoon sergeant [Sergeant First Class] in a truck company, in Fort Polk, Louisiana. Angel said he wasn't quitting the Army until it killed him or he completed 30 years of service, whichever came first. He was married to the Army, and to a sweet woman named Mia, whom he met in Killeen, just off post from Fort Hood. He was also the papa of three boys, all chips off the old block.

Isabella was ten years behind Angel, and two behind Chico. She was an Honor Roll student throughout high school. She graduated in 1958. Then she married Filipe Bolivar, who was employed as a milkman for the Borden Company, whose iconic Elsie the Cow advertisements made the company a household name. Filipe and Isabella had four kids.

Chico was eight years behind Angel. In 1956, he was the first in his family to graduate from high school. He was also a big kid. By age 17, he stood six feet tall, and tipped the scales at 175 pounds of pure muscle. He was enthralled with boxing. He joined a Golden Gloves boxing club in his neighborhood at age 12. He advanced in all the weight classes from flyweight, featherweight, lightweight, welterweight, middle weight, light heavyweight, to heavyweight as he grew bigger and stronger. He was accomplished in boxing with oodles of potential, and many, many amateur wins (73-6). He had never fought professionally although that was his goal.

This is why. Nearly everyone in the barrio played the numbers. It was a simple game and only cost a dime. Nearly every bodega sold chances. The way it worked, a bettor would turn in a slip to his bookie, usually a bodega owner, with any three numbers he desired, from 0 to 9. You could bet the same number, such as 333, if you chose. The winning number was the last three digits of the gross amount wagered that day at a specified major horse track. (Think Churchill Downs, Home of the Kentucky Derby, as an example. The tracks changed whenever the specified track closed for the season.) As such, the winning number was nearly impossible to manipulate, plus it was easily confirmed on the following day's racing sheet which was readily available throughout the nation. The low price of the bet, and the near impossibility for anyone to cheat, is why it was so popular.

Simply stated, if the specified track accepted $78,210 in gross wagers on the day of the bet, the winning number would be 210. The payout was 600 to 1 for anyone betting the winning combination. Ergo, a winning ten-cent bet would collect $60. Of course, it was possible that more than one person could have the same winning number, but not very often. Even if they did, each winner still collected his 600 percent.

Numbers was a massive cash cow to the underworld which

controlled it, especially in the poorer neighborhoods. Nearly everyone could afford to take a chance, and they did. Losing didn't break the family bank, and winning was three week's wages for most people.

Two weeks after Chico graduated from high school, he took a stroll down to the corner bodega to lay down a bet for himself and his papa. He had done this many times in the past. Nobody was too young to place a bet so long as his papa allowed it.

It was mid-morning when he entered the store. Mr. García was standing behind the counter next to the cash register. A thuggy-looking Anglo was also behind the counter, shouting at Mr. García, and shoving his finger deep into Mr. García's chest. No one else was present. The thug threatened to break Mr. García's arm if he didn't pay up by Thursday. The thug suddenly realized Chico was standing there watching his every move and listening to his every word. He shouted, "What are you looking at punk? You want some of this? Get outta here before I break your arm just for kicks!"

Mr. García, with fright clearly showing across his face, looked at Chico and said softly, "He's right, kid. Go on home. Come back later when I ain't so busy."

Chico had known Mr. García all his life. Chico respected him greatly. Mr. García knew his name and all there was to know about him and his family. Therefore, Chico deduced that Mr. García was trying to protect him from the thug by not calling him by name.

Chico left the store, and stepped twenty feet back into the adjacent alleyway. He decided to wait until after the thug left. Then he would go back to check on Mr. García.

A few minutes later, the thug left. He stepped into the alley to light a smoke. He noticed Chico standing there. His eyes lit up like he saw the pot of gold at the end of a rainbow. He glanced down and saw a broken two-by-four about four feet long, laying next to the wall. He picked it up, tapped it against the palm of his left hand, and said, "This is your unlucky day, punk. I warned you. Now you're gonna get the ass whipping Señor Alonzo García deserves."

The thug approached Chico slowly, taking mighty practice swings. He looked like an ugly, overweight, washed up, minor league, baseball player wearing a beige, sweat-soaked cowboy hat, cheap, brown, pinstripe suit with sweat rings under his armpits, bright yellow and green striped, food-stained necktie, scuffed working man's clodhoppers, and a bad haircut.

At first, Chico considered that he might have to duke it out with the thug. So be it. He was prepared, even though he had never fought a man so old; however, he was not ready to face an enraged ruffian viciously swinging a two-by-four. Fist fights were seldom fatal. A thrashing with a two-by-four probably would be.

Chico backed up several steps, keeping his eyes focused on his tormentor. He eased his switchblade knife out of his hip pocket. He flicked it open. "Click!" This was his warning, like a hissing cat or a rattling snake or a pawing bull.

The mob enforcer fixated on the knife and slammed on his brakes about six feet short. He needed time to consider his next move. (Thinking was not one of his strong suits, nor had he been hired to think.) A long, pregnant minute passed. Then he blurted out, "Well, whaddaya know? Another greaser with a blade. Just for that, I'm not gonna just tune you up. No siree! Now you're a dead man, greaser! Get ready to meet your Maker!" Then he charged, mayhem scrawled all across his ugly puss.

He landed a glancing blow with the two-by-four on the left side of Chico's ducking head, notching a gash, and causing blood to course into his left eye. At the same time, Chico swiped his knife-blade across the thug's jugular vein. The slash was five inches long and two inches deep. Blood gushed from his throat like Niagara Falls. The thug collapsed on the ground like a deflated balloon. He shuddered twice, foul-smelling excrement easing out of his voided bowels. The look on his face was one of utter disbelief. Then he expired, shaking hands with the devil. He bled out in a puddle of bright crimson blood nearly four feet in diameter.

Chico looked up. There was no one else around. Nobody witnessed this savage attack on him! He walked back to the bodega and exclaimed, "Mr. García, that guy who was just in here tried to kill me with a two-by-four! Instead, I killed him. Could you call my papa and the cops?"

Mr. García cried out, "Oh, Mother of God! Let me see what you've done! You may have just killed me, too. That guy, Conrad Goetz, is a made man in the El Paso Mafia."

They stepped outside into the alley. Nothing had changed in the minute Chico had been gone. Mr. García said, "Chico, I'll wait here so nothing gets moved. You go back in and call the cops. Then call your papa. Then come back out here. We'll wait together."

Chico made both calls. His papa beat the police to the scene. His papa asked, "Chico, where did you get that switchblade? You know they're illegal!"

Chico responded, "I bought it from a guy in school. Papa, you've got your eyes closed. It's saved me from at least two beatings from the gang kids, except I never had to cut anyone before. Without this knife, I would've been the one bleeding out here, and this gangster would be in the wind without a care in the world."

"Son, this guy is an Anglo, gangster or not. The system already has its mind made up. You don't know it yet, but you're already on your way to prison. Oh, Mother of God! You'll never get your shot at being a professional boxer now! Your life is over!"

"Papa, he attacked me! I was just defending myself! You should be happy I'm alive!"

"Son, wake up! I know that and I am thankful! They're going

to call this murder and blame it all on you! Give me the knife now. I'll turn it over to the cops. I don't want to give them an excuse to shoot you."

Chico handed over the knife. Moments later a marked unit arrived with two patrolmen. Chico told them exactly what had transpired. His papa surrendered the bloody switchblade to the older cop, named Durwood Murphy, whom he knew and respected. Officer Murphy said, "So sorry, kid, but you're going to jail for possession of an illegal switchblade knife. No way around it. That's just the way it is. Turn around so Officer Smithers can put the handcuffs on you."

Smithers cuffed him and put him in the back seat of the well-used and poorly maintained police cruiser, behind the steel mesh shield. In the meantime, Officer Murphy radioed in the dead body. He requested detectives, the paddy wagon, and a hearse. Then he and Officer Smithers cracked the windows, exited the car, locked, and shut the doors. It was already 90 degrees outside. Chico thought he would die of heat exhaustion before the paddy wagon arrived. When it did, Chico was whisked off to the county jail posthaste, where he was examined by the jail nurse and treated for the laceration on his forehead. Then he was lodged by himself in a holding cell.

Hours later, Detectives Armstrong and Bell escorted him to an interview room. Chico told them exactly what had taken place, just like he had done for the patrolmen. The detectives wanted to know if Chico could write. He said he could. They passed him a yellow notepad and a pencil, and told him to write down exactly what he had just told them. He did. They read it and were satisfied with his statement.

When it was all over, Detective Armstrong said, "Chico, we both believe you that this was self-defense. The guy you waxed, Conrad Goetz, is a bad actor, in fact, the worst. Everyone knows him downtown. They call him Cementhead because he's thick between the ears. He never learns from his mistakes, and he's made some doozies. No telling how many times he's been picked up. I know he's done time in the joint at least twice. Nobody in El Paso, except for his boss, is the least bit sorry he's gone. The thing is though, he's connected. He has juice. His boss is a major donor to the election campaigns of several city and county officials, to include the district attorney and at least two sitting circuit court judges.

"Right now, you got two strikes against you. The first is that switchblade knife. A pocketknife coulda cut him just as bad, and you wouldn't have lost the presumption of innocence. The second is the DA. Then if you draw the wrong judge, that'll be strike three. They'll send you away for at least 20 years, no questions asked.

"We all know you ain't got any money. That means you'll get a court-appointed attorney. Some are really good. Some are really bad, and others are in between. We hope you get a really good one, because the deck is stacked against you. It has nothing to do with you being a Mexican either. Don't think it does. It has everything to do with who you know, and neither you nor your sweet old papa know anybody who counts.

"We're both truly sorry this happened to you. We've watched you box. You're real good. Fast. Powerful. Light on your feet. Most definitely professional talent. We both wish you the best, but it'll take a miracle from God for you to stay out of prison.

"Good luck. We both want you to know there's no hard feelings from us or the two patrolmen who arrested you. If it was up to us, the city would give you a medal and a thousand dollar reward for exterminating that lowlife, but it ain't up to us. We got no say. Sorry, kid."

After they left, Chico began to weep silently. This was all so unfair!

It didn't take long. Judge Armand Potter, a well-known lackey within the corrupt political circles, did exactly what Detective Armstrong said he would do. Before pounding his gavel like he was trying to smash marbles into little glass shards, the rheumy Judge Potter with his bulbous, red-veined, alcohol-saturated nose, and red, watery eyes, sentenced Chico to 20 years at hard labor for manslaughter. He remanded Chico to the Texas State Penitentiary in Huntsville, nearly as far across the state as you could get from El Paso, where all the really bad boys did their time. Chico served 15 years before he was finally released on parole.

Life was extremely hard in Huntsville. The only law inside the bars was the natural law of survival of the fittest. Take your choice: fight, become a bitch, or die. Chico quickly became a hard man. He earned a masters degree in crime with a minor in mayhem during his tenure, learning from the masters of deceit, murder, assault, burglary, auto theft, robbery, arson, extortion, forgery, bunco, and trafficking in contraband. He stayed far away from the sex offenders. All the while, he learned how to make alliances; how to sniff out a snitch, and what to do when he did; how to protect himself and what was his from the predators; how to street fight; how to gouge out eyes; how to kill without being caught; how to serve time in the hole for minor infractions; and what it was like to be respected and feared by all the other inmates. Chico was no longer the kind, simple soul he had been when they sent him up the river. By the time he was released from prison, he was a stone-cold killer without a smidgen of remorse.

In the interim, Chico's papa had passed away at age 65, just like his boss, Mr. Stevenson, before him.

Chico's mama was living on her deceased husband's minuscule, Social Security old age retirement benefits check. She had moved in with Isabella and Filipe and their four kids, a son-in-law, and two grandkids in their five-room house.

Angel was still serving in the Army, living with his family in post housing in Fort Polk, Louisiana.

The bottom line was, Chico had nobody and nowhere in law-abiding Texas to return to once he was released on parole. He was on his own, just like he was the moment he entered those prison walls. That being said, he had made a number of useful contacts while he was in stir. He knew no righteous citizen would ever hire him, at least not at a living wage. He would have to live by his wits, just like he did inside. The die had been cast for him 15 years ago. His new livelihood would be in the criminal arena. He would survive and he would prosper, or he would die. C'est la vie. Qué será, será, except it wasn't really quite that bleak. Chico already had a job waiting for him.

The cousin of a former cellmate who was still doing 25 years for murder, and who was also from El Paso, had an opening for a gang enforcer. He wanted to beef up the muscle in his cannabis marketing enterprise. Pick up new territory and with it, new clients. Some of his competitors were already unhappy with what could only be considered his poaching. That's because "they were all plowing the same field".

El Jefe was concerned about having loads hijacked; "corporate" sabotage (as in a competitor calling in an anonymous tip to the cops after planting some contraband on his premises); as well as efforts to suborn his employees (by offering them a better deal for spying on him). Any of these nefarious deeds could result in the collapse of his entire house of cards. Of course, it went without saying that the penalty for disloyalty was beyond severe. It would be excruciatingly painful, and downright gruesome for the weak of heart who happened to discover the body. Everyone in the game knew that.

El Jefe needed someone with Chico's specific skillset to monitor operations and handle pest control. Pedro Ibarra had been able to maintain cover for his primary cash cow in the cannabis trade because he owned a legitimate business called Pedro's Auto Repair Shop, and the shop did very well financially. It was located at the intersection of Hope Street and 16th Avenue. Ironically, it was only three blocks from the house where Chico grew up. Pedro nominally employed Chico as a mechanic. In fact, he already was a skilled mechanic, but he was never asked to turn a wrench. He had much bigger responsibilities, and as such, he was afforded a wide berth by all the other employees. Mr. Ibarra did not employ any dummies. Everyone in his employ could recognize a stone-cold killer when they saw one.

Chico's nominal occupation as a wrench kept his parole officer satisfied with respect to a parolee's requirement to maintain gainful employment and to stay away from the company of known felons, of which El Jefe was not. In fact, he had never been arrested for anything. Nada. Pedro wasn't an honest man, but he was a smart cookie.

What more could Chico ask for? This job was right up his alley, and the pay was more than just good. It was fabulous.

Chapter 2

A First Class Goat Rope

Saturday, March 9, 1974

Saturday's shift started out for Deputy Sheriff Barlow Adams with a whimper, but it ended with a backfire, similar to explosive flatulence in a beauty pageant.

He reported for duty at 2345 hours (11:45) Friday night. He pushed off Deputy Kirk Shoemaker, who commented that the full moon must be affecting everyone. The world had gone batshit crazy. He'd written three moving traffic citations, two of which were for drag racing; responded to one domestic dispute call (easily resolved); made a prowler run at Widow Carson's house; and capped off the evening with a dispatch to the Dry Gulch Saloon where two regulars, Lamar Winston and Dwayne Wilbur "DW" Preston, both of whom were pie-eyed, got in a fistfight out in the parking lot.

Kirk relayed the story of the last incident. "Heaven's sake, both of those knuckleheads work for the Santa Fe Railway, on the same rotation, on the same train, and have for many years. Normally, they're tighter than a pair of engorged ticks on a dog's balls. As you know, they're like Pete and Repeat. You see one. You see the other.

"I know you've met Lamar's kid, Kerry. Tall, skinny, blond. Nice kid. He's a sophomore this year. He's also a sub on our basketball team. So tonight, Kerry blew the second of a one-and-one free throw twelve seconds before the end of the game. Brewster County picked off the rebound, which sealed our 54-53 loss to them in the regional playoffs. Everyone was sorely disappointed.

"After the game, Lamar and DW went to the Dry Gulch Saloon to drown their sorrows. DW just couldn't let it go. Oh, no. He said the loss was all Kerry's fault. That did it. That was all she wrote. Like a flash of lightning, it was the Hatfields and McCoys all over again, except this time in Texas. Lamar and DW were jawing at each other, getting louder and louder, wouldn't settle down, so Old Man Spellman tossed 'em out on their ears.

"Well, they started trading blows soon as they got out in the parking lot. They kicked up such a ruckus that Elmer [Old Man Spellman] finally called the jail. I was just around the corner, so I rolled up in a matter of seconds. Before I could even unass the cruiser, they were down on the ground, wrestling in the gravel, almost completely underneath Elmer's rusty old '56 Dodge pickup truck. You know, the one that's all jacked up. Not the '59 that he refers to as his new truck.

"Anyway, I pulled Lamar out by his legs and shook him like a dog. Told him to settle down or I'd break his jaw. By then, DW had crawled out under his own steam, so I had him sit down by the truck, six feet or so from where I had Lamar. Both were the worse for wear, all scuffed up with black eyes, bloody noses, and the like.

"I shined my flashlight right in their faces, half blinding 'em. I looked at 'em both hard in the eye so they knew I meant business. Then I asked, "Who's gonna 'fess up first before I lock up both you jaybirds for disturbing the peace and maybe for drunk and disorderly? Take your choice."

"It's crickets for a full minute. It was like they both turned stone deaf.

Finally, DW says, "It's my fault, Kirk. I started it when I blamed Kerry for us losing the ballgame. I know he done the best he could and that he's more sorrier about it than me. Go ahead and lock me up and let Lamar go. It ain't his fault."

"So I look over at Lamar.

"That what you want, Lamar? You want me to haul DW off

to jail?"

"No way. Absolutely not. That ain't right. I clocked him first. Lock me up and let him go. Besides, deep down, I know he didn't really mean what he said."

"Anyway, I made 'em apologize to each other, shake hands, and told 'em to go straight home. I gave 'em both a verbal warning. I probably shouldn't 'ave done that because they were both wasted. Lucky they didn't run into anybody on the way home. Then I'd 'ave been in the soup. Anyway, I doubt you'll have any further trouble with either of them tonight. Besides, I was doing you a solid. I didn't figure you'd really want to spend your night babysitting those two jaybirds."

Barlow smiled and replied, "Kirk, you're a great American. One of a kind. The very best. I sincerely appreciate your compassion as well as your thoughtfulness. Just to ease your mind though, if I hear about either one of those two jaspers hooting it up again tonight, I'll put the kibosh on him. Then it'll be Judge Sweeney's turn to twist a knot in his tail."

Kirk nodded and went end-of-shift.

Barlow poured himself a cuppa joe and sat down at the senior deputy's desk. He pulled out his tome on *The Complete History of World War II* and turned to Chapter 44, in a supreme effort to get caught up on his reading assignment. He had 73 factually-detailed pages to scour, and a five-page analysis to write for his Monday evening class.

He took a sip of steaming black coffee and sighed. Then he lit up a stogy. Sarah and he had ten more, agonizingly glacial weeks until graduation. He was hanging on by his fingernails. Five years both working and attending college full-time had exhausted him. This was the primary reason Barlow had saved this particular class until the final semester. He needed a captivating topic to keep him motivated. He wanted to graduate with a bang, not with a whimper. World War II was fascinating to him, especially anything regarding General George S. Patton's

3rd Army, the unit in which his father, Private First Class [PFC] Chester R. Adams, had served.

Chester R. Adams had been a military policeman [MP]. Late in 1944 during the German Ardennes Offensive, otherwise known by the Americans as the Battle of the Bulge, PFC Adams had been assigned fixed-post traffic duties, oftentimes alone, in the middle of recently uninhabited, rural areas of France. Areas like this had been thriving before the war, but now they were ghost towns. It was due to recent military occupation by the German Army; their atrocities committed upon civilian non-combatants; local skirmishes and battles between the German and encroaching Allied forces; aerial bombing; artillery bombardment; and starvation, among other dreadful circumstances. PFC Adams' assignment was to direct military traffic, usually convoys, on unmarked, muddy, rutted roads along the path of General Patton's lightning push to relieve the 101st Airborne Division at Bastogne.

While this was ongoing, unbeknownst to the Americans, a German Army Special Forces unit was conducting a Top Secret mission codenamed Operation Greif, in the area where PFC Adams had been assigned. American-educated German soldiers who spoke fluent English with American accents, dressed in U.S. Army uniforms, impersonated U.S. Army MPs at various crossroads. Sometimes they killed the real U.S. Army MPs, who were the first to be deceived. The German imposters rerouted military convoys to wrong destinations in an effort to disrupt U.S. military operations. They had some sensational successes in the beginning.

At least three German imposters were exposed, captured, and interrogated. They spilled their guts before they were executed by firing squad (two days after they were captured). The American hierarchy quickly disseminated this information to their troops. Nevertheless, knowing there were German soldiers impersonating American soldiers sent a wave of controlled panic throughout the American forces in this area.

U.S. soldiers harshly grilled other U.S. soldiers they didn't know, asking American trivia questions that most Americans should know, such as, "Who won the 1941 World Series?" or "What's the biggest city in Michigan?" Soldiers who didn't know the answers were quickly ratcheted up to the third degree until they convinced their fellow Americans of their sovereignty. Fortunately, Operation Greif only had a minimal impact overall and was short-lived.

PFC Adams survived the war unharmed. He was awarded the Good Conduct Medal, European-African-Middle Eastern Campaign Medal with three Oak Leaf Clusters (for service in three campaigns), and the World War II Victory Medal. He was honorably discharged and returned to his hometown in Arlo, Texas. He married his high school sweetheart, Miss Matilda Lee. He and his brother, Clive, a Navy veteran, went into the auto mechanic business together, opening up their own garage. Chester and Matilda had two children, Chloe and Barlow. Chester R. Adams set the example for Barlow when it was his turn to fulfill his military obligation during the War in Vietnam.

At any other time besides tonight, Barlow would have been salivating to study this savory bit of world history, but tonight he was hungry for some action of his own. Nevertheless, he buckled down and opened the book to Chapter 44 and began reading. You know what they say. Be careful what you wish for.

The hours passed quietly without incident. It was 2:30. Barlow had just stood up to stretch. He was thinking about putting on a fresh pot of coffee when he heard someone open the rear door. Before he could see who it was, he heard voices. It took a couple of minutes, but eight, clean-cut men in dark suits and subtle ties strolled in like they were the Praetorian Guard. The one in front, who looked to be in his mid-40s, loudly proclaimed "Supervisory Special Agent [SSA] Roderick Hurley, FBI. I need to speak to whomever's in charge immediately."

He flashed his commission book open and started to slam it shut, but Barlow surprised him and retrieved it out of his hand. He opened it wide for a closer inspection. Sure enough, the stiff standing before him was a supervisory special agent in the world's second most pompous law enforcement agency, right behind Great Britain's Scotland Yard.

Barlow replied, "Hello to you too, Agent Hurley, and to all your compadres. Since I'm the only deputy on duty right now, I guess that makes me in charge. How might the Quayle County Sheriff's Office be of service to the FBI?

"Let's see. It's been a few years since I've even seen an FBI agent. There were two of them. They were investigating me for allegedly violating the civil rights of some outlaw motorcycle bikers. Seemed like nice enough fellows. They did their jobs and disappeared, never to be heard from again. Are you all here looking for civil rights violators tonight?"

"No. We are not here tonight looking for bad cops, Deputy, although that is indeed a worthy pursuit, putting the rotten eggs in jail, wouldn't you agree, Deputy Adams (reading his name tag for the first time)?"

"Only if your endeavor is to seek the truth, rather than to pursue some political agenda passed down from the Washington puzzle palace. So if you all are not looking for rotten egg cops, what brings eight federal agents, none of whom look like they're from anywhere near Texas, to our doorstep at 2:30 in the morning?"

"Glad you asked. We're here to arrest an extremely dangerous subversive and his protégé, of whom we have reliable information causing us to believe that they're hiding in your county. Deputy Adams, have you ever heard of the Symbionese Liberation Army?"

"The SLA? Is there anyone in America who hasn't? Aren't they the urban commie guerrillas operating in California? In fact, aren't they the ones who kidnapped that newspaper heiress in

Berkley last month?"

"That is correct. Her name is Patty Hearst. They also murdered a public school superintendent in Oakland last fall. His name was Marcus Foster."

"I do remember. So who and why would any California whack job want to hide out in the middle of the desert in southwest Texas? Don't they have the Mohave Desert in California? Besides, it absolutely defies logic. Strangers get noticed in places that are underpopulated, such as Quayle County, Texas, which just happens to be more than 22,000 square miles with less than 3,000 residents. It's a wonder you even found us on the map."

"You'll understand. The man we're after is William L. Wolfe, white male, 23 years of age. He's one of the founders of the SLA. He's supposed to be in the company of a sympathizer named Marley Logan, a former anthropology student at UC-Berkley. To our knowledge, Logan is not known to be violent, but Wolfe's as deadly as an unpinned hand grenade. We have warrants to arrest them both. We need for you to lead us to their hideout. Allegedly, it belongs to Logan's grandfather. Supposedly, it's out in the way beyond of Quayle County. All you gotta do is lead us there and get out of our way. We'll do the rest."

"Well, Agent Hurley, I'd like to oblige, but you do realize that I'm a sworn deputy and we have arrest powers, too. Besides, I don't know any Logans in Quayle County, and I thought I at least knew the name of every resident here. Let me make a call first."

"Do what you gotta do, but hurry it up. We'd like to capture these villains before they wake up."

"Of course."

Barlow said, "Help yourself, if anyone wants to make a fresh pot of coffee." Then he picked up the phone and dialed Sheriff Sol's home. It was inching towards 3 o'clock. The call was picked up on the third ring.

"Hello."

"Sheriff, it's Barlow. Eight FBI agents are in our office. The agent in charge, Roderick Hurley, said he has arrest warrants for two yahoos who are part of that SLA terrorist group in California. You know. The gang who kidnapped Patty Hearst. Their main target is a white male named William Wolfe. Supposedly his partner is a college student from UC-Berkley named Marley Logan. Supposedly they're staying at a house out in the Tulies that belongs to Logan's grandfather. I don't know any Logans here, so I figured I better call you."

"I know who it is, and where he lives. I'll be right there. You call Slick and tell him to roll. I'll call Chief and tell him we need him to man the desk and cover our backsides in case this whole thing goes haywire. The Feebs will leave us and our underwear flapping in the breeze if it does. Soon as you rouse Slick, get a copy of their warrants and get the names of every single agent there. Copy?"

"Copy. See you when you get here."

Barlow hung up and went back to SSA Hurley, who was waiting for the coffee to finish brewing. Barlow said, "The sheriff, Solomon Pratt, will be here in a few minutes. He knows the house you're asking about. He told me to get a copy of the two warrants and the names of each agent here. Soon as he arrives, we'll show you all the way."

"Deputy Adams, you already know my name. Why does he want everyone else's?"

"Truthfully Agent Hurley, I think it's in the event everything turns to shit. He doesn't want to be left with his dick in his hand. Same reason he wants a copy of the warrants. Also, he didn't say it, but I know he'll want to see a photograph of each bad guy. We might know Logan by·sight."

"All right. You all got a copier?"

"No, but they have one upstairs in the county clerk's office."

"Guys, show your credentials to Deputy Adams so he can write down your names. Abner, get the photographs of the targets and the warrants. Go with him upstairs so he can make a copy. I want to be ready to roll as soon as Sheriff Pratt arrives."

Barlow had expected an argument and was surprised he didn't get one.

Sheriff Sol and Slick were waiting for Barlow by the time he had finished copying the warrants. He also made xerographic copies of the mugshots (in black and white) but they did not turn out very well. Then SSA Hurley and Sheriff Sol had a tête-à-tête in his office behind the closed door. Chief Alex arrived a few minutes later. He asked Barlow what the commotion was all about. Barlow told him everything he knew.

A few minutes later SSA Hurley and Sheriff Sol emerged. Sheriff Sol motioned to Slick, and called him over for a private chat. His instructions were sotto voce. "Slick, I hope you grabbed your favorite rifle. I want you to go to the old Briscoe place. Park your car out of harm's way and sneak in on foot. Get a vantage point where you can cover the back door.

"The FBI has federal felony warrants from California on two alleged members of the SLA. If you see this guy (holding up a mugshot of William Wolfe) and he's flourishing a firearm, eliminate the threat. Wolfe is accused of murder. He's listed as armed and dangerous.

"If you see this guy (holding up Marley Logan's mugshot) and he's flourishing a deadly weapon, take your shot, preferably to disable, but if he bites the dust, so be it. He's wanted for harboring a fugitive. You may recognize him. He's Dr. Edwin Delaney's grandson.

"The FBI has insisted on conducting the raid by themselves. Barlow will go with me to observe. If things turn to manure, we'll do what we can to pull the Bureau's chestnuts out of the fire. Any questions?"

"Nope. Give me at least a 15-minute head-start to set up."

"Roger that. They don't have a Chinaman's chance of finding the house without our help, so I can guarantee we won't embark until at least 3:30 (looking at his watch). Cut a chogy, Deputy Oldman. See you when this is a wrap."

In the meantime, SSA Hurley briefed his agents near the back door. He showed them a rough sketch of the house and the curtilage, which had been hand-drawn by Sheriff Sol from memory. Hurley passed out assignments.

Sheriff Sol called Chief Alex and Barlow into his office and told them what he had told Slick. Then he remarked, "I think this is a soup sandwich, but I can't control the FBI, even in my own county. These are their warrants and their raid.

"I sent Slick ahead on overwatch without FBI permission. Rest assured, if this raid blows up in their faces, they will do all they can to make us the scapegoats.

"Chief, I need you here to man the phones and the radio and whatever else you can think of to do in the best interests of Quayle County.

"Barlow you're riding with me to lead them to the site and to help monitor whatever they do. Grab your .30-30. I'll check out one of ours. Any questions?"

None were voiced. Then he said, "Good. I gotta go take a leak. Barlow, grab us a Coke from the vending machine. Here's my keys and four dimes. Go wait for me in my car. We still have to delay another five minutes before we leave without the Bureau catching on, in order to give Slick time to set up. It'll take at least that long for me to empty my bladder."

Barlow grabbed two pairs of binoculars from the property room before he left. He bought the Cokes, and picked up his flashlight, rifle, and bandolier of extra .30-30 ammo from his truck. Then he situated himself in the driver's seat of Sheriff Sol's unmarked, 1969, brown Plymouth Fury, and rolled down the windows. The temp was in the mid-50s. He knew Sheriff Sol would want him to drive, even though he didn't know yet exactly where they were headed. He thought it would be somewhere on the east side of the county, and he was right.

A few minutes later, Sheriff Sol, followed by all the FBI agents, streamed out of the courthouse and piled into their vehicles. The agents were in three, dark-colored, benign-looking, plain Jane, four-door sedans. One was a Ford; one was a Chevy; and one was an AMC. They looked like the type of cars Fuller Brush Company salesmen, old folks, nuns, and poor Protestant preachers drive, except shinier.

Sol told Barlow to head north on Texas Street and turn east on County Road 14. The caravan went about 15 miles before turning north on the old, gravel Wagon Road. They went another couple of miles to a rutted, single-lane driveway going east, where a single mailbox marked 67 indicated that a residence was nearby. Sheriff Sol told Barlow to pull over on the side of the drive and stop. Then he got out of the car and walked back to the first FBI unit.

He went to the front passenger window and spoke to SSA Hurley. "Follow the driveway about three-quarters of a mile all the way to the end. There's an old, one-story, stone ranch house and a couple of outbuildings. That's where Dr. Delaney lives by himself since he's a widower, when he's in town. He's sort of a recluse, but he's a real fascinating guy. He's an archaeologist, and usually he's gone on a dig somewhere. I think he's in Guatemala now.

"Marley Logan is his grandson, and his only surviving relative so far as I know. I've only seen him a few times. He and his parents lived in Nevada, as I recall. He's a nice kid, and I'm surprised that he's mixed up in this mess. We'll wait here for a few minutes to give you all time to get situated. Good luck." Then he walked back to his car and got in. He lit up a Lucky Strike and waited.

SSA Hurley spoke to his men, and then they departed. They crawled down the drive without any lights like a somber, funeral procession led by Helen Keller with three mule-driven buggies driven by her, Ray Charles, and Ronnie Milsap, transporting eight, heavily-armed, gussied-up, deaf and dumb blind men.

Sheriff Sol said, "We'll give 'em about five minutes. Then we'll go down and see what they've found. It wouldn't surprise me one bit if the house is empty. I just hope they don't break down the door. It's anyone's guess when Dr. Delaney will return."

In the interim, when Slick got close to his destination, he turned off his headlights and motored along a desert jackrabbit trail north of the old Briscoe place. He parked his vintage black, 1948 Studebaker pickup truck about 500 yards northeast of the old homestead. He could make it out just fine in the moonlight. He picked up his rifle and walked southwest until he was about a hundred yards east of the backdoor. He checked the creosote bushes carefully all around him as if he were creeping through a minefield. Then he lay prone on a flat, four-foot-wide escarpment with a very slight incline towards the house. It was situated between a bush on either side. His sniper post was unencumbered, and provided him with a clear vantage point of the back door. Even so, it was still dark and civilians didn't have night vision binoculars or scopes back in those days. However, tonight he had been blessed by the desert night god - the one known as Hssss, and for that he was thankful. Rattlesnakes oftentimes repose under desert bushes after dark. They anger and become hostile quickly if a human gets too close. Slick preferred not to lie where angels fear to tread.

The house itself was completely dark. He could not make out any motor vehicles parked in the yard. It didn't mean there weren't any parked inside the barn.

The sky was beautiful - clear with 10,000 twinkling stars and a waxing moon. He had a slight breeze west to east. Slick stuffed a big chew of Mail Pouch tobacco inside his cheek and let it motivate his saliva glands. He would have preferred a smoke, but he didn't want to risk the odor of a burning cigarette, nor the orange glow of the lit end. If it were God's decision for a man to expire this pre-dawn morning, He couldn't have picked a more peaceful, beautiful, bucolic location than right here. This was absolutely perfect.

Slick didn't think death would come to pass tonight, at least by his hands. He couldn't make out faces from here. Unless a man were shooting directly at him, he'd never return fire. How could he identify friend from foe? He wouldn't want to shoot an FBI agent by accident. Not even Squirrelly Hurley.

SSA Roderick Hurley and the seven special agents who answered to him proceeded cautiously in a nearly silent three-car motorcade, in near total darkness. Every bump in the road came as a surprise. They were kicking up clouds of dust. They could barely make out the trail.

They were on a sanctioned manhunt to catch an alleged, demonic killer and his protégé. But . . . this was a setting right out of Rod Serling's television show, *Outer Limits*. Would they experience a close encounter of the third kind [in other words, see a space alien]? They all thought it was creepy out here in Quayle County, Texas. What did folks do here for fun? Go on rattlesnake roundups? Ride bucking broncos? Chase their inbred sisters for sex? What?

One and all, these FBI agents were born and bred big city slickers who were in their element in the urban jungles of the major metropolitan areas. Crime-infested, ethnic neighborhoods did not faze them. Honking horns, traffic congestion, smog, police sirens, 80-story buildings, graffiti, underground subways, trash on the sidewalks, air and noise pollution from commercial airports and bus terminals, street gangs, what's the big deal? They preferred concrete under their feet. But brave? Were these agents brave, as in the FBI motto "Fidelity, Bravery, Integrity"? Without a doubt they all were, save for one, who was a bean counter - a shoe clerk - a reader and writer, not a fucker and fighter.

SSA Hurley had been saddled with SA [Special Agent] Lester

M. (for Manfred) Glockstern, Jr. out of the White Collar Crimes section of the San Francisco Field Office, because he needed one more man, as it were. SA Glockstern was the only available white collar investigator that his supervisor claimed he could spare. Perhaps that was because after three years of hard work, devotion, and dedication to duty as a fully accredited special agent - no longer a probationary employee - SA Glockstern had never made a physical arrest. Not one! (He had a few "paper" arrests in which the U.S. Marshals Service scooped up his man and he took credit, as was the FBI's custom. Remember, FBI Director J. Edgar Hoover had never made an arrest until many years after he became the director, and even then his subordinates set it up for him.) This particular assignment was fully endorsed by SA Glockstern's boss to help him break his cherry. Grow some hair on his ass. Learn to sing baritone or bass instead of soprano. Maybe put a notch on his government-issued Smith & Wesson .38 Special revolver. Man him up. That kind of thing.

As he rode in the back seat of the last unit, SA Glockstern was fighting back tears. Why, oh why, did he ever quit his comfy job as a CPA in a major Los Angeles accounting firm which catered to Hollywood movie stars and other notable multi-millionaires? It certainly wasn't for the money.

Tonight he would probably die. He was only 33 years old with a receding hairline; still lived with his mother; and drove a light blue, 1970 AMC Gremlin, inline six-banger with a 199 cubic-inch engine and manual three-speed transmission (with a top speed of 95 miles per hour going downhill with a sturdy tailwind). He wore highly polished brown wingtips and argyle socks all the time, even when he was off-duty in his pleated beige shorts, baggy, untucked Hawaiian flowery shirt, and his ever-present, thick, tortoiseshell glasses. He was captain of his church league badminton team; superstitious of black cats; wore a pocket protector so he wouldn't get ink on his dress shirts; tucked his ties into the waistband of his trousers; was passionate about strawberry milkshakes; had never been married; and had never, ever been laid.

Lester decided if he lived through this ordeal, he was going to ask Gladys Gobel out on a date. Take her to a matinee. Maybe see *Harry and Tonto*. He heard it was really good. Try to feel up her titties during the show. She had some big ones. Then take her out to eat at a swanky place. Maybe Hoffman's Haus of Weiner Schnitzel. Show her his beloved stamp collection on a second date. Experience some life before he bit the dust in his highly vaunted position as a fearless G-Man. (Think Melvin Purvis.) Go for the gusto. Doing this Wyatt Earp thing was bound to get him killed sooner or later. Lester silently prayed for deliverance, and that Gladys would say yes. His silent prayers were both answered.

SSA Hurley assigned his three most seasoned agents, SA Tom Williams, SA Bernie Farris, and SA Abner Jamison, to enter the front door with him. He sent SA Haywood Thompson and SA Morris Weathers to search the outbuildings. Upon clearing them, they were to post up on the front door for the duration, in the event one of the perps made it past the entry team. SA Al Mazzei and SA Lester Glockstern were to cover the back door. SA Mazzei was quietly instructed to make sure nothing happened to SA Glockstern upon penalty of a swift transfer to Butte, Montana, J. Edgar's favorite agent dumping (banishment) ground.

It didn't take long. SAs Thompson and Weathers reported that both outbuildings were clear. A red, '66 Plymouth Valiant, two-door sedan was parked inside the barn. The hood was cold. SSA Hurley scanned his men. Everyone was ready, sitting on G and looking at O.

Sheriff Sol and Barlow pulled up where they could see the front door. They exited the car with their rifles and stood next to it in the event things broke bad.

SSA Hurley pounded on the front door. He yelled, "Open up!

FBI!"

A few moments later, SA Farris said, "Boss, someone just turned on a light."

Agent Hurley pounded on the door again and repeated his announcement.

They heard footsteps coming to the door. Without the door opening, a male voice asked, "Who is this and what do you want? It's 4 o'clock in the morning for Christ's sake!"

"Open the door. This is the FBI. We have an arrest warrant for William Wolfe."

"He's not here. Go away!"

"Is this Marley Logan?"

"None of your business. Go away!"

They could hear running feet.

SSA Hurley shouted, "He's taking a powder! Farris, kick it in!"

It took three hard kicks, but the door jam finally gave way, and the four agents barged in, Hurley and Farris holding revolvers. Williams had a pump shotgun and Jamison had a Thompson submachine gun with a 50-round drum magazine.

Marley Logan was in his tighty whities and a white tee shirt. He was also barefoot. He opened the back door and turned right into the darkness of his backyard. He ran smack dab into SA Glockstern, both of whom crashed to the ground. SA Glockstern wrapped his arms around Marley, who was thinner and smaller, and squeezed the living shit out of him with a bear hug. SA Mazzei scrambled over to the pair of writhing bodies. He pried SA Glockstern's arms from around Marley, and handcuffed him behind the back. Then he pulled Marley up by the stack and swivel. SA Glockstern jumped up and yelled, "Hey, dipshit! You just assaulted a federal agent! It's your ass now, hotshot!"

SSA Hurley and his three breaching agents blasted through the back door, hot on Marley's heels. SSA Hurley exclaimed, "Great job you two! Put him in my car and keep an eye on him.

The rest of us will toss the house."

SSA Hurley and his three favorite subordinates went back inside and turned on every light in the house. Then they turned the house upside down looking for guns, explosive materials, and SLA propaganda. They came up short. Nada. Nothing there. Not even a girly magazine or a joint. Not even a single BB or a slingshot!

Sheriff Sol told Barlow to look for Slick quietly, and have him head back to the jail. Then he stepped inside Dr. Delaney's house to see what was going on. He said, "Agent Hurley, you all trashed an innocent man's house. You need to return it to its previous condition. You also need to fix his front door."

"He can file a claim with the FBI in San Francisco. We gotta go. We're headed straight to the FBI office in El Paso with Logan in tow."

"Not so fast. First of all, Dr. Delaney isn't even in the U.S. now to file a claim or fix his door. Second, I may be a local yokel sheriff but I do know the law, which says you have to take your prisoner to the nearest circuit court judge, be it state or federal, for an initial appearance and a determination as to whether the prisoner waives his right to a hearing to contest extradition. The nearest circuit court judge is Maxwell Sweeney, right here in Mosby. You're not taking Marley anywhere until you do that."

"We'll take him to El Paso before a federal circuit court judge there."

"That's more than 300 miles from where we stand. That's beyond the limits proscribed by law UNLESS there is no circuit court judge closer. You do that, and I promise you, Judge Sweeney will have called his old law school buddy, Chief Federal District Court Judge Amos Swindler, Western District of Texas, and your shit will be running down your pants leg by the time you get into federal court.

"You do this the right way, to include putting the house back in order, and getting a carpenter, and a locksmith if necessary, out here today to repair the damage to the front door. Otherwise, I will file a formal complaint against you and those of your staff who were negligent. I can promise you my complaint will have a cover letter and endorsement from Texas Governor Dolph Briscoe. [Sheriff Sol stretched truth on the last threat.] Are we clear?

"One last thing. We don't have to part ways as enemies. I know this kid, Marley. He's not some wild-eyed revolutionary. My best guess is, the limit of his culpability is being friends with Wolfe. He's not a harborer of fugitives in the traditional sense. Whatever he does know, I'm pretty sure he'll tell me. He may still have to go back to California to stand trial, and the FBI may have enough to convict him of some kind of chickenshit charge, but in the long run the FBI will be the loser. If this kid is the type of person who bears the brunt of the full force the FBI can rain down on someone, the FBI will end up losing mass public support. Is that really what you want?"

"Fine. Thompson and Weathers, you guys are drafted to pull maid service. Put everything away, and do it right. I better not hear otherwise. Also, look around for some tools to fix the front door. I think all it needs is the door jam being realigned and nailed down. If it's gonna take more than that, pull it to, and come back to the courthouse. I'm sure the sheriff knows a reputable carpenter who can make an emergency repair. The rest of us will take Mr. Logan back to the jail.

"Anything else, Sheriff?"

"Nope. Much obliged. I think that covers it, except your prisoner is barefoot and in his drawers. Is that really the way you all to want to bring him to court before Judge Sweeney? He's old school, with a penchant for proper decorum - a real stickler. Let me know when you all are ready and we'll head back."

When they returned to the courthouse, Barlow and Chief Alex booked Logan, to include taking mugshots and fingerprints. Sheriff Sol called District Attorney Able DeWitt and Judge

Maxwell Sweeney. The judge scheduled an emergency session of court for 9 o'clock. SSA Hurley made his calls. SA Thompson reported that the house was in order, that they repaired and locked both doors.

About 7 o'clock, the incoming day shift deputy, Randy Meacham, brought Marley a breakfast from Betty's diner. After he had eaten, at Sheriff Sol's instruction, Randy brought Marley to the sheriff's office handcuffed in the front, and wearing black and white, horizontally-striped jail clothes and flip flops. Sheriff Sol and SSA Hurley were standing by. Randy left and closed the door.

Sheriff Sol read the Miranda Warning to Marley. He said he understood his rights and that he was willing to talk. He signed the waiver affirming same.

Sheriff Sol said, "Marley, I've known you since you were born. I knew your momma and papa before they died in that plane crash in Tunisia. I've known your grandpa since I was a kid. You know me, and I hope you know that I've got your best interest at heart, sheriff or not. If you want, I can get the public defender, Sam Davis, to come over to counsel you before you say anything. You want me to call him?"

"No. I trust you. I'm not gonna lie. No matter what anyone says about me, I don't believe I did anything wrong."

"That's great, but you understand that whether you say anything or not, you'll still have to go with Agent Hurley to El Paso, and ultimately to San Francisco to plead your case before the federal court. Since he has an arrest warrant, that's a given."

"That's fine. I was planning to go back anyway and pick up at UC-Berkley where I left off."

"Well, we'll hope for the best, but you could get sent off to prison. You do understand that?"

"I do. That scares the living shit outta me, but I didn't DO anything."

"Well okay, then. If you still want to make a statement or

answer questions to someone who knows you, it will have to be now. You have a court appearance before Judge Sweeney at 9 o'clock."

"I do. Okay. This is the deal. I know Willie Wolfe from college. I met him at a Save the Whales rally. Next time I saw him was at a social justice protest. The idea was that blacks and women and other minorities don't get a fair shake in society. They should get a leg up. That's when Willie told me he was a member of a new group called the Symbionese Liberation Army, and that they were going to take some affirmative action in furtherance of their ideals. He introduced me to some members, to include this black dude they called General Field Marshal Cinque and some white chick they called Mizmoon. These two were a matched pair of psychotic, weirded out freaks. They made their own flag and talked about getting some guns and all kinds of scary shit. That was the one and only time I went. These people are fanatics. They acted like they're part of an anti-Christ cult, although they never mentioned Satan. What I did learn is they absolutely hate America. I didn't want any part of them. They were turning peaceful, love-all-of-Mankind protests into a civil-fucking-war. That's it. That's all I know.

"I ran into Willie a few more times afterwards on campus. I really liked him. He wanted me to join their organization, but I said I didn't feel comfortable around them.

"One time early on, I happened to mention that I was thinking about taking a break from school. I told him I might stay at Grandad's house because he was always gone on some dig and he said I could stay there anytime I want. I told Willie it was in the middle of nowhere. Nobody could ever find you if you hung out there, which is why I like it whenever I need to get my head screwed on straight. He said it sounded like a cool place and that he might like to visit me if I went there, so I drew him a map. I never thought another thing about it.

"Wednesday night, real late, I was already in bed. I heard

some idiot pounding on the door, yelling for me to get up and let him in. I didn't know who it was and it scared me. Gramps doesn't have any guns, so I grabbed the fireplace poker and answered the door. It was Willie, with a dopey, dog-eating-shit grin. I let him in, and we basically just hung out. We never went anywhere. Good thing I'd been to the grocery because he ate like he hadn't had a square meal in awhile.

"He was all animated while he was here. Kept saying the shit was about to hit the fan. He never explained what he was talking about, just that people were gonna die. He was all wound up. Couldn't relax. I couldn't make heads or tails about what he meant. Then real late Thursday night or early Friday morning he said he had to go - that they were counting on him. That's all he said. He took all his shit and packed it in an Army barracks bag and left. Said he'd see me around. Then he drove off in a cloud of dust. That's it!

"That's why breaking my door down at four in the morning and locking me up is bullshit! My parents left me a humongous endowment and I'm gonna hire me the best, slimiest, meanest, fucking lawyer in San Francisco. As soon as this thing is dismissed, I'm gonna sue the shit out of the FBI, and especially you, Mr. Supervisory Special Agent Roderick Hurley. That's all I have to say!"

Sheriff Sol replied, "Marley, this whole thing sounds like a first class goat rope - a monumental misunderstanding. Agent Hurley was just acting on the information he was given. It sounds to me like somebody embellished the story. I know the truth is all bound to come out before you go to trial. If a witness lied, or anyone in the FBI pursued this with bad intent, they will pay the price.

"I know you said you're done talking, but I'd like to ask you just two questions. You don't have to answer, but it might be of benefit to you if you're willing."

"What are they?"

"What type of car was Willie driving, and did he ever show you any guns?"

"He had a white, '72 Camaro. It had California plates, and it was stuffed to the gills with everything he owned. I never saw any weapons."

"Thank you. Agent Hurley, are you satisfied?"

"I am. Thank you. Just for the record, all we want is justice, for you, and for everyone else. The SLA are American terrorists and I think you recognized that. I believe that's why you parted ways with them. We're doing all we can to capture them before they kill anymore people, to include Patricia Hearst.

"I'll get to the bottom of this regarding how we obtained the information about you, and if anyone lied about your actions, I'll find out, and I promise to rectify the situation. However, until then, the charge against you has to play itself out in court. That being said, are you going to fight extradition back to California?"

"Oh, Hell no! I want to clear my name as soon as I can."

"I don't blame you. We'll get you back as soon as we can."

At 8 o'clock, Barlow asked Sheriff Sol if he needed him to stay.

Sheriff Sol replied, "No. Thanks for checking. Randy and I have it covered. I'm sending Chief Alex home too. Enjoy what's left of your weekend. Give Sarah my best."

"Will do. Thanks, Sheriff."

Barlow drove straight home in a rush - all mile-and-a-half of it. When he walked in, he thought Sarah was still asleep but she tricked him. When he tiptoed into the bedroom, she asked, "How was your night?"

The shades were still drawn, so the lighting was dim. It was a little hard to see. Sarah was lying on the bed on her side facing him in her fabulous birthday suit. She was petting their dog, Happy, who was slobbering all over the floor. He was preening with all the lavish attention.

Barlow replied, "This may have been the weirdest midnight shift I've ever worked. However, you're wearing my favorite outfit and I don't want to think about anything else right now. Tell you later. What if I feed Happy and let him out in the backyard to dig a hole or bark at our neighbors?"

"I already thought of that Mr. Adams. He's been fed and he's gone potty. Just shuck your clothes and tell him to get in his bed. In fact, give him a Milk Bone. Then hurry back and rub my back and feet. Then maybe I'll let you rub another part of my body with another part of yours, and we'll see what happens. Your magic touch might turn my Prince Charming into a horned toad being you're so horny all the time, but what's a fair damsel to do when she has an itch which needs to be scratched - like with a warm, stiff, succulent, dome-shaped, throbbing, female pleasure-maker?"

"But what if I'm too exhausted to rub your bewitching body? What then?"

"But you're not too tired. I know because Roscoe's already bouncing up and down like the high-dive at the Travelers Rest swimming pool with a 300-pound circus lady who imagines she's about to do a swan dive when what she really does is whale-sized bellyflop."

"What if I do my own swan dive down on your sweet spot right now instead? How would you feel about that?"

"Oh, I'd definitely feel wonderful, but I still want my back and feet massaged first. Then maybe I'll give Roscoe a tongue massage just to see if you really are too tired to quench the lascivious thoughts racing through my mind. Are you ever going to pleasure me, Mr. Adams, or just talk me to death?"

"Perish the thought, Madam. Roll over on your stomach. My lips are sealed."

"Oh, I certainly hope not. Just long enough for you to assuage my sore back muscles and aching feet. I think I was dreaming all night long about rodeoing with my stud muffin husband and got all tensed up. It's all your fault, you know."

Barlow crawled up on the bed and began to gently massage

her back and shoulders. She had some scented body lotion on the bed stand so he used that and rubbed it in. She began to moan softly, so he moved further down her body and began massaging her lower back and perfect derrière. She seemed to respond to that, so he gently pushed her legs apart up by her hips, and began to massage her inner thighs. His hands were slippery and they kept brushing up against her sweet spot by accident. She began to breathe a little heavier, so he did it some more. Then she said, "Not fair, Barlow. You're cheating. It feels too good and I'm losing control of my body way too soon."

Barlow slowly shifted down to her thighs and legs, but he slyly replied, "Sounds like a song. Are you actually accusing me of making it hurt so good?"

"Yes. Now hush up and massage my feet and toes."

So he did, until she asked him to rub her calves and her thighs again. Finally, he worked himself back up to her sweet spot, where he rubbed softly. He could feel her getting wetter. Her hips began to thrust back and forth ever so gently. Her breathing picked up, and she began thrusting more vigorously. She whispered, "Oh, my God. You're making me come. I told you not to do that," except she kept on thrusting, harder and harder, so she must not have really meant it.

He said, "Okay. I'll stop when you do."

She intensified her thrusts and moaning. She barely eked out her response. "If you do . . . . pant, pant, pant . . . . I won't let you do . . . . pant, pant . . . .what you really want to do."

"Are you sure? Do you really mean that?" He continued to massage her wet spot in perfect synchronization with her thrusts.

"No. . . . Don't stop. . . . I'm nearly there."

The dam broke. The gusher erupted. Barlow let her be. She lay panting for a minute before her breathing returned nearly back to normal.

Eventually she spoke softly. She said, "I can't believe you got me off like that with so much intensity. Now it's your turn. Roll over and I'll give Roscoe mouth-to-mouth."

"Just enough to make sure you've got his undivided attention. Then bend over the bed and hang on. Roscoe's throbbing like a broken heart and he needs maximum penetration. If you think what you just got was intense, you ain't felt intense yet. If you don't collapse from sheer ecstasy, my name's not Peterman."

"That's big talk, Mr. Peterman. We'll soon find out if you can deliver. You might not be able to. I may drain you dry and rain on your parade before you even get started."

"Not today, Sweetie. Not gonna happen. I know all your witchy woman tricks."

Talking ceased and pleasure-making commenced. She nearly had him but he utilized the last of his willpower and slipped away. He spun her over on her stomach and slid her up on her knees with her lower legs off the bed. He was a little forceful, which added to her thrill. He stood between her legs and let Roscoe do the rest. The engagement was forceful and it was long. Sarah climaxed again and again and again. He made it "hurt so good . . . ."

Today was Peterman's day. He did everything right. Sarah collapsed on the bed like a little kitten. Barlow lay down and she snuggled up next to him. In less than a minute they were both fast asleep.

Then Happy crept up on the foot of the bed and fell asleep, too.

Author's Note: On May 17, 1974, a month after the SLA robbed the Hibernia Bank in San Francisco, shooting two people, William L. Wolfe (known as Willie and Kahjoh) and five other members of the SLA died in a massive shootout and fire at their hideout in Los Angeles against 400 local and federal officers. It is believed that the fire started from a tear gas canister. Most, if not all members had an opportunity to surrender, but chose to shoot it out instead. It was televised live. William Wolfe is believed to have perished by the flames - not by gunfire.

Chapter 3

AT LONG LAST

Thursday/Sunday, May 16/19, 1974

This Thursday had been a long time in coming, as in five years of righteous toil, all during which Barlow and Sarah Adams had both been employed full-time. One could even say five years of burning the midnight oil for Barlow, since he had been on permanent midnight shift duty as a deputy for the Quayle County Sheriff's Office. Beginning tomorrow, he was available to work on all shift rotations year around, and not just during the summers or school breaks. Yippee ki-yay!

Mr. and Mrs. Adams strode across the stage single file, rigid and precise like West Point cadets passing in review, one behind the other in correct alphabetical order. They were attired in mortarboards and gowns bearing the school colors of scarlet and gray, in the packed to overflowing auditorium at Sul Ross State University where they received their baccalaureate diplomas from University President Norman L. McNeil. Barlow was even wearing an SRSU Lobos tee shirt under his white dress shirt in a private flight of fancy. He was 25 years of age and Sarah was 23. (She wouldn't turn 24 until July.) Barlow graduated magna cum laude, but Sarah graduated summa cum laude. Barlow was ecstatic for her.

It was a monumental day for them both, even though their respective occupations did not call for a college degree. This was something they did just for themselves. It was a matter of pride and self-esteem. Their degrees were in history. They were of the first generation in their families to graduate from college. Ironically, each of them was the second sibling in their families to achieve this honor, not the first. Nonetheless, it was still a big deal. Today was a proud day for Sarah's parents and siblings, as well as for Barlow's older sister, Chloe Kilgore, who was unable to attend because she and her family reside over 500 miles away in Bisbee, Arizona.

Now that the scholastic grind was fast fading in the Adams' rearview mirror, neither of them had a clue as to what they would do with all their free time. The manic push to graduate was finally finito! Certainly, they would catch up on some much-deserved rest, but not tonight. This was a night for champagne, but after tonight, then what?

After *Pomp and Circumstance* they celebrated with Sarah's parents, Arthur and Clarice Baker, her brother and sister-in-law, Cordell and Darla Baker, and Quayle County Sheriff Solomon "Sol" Pratt and his wife Joanna, at the Longhorn Emporium in Alpine. Brewster County Sheriff Leland Waters and his wife, Muriel, even showed up and joined in the merrymaking. Barlow's first toast was to Grandma Bea, who reared him from the time he was in the seventh grade after his parents were killed in an automobile accident. As the saying goes, regarding this particular night, "a good time was had by all".

Then on Friday night, Sarah and Barlow went to the Bijou Motion Picture Theater and watched *Chinatown*, featuring Jack Nicholson, Faye Dunaway, and John Huston. Best show ever!

On Saturday, they took their pooch, Happy, and went horseback riding and shooting down by the Rio Grande on the Baker spread, known formally as the Bar B Ranch, or informally as Casa de Baker. Barlow, in particular, got in some quality time practicing on moving targets with his .41 caliber Smith & Wesson revolver. This time he shot it more than his .30-30 Winchester, his preferred weapon of choice. Sarah devoted her time shooting with her .25 caliber Browning, semi-automatic belly gun. No shots greater than five yards away. She went through rapid-fire, six-shot, shooting sequences like she would do if she were confronted by an attacker. Empty the magazine in his torso and run. Pray he didn't keep coming. She'd experienced something like that in the past, and hoped she never would again.

On Sunday they attended services at St. Paul's Methodist Church in Mosby where they married. Church was followed by a magnificent Southern fried chicken dinner, capped off with cherry pie á la mode at Sarah's family homestead. (They had to stop by the house first and pick up Happy. It wouldn't have been fair to leave him out. He and Arthur's dogs were kissing cousins.)

Monday, they both returned to work - she at the Quayle County Rodeo Grounds on day shift, and he at the sheriff's office on the afternoon shift. Except for the torrid lovemaking Friday night, it was all anticlimactic since the euphoria of graduation.

Anticlimactic doesn't mean nobody has a climax. Perish the thought! Sarah almost wore out her saddle and Barlow nearly wore out his horse.

It was after the weekend when all the drama began.

Who'd a thunk it?

Chapter 4

SHITTING BRICKS

Monday, May 20, 1974

It was already past noon. Geraldo Flores, the courier from Oaxaca (pronounced wah-HAH-kah), Mexico, was three hours late! Armando Cruz, age 24, and Joaquín Pérez, age 19, were both muscular, hardened, career criminals in the prime of their youth. Murder was part of their repertoire. Both were El Paso residents. They had been waiting for Geraldo's arrival in the trees near the Rio Grande behind the parking lot of Gustavo's Cantina in El Paso del Norte since 8 o'clock. The ground under their feet was littered with cigarette butts to prove it. Conversation had been sparse for the past two hours because they were getting anxious.

Geraldo was scheduled to deliver 60 kilos of primo Oaxacan Highland Gold (OHG) marijuana in exchange for $24,000 in new, crisp, uncirculated Benjamin Franklins. As always, both Armando and Joaquín were armed with a .38 caliber Smith & Wesson revolver, and today they had additional firepower in the form of a 12-gauge, Winchester pump shotgun filled to capacity with 00 buck. This site was well known to the local denizens as a drop site for illegal transactions, primarily drugs, but also stolen motor vehicles, firearms, jewelry, etc. Armando and Joaquín were concerned that a rival gang might attempt to steal the dope and the money. They kept checking their surroundings for unwanted visitors, but fortunately, no one showed up.

El Jefe had assigned them to deliver this load of herb to Pepe Aguilar in Del Rio, 400 miles east of El Paso, in exchange for $60,000. They were supposed to make the delivery at 6 o'clock, and return to El Paso by 4 o'clock Tuesday morning. Failure to do exactly as ordered could result in harsh punishment, and perhaps even in death, depending upon circumstances.

Geraldo finally rolled up at 12:15 in a faded red, 1954 Dodge pickup truck loaded down with watermelons. He pulled up next to them and parked. Geraldo was an unkempt, short, portly man about 50 years of age. He looked and acted more like a garrulous, half-witted garbage tipper than a transporter of top-shelf weed. He was as bald as an onion except for around his ears, but he wore a disreputable straw sombrero to protect his pate from the blazing sun, so his baldness went largely undetected.

He piled out of his truck, smiled, and exclaimed, "Hola, amigos! Sorry I'm late. The bandidos who call themselves Federales held me up for a $200 bribe and six watermelons. I thought the greedy bastards were going to steal the load, but lucky for me, money talks and bullshit walks. At least I'm here now."

Armando replied petulantly, "We were worried. We're running way behind. Can you help us load the stuff onto our truck?"

"Sure." Geraldo pulled off his tarp and began moving watermelons. Armando helped, while Joaquín began shoveling the mostly dried horse manure out of the bed of their filthy white, 1970 Ford, F-350 dually pickup truck.

The three of them placed the bricks on the truck bed of the Ford, and covered them up with as much manure as the truck would hold.

Geraldo exclaimed, "Ah chihuahua! You sure anyone will want to smoke this shit when that's exactly what it smells like?"

Joaquín replied, "Who cares? We're just trying to keep nosy cops out of our hair if we get pulled over. Hey, how about spotting us a few watermelons?"

"No problemo. Six enough?"

Armando said, "That'll be plenty. What'll you do with the

rest?"

"Sell 'em at the farmer's market. Jefe lets me pocket whatever they fetch."

Armando retrieved two $10,000, strapped packets of uncirculated hundreds and one $4,000 packet from under the driver's seat of the Ford, and handed them to Geraldo.

Geraldo counted the bills to make sure it was all there. Then he said, "Muchas gracias. See ya next time. Take care. He smiled, scratched his itchy balls, waved, and waddled back to his truck. Soon as the transfer was done, he left for Ricardo's bordello in Ciudad Juárez to get his ashes hauled. Life was good.

Armando waited until Geraldo was out of sight. Then they saddled up and began the long trek eastward. They would take turns driving. They would also have to push it hard if they expected to get back by daybreak. He would call El Jefe when they departed from Del Rio.

Chapter 5

ENFORCING THE LAW

Monday, May 20, 1974

Barlow reported for work at 4 o'clock. Sheriff Sol was out of the office when he arrived. Chief Alex would cover the office beginning at 5 o'clock when Miss Loretta's shift was over. Barlow and Deputy Dewey Carruthers were the two afternoon patrol deputies for the week. Dewey was assigned the east side of the county, and Barlow had the west. Both were in marked units. They had pushed off (relieved) Deputy Ernie Atwater, who was the only day shift deputy this week.

Deputy Atwater said it had been a quiet shift. Nothing much going on except for a capias pro fine warrant (Texas Code of Criminal Procedure, Article 45.045), which he had just picked up from the Clerk of Court, Miss Eloise M. (Marguerite) Goodman.

The capias had been issued for the body of one Delmar S. Higgins, age 36, by Quayle County Circuit Court Judge Maxwell B. Sweeney. Higgins had failed to pay a $35 speeding citation issued by Deputy Kirk Shoemaker over a year ago. Higgins was tried, convicted, and sentenced in absentia because he had ignored three summonses to appear in court after he was cited. Frankly, Barlow was surprised that Judge Sweeney had been so patient. He was usually good for one lapse of judgment after which he lowered the boom, hence his nickname, Maximum Max. Since service of the third summons, nobody admitted having seen hide nor hair of Higgins. That sounded a little bit fishy to Barlow, but he never mentioned it. Since Delmar lived on the west side of town, Barlow said he would serve it. Dewey was quietly relieved because he knew Delmar was a rough character.

He was bound to act up just as soon as he realized what was afoot.

First order of business for Barlow was to drive the 1973, Dodge Polara police cruiser over to Amos Yellow Dog's Self-Service Car Wash on America Avenue. In 1972, Sheriff Sol had altered the paint jobs on all new marked units. Instead of being all white, now they were painted black with a white roof and white front doors, similar to a lot of state police or highway patrol agencies, as well as most law enforcement agencies in California. The black paint was a dirt magnet, so Barlow made a habit of washing inside and out, whichever car he drew at the beginning of each shift. Besides, a clean car always seemed to run better to him, and besides that, the county footed the bill. Mission accomplished, he patrolled the westside beat.

The very next day, with 20-20 hindsight and a lot of reflection, Barlow realized Monday night had been like Erich Remarque's *All Quiet on the Western Front*, which really wasn't quiet at all, but started out like it was. Nevertheless, nothing had been amiss during the afternoon hours. You could even say that Monday began like the television program, *Andy of Mayberry*. Everything was peaches and cream. No thorns amongst the roses. Copacetic.

Barlow waited until 6:30 to ease up behind a billboard advertising the Pecos Bank & Trust, which was located one mile east of the Quayle County/Brewster County line on the south side of US Highway 90, facing west. He wasn't looking to ambush speeders, per se. He knew Delmar Higgins worked as a mechanic at an old, dirty white, concrete block, three-stall garage, adjacent to an automobile boneyard owned by the region's most prolific auto thief, Big Bubba Cretin, not to be confused with his son who was even bigger, Little Bubba Cretin, who was a chip off the old block.

The garage was called Honest Abe Carmichael's Auto Repair Shop. (Think maybe the Cretins and Honest Abe Carmichael were in cahoots? Barlow certainly did, but they were taxpayers of Brewster County, not Quayle County.) The garage was located on the south side of US Highway 90, about a dozen miles west of the Quayle County line. The shop hours were 7-to-7, Monday through Friday, and 8-to-noon on Saturday. Barlow knew Delmar would be running wide open as soon as he got off work in his souped up, metallic forest green, 1971 Chevy Nova, so he could rest his hardworking (not!) ass on his favorite bar stool at the Dry Gulch Saloon in downtown Mosby. That's why it was tough to swallow that nobody had laid eyes on Delmar for months. Perhaps he had been in disguise wearing a pair of the Groucho Marx gag glasses with the thick black frames and the big nose and bushy fake mustache.

Barlow had decided to favor Delmar with a fresh ticket, assuming he was once again in violation of the traffic laws since he was such an obnoxious scofflaw. Ticket or not, he was still getting busted on the capias. That was a given. Barlow also planned to have Buck Boyd tow Delmar's car in the interest of public safety. Make him shell out for the tow and the storage fees. You know, keep his hotrod from being stolen by a band of roving gypsies or sideswiped on the side of the road by an errant tractor-trailer with a full head of steam, bound for the Big Easy in Louisiana.

Maybe this time Delmar would learn his lesson, but probably not. He was known around town as a touchy, insufferable blowhard, who quickly resorted to violence with his fists (which were the size of grapefruits) whenever anyone angered him. Delmar was a size XXL, and he could certainly fight, but Barlow was prepared for that, too. His slapjack was resting comfortably in the slash pocket on his right trouser leg just behind his holster. Size not being an advantage for Barlow in dealing with cop fighters, he had become quite proficient in the fast draw and proper usage of said slapjack when challenged by them. Most never saw it coming, and didn't know what had hit them. They usually thought Barlow had just used his fist, especially if they were drunk.

Meanwhile, while Barlow waited patiently for Delmar to make his appearance, he munched away on his cold supper, consisting of a ham and cheese sandwich, potato chips, banana, and oatmeal cookie, washed down with hot black coffee from his thermos. He listened to the good times radio play mournful, crying-in-your-beer country music - like Dolly Parton's, *I Will Always Love You.*

Tick tock. Tick tock. Time slipped away.

Well, what do you know? Game time. It was 7:14, and Delmar just blew the paint off of Mr. Dinkins' billboard sign. Barlow peeled out and goosed the Dodge. He closed quickly. He clocked Delmar at 115 miles per hour before he finally slowed down and pulled over. Barlow called in the stop. He gave the location, and requested that Buck Boyd bring his wrecker. Then he climbed out of the cruiser and eased on up to the Nova. Sure enough, it was Delmar the Terrible, eyes burning like red hot coals, fists choking the life out of the custom wood and chrome steering wheel. Looked like he was all steamed up and about to blow a gasket.

"Get out of the car, Delmar."

"Hold on a second, Barlow. I wasn't hurtin' nobody. I was just tryin' ta blow the carbon outta my carburetor. It's been sputterin' for days now. I just fixed it."

"Save it for Judge Sweeney. You're under arrest. Last time I'm asking. Please, Mr. Higgins, will you get out of your vehicle, SIR?"

Delmar snorted and piled out. The look on his face was vicious, like a rabid dog ready to bite. He straightened up to his full height of 6-feet, 2-inches, balled both hands into fists, and took a ferocious roundhouse swing at Barlow with his fight-ending right fist. What was that old 1960, Tennessee Williams song, *Sixteen Tons?*

"If you see me comin', better step aside.

"A lotta men didn't, a lotta men died.

"One fist of iron, the other of steel.

"If the right one don't a-get you,

"The other one will."

Delmar just threw his world-class knockout punch.

Barlow was primed. He saw this coming even before Delmar decided to go for it. Barlow took a quick step back, and slapped Delmar hard as he could with the flat side of the slapjack, squarely on his left cheek, smack dab on the cheekbone. Blood started spurting like a water fountain, and Delmar collapsed to the ground like a 225-pound, burlap sack of horseshit falling from a 20-foot hayloft. He was out cold like the proverbial mackerel. Barlow returned his slapjack to its home, stooped, and rolled Delmar over onto his stomach. Then he cuffed Delmar behind the back good and snug. No wiggle room. Then he searched him like he was looking for a stolen buffalo nickel. No weapons. Not even a pocketknife.

Barlow walked back to his cruiser and popped the trunk. He retrieved two ace bandages and some gauze pads from the first aid kit. He wiped the blood off Delmar's face with some pads, held tight, and tied an ace bandage around his face, squeezing and wrapping the bandage as hard as he could to staunch the flow of blood. It looked like Delmar had about a one-inch cut. He would probably have a permanent scar. Now from this day forward, each time Delmar looked in the mirror to shave, he would see the scar. It would be a constant reminder. DON'T FIGHT WITH THE COPS, ASSHOLE!

When Delmar finally roused, Barlow helped him up, and placed him in the back seat of the cruiser behind the wire mesh shield. Then he locked Delmar inside, and walked back to his hotrod and gave it a thorough toss. It was tidy and clean. No contraband. Registration and insurance papers along with an owner's manual in the glovebox. Nothing under the seats or sun visors. Nothing but a spare and a jack in the trunk. Nothing which needed to be inventoried. Good news for Barlow. Made his job easier.

Buck arrived and towed the car back to his Phillips 66, full service gas station, and parked it in the fenced and locked tow lot.

Barlow called in his arrest and his ETA to the jail. He requested that Doc Boykin meet him there. Chief Alex thought out loud, "Can't wait to see this. It's been along time coming."

When Barlow arrived, Chief Alex assisted him in conducting another thorough body search of Delmar, and swapping out his civvies for horizontal, black and white striped jail duds and shower clogs. Chief fingerprinted, mugshotted, and lodged Delmar in the left cell (Number 1). He was sullen, but he kept his trap shut. He acted like this was the very first time someone had beaten the snot out of him. It came as a complete surprise. He was accustomed to being the victor, especially if he got in a sucker punch.

In the meantime, Barlow completed the booking slip, incident report, criminal complaint for speeding 115 in a 55 mile-per-hour zone, resisting arrest, and simple assault on a law enforcement officer. These were all misdemeanor charges. He also signed the executed capias pro fine warrant.

Doc Boykin arrived late because he was on an unexpected house call. He gave Delmar a thorough examination. He checked for obvious signs of a concussion, but didn't notice any symptoms. Then he cleaned the laceration and sutured it with seven stitches. He told Chief and Barlow to give him a call if they noticed any unusual behavior by Delmar, such as vomiting or dizziness. Doc didn't think Delmar had a concussion, but absent a trip to the hospital in Del Rio for X-rays, he couldn't be sure. He said he would check him again tomorrow before his 10 o'clock appearance in court before Judge Maxwell.

As Barlow was escorting Doc out of the jail, he said, "Boy, Barlow, you clocked him good."

"I know, otherwise I might still be lying out there on the side of the highway in worse condition than he's in now."

"No doubt. I know he had it coming. Just keep in mind, Delmar's the type of guy who'll be looking for some payback. Don't ever let him sneak up behind you."

"I won't. Thanks for your insight."

After Doc left, Barlow returned to the jailer's desk where Chief was sitting. Barlow said, "Thanks, Chief. I've got it now."

Chief smiled and replied, "No problem. It's already 9:30. I've got this until Randy shows up. Why don't you take a spin around your half of the county? Put the good citizens of Quayle County to bed before your end of shift."

"Will do. Much obliged."

Barlow traveled up and down the west side county roads way out in the sticks. There had been virtually no traffic throughout. Most folks were at home, watching television or getting ready for bed. Barlow returned to town, and took one final spin around the northwest side of Mosby before turning south onto Sam Houston Street. It was 11:30. As he was approaching US Highway 90 (America Avenue), he saw a white Ford pickup truck barreling eastbound without regard for the in-town, 45 mile-per-hour speed limit, down from 55 outside of town. Barlow turned left and got behind the truck. He clocked it at 67 miles-per-hour as it crossed the main intersection at TX 651 (Texas Street). He flicked on his oscillating blue light and tapped his siren. Not only did the truck keep on going, it sped up, now attaining 75 miles-per-hour. Barlow called it in on the radio.

Dewey Carruthers responded, "Quayle 6, this is Quayle 8. I'm headed west on 90 just east of the Rodeo Grounds. I'll set up a roadblock there."

"Roger that. He's up to 90 now. Be ready to get out of the way if he doesn't stop. The truck is loaded down with something heavy. Two guys in the cab that I can see."

Seconds later the truck spotted Dewey's cruiser with it's blue light flashing. The driver slammed on the brakes and stopped.

Barlow jerked to a screeching halt behind the truck. Just as if everything were choreographed, Barlow and Dewey bailed out of their units simultaneously, revolvers drawn. The driver and passenger both jumped out of their truck armed, too, loaded for bear.

The passenger wielded a pump shotgun which he aimed at Dewey, who wisely ducked behind the passenger side of his unit a split-second before the offender sent a load of buckshot into the driver's door where Dewey had been standing. At the same time, the driver aimed his Smith & Wesson revolver at Barlow, who beat him to the draw and shot first, striking him center of mass. The driver tumbled to the ground and lay inert.

Dewey fired back at the passenger, who stood erect without benefit of cover while chambering another shell. Dewey's shot missed high, but Barlow's didn't. His round hit the the pistol grip of the shotgun, which was up near the passenger's chest, demolishing his hand, and showering bullet fragments and splinters from the shotgun stock into his face. He shrieked and dropped the shotgun, falling to his knees, hands rubbing his eyes out of Barlow's sight. Dewey scrambled over to the assailant, pointing his revolver at his head. Barlow glanced at the driver's inert body to make sure he was out of commission before he kicked his revolver away from his body. Then he ran in front of the truck to render assistance to Dewey.

Dewey was in control. He yelled, "Face down on the ground with your arms stretched all the way out, fingers open, or the next round will be in your brainpan, asshole!" Dewey's voice was quivering and his hands were shaking. For a moment, Barlow thought the perp was headed to perdition posthaste, not that it would have mattered one whit to Barlow if he were. However, the perp must have sensed his hairsbreadth from Hell, and he did exactly as he was told. Barlow covered the perp with his revolver to give Dewey the opportunity to cuff him behind the back. Then Dewey yanked the perp up onto his feet and searched him roughly like he was looking for a hidden diamond while wearing bear-claw mitts. He didn't find one, but he did find a Smith & Wesson revolver jammed deep down into his waistband.

Dewey perp-walked the offender back to his cruiser and shoved him face down on the back seat behind the wire mesh cage. He slammed the door shut, and leaned up against it. He turned his listening ears off, and closed his mind to the perp's agonized howling. Sounded like a hyena with his foot caught in a bear trap. Fuck him! He brought this shitstorm all on himself!

Dewey lit up a Pall Mall cigarette. His hands were shaking so much, he almost singed his right eyebrow lighting up. At last, after his third smoke, his heart began to approach its normal range of heartbeats like he had just completed the mile-and-a-half run on his Army Reserve annual physical fitness test. Even so, he still had a slight case of the shakes.

In the meantime, Barlow radioed the office. He knew Chief was in the cellblock keeping an eye on Delmar, so he thought he might have a slow response. He didn't.

"Quayle 2 from Quayle 6. Can you call out Quayle 7 (Ella Mae Gillespie) and meet Quayle 8 and me in front of the rodeo grounds? Ditto for Doc Boykin, Pete Ricketts, and Buck Boyd. Tell Buck to bring his big wrecker."

"Roger that, 6. Quayle 7 might beat me there. I'll call Quayle 9 (Randy Meacham) and get him to relieve me early. I'll also call Quayle 1. I'm sure he will want to see this."

"Roger that, 2. Quayle 6 out."

Quayle 1 was the first to arrive, as within ten minutes. First thing he did was check to confirm that both Dewey and Barlow were uninjured. Then he had Barlow walk him through the sequence of events. At the end, Sheriff Sol asked, "Do you know what precipitated the shooting? Surely it wasn't just because of a traffic stop for speeding?"

"No, Sir. Either they just robbed or killed somebody, or they're running contraband, or perhaps they have outstanding felony warrants somewhere else. I have no idea. All I know is they piled out of the truck ready to light Dewey and me up. Trying to sweet talk me out of a ticket was not on their agenda. We'll have to sift through all that manure in the back of the truck just to see if they've got a body or something buried under it. Probably be best, though, if we did that at the storage lot."

"You got that right."

Next, Sheriff Sol had Dewey walk him through it. Sheriff Sol could tell that Dewey was fighting hard to hold himself together.

Dewey sputtered and said, "Sheriff, Barlow saved my life. He shot 'em both! I probably would've been a goner. That asshole shot at me first with a shotgun, but thankfully he missed. Praise the Lord. Instead, he demolished the driver's door. I fired back once, but I missed. I couldn't see my front sight in the dark or tell where I was aiming at. Then he was fixing to let go with another blast. I saw him chamber another shell when Barlow winged him. Shithead howled like a gutshot Comanche. I was so relieved.

"He might've been partially blinded from Barlow's shot. Not for sure. It tore up his hand pretty good and shattered the pistol grip. I saw blood running into his eyes. He might've got splinters in 'em. I didn't check his face all that good. Right now I don't care if he can see or not. I'm pretty sure he ain't terminal, but for damn sure he's in a heap of pain. Serves him right, too."

Sheriff Sol responded, "He probably wouldn't look at it this way, but today was his lucky day. If he hadn't been holding that shotgun up next to his heart, he'd be pushing up daisies right now. Soon as we get some reinforcements out here and Chief gets the crime scene photographed and processed, I'll have a couple of deputies run him to the hospital in Del Rio. Make sure you clean all the blood out of the cruiser before you drop it off over at Boyd's for repairs. Otherwise, it'll stink and nobody's gonna want to drive it.

"After that, go on home and get some rest. Hug your wife. Say your prayers. And Dewey, you did a great job. Remember that.

I'm thankful you didn't get hurt.

"See you tomorrow. In fact, I'm switching you and Ernie out tomorrow. I want you on days so you can write your statement and do anything else Chief needs. Copy?"

"Copy."

It took the better part of an hour to process the crime scene. Afterwards, Buck Boyd towed the F-350 pickup truck to the impound lot at his Phillips 66 service station. Pete Ricketts transported the corpse to his mortuary. Doc Boykin examined the wounded perp and cleaned him up somewhat, trying to do no further injury. Then Deputies Kirk Shoemaker and Randy Meacham transported him to Baptist Hospital in Del Rio for treatment prior to incarceration in the Quayle County Jail. Sheriff Sol told them he'd send someone to push them off (relieve them) as soon as he could IF the prisoner was not being released from the hospital.

Dewey drove his unit to Buck Boyd's shop. He used Pine Sol to scrub down the interior of the projectile-riddled cruiser. This was the first time Dewey ever thought how insightful it was of Sheriff Sol to always purchase cars with vinyl floors and seats. Now he clearly understood why. You'd never get the blood and guts out of the upholstery or carpet otherwise. He left the unit at Boyd's for repairs. Then he called his wife to come pick him up.

Deputy Ella Mae Gillespie began her early call-out guarding Delmar for Deputy Randy Meacham, who was tied up with the prisoner at the hospital.

Chief Alex went to Ricketts Mortuary to photograph and examine the corpse before Pete transported it to the Val Verde County Medical Examiners Office in Del Rio.

Sheriff Sol and Barlow went to the impound lot to search the truck. It stunk to high heaven, so bad in fact, that the stench brought tears to Barlow's eyes. It was because not all of the manure was dried, especially the portion deep in the middle of the pile, which was still somewhat steamy.

First, they searched the cab. The glovebox contained the vehicle registration. This was certainly helpful. It reflected that the truck belonged to one Diego R. Cruz, 214 Cottonwood Street, in El Paso. It also contained six, Remington, 12-gauge, 00 buck shotgun shells, a partial box containing 28 Western brand, .38 Special bullets, two unopened packs of Phillip Morris cigarettes, a packet of matches, the Ford service manual, and a Texas state roadmap. Nothing was under the bench seat except for an empty Budweiser beer can. Ditto above the sun visors - all clear. A pair of worn, leather work gloves was in the passenger door pocket. The driver's door pocket was empty.

Next, they got down to business and searched the bed. Barlow used the shovel from on top of the pile to dump manure onto the ground. Within a couple of minutes, they discovered the marijuana bricks. There were 60 kilos overall.

Sheriff Sol left, and stepped inside the service station to phone the jail. Gillespie answered. She said Chief had not returned yet from the mortuary.

Sheriff Sol said, "Call over there, and ask Chief to stop by the impound lot as soon as he finishes up. We need him to take photographs and help inventory the 60 kilo bricks of marijuana we recovered. That's gotta be worth $60,000 at a minimum. Somebody's gonna be awful disappointed.

"You're a smart cookie. Out of curiosity, you got any fresh ideas where we can secure the dope? The bricks were buried under a ton of horseshit, and that's exactly what they smell like. No way they're going into our evidence room at this time."

"What about Slick's ranch or Archie's? They could maybe lay them out in the sun to air out. Maybe Judge Maxwell or DEA [Drug Enforcement Agency, successor to the old Bureau of Narcotics & Dangerous Drugs] would authorize burning them after we've taken a sample from each brick."

"Great idea, Gillespie. After you call Chief, call Slick and tell him what we need. Ask him if he would be willing to do that until

I can get a burn order from Judge Maxwell. If he says yes, ask him to come over to Buck's right away. If he won't, give Archie a call. Copy?"

"Copy."

It was sometime after 3 o'clock by the time Slick left with the odiferous contraband in the back of his 1948 Studebaker pickup truck. It was going to be even a longer call-out for him, because Sheriff Sol asked if he would mind pushing off Kirk at the hospital once he dropped off the evidence at his ranch. Sheriff Sol said he would prefer having a combat-experienced deputy working on the midnight shift. He also said he would send Gillespie to push off Randy for the very same reason. Slick said he would get there as soon as he could. Then Sheriff Sol, Chief Alex, and Barlow returned to the jail.

Upon their arrival, Gillespie reported, "Kirk called in. He said our prisoner, Joaquín V. Pérez, DOB October 12, 1954, of 505 Primrose Street, El Paso, has three shattered metacarpal bones in his left hand. Most of those bones are missing. He may have to have that hand amputated. They're worried he might get gangrene. The only fingers still functional are his thumb and little finger.

"He also lost the sight of his right eye and they had to remove it. They extracted a splinter about half the length of a toothpick from the pupil. He's in a lot of pain. The attending physician, Dr. Patrick D. Sincox, says Pérez is unfit for travel, and needs to remain in the hospital at least until Friday. Kirk left a callback number for you."

Sheriff Sol replied, "That's worse than we thought. The silver lining is that this is going to hamper Mr. Pérez's criminal ways in the future. Chief, do you have the identity of the driver?"

"Yep. Armando B. Cruz, DOB February 9, 1950, of 214 Cottonwood Street, El Paso, which is where the truck is registered to a Diego R. Cruz. I haven't had a chance to run 'em yet."

Sheriff Sol replied, "No doubt. Look, everything we've got here can wait until normal work hours. Chief, you and Barlow go on home. Both of you come back about noon. Barlow, you can write your statement then. Chief, tomorrow you can touch base with EPSO, EPPD, DEA, and any of the other alphabet soup agencies you think might be helpful.

"Most importantly, call the District Attorney's Office and ask Able DeWitt to scramble the Grand Jury so we can present the Pérez case, and both our line-of-duty law enforcement shooting cases. In fact, see if they could schedule the LEO shootings this afternoon.

"Barlow, you can't return to duty until you get cleared, so Chief, try to get that scheduled by Wednesday, if not sooner. We're going to be real shorthanded so long as Pérez remains in Del Rio and Delmar's cooling his heels here.

"You all think about this. All of Delmar's charges are misdemeanors. He's already proven that he won't pay a fine. That means we might be babysitting the asshole for the next year or two. We all know he needs to be taught a lesson, but his lesson is likely to be more painful for us than it will be for him."

Chief Alex queried, "I wonder if Judge Maxwell would let us farm him out to the Brewster County Jail. Sheriff Waters has a chain-gang he works five days a week. Heck! If Delmar were sentenced to hard labor, I bet Leland (Sheriff Waters) would take him off our hands for free. See, the SO over there gets paid $2-per-hour by the county for each inmate, whenever they use 'em on a road gang. Ten inmates each working 40 hours a week, is 400 hours, times $2-per-hour, equals $800 a week extra in Sheriff Waters' budget. Whaddaya think?"

"I think I'll call Leland later today. If he's willing, I'll go see Judge Maxwell. This just might be the solution to our problem. Just think if he got a year! Wouldn't that be sweet?"

Chief Alex replied, "Like manna from heaven for us and Leland."

Sheriff Sol said, "Okay. Back to our most pressing problem. I'll call Val Verde County Sheriff Will Shive in a few minutes to see if he can shake loose a deputy to give us a hand. Tell you the truth, I don't feel good about only having two deputies to guard this prick in an unsecured hospital. The weight these pendejos were carrying leads me to believe they're working for a well-organized criminal syndicate. The fact that they went for their hardware before trying to charm their way out of a lousy speeding ticket tells me all I need to know about the folks they work for.

"Folks, we've grabbed a tiger by the tail. It's not the first time, nor will it be the last, but we have to be smart and extra vigilant or someone else will get hurt.

"Gillespie, I need a favor. Could you push off Randy and guard Pérez with Slick tonight? I really hate to ask, but I'm all out of deputies until Barlow and Dewey get cleared by the Grand Jury."

"Sure thing, Sheriff."

"Thanks. Chief, you and Barlow get on outta here. I got some calls to make. Gillespie, before you go, check on Delmar one last time. If he causes you any problems whatsoever, get out your skunk oil. That'll fix his little red wagon. I'll stay behind and babysit him until Kirk returns from the hospital. Then it will be up to him."

"You got it, Sheriff."

Sarah was still up and wide awake at 4:30 when Barlow returned home. He was surprised, because he hadn't had a spare moment to call and say he'd be late. She sprang up and leapt into his arms the moment he walked through the door. She cleaved to him like he was the most precious person on Earth. That's because to her, he was. He started to speak, but she whispered, "Hush. I know all about it. Joanna (Pratt) told me. Hold me tight and never let go."

He whispered back, "It's okay. I'm okay. I'll never let you go.

You're always in my heart, whether I'm physically with you or not."

Sarah held on for nearly five minutes before he could close the door. When she let go, she asked, "Could I get you something?"

"Well, I can see that except for that old Army shirt of mine, you're wearing my favorite outfit. You know the one. The one that doesn't leave anything to my imagination. The one where you look like Eve in the Garden of Eden before she took a bite from the apple and covered herself with a fig leaf. You know exactly what I'm talking about. But before you prance around for me in your fabulous birthday outfit and tease to please, maybe you could pour me a tall Old Fitz on the rocks while I shuck my outer skin. I probably ought to shower, too."

Sarah's heavy-hearted countenance evaporated like the morning mist at the break of dawn, even though you could still see tears in the corners of both eyes and the tear tracks on her cheeks. She flashed a smile, and removed the oversized tee shirt like a strip tease artist, twirling it overhead, and tossing it into a corner. She slowly ran her fingers down her breasts and sides.

For the first time since he walked in the door, Barlow noticed her fingernails and her toenails. She must have given herself a mani and a pedi before she heard about the shootout. Her nails were a jade green, just like her eyes.

Sarah put some ice cubes in the tumbler, and topped it off with more than just a splash of seven-year-old, Old Fitzgerald, straight from the hollers of old Kentucky. She waited until Barlow had stripped off all his armor, and sat down in the cane-bottom, ladder-back chair in their small, and simple boudoir. Then she handed the frosty glass to him.

She noticed that Barlow hadn't bothered to put anything on over his taut body. His posture reminded her somewhat of Auguste Rodin's sculpture of *The Thinker*, except with a massive, raging erection. Barlow feigned being oblivious to Roscoe bouncing up and down like he was bobbing for apples. Sarah dipped her fore and middle fingers into his drink, and rubbed the chilled elixir all over Roscoe's shiny bald head. Then she went to work on Roscoe like he was a red hot, throbbing, bourbon-flavored ice cream cone.

It didn't take long. Sarah made it feel so good. Barlow gently lifted up her head. He gave her a soft kiss. Then he scooped her whole body up and gently placed her in the middle of the bed, minus the quilt. Then he ran out of gentle.

Roscoe honed in on her sweet spot like a guided missile, full of thrust and retro thrust, back and forth, like a demented demon until she was weeping with joy, begging him not to stop, so he didn't, for as long as he could. And then he couldn't anymore, but it was all right by then. All her nerve endings in the area that mattered the most were tingling with sensory overload. She was all out of breath, soaked in perspiration, her entire body feeling a soft warm glow all over. The Sandman was tugging ever so softly on her eyelids. Barlow rolled over, and she cuddled up with him in the sheets, completely embraced by an overwhelming sense of nirvana.

Barlow asked softly, "Are you going to work today? It's already 6 o'clock."

She mumbled, "Shush. No. Go to sleep."

So he did.

Chapter 6

A BEAR WITH A SORE TOOTH

Monday/Tuesday, May 20/21, 1974

R ing! Ring! Ring!
    "Hola. Pedro's Auto Repair Shop. Ruby speaking. How may we be of service?"

"Hola. This is Pepe Aguilar. May I speak with Señor Ibarra?"

"Wait while I transfer your call." Ruby pushed the fourth button on the phone to switch the call to her husband's private line."

"Señor Ibarra speaking. Whom may I ask is calling?"

"Señor Ibarra, this is Pepe Aguilar. Those parts for my 1960 Mercury have not arrived yet. I was expecting them about 6 o'clock. They're more than four hours late. Have you heard anything?"

"No. Armando and Joaquín left about 8 o'clock this morning to pick them up. They were supposed to call me after they left your shop. They haven't called yet. That's the only reason I'm still here."

"Do you think they have had an accident?"

"Well, I'm sure they didn't have one at my end, or I would have heard something a long time ago. Both of them are reliable employees. Something must have happened to them along the way. Let me make a call to be sure they got the parts. Stay where you are. I will call you back as soon as I know something. It might be an hour or two, but I will call back."

"Sí. Gracias."

Pedro Ibarra checked his Rolodex for the number of Ricardo's bordello over in Ciudad Juárez, right across the border. That's where most of his employees went to get their ashes hauled when they didn't have a woman giving it up for free here in El Paso, which normally they did. It was a pretty nice place. Pedro had been there a few times himself when he felt like getting some strange. Ricardo had some señoritas on his payroll who had amazing talents in the erotic arts. Whatever floats your boat. Besides that, it was cheap. It only cost $10 to go around the world. Not only that, Ricardo Guerra was his compadre.

Pedro dialed the number.

"Hola."

"Hola. This is Señor Ibarra. May I speak to Ricardo?"

"Señor Ibarra. This is Rosa. It's been too long since we've seen you. You may have to wait. Señor Guerra might be indisposed right now. He's trying out a new girl. Her name is Carmelita. She comes well recommended by all who have known her. You should come see for yourself. You remember. Satisfaction guaranteed or your next ride is half price. Besides, she has grande bosoms. You will like."

"Rosa, you're speaking my language. I will come soon, but now I have an urgent matter. Would you check to see if Mr. Guerra could give me just a few moments, por favor?"

"But of course. Just a minute while I check."

Pedro lit up a fresh H. Upmann cigar and blew out an enjoyable billow of aromatic smoke.

"Pedro. Good to hear from you. I only have a moment. I'm taking a new girl out for a spin. Rosa said this is a matter of great urgency."

"Sí. Gracias. Have you seen Geraldo Flores or Armando Cruz or Joaquín Pérez today?"

"Sí. Geraldo has been here all evening. He has engaged Anita for the entire evening. You remember who she is, don't you? She's my roly-poly artisan."

"But of course. How about Armando or Joaquín?"

"Sadly, no. What is the problem?"

"Armando and Joaquín were supposed to deliver some parts for me, but they never showed up. I can't find them anywhere. Would it be possible for me to speak to Geraldo?"

"Sí. I will ask Rosa to fetch him for you. What was the value of the merchandise?"

"Don't ask. Enough to purchase three or four houses."

"Ah chihuahua! I hope you find them. They are fine boys. Very trustworthy. Hold the line while Rosa finds Geraldo for you. Good luck. Come see us soon. Buenos noches."

"Buenos noches."

Pedro held the receiver in his left hand, while he poured himself another shot of tequila - the top shelf kind - José Cuervo Gold - not that rotgut Escupidura Lagarto, known to the Anglos as Lizard Spit. He savored the taste while he waited.

"Jefe, this is Geraldo. Why do you seek me?"

"Did you see Armando and Joaquín today?"

" Sí, sí, but I was very late. I had some problems at the border. I didn't get there until a little after noon. Everything was fine. Why do you ask?"

"Because they never made the delivery! Are you sure everything was fine?"

"Sí. I took the payment to Jefe Castíllo before I went to the farmers market. You can call and ask him. Do you have his number? I can give it to you."

"No need. I believe you. Besides I already have it. If, perchance, you see them, would you ask them to call me right away?"

"But of course. I hope you find them. Now I'm worried, too. Buenas noches, Jefe."

"Buenas noches."

Pedro dialed Pepe Aguilar's number.

"Hola. Is that you?"

"Sí. I confirmed that the boys picked up the parts, but the delivery was late - not until after noon. Even so, they should have been there hours ago. In the morning, I'm sending Chico Salazar along the route to see if he can find them or evidence of a mishap. He will stop by your business whether he does or he doesn't. If they do show up, or if you hear something, give me a call right away. In the meantime, I will order some more parts. It will take me two days to get them to you. Is that satisfactory?"

"Sí. Gracias. I will be in touch if I hear anything. Buenas noches."

"Buenas noches."

Pedro exited the back door of his shop and crossed the gravel parking lot to the cabaña on the left. It was the smallest of three, with only one bedroom. The others had two. He let his most trusted employees live in them for free if they so elected. Right now Chico was his only tenant, and he needed only one bedroom. Pedro knocked on the door, saying, "Chico, it's me."

Chico answered the door in his white boxer shorts and sleeveless undershirt. He said, "Jefe, come in. Would you like a snort of Escupidura Lagarto?"

"No, gracias. I won't be here but a moment. I have something very important I need you to do for me."

"But of course. Anything."

"Something happened to Armando and Joaquín. They never delivered the load today. I know they left El Paso about 1 p.m. I need you to try to find them. Take a couple days' clothes.

"They were supposed to have taken US 90 all the way to Del Rio. The package was going to Señor Pepe Aguilar, at 110 Liberty Street in Del Rio. It's called Pepe's Scrap Metal. His telephone number is 455-6669. Write that down. It's a fucking junkyard with six or seven vicious German shepherds. It's on the east side of town on the north side of 90. Turn north just past the Dairy Queen, which by the way, has the best chocolate soft serve ice cream I've ever had. Get the biggest cone. It only costs 45 cents. Anyway, you can't miss it. Señor Aguilar is expecting you sometime tomorrow evening. Look along the way for signs of an accident. They were driving the white F-350.

"Look, I want you to call me along the way, starting at Van Horn, and continuing at each major junction until you get there. I will provide you with any updates. Maybe save you some time. Here's $300 to cover expenses. Be careful. There's always a chance the Tres Deuces got them, or God forbid, the cops. That load was worth $60,000 to me. Comprendes?"

"Sí. Do you mind if I leave now? The highway will be empty and I can search with less difficulty. I won't call you until breakfast time unless I find something. Okay?"

"Sí. Take your .45. You might need it. Got enough ammo?"

"Sí. Two full boxes and one half-box altogether. If I need more than 15 rounds (two 7-round magazines plus one in the pipe) for this trip, I'll be fucked."

"Don't even joke like that. Any questions?"

"No. I'll be in touch."

Chico packed an extra chambray shirt and three sets of underwear and socks into his gym bag. He figured he could get by on the pair of Wranglers he had on. He also put in his shaving kit, a carton of Camel regulars, and an extra box of ammo. He slipped on his new Tony Lama's, stuck his Colt automatic in his waistband, checked his jean jacket to make sure his extra magazine was still in the side pocket, adjusted his new Stetson, grabbed his bag and thermos, and stepped out of his digs.

He checked the lot to see which vehicles were available. He selected the pale blue 1968 Dodge A100, short wheelbase cargo van with a three-inch-wide lateral white stripe along both sides, and a 225 cubic-inch (3.7 liter) Slant 6 engine and "three-on-the-tree" manual transmission. It had new rubber, and except for a slight rattle they couldn't nail down, drove like it was brand new. He picked this particular truck because he wanted to blend in like a workman.

He stopped by the Petro Truck Stop on the way out of town. He topped off his tank, filled his thermos with coffee, and purchased two prepackaged bologna and cheese sandwiches, a Tootsie Roll, and a Texas roadmap. He studied the map, and then he was ready to roll. This was the first important on-the-road assignment that El Jefe had given him. He was ready to prove his worth.

He didn't concern himself much with Greater El Paso. When he crossed into Hudspeth County, he began searching both sides of the road in earnest. It wasn't that difficult. The road was flat, the ditches were shallow, and there wasn't much traffic. Besides, he never drove over 50 miles per hour.

He only encountered a half-dozen vehicles between Fabens and Van Horn. It was even more sparse between there and Alpine, where he came upon a dilapidated adobe, all-night, two-pump, DX gas station. It was operated by a small, grizzled, Hispanic octogenarian in overalls and a dirty white tee-shirt, worn out Jethro Bodine boondockers, and a disreputable straw sombrero with two holes in the crown where the straw had been broken. He was puffing away on a corncob pipe. Two empty, and one half-full Mountain Dew soft drinks in green glass bottles stood in a straight line on the ground beside him like glass soldiers at parade rest.

The old codger arose from his rusty, chrome-framed kitchen chair with a torn red padded plastic seat and back, which was situated outside the front door of the tiny building. He greeted Chico warmly, only his second customer of the night. He pumped the gas, checked the oil and tire pressures, and washed the bugs off the windshield. In the meantime, Chico stretched his legs and helped himself, purchasing a cold, six-ounce bottle of Coca-Cola for two thin dimes from the antique vending machine next to the front door. The old guy greeted him in Spanish, so Chico responded in kind.

While Chico took a break and polished off his Coke, he chatted with the old man. He said his name was Bembe, which means means Son of Prophecy. He was born 82 years ago in

Ojinaga (Mexico). He'd been living in Alpine since he was nine years old. He was a sheepherder all his life, but now he is too old. Now he does this. His wife is dead, as are two of his sons. The other son ran off when he was 15 and hasn't been seen since. His only daughter married a man as strong as a bull and twice as dumb. He digs graves for a living, in addition to being the caretaker of the church cemetery. He likes to lose his money on Tuesday nights when they have cockfights. Now his daughter is 60 years old and has five sons, two daughters, eleven grandchildren, and two great-grandchildren. There haven't been any traffic accidents around these parts for at least a month. He doesn't remember seeing a white Ford F-350 loaded down with horseshit and two hombres, but most likely he wasn't at work when they passed by. He wished Chico luck finding them.

Chico thanked Bembe and moved along. He passed through Mosby in Quayle County, which reminded him of every other little desert burg he'd ever driven through. He hadn't seen any sign of a motor vehicle accident or the truck. It was approaching 7 o'clock, when he rolled into Del Rio in Val Verde County. He topped off again, this time at a Sinclair service station with a large, green, concrete dinosaur. He stopped for breakfast at Belinda's Diner. He ate a stack of pancakes with patty sausages, washed down with orange juice. When he was sated, he stepped outside and belched loudly. Then he called El Jefe. It was almost 8.

Jefe asked, "Where are you?"

"I'm in Del Rio. Sorry, but I didn't find anything."

"Listen to me. Señor Aguilar called me an hour ago. He was listening to a local radio station, 790 on the dial. He heard a report that the Quayle County Sheriff's Office made a traffic stop last night. They got into a shootout with the two men in the vehicle. One was killed. The other is in the hospital in Del Rio. The names have not been released pending notification of next of kin. The man in the hospital is under arrest, pending a court appearance in Mosby.

"I bet they're talking about Armando and Joaquín. Go talk to Señor Aguilar and see what you can find out."

"Sure thing, Jefe. I will also tune in 790 to see if they report this again at the next broadcast. It's almost 8. I'll call you back in a little bit."

Chico tuned in the radio just in time to catch the "News at the Top of the Hour." The lead story by Dwayne Arbuckle was this. "Quayle County Sheriff Solomon Pratt reported a late night shooting last night between sheriff's deputies and two out-of-town men as the result of a traffic stop. The men were traveling at a high rate of speed in the central business district of Mosby when they were stopped. The driver and his passenger exited the vehicle with drawn firearms. After an exchange of gunfire, the driver was killed and the passenger was wounded. No lawmen were injured. The wounded man was arrested and transported to Baptist Hospital in Del Rio, where he is listed as being in serious condition. Upon release from the hospital, he will be transported back to Quayle County for his arraignment on criminal charges. The names of the deceased and the wounded man are being withheld pending notification of next of kin. On an unrelated matter, Val Verde's Farmers Bank . . . ."

Chico turned off the radio. This had to be Armando and Joaquín. If the broadcast were factual, they must have left their brains at home. Why would they speed through a small town carrying a load? Why would they jump out with weapons drawn? It didn't make any sense. True or false, it meant the cops had the load, but did they realize it yet? Could it still be buried, undetected in the load of manure? Who did the truck registration come back to?

Chico followed Jefe's instructions to Liberty Street. He turned north and followed it a quarter-mile before he found the junkyard owned by Señor Pepe Aguilar. Chico stepped out of the van, checking carefully for the vicious junkyard dogs.

Fortunately, they were behind a chain link fence which separated the old junkers from the newer ones. That was good. Pulling his concealed .45 and shooting the man's dogs would not make for a favorable introduction. He stepped inside the near darkness of the metal garage and waited for his eyes to adjust. He saw several muchachos. He guessed correctly that the older one wearing spectacles and seated behind a desk working on invoices was Señor Aguilar.

Chico waited until Señor Aguilar noticed him. Señor Aguilar stood up and took off his reading glasses. He walked over to greet him. Señor Aguilar was about 45 years-of-age. He stood 5-feet, 9-inches tall, and weighed a buck-fifty. He had thick black, curly hair sprouting from the open collar of his shirt and on the back of his hands and fingers, not to mention a bushy Pancho Villa mustache. He was wearing black dress trousers and a white, western cut, long sleeve shirt with mother-of-pearl buttons. His thick black coiffure was mostly concealed under an expensive straw, 15X Stetson. He wore shiny black, lizard skin, Tony Lama boots, and a hand-tooled black, lizard skin belt with a magnificent oval, sterling silver belt buckle displaying an inset of a turquoise lizard. His hairy left pinky sported an engraved silver ring with a turquoise stone designed to look like an eyeball; however, the most impressive aspect of Señor Aguilar's ensemble was a black, hand-tooled, El Paso Saddlery, cross-draw holster, securing a nickel-plated, four-inch Colt Python, .357 Magnum revolver, with checkered, turquoise grips. Señor Aguilar did not portray the image of a man running a junkyard that Chico had expected. Instead, he exuded confidence, power, strength, intelligence, and class, all with panache. He certainly was impressive.

He said, "You must be Chico. I was expecting you."

"Nice to meet you, Señor. I hope to be of some assistance to you and to Señor Ibarra.

"I heard the radio broadcast on my way over here. It sounded like the parties involved are probably Armando and Joaquín, especially since they have dropped off the radar. Under the circumstances, we are reluctant to contact the authorities. We don't know if the authorities have discovered the load they were carrying. It was buried under a mountain of dried horse manure, but we must assume that they have. Is there no way, Señor Aguilar, that you could make a discreet inquiry at the hospital to learn the name of the survivor and the extent of his injuries?"

"Naturally, I have been reluctant to do so for the same reasons. Now that you mention it, I might know of someone who could at least find out his name without arousing suspicion. What are their surnames?"

"Armando Cruz and Joaquín Pérez."

"Why don't you have a soft drink from my machine while I make a call? I have all the Mexican flavors, watermelon, peach, strawberry, raspberry, lime. I have each flavor, and they only cost a dime."

"Thank you, Señor. I haven't had a watermelon soda in quite some time."

While Chico sought out a cold beverage, Señor Aguilar made a private call from his desk. About ten minutes later, he arose and sauntered over to the soft drink machine. He said, "I was fortunate. I was able to speak to someone in the know. The survivor is Joaquín Pérez. He was delirious with pain when he arrived. He's maimed for life. They had to amputate the middle three fingers on his left hand. He also lost his right eye. He's under heavy sedation. He's also under heavy guard at the hospital. So long as he does not deteriorate, they will transport him to the Quayle County Jail on Friday. That's all I could get. If you're thinking about pulling off a rescue, forget about it. It would take an Army to do so successfully, and even then you would lose even more compadres. Do you wish to call Señor Ibarra or should I?"

"Thank you, Señor. No. It is better if I make the call. He's expecting me to call."

"But of course. Could you ask if I can expect a delivery tomorrow as he promised?"

"Yes. May I use your phone?"

"I'm always leery of this line being tapped. When we speak of business, it's always in code. I do have a payphone out back. It only costs 55 cents to call El Paso for three minutes. Here, I have the change."

"That's okay. I have a pocketful of change, but thank you anyway. I'll go make the call and let you know what he says. Be right back."

Chico went out back and made the call.

When Jefe answered, Chico said, "It's them. Joaquín is alive, but he's maimed for life. He lost the middle three fingers of his left hand, and his right eye. He's under heavy sedation. The hospital is full of guards, but if all goes well, they will transport him to the jail in Mosby on Friday?"

"Do you know if he squealed?"

"No, but they said he was delirious with pain upon arrival, and he's under heavy sedation now."

"Then there's no way to know for sure. Besides, he's got three more days to change his mind if he hasn't.

"Tell you what. Cruise through the hospital lot to see how many cop cars are parked there. Don't forget Quayle County. Then find a motel in Del Rio and check in. Get some rest.

"Check it again during the midnight shift. Then go check out the jail in Mosby. See if you can figure out how they will take him in. Then see if you can find the safest way to get from there to here without getting busted by the cops.

"What I want is for you to wax him before he walks through those jailhouse doors. Try not to kill a cop unless you wanna be on the run for the rest of your fucking life. Those bastards will hunt you down like a rabid dog if you do. You'd probably have to live in Mexico for as long as you live if it came down to that.

Check everything, e-v-e-r-y-t-h-i-n-g, including your escape route on Wednesday night, too. Then Thursday night, you duck in a hidey-hole where you can watch the Mosby jail parking lot, somewhere near the entrance without getting rousted. The idea is to do a hit-and-run, quick as a flash. Do the deed and come back home. I hate that this must be done, but much is at risk. Can you do that?"

"Let you know for sure on Thursday.

"By the way, Señor Aguilar asked me if he can still expect a delivery tomorrow."

"Yes. Tell him he'll have it sometime tomorrow night. Velásquez and Jiménez will bring it, but via a different route, so they may not arrive until 8 or 9."

"I know he will be pleased."

"Okay. Call me by 8 p.m. on Thursday."

"Sí, sí. Adiós."

"Adiós."

Chico rang off and went back inside.

Señor Aguilar asked, "How did it go?"

"I think it was about like he expected. He wasn't happy, but what can we do? We'll have to wait and see. He also said your delivery will be here tomorrow night. It may not arrive until 8 or so, since the muchachos will be taking a different route. He hopes this doesn't inconvenience you."

"Not at all. We're still in business. This was just an unfortunate set of circumstances."

"He also told me to express his appreciation to you for getting the details."

"Glad to do it. What will you do now?"

"Get some sleep. Work my way back home. He told me to take my time."

"Well Chico, it was my honor to meet you. Call me if I can ever be of service."

"Gracias. Adiós."

"Adiós."

Chico cruised the Baptist Hospital lot. He saw three marked units - two Val Verde and one Quayle County. There may have been one unmarked unit. He wasn't sure. He was thankful El Jefe didn't want him to do the job here.

Then he checked in at the Primrose Inn a couple of blocks back behind the hospital. It was a 1950s era, tan stucco, single-story motel with 16 rooms, a little off the beaten path. He hoped to remain undetected by Señor Aguilar. He wasn't sure if anyone had noticed his van at the junkyard in the midst of all the other vehicles which were parked willy nilly. He hoped not.

Chapter 7

Running Out Leads

Tuesday, May 21, 1974

Chief Alex didn't sleep very well after he went home in the wee hours. He knew he had a full plate on his desk, and that he was behind the power curve. This was doubly so with Gillespie pulling the night shift guarding the prisoner. She took care of all the minor investigative details for him while he was frying bigger fish on their major felony cases, and she did it very well. Always cheerful. Never a complaint. He didn't have to double-check her work.

He arose at 8 o'clock and got ready for work, but at a weary snail's pace. His wife, April, was concerned about him. The doctor said if he didn't slow down he would likely have a heart attack. She watched what he ate like a stingy dietitian in charge of a fat farm.

This morning Alex got a bowl of shredded wheat with only one teaspoon of sugar, a four-ounce slice of ham, fresh strawberries, orange juice, and black coffee. April sent him to work with a lunchbox lovingly filled with tunafish salad, eight saltines, a cup of cottage cheese, a large dill pickle, an apple, a small thermos of milk, and one oatmeal cookie. Alex complained that the inmates ate better than he. She responded that she didn't care what they ate. She only cared what he ate. She asked him not to stop by Crabtree's for an afternoon milkshake, because he would get some ice cream after dinner. Chief decided this was a fair trade-off as he moseyed out the door, mind already racing with leads he needed to pursue, but his body was balking, and not in sync with his mind.

Sheriff Sol was also running on fumes, but he was younger and in better health than Chief Alex. Also nobody put him on a diet, but he was cutting back anyway. Nevertheless, he no longer measured his weight in pounds. Now he calculated his weight in stones (14 pounds to the stone) like the British. Right now he was down to a trim 16-1/2 stones.

Sheriff Sol was a commander who led from the front. One who never asked of his troops anything he wouldn't do or hadn't done himself. He routinely put in more hours than any deputy except for Chief. Now he was working in concert with April to reduce the number of unpaid hours of overtime that Chief put in. Easier said than done.

Sheriff Sol beat Chief Alex to the office by two hours. First thing he did was call Baptist Hospital and ask the receptionist to patch him through to Deputy Clarence Oldman (Slick), or to Deputy Ella Mae Gillespie. Gillespie picked up.

"Gillespie, how you holding up?"

"Oh hi, Sheriff. I'm fine. I wasn't expecting a call from you. Anything going on? Need us to work another tour?"

"Maybe if we were in World War III, but not today, Ella Mae. Thanks for inquiring. What's the status of Mr. Pérez?"

"He's in pain. No question about it. Unless he starts feeling better, I don't see how we could possibly care for him in the jail."

"That's what I was afraid of.

"Okay. Listen. Randy's back on afternoons at the jail. You're working days with Chief tomorrow for as many days as he needs you. Also, Ernie and Chunk should be there shortly to push you all off. Do you have any questions?"

"No. Thanks, Sheriff."

"Thanks right back at you. Appreciate you stepping up last night when I really needed you. Could you get Slick on the phone for me?"

"Sure thing. See you tomorrow, Sheriff."

Gillespie went back happy as a lark, to Room 211, where Pérez was feigning abject misery and plotting his escape. He still hurt miserably, but he needed to free himself before Jefe decided that he was snitching, something he would never do. He would die first.

Slick was seated in a padded office chair (without rollers) in the hospital room, trimming his nails with the U.S. Marine Corps K-Bar knife he liberated from them at the conclusion of World War II (when he was honorably discharged). He would have liberated his M-1 rifle if he could have gotten away with it.

Val Verde County's Deputy Hans Johansson and Reserve Deputy Clifton Mueller were sitting in the same type of chairs outside the room, wondering how long this incredibly boring assignment of being jail guards for Quayle County's prisoner would last. Both would have much preferred being on patrol doing real police work. This was pure torture.

Gillespie returned to the fold and pushed off Slick so he could take the call down the hall at the nurses' station.

Slick inquired, "What's up, Sheriff?"

"Just making a wellness check on my troops. Thanks for coming in last night, and for securing and fumigating our seizure."

"Think nothing of it. Now I told Matilda (Slick's new favorite horse) not to eat those herbs, but she's got a mind of her own. She don't always do what she's told. She can be ornery."

"Well if she does, just box up her eye-watering deposit and put an evidence tag on it. If she gobbles up an entire kilo, I expect she'll unload an entire kilo. Just make sure to store that evidence box in your bedroom closet for safekeeping.

"Look, Mr. Smartypants, the reason I'm calling is to ask your assessment of the security arrangements on our prisoner, and what your thoughts are regarding a possible rescue attempt."

"Well, this ain't no secure location, but you already know that. We got two local deputies, but they say their boss insisted that they stay on the door. I'd much prefer one down by the elevator, with the other'n as his relief - maybe hang out at the nurses' station when they take turns on relief. Then we post one of us in the room with the turd and t'other one outside the door. I'm even happy to make this a four-man rotation, 30 minutes at each post, but they say they aren't allowed to deviate from their orders."

"Did Will send over some solid guys?"

"His regular deputy, Hans Johansson, is as solid as they come. Let's just say the reservist couldn't break up a fight between a couple of Brownie Scouts without getting his ass whipped. My understanding is that Will didn't have much say in the matter of hiring this Clinton Mueller character, at least as a reservist, because his old man is a major donor to Will's re-election campaign. Ever heard of Mueller Truck Lines? Big deal over here. That's his old man."

"Nope, but I'll take your word on it. I'll call and see if Will will budge on how we deploy you all. What's your assessment of a possible rescue attempt?"

"We know anything yet regarding which El Paso gang we're dealing with?"

"Not yet."

"Well, whoever they are, they shoot first and ask questions later. I'd say it's a serious risk."

"That's my concern, too. Okay, I'm leaving you on the midnight guard detail for now. I consider it the riskiest. I'll send Barlow with you too, until we get this jasper properly secured and tucked into our own jail."

"What about the Grand Jury regarding the officer line-of-duty shootings? Isn't Barlow sidelined?"

"I'll make a couple of calls on that, too. We don't have the luxury of putting Barlow and Dewey on ice. I'm pretty sure I can get that worked out. In the meantime, you and Gillespie trade off on the room and the nurses' station. Tell Ernie and Chunk the same thing. This will have to do if Will won't change his mind.

Look. I gotta go. Adiós."

"Adiós."

Next, Sheriff Sol called Judge Sweeney at home on his business line. Judge Sweeney picked up on the first ring. "Hello?"

"Judge, Sheriff Sol here. Sorry to call so early."

"Is this about last night's shooting?"

"Yes, Sir. How did you hear about it?"

"Sheriff, this is a small town. Everyone knows, including Del Rio's news reporters on television and the radio. You must've briefed them. What is so important that it can't wait until 10 a.m.?"

"A couple of things, Judge. Most importantly, the public doesn't know we seized 60 kilos of marijuana from the truck those El Paso bandits were driving. Right now we're holding that close to the vest.

"Next, I've got two deputies guarding the prisoner at the Val Verde hospital. Sheriff Shive has also assigned two of his men. We're grateful for that.

"Third, Barlow scooped up Delmar Higgins last night on that capias. He's cooling his heels in our jail as we speak.

"I'm asking if it would be possible to have the Grand Jury hear the officer line-of-duty shooting cases on Dewey and Barlow this morning so I can put them back to work. We're severely strapped for personnel, plus we haven't even begun the investigation on the drug case yet."

"Sol, you know I don't dillydally on criminal cases. Have you spoken to Able DeWitt yet?"

"No, Sir. I just wanted to secure your blessing first."

"You got it. What else?"

"Judge, if we had a prisoner convicted of one or more misdemeanors and he was sentenced to jail time at hard labor, would you object if he did his serve-out in Brewster County, where Sheriff Waters' office gets paid $2 by Brewster County for every hour prisoners in his custody perform road gang duty?"

"Is this true? Brewster County actually does that? Where do they get the revenue to pay for this?"

"My understanding is that the sheriff is allowed to farm out convicted prisoners, under supervision of course, if their sentence specifies hard labor. The county contracts with various public and private concerns, Texas DOT, construction firms, and the like, to provide available inmate labor for $4 per hour. The county treasurer's office keeps $2, and the sheriff's office keeps $2.

"I was thinking that Sheriff Waters would probably house any hard labor inmates we have if he got to keep the $2 per hour. Since this is just a hypothetical question, I haven't asked him yet."

"Tell you what. I need to do some research on this and get an opinion from the Texas Attorney General's Office. I'll also ask our illustrious Texas State Senator Darnell Sweeney to make some inquiries. If the answer is that it's legal, I don't see why we shouldn't start doing that as well. Of course, we seldom have more than one or two inmates, but it would certainly help with the inadequate staffing of your office, assuming Brewster County did agree to take these inmates off our hands for the revenue they would receive. I'll get back to you on that. Anything else?"

"No, Your Honor. Thank you.

"Good day, Sheriff."

"Good day, Judge."

Next, Sheriff Sol called District Attorney Able DeWitt. After the greetings, Sheriff Sol asked, "Is the Grand Jury going to be impaneled today?"

"I'm way ahead of you. I spoke to Chief Alex last night. Yes. They're coming in at 9 o'clock to handle the officer line-of-duty shootings. Do you have something for me on Pérez yet?"

"No. Did Chief tell you we seized 60 kilos of pot?"

"No, he didn't. Wow! He must have been really tired. It was after 4 o'clock when we spoke."

"We're not talking about that publicly just yet. We don't think the shipper knows we recovered it - yet. We could go for attempted murder today if you want. Otherwise, we'd like to wait until Thursday. Our understanding is that the hospital won't release Pérez until Friday."

"Thursday works. What about Delmar and his capias?"

"We'll bring him to 10 o'clock court. Just so you know, we found out Brewster is allowed to put inmates to work if they're sentenced to hard labor. The county pays the SO $2 for each hour of inmate labor. I don't know all the details yet. Judge Sweeney and his brother are looking into it. As a result, Delmar could be looking at a hard labor sentence."

"Interesting. Now, if he does get a hard labor sentence, it might truly have an impact. Let me know."

"Will do. We're hoping that we could farm Delmar out to Brewster County for the revenue. That would really help us here with our shortage of manpower. It would be a win-win for everyone except for Delmar."

"You know what they say. If you can't do the time, don't do the crime. Good day."

Next, Sheriff Sol called Sheriff Leland Waters. Leland said his DA, Bradford Delaney, already had a written ruling by the state AG. He said it was perfectly legal, but to make sure the paper trail regarding the money was well-documented and crystal clear. All revenue coming in from inmate labor, and how the county and SO utilized those funds, had better pass the smell test unless the county officials were prepared to do some hard time themselves.

Leland said he would accept any of Quayle's inmates who were sentenced to hard labor, so long as they worked and/or until they received a serve-out.

Sheriff Sol relayed this message to Miss Eloise Goodman, Judge Sweeney's clerk.

Next he called Sheriff Will Shive to thank him for assigning two officers to assist in guarding the prisoner. He asked if it would be possible to implement an integrated four-man rotation on 30-minute intervals, putting one deputy in the room with the prisoner, one on the door outside the room, one at the elevator, and one at the nurses' station as a relief post. He said it would give them a heads up if the prisoner's employer decided to stage a rescue. Will concurred, and said he would have the patrol captain notify his deputies. Sheriff Sol thanked him again and said he was always ready to return the favor.

Neither Chief Alex, nor Dewey, nor Barlow had made an appearance at the office by 8:50. Truthfully, he had told them to come in around noon, but now he was in a bind. He was there by himself. Fortunately Miss Loretta walked in, so at least the phones would be covered.

Sheriff Sol walked upstairs to the Grand Jury Room and met with District Attorney Able DeWitt. He testified as the lone witness regarding the officers line-of-duty shootings. Normally Chief Alex would have done that. Sheriff Sol swore under oath as to what he observed at the crime scene, and the statements made to him by Deputy Dewey Carruthers and Deputy Barlow Adams. He also testified regarding the nature of the injuries sustained by both assailants.

When asked by a grand juror, he did not speculate as to why the assailants initiated the gunfight. He stated that the criminal investigation was in its infancy, and that they had not completed a background check on either assailant.

He summed up by stating that someone from his office would return on Thursday for a proposed indictment of Joachín Pérez, the surviving assailant, for aggravated assault. He said the deputy presenting the proposed indictment would have personal history information on both assailants by then.

Sheriff Sol was excused.

District Attorney DeWitt read the four possible indictments to charge or exonerate one or both deputies for (1) criminal responsibility regarding the death by gunfire of one Armando

Cruz, and/or for (2) criminal maiming of one Joachín Pérez by gunfire. Then Mr. DeWitt stepped out of the room so the jury could vote to return true bills or no bills or a combination thereof.

Two minutes later, the foreman of the jury asked DA DeWitt to come back in. By a unanimous decision, the Grand Jury voted four no bills. DA DeWitt informed Sheriff Sol. By the time he returned to his office, everyone he needed was present.

Sheriff Sol reported the Gran Jury's decision to no bill both Dewey and Barlow for the line-of-duty shootings. He told Dewey that once he completed his formal written statement, to go home. Both he and Kirk were on afternoon shift duty at the hospital until Pérez was lodged in their jail.

He told Barlow he was assigned the midnight shift with Slick. Then he told Barlow to try to complete his line-of-duty statement by 9:50, unless he hadn't completed the criminal complaint on Delmar, reason being, he needed to take Delmar to 10 o'clock court. Sheriff Sol said he would go with.

Barlow responded that Delmar's complaint was done.

Finally, Sheriff Sol asked Chief Alex to grab some coffee and meet him in his office. He said they needed to map out the investigation.

Everybody got to work.

At 9:55, Sheriff Sol and Barlow were sitting in court with Delmar, who was trussed up in leg irons, handcuffs, and belly chain, wearing jailhouse stripes and shower clogs. He reminded Barlow of a big fish about to be tossed into the ocean for shark bait from the back of a fishing trawler. You could see the anger in his eyes, and by his body language. Delmar was in a foul mood, ready to erupt at any moment. Barlow prayed that he would hold off until court was in session. Since this was the only case on the morning docket, Delmar would have Maximum Max's undivided attention - the only pigeon in the purview of a hungry, circling hawk.

At 10 o'clock, the bailiff, August Bellweather, called everyone gathered in the courtroom to order - all six of them. He was followed in by Judge Maxwell B. Sweeney, who swooped in with a flourish, and alighted in his rightful position on the throne-like chair with rollers as smooth as glass, prominently situated behind the bench.

After surveying his six-person audience, all of whom were standing erect with reverence, Judge Sweeney said, "Please be seated." He looked at his clerk, Miss Eloise Goodman, and asked, "What do we have on the calendar this morning, Miss Goodman?"

"Judge, we have one defendant, but two docket numbers. The first is The State of Texas versus Delmar S. Higgins, docket number 74-01-0006. The second docket number is 74-05-00431."

"Ahem, I see. Will counsels make their appearances for the record?"

"District Attorney Able DeWitt for the State, Your Honor."

"Samuel Davis, Esquire, representing Mr. Delmar S. Higgins, Your Honor."

"Mr. Davis, regarding Docket Number 74-01-00006, I see that I have already found Mr. Higgins guilty in absentia for speeding 50 miles-per-hour in a 35 miles-per-hour zone because he failed to appear on three separate occasions after he had been served with summonses. I sentenced Mr. Higgins to pay $35 plus court costs. I have decided to vacate that judgment and offer Mr. Higgins the opportunity to go to trial today on that charge. What say you Mr. Higgins?"

Mr. Davis responded for his client. He said, "Your Honor, Mr. Higgins wants to plead guilty to that charge."

"Is that true, Mr. Higgins?"

"Yes, Your Honor."

"Very well. We will revisit this in a moment. Miss Goodman, please read the charges on the new docket number."

"Your Honor, there are three charges re Docket Number 74-05-00431. These include speeding 115 miles-per-hour in a 55 miles-per-hour zone; resisting arrest; and simple assault on a police officer."

"Mr. Davis, is Mr. Higgins prepared to go to trial today on these new charges?"

"Your Honor, my client has decided to plead guilty on all three of those charges."

"Is that true, Mr. Higgins?"

"Yes, Judge."

"Very well. Mr. Davis and Mr. Higgins, please have a seat. Mr. DeWitt, does the State have a witness present to make an allocution?"

"Yes, Your Honor. The State calls the arresting officer, Deputy Sheriff Barlow Adams."

Barlow went to the witness chair and stood while Miss Goodman swore him in. Then he took his seat.

DA DeWitt stood up from the prosecution table and said, "Deputy Adams, please tell the court what transpired at approximately 7:14 p.m., the evening of Monday, May 19, 1974, in Quayle County, Texas, resulting in the arrest of Mr. Higgins."

"Yes. I had a capias pro fine warrant to serve on Mr. Higgins. I knew he worked for a company in Brewster County, that he drove a green Chevy Nova, and that he got off work at 7 o'clock. Therefore, I set up on the east side of the billboard on US 90, which is roughly a mile east of the Brewster County line. At 7:14, Mr. Higgins passed me at a high rate of speed. I set out after him and paced him at 115 miles-per-hour before he slowed down and pulled over.

"I asked him to step out of the car. This must have set him off, because after he got out, when I told him he was under arrest, he took a vicious swing at me. I stepped back and returned force with force, striking him once on his jaw. He fell to the ground, unconscious. I placed him in handcuffs and administered first aid. I transported him to the jail, where he was examined and sutured by Doctor Boykin. I had his vehicle towed to Boyd's

Phillips 66 lot."

DA DeWitt asked, "Anything else, Deputy Adams?"

"Not that I can recall."

"Very well. You may step down unless the defense or Judge Sweeney have some questions."

Mr. Davis whispered something to his client, who was visibly disturbed. Then Delmar jumped up and pointed his finger at Barlow as far as he could extend it from the waist chain. He screamed, "You set me up, you son of a bitch! You were hiding behind that billboard all the time, just like a yellow dog pussy! This ain't over, Adams!"

Judge Sweeney banged his gavel rapid fire as hard as he could. It sounded like a woodpecker.

Sheriff Sol jumped up and body-slammed Delmar to the hardwood floor. Then he rolled Delmar onto his stomach, and jammed his knee into the small of his back until he calmed down and quit screaming. Then he lifted Delmar up by the stack-and-swivel like he was a 225-pound gunny sack full of rotten turnips, and slammed his backside hard into his chair, shouting, "Shut up, Delmar!"

Delmar did exactly what he was told.

Judge Sweeney asked, "Mr. Davis, does your client still wish to plead guilty to these three charges described in Deputy Adams' allocution?"

Sam whispered something in Delmar's ear. Delmar replied, "Yes, Sir! I apologize for my outburst."

"Very well. Please stand while I accept your plea and pronounce sentence."

When everyone except for Miss Goodman and Judge Sweeney were on their feet, Judge Sweeney stated, "Mr. Higgins, the Court finds you guilty on all counts. Regarding Docket Number 74-01-00006, on the charge of speeding, I sentence you to serve two months in jail.

"Regarding Docket Number 74-05-00431, on the charge of

speeding, I sentence you to serve four months in jail. On the charge of resisting arrest, I sentence you to serve six months in jail. On the charge of simple assault, I sentence you serve one year in jail. Then I order that all sentences are to be served consecutively at hard labor.

"Just to be clear, Mr. Higgins, I just sentenced you to serve two years in jail at hard labor. Furthermore, Sheriff Pratt, if your office has an agreement with the Brewster County Sheriff's Office, I hereby order that Mr. Higgins be transported there forthwith to begin execution of his sentence.

"All business of this Court having been concluded, I hereby adjourn it."

Bang, bang, bang went the gavel! Judge Sweeney disappeared like a wisp of smoke through his back door.

Sam Davis had a quizzical look on his face. Able DeWitt asked him to come to his office. Barlow had a cat-eating-a-canary grin. Sheriff Sol put the "habeas grabbis" on Delmar and bounced him all the way down the stairs and back into his jail cell. Delmar hadn't expected that - being tossed around like a fat sheep by a pissed off grizzly bear. Sheriff Sol told Barlow to let Delmar change into his own clothes, because he was leaving ASAP for Alpine to begin his sentence at hard labor.

Delmar exclaimed, "Anyplace would be better than this shithole, Sheriff!"

Then Sheriff Sol spun around and looked hard at Delmar. He pointed his finger at him like a gun barrel and said, "Delmar, you better never ever let me catch you setting foot in Quayle County again. You won't get off with just a little tap on the jaw like Barlow gave you. You better move closer to your job in that hot car shop over in Brewster County. You think I don't know how you make your money? You hear me, Delmar? This is your one and only warning."

Then Sheriff Sol strutted away and returned to the office. He saw Chief, who was sitting at his desk with an open file, drumming his fingers. Sol asked, "Anything new, Chief?"

"Very little. I ran NCIC, NLETS, and DMV checks on both Cruz and Pérez.

"Armando Cruz lived at 214 Cottonwood Street, where the truck was registered to a Diego Cruz, presumed to be his father, but who knows. It doesn't matter anyway. Diego died of a massive stroke a year ago. Armando's rap sheet only reflects one bust, back in 1968, for illegal possession of a firearm. He served a month in jail on the misdemeanor beef. That's it.

"Joaquín Pérez's address on his DL is 510 Denton Street. I'm waiting on a callback from my old pal, Captain Stan Howard on that, as well as some other things, one of which is information on the bigger or more aggressive Latino drug-trafficking gangs in El Paso County. Pérez is only 19, but he has a misdemeanor collar for possession of marijuana a year ago. He paid a $100 fine. Right now, he has a pending charge for auto theft. He's out on a $1,000 bond. Next court date is August 16th."

"What about DEA in El Paso?"

"I spoke with SA [Special Agent] Carmine Valenzuela. Nice guy. He commended us on our bust. He asked if the bricks had any markings, a brand so to speak. I said I wasn't sure, but I thought it had something which looked like a black rooster. He said for us to check and get back to him. He also said that the U.S. Attorney's Office there will adopt cases with an aggregate of 100 kilos or more from the same group.

"He said most of the pot trafficking they've encountered is going north to New Mexico, and west to Arizona and maybe California. He said this sounds like one of the bigger groups might be expanding their routes. He also said they'd do a chemical check on a sample to see where the dope originated, and to test its level of THC. Finally, when we are ready to destroy the dope, they have a big incinerator and they would be glad to help with its destruction. Told him I'd get back with him tomorrow."

"That means you're free and could help me take Delmar over

to Brewster County. Leland said he would take any prisoners we have with a hard labor sentence. I'll have Miss Loretta get us another original of the Judgment and Commitment order at the Clerk's Office. Then I'll go grab a bite at Crabtree's. You eat April's lovingly-packed lunch. Then we'll go. Chunk will be in for the afternoon shift. When we get back, we'll call it a day. Whaddaya say?"

"I'm all in. Go eat. Bon appétit."

"Good deal. Be back in 45 minutes. Would you call Leland and let him know we're coming?"

"Of course."

"Oh yeah. I forgot. I left Barlow in the jail with Delmar. Barlow's pulling midnights at the hospital. When you break free, would you send him on his merry way?"

"I will. Go eat. Today's Italian over at Crabtree's."

Chapter 8

OPPOSITION RESEARCH

Wednesday, May 22, 1974

Chico didn't wait until darkness to begin his reconnaissance of Mosby, the Quayle County Jail, and an escape route. He started at 5 o'clock while he still had plenty of daylight.

By the time he arrived, most downtown workers had already completed their workday. An American Legion baseball game was ongoing at the diamond behind the public school. What a crowd! At least a hundred spectators. By comparison, he only saw four cars at the local tavern, called the Dry Gulch Saloon. This spoke volumes with respect to the preferred method of entertainment in this one-horse, one-traffic-light town.

He continued slowly westbound on US 90, slowing to a crawl when he drove past the county's seat of local government. It was a classically designed, three-story, sandstone block building, located on the northeast corner of US 90 and TX 651. This was the epicenter of town.

The front of the edifice faced south. The main entrance was precisely centered. It had a dozen or so steps, 20-feet wide, leading up to metal, double doors, over which, proudly chiseled in stone for all to see, was its name. It read QUAYLE COUNTY COURTHOUSE with 1910 centered on a second line. Unquestionably, this was the public entrance, always locked after hours. Very doubtful they'd bring in a prisoner this way.

He approached the only traffic light in Mosby, which was green, and turned right (north) at the corner onto TX 651, also marked as Texas Street. The courthouse had a single metal door with no window on this, the west side of the building. However, the door had a sign which read NO ADMITTANCE. No doubt this door was always locked.

He turned right again into the parking lot of the courthouse, which spanned both the north and the east sides if the building. They had parking spaces for maybe 50 cars. He saw one marked QCSO unit parked on the east side. There were only a half-dozen cars altogether, which were parked on both sides of the building at this time of the early evening.

That being said, the rear of the building (north side) had a metal door under a green canvas awning. The door had a sign which read SHERIFF'S OFFICE. This had to be the entrance they would use to bring in a prisoner. Then he noticed one window with iron jailhouse bars on the first floor on the east side of the building near the rear parking lot. Bingo! That was a jail window! This confirmed that prisoners were normally brought into the building through the Sheriff's entrance. That's all he needed to see here for the time being.

He turned around and drove north on Texas Street until he reached the outskirts of town. He pulled into a plumbing business which was closed for the night. He studied his Texas state roadmap, which he had folded so he could see this portion of the state.

The boundaries of the counties were printed in gray ink. Not surprisingly, Quayle County, population 3,000, was nearly bereft of any other markings. Mosby was a black dot in the southwest portion of the county. This was the only town. US 90 was a thin blue line going east and west, reflecting its status as a US highway. TX 651 intersected with US 90 at Mosby. It was a thin red line, reflecting its status as a state highway. From Mosby, TX 651 went about 80 miles northeast, intersecting at Interstate 10, which was a thick blue line, reflecting its status as an interstate highway.

TX 651 also ran 20 or so miles south of Mosby, where it dead-ended at the Rio Grande. Mexico, to the south, apparently had been snubbed by Texas DOT in this region. The map didn't depict any roads or towns in Mexico south of Quayle County. By way of contrast, the map showed a fair amount of detail south of El Paso County. Chico knew there had to be something south of Quayle County.

There were so few roads in Quayle County, with the greatest being US 90, that Chico knew there would be no viable escape on it in the van from high-speed pursuit units. Ditto for trying to skedaddle to I-10. Besides, the highway patrol would be swarming on the interstate. That only left south into Mexico as an escape route, assuming he could find a crossing.

Chico drove south on TX 651 for about 20 miles when he came to a thick, corrugated metal railing at the dead-end of the road. He realized that he had seen neither a house nor a building of any sort once he left Mosby. Besides, the river appeared to be too deep for his van at this location anyway.

He turned around and began creeping back north. He went maybe two miles when he saw a dirt, one-lane, goat path on the west side of 651, going southwest. It was fenced in, blocked by an unsecured farm gate. He let himself in, shutting the gate behind him, and followed the path.

Two miles later, he came to another farm fence, which blocked passage to the river. He got out of the van. He observed where the fence had been cut and spliced many times. He also noticed faint tire tracks from the fence, leading south to the river about 50 yards away, and coming out on the south side about a half-mile away. There, it disappeared into the horizon, going up a slight rise. That meant the river had to be shallow at this spot.

He cut the fence and pulled it back far enough so he could drive through. He stopped at the waters edge and surveyed the river again. He knew the poverty-stricken Mexicans drove old, dilapidated vehicles, if they had any vehicle at all. If their junkers could make it, so could this van.

Chico decided to go for it. He slowly inched his way across, using the tire tracks on the south as his point of reference. Hallelujah! He made it!

Now he had to find a road going west, but the only tire tracks he saw continued south. Ergo, he followed the tracks south maybe three miles, he hadn't kept track, until he found a small village of sheepherders. He observed an old man and his dog walking west, away from this cluster of 15 or so, small, sad-looking adobe houses, each occupied by hard-scrabble sheepherders and subsistence farmers. Clucking, scraggly chickens and hungry, barking chihuahuas were disturbing the peace. They were trying to eke out a living, too, amongst the rattlesnakes, lizards, and roadrunners.

Chico wondered how far the old man would have to walk to find sustenance or refreshment, so he inched his way up to him. Chico stopped, and speaking in Spanish, asked, "Sir, what is the name of this village behind you?"

The man replied, "You must be completely lost. The people call this place Diminuto (meaning Tiny)." Then he queried, "Señor, are you running away from someone or to someone?"

He replied, "I guess you could say a little of both. I'm looking for a place farther west where I could ford the river without being detained by the Border Patrol."

The old man laughed with gusto, slapping his bony knee. Finally, he spit and said, "I know of a place, Señor, but it's at least 70 miles away. Are you sure you have enough gasoline?"

"Sí."

"They call it El Pozo de Serpientes (The Snake Pit). Many bad hombres - all murderers and bandits. From there it is just two miles to a hidden crossing. If you break down or stop to talk to anyone while you are there, they will kill you and steal your money and your truck. Your body will be lost forever."

"Once I locate the crossing, where will it put me in Texas?"

"There is a dirt road on the other side. If you follow it west about 20 miles it will intersect with a highway called 385. North will take you to Marathon. South will take you to a highway called 170. That road will take you to Presidio. Those are the only two places where you will find gasoline."

"How do you know of this?"

Laughing again softly, he replied, "Once long ago, when I was a young man and I tired of being a sheepherder, I used to be a coyote. Today I am too old for that nonsense. Now, once again, I am a poor sheepherder. I no longer walk such a precarious path."

"What is your name?"

"They call me El Pato Extraño (The Odd Duck), but my real name is Carlos Javier Gonzales."

"How do I get to El Pozo de Serpientes?"

"Follow this path south another 20 miles to a village named Agua Buena. It has a small Catholic Church. The priest there is very fat and ill-tempered. The archdiocese fired him from his posting in Ojinaga and sent him there to die. It is rumored he copulated with goats. Before Father Leonardo arrived, the church in Agua Buena did not have a herd of goats. Now they do. Is this a coincidence? I sometimes wonder.

"Anyway, there is a cantina there named Paco's where it is safe to eat. Sometimes the Esso station is open and it has gasoline. Sometimes not. From there, take the dirt road heading west about 50 miles to El Pozo de Serpientes. Do not stop for any reason.

"Turn north at the cantina and go two miles. You will see a creek to your right called Maravillas. Follow the dirt road which runs beside it northwest to 385. From there you are home free. If you goof and get on the paved road called 2627, which also goes to 385, you stand a good chance of being stopped by the Border Patrol. They are always looking for smugglers on that paved road."

Chico pulled out his wallet and handed the old man a $20 bill. Then he said, "Gracias, El Pato Extraño. Do you need a ride in the direction I am going?"

"Gracias, Señor. No, I am going that way (pointing west) to

see my daughter. She promised me a chicken if I fix her fence. Ir con Dios (Go with God.)" Then he turned and walked away. The dog trotted slowly by his side.

Chico followed the Odd Duck's instructions. He stopped at the village called Agua Buena. He didn't see a fat man copulating with a goat. Maybe it was still too early. He did see a dozen goats grazing in the churchyard. The Esso was open, so he topped off. Then he parked and went to Paco's Cantina and topped off himself with a plateful of enchiladas, beef tacos, and refried beans. He washed it down with a frosty mug of draft beer that the locals called Orina de Burro (donkey piss).

Refreshed, he turned west, paying close attention to his odometer, until he finally arrived at El Pozo de Serpientes. He pressed on at a snail's pace. He took in a few hard looks from some hard young men, but he avoided eye contact. He saw a thriving cantina and turned north, proceeding to the river. It was dark now. All through El Pozo de Serpientes, he steered with his left hand, and held his cocked .45 in his right. He found the crossing with ease. It was only ankle deep and not much more than a quarter-mile wide. No wonder the Border Patrol camped out in this sector.

He stayed on the dirt road until he intersected with US Highway 385. Tonight he went north to Marathon, where he gassed up again. After the deed was done, he would take the southern route to Presidio, and from there north to Marfa, to US 90, and onto El Paso.

It was after midnight when Chico arrived back in Mosby. He cruised the courthouse parking lot and the adjacent area, looking for a daytime hidey-hole. Nada!

What he did see was an empty space next to the Sheriff's entrance. It had a sign painted on the pavement which read RESERVED SHERIFF ONLY. He also saw two marked units parked near the Sheriff's entrance.

The rear entrance area under the awning was illuminated

with a glass globe light over the door. The light was a single yellow, incandescent lightbulb designed to ward off pesky flying insects. It didn't seem to be working very well tonight. Moths were swarming all around the light. Two lizards were perched on the wall next to the globe at this happy hunting ground. They were devouring moths by the dozens. He wondered if the lizards were deputized to use deadly force.

Chico confirmed his initial assessment that the courthouse parking lot and the adjacent area within eyeshot were too populated during regular business hours to park for any length of time without raising eyebrows. Sooner or later he'd get rousted. Chico needed to be invisible until he struck in order to have any hope of escape. If he couldn't get away clean, he wasn't going to do the hit. He had done all the prison time he was going to do. He also had no intention of committing suicide.

Finally Chico figured it out. With a little preparation and luck, he could pull this off. Issue settled in his mind, he drove back to Del Rio and went to bed.

Chapter 9

INVESTIGATIVE LEGWORK

Wednesday, May 22, 1974

On Wednesday morning Chief Alex phoned Captain Stanley Howard, Chief of Detectives for the El Paso Sheriff's Office.

Chief Alex was lucky because he caught Captain Howard at his desk, and he picked up on the first ring. "Howard here."

"Stan, this is Alex Snodgrass. Did I catch you at a bad time?"

"Alex, by now you should know it's never a bad time for you. How's your dobber hanging? Heard you'd been off sick."

"You heard right. My ticker was causing me some problems. Now I gotta take it a little easy, swallow a few pills every day, and watch what I eat and drink. The wife's got me on a lettuce diet and only one adult beverage per night, but it's a big one. Heck, if I'm going to kick the bucket, I'd prefer to go with a little buzz. I'm doing much better now. How about you?"

"You know me. As long as I can still get it up for at least one rodeo, I'm standing in tall cotton. The day I can't, they better start digging my grave."

"I hear you. Say, the reason I called is, Monday night Barlow and Deputy Dewey Carruthers pulled over a pickup truck for speeding downtown. The assholes jumped out of the truck pointing guns. Barlow killed one and shot the other one's right eye out and blowed off the three middle fingers on his left hand. They had 60 kilos of weed in the truck. You know already right now why I'm calling. The pricks were from El Paso. Both are young Latino hombres. Can you help us out?"

"You know I can. Gimme their names."

"The live one is Joaquín V. Pérez, 10-12-54, of 505 Primrose

Street. The dead one is Armando B. Cruz, 2-9-50, of 214 Cottonwood Street. The truck they were driving is registered to Diego R. Cruz, at that same address. I think he died earlier this year."

"OK. Got it. Anything else?"

"Well, I spoke with DEA Special Agent Carmine Valenzuela from over there in your neck of the woods. Know him?"

"I do. Solid guy. Not like some other Feds we know."

"He was interested in our 60-kilo bust. He said if this load could be tied into any other loads in which the gross weight was 100 kilos or more, the U.S. Attorney's Office would adopt the case federally. Then he asked if the bricks had any markings. I wasn't for sure then. I went back and double-checked. Not positive, but the markings looked something like a rooster."

"Take a picture of it and send it to me. Not sure I've seen a rooster marking before. Anything else?"

"I don't think so. Do you know the names of any barrio gangs which handle this much weed at one time?"

"I know a few - the Los Escorpiones, or Scorpions to you and me; the El Ejército de Satanás, otherwise known to us Anglos as Satan's Army; the Tres Deuces, who have a house on 32nd Avenue; and there's a new group - at least new to us - calling themselves the Hope Street Boys. There's a dozen or so smaller groups, but I don't think they're selling 60-kilo weight. Also, we've had the occasional gangbanger shooting, but nobody's tried to take on the cops yet.

"I'll have Sergeant Julio Elias from Intelligence nose around. If he doesn't pick up a scent, I'll call Lieutenant Fred Wendell who runs Narcotics. Fred does a great job, but he's on the stingy side when it comes to sharing information with other agencies. Always afraid someone's gonna interfere with some operation he has going on. However, if anyone knows the drug gangs in El Paso, it's Fred. Anything else?"

"Not that I can think of right now. Just so you know, Sheriff

Sol made a press release early Tuesday morning, but he didn't identify the skells and he never mentioned the seizure. The weed was buried at the bottom of two tons of horseshit. No doubt the gang figures we've found it by now, but that would be just a hunch on their part."

"When do you go to court?"

"We got the Grand Jury tomorrow to indict Pérez for attempted murder of a law enforcement officer, but I don't think Sol plans to charge him with the dope yet. Pérez is in the hospital in Del Rio, but if things go as planned, we'll bring him back to Quayle County on Friday."

"Well okay, then. I'll see what we can dig up and most likely give you a call on Friday. That work for you?"

"That'll be just fine. Thanks a million, Stan. Adiós."

"Adiós."

Chief Alex hung up. For the time being, he was all out of leads. He photographed the stencil image of the rooster(?) on one of the bricks with a Polaroid camera, putting two photos in the file, and mailing one to SA Valenzuela and the other to Captain Howard. Except for paperwork, he was done for the day. He felt like he needed to do something, but what?

He called Slick's house and left a message with his sister-in-law for him to bring the contraband to the jail on his way to work tonight and store it in the Evidence Room IF the smell had subsided. If not, tell Slick to just leave him a note on his desk.

He checked today's line up. Ernie Atwater and Dewey Carruthers were on days guarding Pérez. Ella Mae Gillespie was on days in town. Kirk Shoemaker and Randy Meacham were on afternoon guard duty. Barlow Adams and Slick Oldman were on night guard duty. Chunk Bustamante was the only deputy off today. Sheriff Sol and he were the only ones besides Gillespie who were available to make a run right now if they got a call. What a way to run a railroad! Surely the Board of Supervisors could find enough money in their budget to hire just one more deputy!

He went in to see Sheriff Sol. Chief Alex said he and Gillespie were caught up for the time being. The only thing he had going on tomorrow was the Grand Jury at 10 o'clock. Chief suggested that Gillespie and Randy Meacham take tomorrow off. Put Chunk with Kirk on afternoon guard duty. Then by Friday afternoon, assuming the hospital released Pérez, they wouldn't need guards on duty at the hospital. They could give Kirk a day off on Friday. Dewey and Ernie could stay on the day shift Friday transporting Pérez to the jail.

Sheriff Sol concurred. He told Chief to make the notifications. Then he told Chief to give himself the rest of the day off.

It wasn't much, but it did help with morale.

Chapter 10

CRIME NEVER SLEEPS

Thursday, May 23, 1974

Rodolfo Velásquez and Tomás Jiménez made the pickup at the regular location by the river behind Gustavo's Cantina at 9 o'clock. It would be the very first time that they made this drop off. They were pumped that El Jefe had finally realized that they were just as smart, resourceful, and loyal as Armando and Joaquín.

They drove the metallic blue, 1970 GMC van. Unfortunately, it did not have air conditioning, but it ran like a scalded dog. They would hide the bricks in a locked, lateral ice chest, where they also stashed full, opened, two-pound metal coffee cans to help mask the odor of pot. Then they placed miscellaneous metal cabinets and office furniture between the freezer and the rear doors of the van as more camouflage.

This time Geraldo Flores was on time. The transfer went smoothly. Tomás commented that Geraldo was old and fat and bald. He probably hadn't scored any pussy in 10 years. His jefe should fire the old goat. What could he possibly do if someone decided to hijack him? Nothing! That's what!

Rodolfo and Tomás were 21 and 20, respectively. They carried the Model 10, Smith & Wesson .38 Special revolvers that Jefe bought for all his employees, but they shot up all the standard loads (158-grain, lead round-nose bullets) which he provided with the guns. Rodolfo bought each of them a box of .38 Special Super Vel bullets, which were the hottest loads on the planet. Super Vels would fuck you up! They were both primed and itching to prove themselves ready for a fight.

El Jefe told them to take the long way as a precaution. They took I-10 east to Sonora and turned southwest on US 277. The trip was about 500 miles this way. They gassed up and ate lunch in Fort Stockton. They refueled again in Sonora and Del Rio before they made the drop. They arrived at the junkyard at 8:30. Mr. Aguilar and three workers and eight vicious dogs were waiting for them. Everyone except for the dogs was openly wearing handguns. Rodolfo and Tomás suddenly snapped to the reality that they would be in a hurt locker if this were a rip.

Rodolfo said he would do all the talking. He also told Tomás to keep a sharp eye out.

They exited the van and slowly walked up towards the garage, which was still lit up with long fluorescent lights. Except for perimeter pole lighting, the gravel lot was pitch black. Four dogs were behind a chain link fence separating the back lot from the front. One was chained up on either side of the building. Two were in cages inside the building. Only the dogs behind the fence were barking. Mr. Aguilar made a downward motion with his left arm and the noisemakers shut up, too. Impressive.

Señor Aguilar walked up to them and put out his hand for a shake. He said, "Welcome. You must be Rodolfo Velásquez and Tomás Jiménez. I am Señor Aguilar. We are relieved that you arrived here safely. Did you encounter any trouble along the way?"

Rodolfo and Tomás shook Señor Aguilar's hand. He had a grip like a vice. This dude with his fancy duds and nickel-plated Colt Python was nobody's bitch, even though he was dressed like a movie star. No doubt he scored a bunch of women.

"Rodolfo replied, "Thank you, Jefe. No. We did not have any problems.

"Señor Ibarra instructed us to drop off 60 kilos of top-grade Oaxacan Highland Gold cannabis for $60,000 in US currency. Is that your understanding, too?"

"It is. I assume you would not be standing here if you did not have the product. Mr. Ibarra and I have been doing business for years. I was horrified to learn that Armando and Joaquín ran into some difficulties with the law Monday night. What you are bringing me today - is it a different load than they were carrying?"

"Sí, sí. We just received this load this morning. If you show me the payment, we will unload your merchandise."

Señor Aguilar snapped his fingers twice. A gorilla the size of King Kong with a face which would terrify a club of Hell's Angels walked up holding a thick, white business envelope with a rubber band around it. He pulled off the rubber band and retrieved six packets, each strapped with a bank label binding 100 Benjamin Franklins. Rodolfo flipped through each packet to ensure all the notes were $100s. They were. He smiled and returned the packets to King Kong, who placed them back in the envelope and secured them with the rubber band.

Rodolfo said, "Thank you, Sir. If you loan us a couple of your men, we can retrieve the product more quickly. It's in the very front of the van behind a mountain of furniture."

The two otherwise unoccupied employees joined Tomás in pulling out the furniture so they could retrieve the bricks from the freezer. King Kong handed the first brick to Señor Aguilar, who sniffed the outer wrapper before slicing it open with his beautiful, sheathed pocket knife. It looked like a Buck Folding Hunter except the handgrips were made of turquoise. He stuck the brick and pulled a little cannabis out on the blade, extending the blade towards King Kong. Then King Kong pulled out a cigarette wrapper and rolled a blunt. He made an excellent job of it. Next he pulled out a Zippo lighter with an 82nd Airborne Division logo on the side, and fired up his smoke. He took several long draws. Then for the first time, he smiled.

Señor Aguilar asked, "Is it as good as all the rest we have received?"

King Kong replied, "Maybe better."

Señor Aguilar smiled and said, "Okay. Get the rest and place it on the table inside. Then help these men put all that stuff back into the van like you had never taken it out."

When they were done and everyone could count 60 bricks with the rooster logo stenciled on the top, King Kong handed the fat envelope to Rodolfo.

Mr. Aguilar shook their hands again. He said, "Give my regards to Señor Ibarra. I hope to see you muchachos when we get our next load. Adiós."

"Adiós, Señor. Gracias."

Rodolfo and Tomás drove off and found a secluded place behind a grocery store which was closed. They got in the back of the van and pulled out just enough furniture to stash the cash in the freezer before locking it up again. They drove back to Sonora and secured lodging in the Desert Rose Inn, just as they had been instructed to do. They would return to El Paso tomorrow. Rodolfo used the payphone on the front of the building to call El Jefe. It took less than a minute to put a smile on Señor Ibarra's face. Then Rodolfo and Tomás went to bed. It was almost midnight.

Well before Rodolfo and Tomás lay their heads down to sleep, Chico was on the move. He picked up a couple of days' worth of pre-made sandwiches, snacks, and iced beverages, which he put in a styrofoam cooler when he refueled at the Pure service station in Del Rio. Then he drove to Mosby and conducted another recon.

Tonight there were two marked units parked at the cop shop. One was still at the hospital in Del Rio. The sheriff's marked parking space was empty. That meant Quayle County had at least four units.

The older marked unit was a 1971 Ford LTD. The newer one was a 1973 Dodge Polara. It looked to be in much better condition than the Ford. Besides, it was newer. If he were to choose which one to drive, he'd pick the Polara.

He double-checked to make sure no one was around. The

coast was clear. He opened his glovebox and selected two of the four potatoes he had purchased yesterday. They were all fairly small to suit his purpose.

He strolled over to the Ford and stuffed the potatoes up into the exhaust pipes as far as they would go. He cut off the excess and put it in a small paper sack to discard elsewhere. Then he used a piece of broom handle to push the potatoes in as far as he could. He wanted to make sure they would not be seen unless someone took a good hard look.

Mission accomplished, he drove away. Now if someone tried to start the Ford, the engine wouldn't turn over because there was no place for the exhaust to be expelled. He didn't stuff potatoes into the Polara because he had to figure at least one deputy would need to go someplace before it was time to consummate the hit. Tomorrow, at the last moment, he would sabotage any other parked fuzz mobiles he could identify.

Next, he drove south on TX 651. He checked both fences which were the gateway to his escape. Still no lock on the first gate and the fence by the river was still just as raggedy as before. He went ahead and cut and rolled it back for a quick getaway. Then he checked the river. It too, had not changed. The water was still shallow. He drove back to Mosby and parked in the junior college lot. He took off both license plates and put them in an old cardboard box in the back of the van. Then he saw a worn out piece of shit Ford Maverick with a New Mexico license plate. New Mexico only issued one plate, so he stole it and screwed it on the van. Subterfuge is always a worthwhile endeavor, especially when you're a crook. He smiled to himself as he drove away.

It was 3 o'clock Friday morning. The whole town was devoid of people as if everyone were in prison lockdown mode. He was the only motorist on the road. He could never get used to these small town ways. Hopefully, after today he would never need to come back.

Chico didn't know what time to expect Joaquín to arrive in Mosby via Special Delivery. Heck! It was possible that they might not even release him from the hospital today. All he could do was wait while trying to be inconspicuous. In this hamlet, that was like asking Lady Godiva to ride though the town naked on a white horse without being noticed. This burg was so small, so staid, so regular, so everyday, that everybody here would notice if the local diner were five minutes late in opening. Oh my gosh! What if something is wrong? Why did you open late? I hope everyone is okay!

Anonymity in Quayle County? No such thing. He wondered. How could folks possibly survive here? He would die of boredom. In fact, it was all he could do right now not to croak himself. Want to punish a lawbreaker? Sentence him to live here for a whole fucking year. That'll learn him!

Finally, cruising around, he found himself a temporary hidey-hole. It was in the back of the saloon parking lot. He could pass a few hours here, and insomniacs who ventured forth in the darkness of night, unwittingly in the presence of demons would think he was just another drunk sleeping it off. H-Hour couldn't come soon enough for Chico.

Chapter 11

PUNCHING A TICKET - ALL IN A DAY'S WORK

Friday, May 24, 1974

It was 7:30. It had been another long, boring night on hospital guard duty for Slick and Barlow, and for Val Verde Deputies Johansson and Mueller. Those two guys had pulled midnights here every single night from the very beginning. Johansson was solid. Mueller was a dick. Slick wondered what Johansson had done to be sentenced to spend this much time in purgatory. Anyway, Ernie Atwater and Dewey Carruthers should be here soon. Pérez had finally been cleared for release to the Quayle County Jail. Soon each of them except for Pérez would be out of purgatory. At least guard duty in your own jail has a few more amenities, not to mention no more two-hour commutes each way.

7:45. Relief was finally here. Slick briefed Ernie, confirming that Pérez should be released soon. He passed Pérez's release documents to Ernie as the incoming senior deputy. Slick and Barlow said their goodbyes to Johansson and Mueller. Then the two compadres hit the dusty trail like the proverbial cow turd. Splat. When they arrived at the courthouse, they swapped out the marked 1973 Plymouth Fury for their POVs [privately owned vehicles].

Slick headed home in his 1948 Studebaker pickup truck, and Barlow followed suit in his 1965 Dodge 100. They both had big plans for this evening after they copped a few winks.

Slick had a date to romance a local cougar who had been widowed way too early in life. Slick was a firm believer that she absolutely copulated her husband to death. His 15 years of marriage had to have been unadulterated wedded bliss - until his ticker gave out (while he was still in the saddle, or so it was said). If he weren't physically fit and so full of baby juice, Slick would have taken a pass on this widow woman and taken on one of the others who was only good for one rodeo. Finito. Done. Go home. Normally, Slick reserved one of the one-and-done ladies for the end of an afternoon shift so he could cut off a slice and go home early fully refreshed. His date for tonight with the Merry Widow-Maker always left him breathless and lap-legged. Sapped of all energy. Usually took two days to recover.

Barlow had similar plans for Sarah, except they were going to grill some steaks at home first. Then go to the Bijou to see the Great Gatsby featuring Robert Redford and Mia Farrow. They heard it was great. Afterwards, they would cap off the night with some of Henry McKenna's straight Kentucky bourbon. Then, he would strip her naked and pleasure her exactly the way she liked it. Her cup would runneth over, and she would collapse before he was fully sated. Then she would make up for it in the morning. That's the way it usually worked. Neither of them wrote to Dear Abby or Ann Landers to voice marital dissatisfaction.

Slick took a steamy shower and then he fell into bed, all cashed in.

Sarah was already at work when Barlow returned home, so all he did was strip naked, brush his teeth, and crawl in the sack. Happy snuggled up at the foot of the bed. If he had been a cat he would have purred.

In the meantime, Chico was sitting in Crabtree's diner eating the Home Run breakfast consisting of three pancakes with real maple syrup, two fried eggs, two strips of bacon, and two sausage patties. He washed it down with a large glass of milk and a half-gallon of black coffee. It was 10 o'clock. He could see the rear courthouse parking lot from his window booth. The meal was $1.95 plus tax. He left a $5 dollar bill on the table and slipped out the door.

He walked past his van which was in the diner parking lot, and strolled across the street to the rear courthouse parking lot. He'd had plenty of time to study the back door area to the sheriff's office. He saw the sheriff arrive in his unmarked, brown, 1969 Plymouth, and go inside. Later, he saw an older man in plain clothes park a light blue, 1967 Jeep Wagoneer, and go into the jail entrance. This man was wearing a holstered pistol on his belt - another cop and another cop car. He watched two uniforms park a marked, 1973 Plymouth Fury and then go their separate ways in pickup trucks. These three units, plus the marked, 1971 Ford which was still dormant where it had been parked last night, would indicate that the department owned five cars.

Chico walked leisurely through the lot. No pedestrians. Not a creature in sight. He used his handy ice pick to puncture the two right tires on the sheriff's car, the two left tires on the Jeep, and both front tires on the marked Plymouth. He slipped his ice pick into his side jacket pocket and slowly sauntered back across the street to his van. He unlocked it and climbed in. He rolled down the windows. Then he opened the vent windows. He lit up a Camel and watched the courthouse parking lot some more. He smoked two cigarettes. He only had to wait 15 minutes. Today Fate was with him.

A marked, 1972 Dodge with two uniformed deputies drove up from the east parking lot entrance. They stopped right in front of the rear jail entrance, facing south. The deputy in the right front seat, who was a little on the portly side, got out of the car and started to assist Joaquín exit from the back seat.

Chico pulled his bandanna up over his face. He started up his van and slowly drove to the rear courthouse parking lot. He continued rolling very slowly until he had a clear line of sight through his passenger window to the open rear door of the cruiser. Then he stopped. He slipped the .45 out of his waistband. Traffic was light on TX 651 and he had experienced no complications up to this point. By then, the deputy driving the cruiser, a tall, thin, drink of water, walked around from the driver's side and around the rear of the unit to assist the other deputy, who was having problems getting Joaquín out of the car. Apparently they finally realized the man driving the van was watching them. Both deputies turned to face him. As soon as Chico had a clear shot, he fired three .45s rapid fire into Joaquín - the first two in the chest, and the last one into his slumped head. It exploded like a dropped watermelon. Blood and brain matter splattered both deputies, to include their faces.

The heavy set deputy from the passenger side froze - hands in the air, eyes wide open with fright. The tall, skinny driver pulled his gun, but before he could draw a bead, Chico capped him in his upper right chest. He did his very best not to kill him.

The deputy fell to the ground on his side. His revolver lay just out of reach. He was writhing in agony, waiting for the coup de grâce.

Chico told the heavy set deputy to unbuckle his gun belt, and toss it with the holstered revolver as far as he could if he valued his life. Ditto for his partner's gun. The scaredy cat complied with no further thought, tossing his rig and his partner's gun twenty feet or more. Then Chico pulled the van up a few more feet and fired two more shots - one each into both driver side tires of the Dodge. By then, he could hear the sheriff and probably the plainclothesman tearing out the back door but he didn't tarry to see what they wanted. He goosed the van out the east side parking lot entrance. He turned west onto US 90. He ran the traffic light at TX 651, both highways being devoid of other vehicles at the time. He turned south and let 'er rip. As far as he could tell he had no pursuit, but he made haste anyway. Not only that, he didn't think he had any witnesses except for the cops. What were the odds on that?

Finally, he arrived at his portal into Old Mexico. He opened the farm gate on the west side of TX 651. No other vehicles were anywhere in sight. Once he entered the pasture, he took time to fasten the gate back the way it belonged. After he drove through the rolled back fence on the north side of the Rio Grande, he took time again to reattach the fencing as good as it was the first time he drove through. This time he could actually see when he forded the river. The fording was smooth as silk - a virtual cakewalk.

Chico suddenly realized when he entered Mexico that he was still wearing the bandanna up over his face, so he pulled it down and stuffed the front into the neck of his shirt. He also realized that his gun was cocked with the safety off; that he had one round in the pipe and only one in the magazine, so he stopped. He put the gun on safe, dropped the magazine, added six new rounds, put it back into the gun, and tucked it back into his waist band.

Then as long as he was taking care of details that, if left unattended, might undo him, he decided to switch out license plates again. He got out and put the Texas plates back on. He would ditch the New Mexico plate as soon as he came across a hidey-hole which would disappear it for at least a decade. No reason to leave the law dogs any breadcrumbs to assist in leading them to his doorstep.

Just as on his trial run, he stopped at Agua Buena and topped off the van at the Esso service station. He left the attendant a buck tip to fog up his memory on the remote chance the cops picked up his scent. Then he ate a satisfying lunch at Paco's Cantina, leaving a two-dollar tip for the same reason. Refueled, full tummy, and empty bladder, all was in harmony. He headed straight for El Pozo de Serpientes. It looked even worse than before now that he could see it in broad daylight. Wisely, no one made an effort to molest him. In that respect, they were fortunate. Today Chico was taking no prisoners.

He turned north at the cantina, forded the river, and once again returned into the fold of Lady Liberty. He followed the dirt road until it intersected with US 385. This time he turned south onto TX 170 to Presidio. Then he went north on US 67 until he came to Marfa on US 90. He would have liked to rent a motel room and spend the night, especially if it came with a full-figured, hombre-pleasing puta; however, the cops were surely searching for this blue and white Dodge van, which, due to his forethought, had a New Mexico license plate on it when they saw it.

He drove all the way back to El Paso without incident. It was 0-Dark-30 when he arrived at the garage. He parked the van inside and walked back to his cabaña. He drank the rest of his Lizard Spit. Exhausted, he fell into bed into a deep, peaceful slumber.

Tomorrow would be a new day. He hoped El Jefe would pay him for a job well-done and give him a few days off. He needed some R&R [rest and relaxation]. He wanted to visit Ricardo's bordello over in Ciudad Juárez to blow off some steam and release some of the tension which had built up over the past few days.

He was not disappointed. Señor Ibarra let him keep the remainder of the $300 in expense money, plus he paid him $500 for his work. He told Chico to drive the badly faded, rust-free, white-over-orange, 1960, GMC 1000, V-6, half-ton pickup truck because it looked old and decrepit; however, like all of Señor Ibarra's vehicles, it ran like a striped-ass ape. Jefe said he would get Ramón and Esteban to repaint the Dodge van a pale mint green. Then he reminded Chico that his parole officer would be stopping by the garage at 10 o'clock on Tuesday morning, so he needed to be back by then.

Chapter 12

TENDING TO THE WOUNDED AND DIGGING OUT OF A HOLE

Friday, May 24, 1974

Chief Alex had just returned to the office from the Grand Jury. Joaquín Pérez was indicted for attempted murder of a police officer as a result of Chief's testimony. The Sheriff's Office still had not released to the public that they were sitting on a significant seizure of marijuana. Now Sheriff Sol and he were hard at it again, discussing whether there was any benefit this late in the game by not making a press release.

They were the only two officers on duty in Quayle County this morning. They expected Ernie Atwater and Dewey Carruthers to make their appearances soon, escorting Joaquín Pérez to the jail from Val Verde County. Sheriff Sol had told them to stay off the air unless they had an emergency. He did not want the press or the public swarming them or the prisoner before they could get him safely behind bars. The last time they had heard from Ernie was about two hours ago, prior to their departure from the hospital.

Suddenly, they heard gunshots from the back side of the courthouse. Pow! Pow! Pow! Pause. Pow! Long pause. Pow! Pow!

It took them a moment to respond. They drew their sidearms on the way out of the office. Sheriff Sol was carrying his nickel-plated, .357 Magnum Colt Python with a six-inch barrel. Chief Alex had a blue steel Browning Hi-Power, semi-automatic, 9 millimeter pistol. Sheriff Sol was a pretty good shot. Chief Alex was not. Hence his 13-shot pistol. If he threw enough lead at the target, sooner or later he was bound to hit something. At least that was his assumption.

The last two shots occurred just as they were clearing the back door. A marked unit was parked, facing the the back door with its green awning covering the path to the sheriff's office. That was the first thing they saw. Then they noticed Ernie kneeling over Dewey. Ernie was not wearing his gun belt. He had a blank look on his face. Obviously, he was in shock. A split second later they saw Pérez's body. Half of his head was missing. Both Dewey and Ernie were awash with blood, pieces of bone fragment, and brain matter.

Chief checked on Dewey, who was fading fast. He whispered, "Chief, he shot me before I could shoot him." Chief responded, also in a whisper, "It's okay. You're gonna be okay. I don't think he hit anything vital. Stay with me."

Then he said, "Ernie, press down hard on his wound, front and back, to help stop the bleeding. Do not let him fall asleep. Can you do that? I'm going inside to call an ambulance. Be right back." Then he ran back into the office.

Sheriff Sol saw that Ernie was spazzing in place and unable to comprehend what he had been asked to do. He grabbed Ernie by his left wrist to get his attention. Then he said, "Ernie, I need you! Ask all these nice folks to stand back and give us some room. Okay? We need more room here. Understand?" Then he rolled Dewey onto his side so he could use both his hands to apply pressure on the bullet entry and exit holes.

By now bystanders had begun showing up one-by-one, gawking at the tragedy. They all knew Dewey and Ernie. The court bailiff, Mr. August Bellweather, approached the crime scene, carrying Ernie's gun belt with his revolver still snapped into the holster, as well as Dewey's revolver. He said, "Sheriff, I found these over there," pointing towards the east side of the parking lot.

Sheriff Sol replied, "Thank you, Mr. Bellweather. Could you take them in my office and place them on my desk? I would be much obliged."

He responded, "Of course, Sheriff. Anything I can do. Don't hesitate to ask. Be right back."

Sol answered, "Thanks. After you drop them on my desk, could you help us to keep everyone back? You're the only other law officer here. Ernie doesn't appear to be up to it right now. I really could use your help."

"You got it, Sheriff."

In the meantime, Chief Alex called O'Reilly's Ambulance Service on their "back door" line. He must have had a lucky charm in his pocket. The owner's wife, Ambrosia O'Reilly, answered the phone.

Chief said, "Ambrosia, this is Alex Snodgrass. Deputy Carruthers, has been shot in his upper right chest. He's in our back parking lot. Sheriff Sol's out there with him now. Could you come right away?"

"Yes, of course. I know Dewey. You all happen to be in luck. As it turns out, we have an ambulance coming your way to get an oil change at Buck Boyd's. I'll call him right now. He should be there in a few."

"Thanks. We owe you big time."

"The heck you say! It's we who owe all of you over there in the sheriff's office. Larry and Tim will be right along. Bye bye."

Then Chief called Pete Ricketts and told him to bring his meat wagon. Said for him to come in through the west entrance. While he was on the phone, August Bellweather brought in the gun belt and both revolvers. Chief thanked him and locked them in his file cabinet for safekeeping. Then he went back outside to see what else he could do.

By the time he returned, he could hear the ambulance siren, coming from the east. Thank goodness!

Sheriff Sol, by his calm demeanor and presence alone, assuaged Dewey's fears. He was hurting, but his breathing was back to near normal. He was no longer in a panic. The crowd had swollen from 10 to upwards of 25 people. August Bellweather had pacified them all like a hillbilly snake charmer from the mountains of Eastern Kentucky. Everyone present was subdued and pensive, and a few were praying, everyone that is, except for Ernie. He looked dazed and confused, staring into oblivion with a vacant look on his face. He didn't seem to be aware of his surroundings. Fortunately, August had noticed this too. He asked Ernie if he would like to take a seat on the bench just to the right of the back door. Ernie complied without a word as August took his hand and lead him there.

As Chief was coming back out of the building, he noticed that two tires on both his car and the sheriff's were flat. He had already observed that the shooter's last two shots had flattened two tires on the Dodge Ernie and Dewey had been driving. He walked over to the marked Plymouth and saw that two tires were flat on it, too. Thankfully, the marked Ford was still intact. He reported his findings to Sheriff Sol in a whisper.

Just then the ambulance arrived, lights flashing. Medics Tim Richman, former Navy medical corpsman assigned to the Marine Corps, and Larry Taylor, former Army Green Beret medic, both distinguished Vietnam veterans, bailed out of the truck. They rolled a collapsible gurney with a large medical kit situated in the middle of the mattress over to where Dewey was lying. Sheriff Sol backed away to give them space to work. Tim peeled off Dewey's gun belt and handed it to Sheriff Sol. Larry cut off Dewey's shirt with its badge, and his tee shirt, and handed them to Sheriff Sol, too. He in turn, passed it all to Chief Alex.

They put an oxygen mask on Dewey's face. Larry took Dewey's vitals while Tim opened two airtight bandages to place over the entry and exit wounds. Then they bound his chest tightly, mummy-like with thick, white bandages. They gently lifted him onto the stretcher, raised it up, covered him with a blanket, and wheeled him to the ambulance. They loaded him into the back. Larry looked around and asked, "Sheriff, anyone coming with us?"

"Me." He looked over at Alex and said, "Chief, you're in charge. Get Ella Mae over to Dewey's house ASAP before Elsie hears about this through the grapevine. If she's not there, she'll be at their Thrifty Scot Second Hand Shop. Tell Gillespie she might have to drive her POV. Make sure she's the one who drives Elsie to the hospital. Okay? Elsie's mother can take care of the kids while she's gone. Call out anyone else you need for assistance. In fact, get both Slick and Barlow on this soon as you get a chance. We don't even know who we're looking for or what kind of vehicle they were in. Now I wish I would have put those two on days instead of nights. Mistake on my part. I just didn't see this coming. Any questions?"

"Nope, we got it all covered, Sheriff. Call us when you can. Adiós."

"Adiós, I'll be in touch. Larry, we're ready to roll."

Sheriff Sol jumped into the back of the ambulance and closed the door. Tim put the pedal to the metal, lights flashing and siren deafening anyone within 50 feet. Val Verde County Baptist Hospital, here we come!

August Bellweather graciously maintained security of the crime scene while Chief went inside to make his calls. Fortunately, his crime scene kit was already in his disabled Jeep. That reminded him to call Buck Boyd and get him over here to get the vehicles operational again. Not only were they short of deputies. Now they were short of operational vehicles! Mercy!

When Chief realized Ernie was still out back, he went outside and ushered him indoors. He told Ernie to sit at the senior deputy's desk while he made a few calls. First call was to Gillespie. Next was to Buck Boyd. He decided not to call Slick or Barlow just yet. What would he have them do? Who would they hunt down? Sheriff Sol wasn't thinking straight. Finally, he called Gertrude Atwater. Fortunately, she was at home. He said Ernie was feeling bad and asked if she could come by the jail right away. He said he would fill her in once she arrived. She said indeed, she would come. The mopping would just have to wait until she got back home.

Chief went back outside to the crime scene. Many of the bystanders had moved on. Just a half-dozen or so hardcore gawkers remained. He asked if August could be his second investigator for the crime scene. August said he would be delighted. Just as Chief started taking measurements, Pete Ricketts showed up with the meat wagon. He apologized. Said he had to hurry up last minute details for the Elvis Thornton funeral. Pete's son was sick today and unable to report for work. Chief assured him that all was fine. He said he still needed to take some photographs and complete the measurements first anyway.

It didn't take long. The critical portion of the crime scene was the area around the police cruiser with Pérez's corpse, which was all crumpled up and visible for any and all to see. Ghastly! Ernie and Sheriff Sol were a bloody mess, too, except they were uninjured. Chief made an assumption that the killer drove from the west entrance but no one had confirmed that yet. He took photos of the way the parking lot was now, depicting which vehicles were parked where. He hurried up, so Pete could take the corpse back to his mortuary. Heck. He didn't even know whom to notify. Probably better for him right now anyway. He had so many other things to do.

In the meantime, Buck Boyd showed up with his wrecker. He surveyed the flat tires. He said he had four tires which he could put on one marked unit and Sheriff Sol's car, or on two marked units. Chief told him not to worry about the marked Dodge yet. It still needed to be processed. Buck said he would go back and pick up the tires he had in inventory. He checked the type of tires on the Jeep and said he would order tires for it and the Dodge. If he were lucky, he'd have them by the afternoon. Then he asked, "Chief, all four of your tires are nearly bald. You want me to order you a whole new set?"

"Yes."

"What about the Ford? Have you checked to make sure it's operational, considering the circumstances."

"No. You know where we hang the keys. It's inventory number is 98, I think."

"Nope. It's 99. Chief, I know your cars better than you do since I maintain all of them. You drive just the one. Besides, 99 is the onliest Ford you all have. I can tell the different makes of car keys from a mile away. Each brand is different. Be back in a jiffy."

He returned moments later with a set of keys for the Ford. It wouldn't start. He checked under the hood. Plenty of gas plus a spark. Finally he crawled under the car on a creeper. After a thorough examination, he shouted, "Chief, some prick stuffed a potato deep into the exhaust pipes. They're so far up there I can't get 'em out. I'll have to tow it in. I hope not, but we may have to install new exhaust pipes."

"Do what you can to get her running as soon as you can. Right now we need that unit more than ever. This '72 Dodge is going to need a rear seat at the very minimum. The blood has seeped in over everything. We may have to replace the front seat, too. I know it'll be out of commission for several days before you can get it repaired."

"Yep. I'll tow it too, once I put tires on the two Plymouths. See you in a few."

Chief had done all he could outside, except to park the crippled Dodge in a proper parking space, which he did. At least the driver's portion of the front seat was not soaked in blood. He figured there were probably two or three spent projectiles in the car somewhere but he didn't have time now to search it. He thanked August for all his help, and went back inside. Now it was time to let his fingers do the walking.

First call was to the Quayle County Volunteer Fire Department. He asked Big Billy Bear Blanchard if they could bring the pumper down to the rear lot of the courthouse to spray off the blood. He said they had a murder out back, and it would make the citizens who had to park there very happy not to have to drive or walk through it. Typical of Big Baby Bear, he replied superciliously that Chief should understand that they were in the middle of a drought and they couldn't spare a drop of precious water for something which wasn't burning on fire.

Chief shot back, "Tell you what, Big Baby Bear. I'll just call Judge Sweeney upstairs and ask him to call Water Conservation District Supervisor Nathan Hilliard to see if it's okay. Just forget I ever called, but you might want to clean out your locker and mosey your ass on home. I'll bet they have your replacement with his compliant ass occupying your chair with his nameplate front and center on your desk before the end of the day."

"Hey, Chief, no reason to get your panties all twisted. I was just letting you know I'm doing this in the middle of a drought as a special favor just for you. That's all. We'll be right out. No problemo."

"Thank you, Big Baby Bear. I'll let Judge Sweeney know what a swell guy you are." Then he slammed down the receiver.

Soon as he did, Gertrude Atwater waltzed in. She was a thin, small woman, with lots of wrinkles. She looked to be 65 or 70, but was most likely only in her 50s. Her light brown hair with silver streaks was done up in a small bun underneath, which was covered with a folded red bandana tied around her head to keep hair out of her eyes. She was wearing a pink and white gingham house dress which may have fit once upon a time, but was two sizes too large now. She wore silver, wire-rimmed glasses, which could not conceal the intensity of her bright blue eyes. The only thing which was out of character for her was that was wearing her slip-on, pink, terrycloth house slippers. Chief wondered if her bunions were bothering her. She carried a large, thin, rectangular, brown leather purse with a loop handle. Looked more like a book satchel. Big enough to carry a county telephone book plus an atlas.

She took one look at Ernie, who was sitting in a rolling, oak desk chair with his hands folded in his lap. His face looked like he just had the living shit scared out of him. She noticed that he wasn't wearing his gun belt and that his shirt had dried bloodstains and other matter all over the front, not to mention his face and hands. He was a total mess. He looked up at her, but didn't utter a word or even seem glad to see her.

She blurted, "Chief, what's the matter with my husband? Look at him! He acts like he's been struck by lightning."

He replied, "Gertrude, I'm glad you could come right away. Just so you know, we are the only ones here right now, so you can speak freely without fear of anyone else listening.

"As I'm sure you know, Ernie and Dewey picked up a prisoner at the hospital in Del Rio this morning. None of us were afoot in the parking lot when they arrived. He and Dewey were taking the prisoner out of the cruiser when person(s) unknown drove up. They shot and killed the prisoner. They also shot Dewey. He's en route to the hospital as we speak. Sheriff Sol is with him. The bad guys got away clean. We don't even know yet what he, or they, were driving or which way they went.

"As soon as we heard the shots, Sheriff Sol and I ran outside, but by then it was all over except for the weeping and gnashing of teeth. Ernie's been like this ever since. He hasn't uttered a solitary word. He's obviously had a terrible shock. I don't know if it would be best to take him home, or if he should go straight to the hospital to be evaluated by a medical professional. If that's what you think, I will call another deputy to take you."

"Is Dewey going to be okay?"

"We think so. He was shot in the chest, but we don't think the bullet hit any vital organs."

"Oh, praise the Lord! Let me talk with Ernie alone for just a minute. Would that be okay with you?"

"Certainly. Would you like for me to get you a cup of coffee or a soft drink?"

"No, thank you. Maybe a cup of cold water if you have it.

Don't put yourself out."

"I'll fetch a glass and pour some refrigerated water out of the fountain. I'll be back in a moment."

"Thank you."

Chief left the office. He waited five agonizing minutes before returning.

He handed Gertrude the water. She took a sip. Then she held the glass for Ernie to drink. He looked at her for a long moment before he accepted the glass. He drank every last drop and returned the glass to her.

She said, "I know he recognizes me, but he won't speak to me either. I think he needs to go to the hospital. I would be much obliged if someone could take us. The problem is, I can't get back home before school's out. My sister, Vera, works at the dentist's office. I suppose I could call over there and see if Dr. Tinsley would let her off a little early. Hilda is 16 and Winston is 12. Normally I could leave them alone for a little while, but I'm afraid to do it under these circumstances."

"Of course. Why don't you give Vera a call and see. In the meantime, let me rustle up a deputy to take you. You can use the phone on the desk next to Ernie. I need to make a couple of calls myself while you're doing that."

Chief walked back to his desk and called Barlow. He answered after a half-dozen rings.

"Hello."

"Barlow, this is Chief. Hate to bother you, but we're in a bind. Sheriff Sol told me to call you and Slick. I didn't think it would be necessary, but it is."

"Gosh! Whatever you need, Chief."

"Dewey and Ernie were ambushed in our parking lot when they were bringing Pérez back to the jail. Unknown assailant(s) - actually not sure how many - shot and killed Pérez. They also shot Dewey, but we think he's going to be okay. Sheriff Sol went with him to the hospital and I haven't heard back yet. Ernie is in what I would call a catatonic state. He hasn't uttered a word. Otherwise, physically he's okay. He and Gertrude are in the jail with me now. I need you to take them to the hospital. By the way, the bad guys disabled every single unit we have in our fleet, so you'll have to drive your own vehicle. Wear civvies. Any questions?"

"Yes. Would it be okay if I got Sarah to follow us over there? I could drive them in Ernie's car. That would allow Sarah and me to come back home when we are no longer needed."

"That's perfect. We'll see you all when you get here."

"Roger that. Be there in a few."

Next, Chief called Slick. He gave Slick the same rundown. Then he said, "Slick, I think the shooter(s) must have entered our parking lot from Texas Street. I need you to canvass the businesses there near the courthouse. Just ask if anyone saw anything or anyone looking suspicious anytime up to 10:30 or so. Problem is, we don't have a description of the doers or the car. We don't know where they fled, but there's only four ways to go, plus we think they're from El Paso. I'll be here at the office until Randy comes in for the midnight shift. Let me know what you find, okay?"

"You got it, Chief. Guess I'll be driving my own truck."

"Be sure to stop by here first. Buck may have some new tires on the '73 Plymouth before you head out."

"Roger that. See you in a little bit."

When Chief was done, he walked over to Gertrude and Ernie. Chief asked, "Is Vera able to give you a hand?"

"She is."

"Good, if you need to use the restroom, it's over there. Barlow will be here in a few minutes to take you."

"Thanks, I believe I will. By the way, where's Miss Loretta?"

"Oh, she's got a cold and a sore throat. We're hoping she'll be able to come back to work on Monday."

"When it rains, it pours, don't it?"

"No truer words were ever spoken."

Chief went back to his desk and called the Emergency Room at the Val Verde Baptist Hospital. He asked if Sheriff Sol were there. A few minutes later, he picked up the line. "Sheriff Pratt speaking."

"Sheriff, it's me, Chief Alex. How's it going?"

"Dewey's in surgery now. Did you get ahold of Gillespie?"

"I did. She and Elsie should be on the way. The reason I called is, Ernie's still catatonic. Barlow and Sarah are going to take him and Gertrude to the hospital in a few minutes to have him checked out by a psychiatrist. They'll have Ernie's car and Sarah's bug. Unless we call someone else, that will be your ride home."

"Thanks, but I already called Joanna to come get me. We may be here awhile. What's the status on our fleet?"

"Buck's got tires on hand for your car and the '73 Plymouth. He hopes to have tires for the Jeep and the Dodge later on today. The bad guys stuffed a potato up deep into the Ford's exhaust pipes. He may have to replace 'em. The '72 Dodge is still a crime scene, plus it will take a few days to get it operational with the blood and all.

"Did Dewey tell you anything?"

"Yes. A lone white or Latino gunman in a blue and white Dodge van. No plate number. He had a Government Model .45. He turned westbound on 90, but no idea where he went from there."

"Well, at least that's something. I'll tell Slick soon as he gets here. I've got him canvassing all the nearby businesses on Texas Street."

"Good job. Look, I'll call you later when Dewey's out of surgery."

"Roger that. Adiós."

"Adiós."

Next Chief called the El Paso Sheriff's Department. Lucky for him, they were able to flag down Captain Howard just as he was leaving the building.

"Chief, I was just fixing to go to lunch. Can I call you back in a little bit?"

"Of course, I'm really sorry to bother you, but we've had an incident. Parties unknown ambushed two of our deputies outside our office as they were bringing Joaquín Pérez back from the hospital. They killed him and wounded one of the deputies. He's at the hospital now. Also, the doer(s) did a first-class recon on our fleet of cars. They spiked the tires on all of them such that we couldn't even begin a cold pursuit. Anyway, call me back when you can, so we can discuss the more dangerous drug gangs in El Paso."

"Damn! The deputy going to make it?"

"I think so. It's Dewey Carruthers. I don't think you know him. He's originally from El Paso. Shot in the upper right chest with a .45. Doer (or doers) was driving a light blue and white van. Think it was a Dodge. Nothing further at this time."

"Look, as it so happens, I'm meeting Fred Wendell and Julio Elias for lunch at the Burger King. Won't take long. They're supposed to have some information for me on our pot gangs. I'll tell them about this. Maybe someone knows who owns this van. I'll call you back in an hour. That okay?"

"You bet. Thanks."

"Sure thing. Adiós."

Next, Chief called SA Carmine Valenzuela of DEA in El Paso. He was out, but the receptionist said he left a message for him. It read, "Weed comes from Oaxaca, Mexico. Big operation. Controlled by warlord named Victor Estrada and his brother Mateo. Many tentacles. Check with Lieutenant Wendell from El Paso SO. Call if I can be of further assistance. Carmine."

While he was waiting for a callback from Captain Howard, Chief Alex decided to put out a BOLO [Be on the Lookout For] on NLETs [National Law Enforcement Telecommunication System] on the getaway vehicle. It read, "Quayle County, Texas

Sheriff's Office is looking for a late model blue and white Dodge van, license plate unknown, involved in the murder of a prisoner and shooting of a deputy sheriff this date. If encountered, approach with caution. Contact Chief Deputy Snodgrass at 905-671-3343."

Chief felt like he was sitting around with his finger up his ass. He began the tedious process of writing today's incident report, referencing Barlow's traffic stop shooting; creating a case file; drawing a detailed crime scene sketch; and, filling out the packet with the roll of 35 millimeter film of the crime scene for development by the drug store.

Then he got in his file cabinet and checked both Ernie's and Dewey's revolvers. Ernie's had been protected by his leather gun belt, but Dewey's wooden handgrip on the right side was scuffed up a little bit. He thought it could probably be rubbed out with some very fine sandpaper. Other than that, both revolvers were fine. Dewey's tee shirt and uniform shirt were beyond repair. He put them in a plastic bag and dropped them in the dumpster out back. Chief washed the blood off Dewey's silver star and then he polished it. He put it back in the file cabinet with the guns and locked everything up.

He was itching to process the 1972 Dodge as a crime scene, but there was no one available to assist or cover the phones.

He scratched his ass and wondered. How would Sheriff Sol man the shifts with two deputies on the Injured Reserve List. There were 21-man days (shifts) each week, if each shift only had one officer. Leaving Sunday unmanned, reduced it to 18 man-days (shifts). Eight officers (including the sheriff) equals 24-man days available. However, if each officer got two off-days each week instead of just one, they would be down to 16 man-days to cover 18 shifts. Ergo, there weren't enough personnel to give each employee a second off-day each week unless they put in some 12-hour shifts (without overtime pay, of course). The budget had always been too lean to pay overtime and the Board of

Supervisors was well aware of it. That's why Sheriff Sol gave deputies comp(ensation) time off whenever he could to help make it up as best he could. The troops appreciated it, but it still didn't make up for all the uncompensated work hours.

Furthermore, this one-officer model did not take into account the additional manpower needed to guard prisoners 24/7 (when they had them), or deputies attending mandatory POST training, or court appearances on off days, vacation days, holidays, sick days, or annual military training for the national guardsmen or military reservists (of which they had one of each right now). To put it in perspective, the police personnel administration manual calculated that it takes 14 officers to provide 8 officers for 24/7/365 coverage for just one shift, or 42 officers to provide 8-man coverage for all three shifts. Extrapolating, they need 10-1/2 officers to man three 2-man shifts everyday.

Chief wondered what Sheriff Sol would come up with. It would have to be creative. Hell, the federal labor laws would never permit what they had been getting away with for years. Things had changed substantially since World War II, except for the application of federal labor laws here in Quayle County. Here they were anachronistic. Chief was thankful he didn't have to make this decision.

Ring! Ring! Ring! "Quayle County Sheriff's Office. Chief Snodgrass speaking."

"Alex, it's Stan. Got some good news, I think."

"Let's have it. Good news is in very short supply here."

"The pickup truck you all seized did belong to Diego Cruz, age 54, recently deceased. Cancer, I think. Your first decedent, Armando Cruz, is one of his sons. He's got several, all a chip off the old block. Diego was an ex-con, mostly burglaries and auto theft. Between stints in the joint, he worked for Pedro Ibarra, who owns a garage at 900 Hope Street, corner of 16th Avenue, called Pedro's Auto Repair Shop.

"Pedro Ibarra is 55 years old, El Paso High School graduate,

Class of 1940. Never been arrested. World War II Army vet with two Purple Hearts. He's as shady as the inside of Mammoth Cave. He's also a prominent figure in the Latino section of El Paso where he grew up, which is where his business is located. Prosperous. Articulate. Well-respected in his neighborhood. Big donor at St. Boniface Catholic Church. Buys uniforms for the kids on the neighborhood American Legion baseball teams - both of them. Employs about a dozen workers. Get the picture?"

"I do."

"Good. So both Armando Cruz and Joaquín Pérez are associated with Ibarra. Might have been employed by him one time with W-2s, but not for at least a year. Officially, they are not his employees. Both are known nickel-and-dime pot dealers.

"Narcotics has long considered Ibarra a small-time source for weed, but he never rose high enough on their radar to pursue. For one thing, DEA has never been all that interested in weed. They're after Mexican tar in particular, but on occasion, no matter what type of controlled substance it is - think LSD - they'll get involved IF it's newsworthy. Truthfully, it's not really DEA. It's the U.S. Attorney's Office. No headlines? Take it local. Problem is, our local DA and the judges who have to get elected every four years are not interested in prosecuting someone of Pedro Ibarra's stature in the Latino community. He's never gonna get prosecuted by them unless he gets caught raping Mother Theresa in public.

"But there is some good news. Turns out that Ibarra is a blood relative to Victor and Mateo Estrada down in Oaxaca, Mexico. Allegedly those two pretty much control the market on a new, potent strain of pot called Oaxacan Highland Gold, otherwise known as OHG. The kilo bricks of weed with the rooster logo is their product. It's suddenly become the weed of choice in the American southwest. Also, word on the street is that recently, Ibarra and his criminal associates have been tagged with the label, Hope Street Boys. Not only that, allegedly Ibarra has quit making nickel-and-dime sales. Supposedly, now he only sells in kilo-size quantities or more. In addition, he's supposed to be in a turf war with another gang called the Tres Deuces, who by the way, do not have access to OHG.

"There's also some shitty news. Nobody in local law enforcement here has got an in with the Hope Street Boys. Even if we did, none of us have the budget to purchase a half-dozen bricks of their dope at $2,000 a kilo, although the price goes down the more keys you buy at one time. Also, although it appears that your shooter is working for Pedro Ibarra, no one has any notion as to who he is. He's a ghost, and certainly a whole lot smarter than any of the weed gang hit men Narcotics has identified. You can tell that by the way he pulled off the hit in broad daylight, plus the fact that he managed to disable all your cars. That's a first for us. Does any of this help at all?"

"It does. I just don't know how we can proceed from here. Guess our first goal is still to identify the shooter. If we could do that, maybe arresting him would bring Pedro Ibarra out in the open. That should be good for you all or DEA. Our problem is a hundred times worse than yours, though. Right now we're down to eight badge-toters; we're 300 miles from El Paso; and, our budget is - let's just call it paltry.

"When Sheriff Sol returns from the hospital, I'll run all this by him. Probably give you a shout Monday. Listen, I appreciate everything you all have turned up. Thanks a million."

"De nada. Don't lose hope. What you all need is some more taxpayers to feed the hungry beast."

"That's just it. They claim our population is down 10% since the 1970 census. We're going backwards."

"That's a chilling thought. Hopefully that will turn around. In the meantime, we'll figure out our joint weed problem together, Amigo. We're here to help. You know that. Adiós."

"Adiós."

Chapter 13

TRYING TO KEEP THE BALL IN THE AIR

Friday, May 24, 1974

Sarah followed Barlow, Gertrude, and Ernie to the hospital. From what little bit she could observe of Ernie, he might as well have been a potted plant. She wondered what would become of him. She felt bad for him and his family, but she thought he needed to find another job. Something less stressful, like a milkman or a soda jerk at the pharmacy. No one on the sheriff's office would ever trust him again. He almost cracked up a few years ago when he shot and killed the rustler who tried to run over him in the tractor semi-trailer.

When they arrived at the ER, they saw Joanna Pratt, who was working on a needlepoint in the waiting room. Then two orderlies escorted Ernie and Gertrude up to the top floor where the psyche ward was closed off from the rest of the hospital. Ernie went blithely along. He still had a vacant stare on his face.

Joanna said Dewey was out of surgery. Everything was fine. He would stay tonight and Saturday night, and be released on Sunday. Sheriff Sol and Ella Mae had gone to his room to wish him well before they left.

While they were chatting, Gillespie and Sheriff Sol showed up. He asked about Ernie. Barlow filled him in. He replied, "That's worse than I thought. Ernie's in for a tough time. We need to look in on Gertrude and the kids at least once a day for awhile to see if they need any help."

Barlow asked, "Do you know if Elsie is staying?"

"Yep, for the time being. Her mother is bringing the kids up to see Dewey for a little bit. Then they're all going back home. I'll be back sometime tomorrow to check on him and Ernie. We're all done here for tonight. You all have any dinner plans?"

Barlow said, "Not anymore. How about you all?"

Joanna responded, "Well, there's a nice little Italian restaurant called Benedetto's about two blocks from here. It's early enough that we shouldn't have a wait. Would you all be interested in joining us?"

Sarah said, "Of course. I doubt Barlow's eaten since he went to work last night. I used to eat there sometimes when we would visit with my grandmother and aunt. What do you say, Barlow?"

"Lead the way, garçon. Right now I could eat a dead possum marinated in a septic tank."

Sheriff Sol asked, "You in, Ella Mae?"

She replied, "Absolutely. Let's go. I'll follow you all."

Normally talk about the job would not have been discussed over dinner, but tonight it was a necessity due to the inordinate amount of violence directed at them in such a short time.

After they placed their orders and had an adult beverage, Sheriff Sol said, "I know you all can see the predicament we find ourselves in. Dewey's likely going to be off for the next couple of weeks, and even then he may be restricted to desk duty for awhile after that.

"As far as Ernie's concerned, depending upon the severity of his situation, he may never return to work. He's got 21 years on the job, plus three years in the Army which also counts. Problem is, he's only 42 years old. You need age 50 plus 20 years service in order to retire. I know there are provisions for a medical retirement, but it's never come up before here in Quayle County so I don't know how it works. All I know is that after ten years of service, an officer is vested, but the payout doesn't take effect until age 65. Guess we'll just have to wait and see.

"All of which brings me back to the dilemma on how we run the office with only eight of us. Eight officers working five, eight-hour workdays a week means we can cover 40 eight-hour shifts.

Snake Pit 131

Already no one works on Sunday unless he's playing catchup (referring mostly to Chief) or unless we get a duty call.

"Stay with me. If we dispense with the midnight shift, we can staff three officers on two shifts for six days with four man-days left over. That's not anywhere near enough personnel to cover holidays, sick days, vacation, training, guarding prisoners, or responding to true emergencies. One person takes a week off, we're already short on one shift; however, for the time being, that's all we've got. Savvy?"

They all nodded their heads.

"Okay. Last year, I told the patriarch of this outfit, County Board Supervisor Archie Willis, that we've been in a crisis mode for several years due to an uptick in crime and a lack of staffing. He already knew that and agreed with me wholeheartedly. Problem is, Quayle County is flat broke. As you know, the property tax referendum did not pass. Also, as I understand it, our population is shrinking. That means fewer taxpayers. Archie suggested reducing down to only two shifts as an alternative, which I really did not want to implement, but under the circumstances, it's all we can do.

"So, beginning Monday, we will no longer have a midnight shift unless we're housing a prisoner. We'll operate three-man day and afternoon shifts. Two permanent fixtures on days are Chief and yours truly. Any duty calls on Sunday will generate a response from the day shift deputy. Calls on the midnight shift will be handled by two of the afternoon shift deputies. Ditto if we have any overnight prisoners. We'll make adjustments as needed. For example, Ella Mae, you may be called in to assist Chief on investigations. Barlow, you and Slick will still be my primary bloodhounds. Is this clear to both of you?"

They both nodded their heads. Barlow had a dog-eating-shit grin he couldn't wipe off his face. Ella Mae Gillespie was more circumspect, but she was just as excited as Barlow.

"Okay. I've been working on a new schedule while I was

cooling my heels in the waiting room. Barlow, you and Ella Mae are on afternoons beginning Tuesday since Monday is Memorial Day. Check the rest of the two-week schedule when you report for duty.

"Okay, now that's over, who wants to talk baseball or opera or anything else?"

On the way home, Sarah asked what Barlow thought would happen to Ernie. He replied, "Well, first of all I hope he makes a full recovery. He's a good guy and he knows police work inside and out. He knows how to talk to people and get the best out of them. However, I think he's done. Nobody will ever trust him again to be there when the shit hits the fan. You definitely can't send him out alone. That would be like letting an infant walk too close to a ledge. He'd wind up falling off. I pray he recovers to the extent that he can find work in a low stress occupation. Sell fire insurance or be a barber or something. As much as everyone likes him, I can assure you that nobody will ever want him for a partner or a back-up. He would be a pariah."

"That's pretty much my take on it, too."

When they arrived home, they took Happy for a walk. Then they stripped off and bounced into bed. Barlow hadn't had much sleep and he was exhausted, but once Sarah cuddled up next to him, the pheromones kicked into overdrive and he was raring to go. The thing nagging him tonight was worry over his stamina. He didn't want to be a Minute Man in the physical sense of the term.

He needn't have worried. Sarah read him like he was a first-grader and she was the teacher. She rolled over on top, tightened the cinch, and began a slow canter. It was rhythmic, like ocean waves lapping up on the beach. She was in no rush. She took her time. Then Time overtook her. She could no longer control the pace. She was riding faster and faster. Her breathing became sporadic. She clinched his shoulders and his love-maker. She was gushing wet and about to fall off her steed. Barlow increased the pace even more, wrapping his arms even tighter around her waist so she wouldn't slide off.

Then it happened. She crossed the threshold into Nirvana, carrying him with her. Barlow was spent like an empty tube of toothpaste. Sarah collapsed like a sandcastle erected too close to the encroaching tide.

Night, night, sweet prince and princess. Sleep tight.

* * * * * * * * * *

Sheriff Sol dropped off Joanna at home. Then he stopped by the jail. Chief was by his lonesome, working on his notes and assembling those portions of the criminal case file that he could. The office smelled like Hoppe's Number 9 gun solvent.

Sheriff Sol asked, "Cleaning guns now?"

"Yep.

"I'm basically at an impasse until I conduct the crime scene on the Dodge. I also need to tell Pete what to do with both bodies. Probably need to find next-of-kin first. Also, we need to decide whether or not to make a press release on the dope. Almost forgot. If we want to, we can seize the truck for hauling contraband or we can just let the next-of-kin come pick it up.

"Anyway, I was spinning my wheels, so I decided to clean my pistol. That didn't take much time, so I cleaned Ernie's and Dewey's. Ernie's ammo was so old, the brass casings had a green patina from oxidation all around the primers, plus the lead bullets had turned brittle with some kind of white powdery substance like arthritis coating them. Even the spare cartridges in his belt looked like they were Civil War artifacts. I scooped up all his ammo and I'll dispose of it tomorrow. I'll also stop by Jake's and buy him a new box of bullets."

"Charge 'em to the office account. Also just buy standard round-nose .38s. He won't be needing .357 Magnums anymore."

"Will do. Sorry, Sol, for rattling on. Anything I need to know?"

"Chief, did you eat today?"

"Sure did. April brung me a Care package a little while ago. She knew I wouldn't be home 'til late. You know what she brung me?"

"What?"

"A big bowl of beef chili, still hot. It was in a Tupperware bowl with a tight lid. A sizable piece of French bread, some sharp cheddar cheese, semi-dill pickles, artificially sweetened lemonade, and a cold bowl of applesauce. It's more food than I get in two days. I've lost three pounds this month, but that'll probably undo it all. What can you do? You only live 'til you die."

"You got a point there.

"Looky here. Dewey's gonna be fine. Might be off a couple of weeks but that's it. He'll come back stronger than ever. Being in two shootouts in one week has stiffened his backbone.

"Chief, I finally got it out of Dewey. Ernie froze up, plain and simple. Soon as the perp shot Pérez, Ernie gave up. Hands reaching for the sky. Dewey had just drawn his gun when the perp shot him. He went down, dropping his gun. It was just out of reach in front of him. He was trying to reach it when he looked up. The perp was eyeing him with his .45 aimed right at his head. Dewey was waiting for the guy to finish him off, but he didn't. Instead, he told Ernie to ditch his gun belt and Dewey's gun. Ernie never went for his gun the whole time, even when the perp was distracted. Just did what he was told, and then continued reaching for the sky like that's his normal posture.

"The perp was dead calm. He didn't leave until he heard you and me coming. Then he shot out the Dodge's tires and sped off around the corner.

"That's how it went down. No sugarcoating it. I've made up my mind.

"I pray that Ernie has a complete recovery, but either way he's a gone pecan. He can take an early retirement or maybe a medical one, or he can make me do the hard thing and fire him. Hopefully, I'll never have to tell him that. Give him the opportunity to do the right thing without feeling like he was forced into it. In fact, I plan to go see Archie tomorrow to see if he can clue me in as to what the best retirement option would be for Ernie. Just don't mention any of this to anyone, okay?"

"Of course."

"Also, at least for now, beginning Tuesday since Monday is a holiday, I've eliminated the midnight shift. The afternoon shift will cover any midnight call-outs as well as midnight jail duty when it's necessary. Day shift will handle all Sunday calls. I've already rewritten the schedule for the next two weeks, which I'll post by the coffee pot after I take the other one down. I'll call the guys tomorrow to give them a heads up. Barlow and Gillespie already know.

"So did you have any luck today?"

"I did. Cliff Notes version is that the weed is an extremely potent product known as Oaxacan Highland Gold, referred to as OHG. The rooster on the wrapper is the OHG trademark. Right now, DEA and EPSO believe there's only one importer in Texas. An auto repair shop owned by a Mexican named Pedro Ibarra is believed to be that source. His business is on Hope Street in El Paso. Hence, the name of his cannabis enterprise is known as the Hope Street Boys. Word is, another gang called the Tres Deuces is at war with the Hope Street Boys. Also, both Armando Cruz and Joaquín Pérez are associated with Ibarra.

"Ibarra has essentially been hands off by the locals because of his stature in the Latino community - a war hero and big donor to all the right causes. Also allegedly, now Ibarra deals only in kilo or larger size quantities. A single brick sells for $2,000. EPSO doesn't know who might've been the assassin, or if Ibarra's crew has a blue and white van, but they're working on it as we speak.

"Also Slick spoke with Molly Maloney at Crabtree's. She said they only had one stranger during the morning shift. It was a Mexican male, maybe 35, very handsome like a movie star, with black hair, and brown eyes. Nice, thick mustache like the actor

Tom Selleck. Molly noticed two distinguishing marks. One was his left pinky fingernail was black or blue. It looked like maybe he'd hit it with a hammer or something heavy. The other was he had a wart on top of his left hand between his thumb and forefinger.

"He was sitting in booth five, which is right next to the front window where he had a clear view of the rear courthouse parking lot. He ate breakfast and drank several cups of coffee. He was very polite, good English like he was American-born. Left a generous tip. He was wearing jeans, jean jacket, blue chambray shirt, and a beige Stetson. Not sure what he was driving. However, there was a blue and white van with a New Mexico license plate parked facing east where he could keep an eye on it if he was of a mind to.

"Slick also spoke with Aaron Booth from the Rancher's Co-Op next door to Crabtree's. He was in Crabtree's getting carry-out coffee. He saw this same guy, whom he said was mid-30s, about 6-feet tall, 170-180 pounds, rugged looking, who had just walked out of the diner as he walked in. Said the guy had a confident aura about him. While Aaron was checking out, he noticed that the guy was walking across the street to our rear parking lot. Never noticed a vehicle that he associated with the guy. That's it."

"That's a helluva lot. That's gonna be our perp. Now maybe we can get an ID on him from El Paso. Well, okay then. Hey, you want me to help you do the crime scene on the Dodge tomorrow?"

"That would be great. About noon?"

"You got it. See ya then."

Chapter 14

BARLOW CONTRIBUTES TO THE INVESTIGATION

Saturday, May 25, 1974

Barlow awoke early. They were supposed to go horseback riding today down by the river, but Barlow had a better idea.

It couldn't keep. He hopped out of bed, set up the percolator, and turned it on. He went back to the bathroom to shower and clean up while waiting for the percolator to perform it's magic.

The running shower awakened Sarah. This was not Barlow's custom on a Saturday morning. He had to have the kinks in his swollen love muscle worked out as soon as his eyelids popped open. Sarah always looked forward to this family custom. Something was afoot.

She entered the bathroom in her nudies and asked, "What's going on so early today that my horn dog husband didn't come to me for our Saturday morning rodeo? Did I break your thingamajig last night?"

He was done, so he turned off the water, pulled back the curtain, and began drying himself. He replied, "No, Sweetie. I'm practicing delayed gratification, as in waiting until this evening. I had an epiphany before I woke up. I'm fixing to do something I've never considered before."

"What's that?"

"I have a hunch the killer slipped through the fence at the same location where the sheep rustlers did four years ago. I've decided to find out. If he did, I'm going straight to that little village called Diminuto three or four miles south of the breech to see if anyone saw him."

"Are you planning to go on horseback?"

"Yep. Head to the river from your Dad's ranch and follow it east to the breech. If there are no signs of recent motor vehicle tracks, I'll turn back around. If there are, I'll go to Diminuto."

"So you're going armed?"

"Yep. I doubt there are any local policia in that area. Just plan to ask my questions and come back home."

"Barlow, your Spanish is pretty bad. Mine, on the other hand, is pretty good, so I'm coming with."

"I don't think that's a very good idea. I could run into some trouble."

"Darn right, you could. That's another reason. Besides, did you forget I shot that kidnapper at the rest stop - in fact, three times while he was abducting that girl because he thought she was me? I'm taking both of my guns, too."

"Sarah, if your dad gets even a hint I let you come with me, he'll be sore as hell."

"Then don't tell him. Also, why don't you call Slick? I bet he'd want to go, too."

"Hey! That's a great idea."

It was just a quarter after six, but Barlow figured Slick would already be up. Barlow dialed and let it ring. After the 27th ring, Slick picked up and said, "Oldman's."

"Slick, it's Barlow. I've got a very bad idea, but I thought you might be interested."

"You have my undivided attention. Is it worse than tearing shingles off your barn roof and then replacing them by yourself?"

"Could be unless you fall off the roof. Look, I think the killer fled the scene by breeching the fence where the rustlers did in 1970, and then looping back around into the U.S. somewhere one or two counties west of us. I'm planning to saddle up at the Bar B and follow the river to the breech site. If there's recent car tracks, I'm riding over to Diminuto and see what I can find out."

"I like your idea. Shoulda thought of that myself. Got a description of the killer?"

"No, just the van. Do you?"

"I do. How long it take you to meet me at the breech?"

"Two hours. Maybe a little more."

"Okay. See you 8:30-ish. You know if we get spotted by one of those crooked Mexican cops we may have to shoot it out."

"Yep. That's why I tried to talk Sarah out of coming along but she's made up her mind."

"Sarah's a plucky woman, and she's a whole lot more fun to talk to than you, plus she's easy on the eyes. Remind her to take her hideout gun in addition to her revolver."

"I will. See you in a couple of hours."

Barlow hung up. "Okay, Sweetie. We meet him 8:30-ish. We gotta get a move on."

It took a little longer than Barlow estimated. It was either that or forego breakfast. Sarah made them a couple of quick fried egg and ham sandwiches and brought two bananas to go. She also packed six ham and mustard sandwiches and three apples for lunch. They didn't arrive at the breech site until 8:40. Slick was already there studying the tracks.

He said, "Glad you ladies could make it this afternoon. It's a fabulous day to be a lawman on the hunt with nothing but an unsecured international boundary in our way. Me and Archie's done this numerous times and it's a hoot, but you need to keep your eyes peeled and be prepared for fight or flight, whichever option seems best at the time. Also, you need to keep this escapade to yourselves. I'll mention it after the fact to Sheriff Sol if we pick up any leads.

"Sarah, you being along just might make things a little easier for us, except everyone can see we're packing heat. Nobody over there's gonna have a gun unless he's a bandit or a cop, which is basically synonymous, meaning they'll know we're American lawmen right off, especially now everyone knows we got a female deputy.

Pointing down to the ground, he said, "Looky here. As you

can clearly see, there are two sets of tracks right there, and I can definitely see at least one set on the other side. Over here's a place with a very clear tread mark. If you can, memorize the pattern. This tire is new. You can see the tread is deep. No paisano has a tire this new, so this is most likely our guy.

"Barlow, yesterday I got a great description of our killer - Latino male, about 35, 6-feet tall, 175 pounds, ruggedly handsome, black hair, brown eyes, shares your and my appreciation for our style of mustache, wearing the same thing we got on, has a dark fingernail on his left pinkie, and a wart between his thumb and forefinger on his left hand.

"It's highly unlikely we'll run into him today. He's probably in El Paso holed up with a chica who appreciates his money and good looks, but you never know. If you see him, you better slap leather first. This hombre knows his trade all too well. Okay. Let's do it."

They rode in single file. Slick took the lead. Sarah was in the middle, and Barlow trailed. Both Sarah and Barlow were pinging. This was like the days of yesteryear, hunting bandits across the border, except this trip was unsanctioned. You know. "The government will disavow all knowledge if you get caught." On the south side of the border, being armed automatically made them the outlaws. At the same time, you'd have to have rocks in your head not to be.

On the south side of the Rio Grande, the tracks were clearer. This path going south had been used many times, but the newest tracks stood out like neon lights in the dark. Sure enough, about an hour later, they came up on the little village of Diminuto. Paisanos were out and about attending to their business, shooing away feisty roosters, shouting at rambunctious kids and yapping chihuahuas, or chatting with neighbors. They seemed curious enough about the horsemen, but in a friendly way.

They spotted an old man with a staff and a dog start walking towards them. He looked to be the oldest person in sight - 80 at least. If this were a proper city, he would probably be the alcalde, or maybe not. He looked more like an ancient Mexican Jesus - too poor, too honest, too virtuous to be a politician.

Slick was on the left, then Sarah in the middle, then Barlow. It surprised them that the old man approached Barlow first, in that Slick was obviously the most senior of them. Slick also looked more distinguished to Barlow than he looked to himself.

Barlow started to speak but the old man waived him off. Speaking excellent English, he said, "I know who you are. We all do. Your name is Barlow Adams. They call you El Vengador de los Inocentes."

Barlow looked at Slick and asked, "What?"

Slick replied, "The Avenger of the Innocents. They must really like you over here, Barlow, even better than we do. Ha!"

The old man looked over at Slick and said, "You are Señor Slick Oldman. Your family has lived in these parts for a hundred years. They call you El Fantasma de Wyatt Earp."

Sarah uttered softly, "The ghost of Wyatt Earp. Slick, they must hold you in high regard, too."

The old man walked closer to Sarah and said, "You are Sarah Adams-Baker. Your father is Señor Arturo Baker. Your mother is Señora Clarice. They are true friends to the Mexican people. They rescue those who need rescuing, and give them jobs and a place to live. They are very fine people."

Slick asked, "What is your name, Señor? I don't think we've ever met."

"My name is Carlos Javier Gonzales. They call me El Pato Extraño. We met once many years ago when I was a shepherd. You and Señor Archie Willis were tracking a murderer named Jesús Oswaldo López. He was a very bad hombre. You tracked him to my flock and asked me if I had seen him. I pointed the way he went. We never heard of him again."

"That's because we found him. He was already dead. He was bitten multiple times by rattlesnakes. Guess human snakes are despised by the reptile variety same as by humans. We found a recess in a bluff and put him inside sort of like a sepulcher. Made more work for the vultures. His bones are probably still there."

Barlow interrupted. "What's the meaning of El Pato Extraño?"

The old man replied, "The Odd Duck. The people think I'm afflicted, perhaps. I like it, and anyway the name stuck.

"I know whom you seek and the direction he went. He's a murderer too, like Jesús Oswaldo López."

Slick replied, "Please tell us."

"The first time I saw him was early Wednesday evening. He wanted to know a different location to ford the river than the one you just crossed. I directed him to the one near El Pozo de Serpientes, which leads to Brewster County. It's about 70 miles from here - maybe more. He was driving a light blue and white Dodge van. It had Texas license plates. He never told me his name. He's Americano of Mexican descent. I would say he's between 30 and 40. He has a thick mustache. He gave me $20 for my help.

"The only other time I saw him was yesterday about lunchtime. He didn't see me. That was probably my good fortune. He was wearing a bandanna over his face, but he pulled it down. He got out of the van and took off a New Mexico license plate, and changed it out with Texas plates. I could not make out the number. Then he hurried along his way."

Slick said, "Thank you Pato Extraño. You have been most helpful once again. Is there anything we can do to repay the favor?"

"Next time you come back this way, bring me a live chicken."

"Slick replied, I can do better than that. I can bring you several live chickens. In the meantime, here's $20 to buy a few to hold you over. Gracias and adiós."

"Thank you and goodbye. Go with God."

El Vengador de los Inocentes and Señora Sarah Adams-Baker

smiled back and thanked him, too. They bid him adieu as well. Then they pointed the horses north and headed back to Texas.

On the ride back, Slick said, "Our killer is cunning. He changed out his license plates. He scouted the area until he found the safest escape route. He's a thorough planner. He identified all our cars and disabled them. He's a good shot. He knows how to charm people, and he knows how to fade into the woodwork, but we have a leg up on him. We have an excellent description of him and we know how he operates. We even know which neighborhood in El Paso to begin looking for him, although we have to be discreet, or he'll evaporate like smoke on a windy day. It makes him a worthwhile adversary."

Barlow said. "That's all true, but wasn't it a little spooky that El Pato Extraño and apparently all the other citizens in Diminuto know who we are to the extent that they've even given us nicknames?"

Slick answered, "You should be flattered. You have an honorable reputation amongst them. Do you not understand yet that man and beast alike are always watching? They know you better than you know yourself. You better think twice before you take a leak behind a cactus again. Even the lizards are watching. If you have a small winky, all the beasts in the kingdom will know."

Sarah started laughing. Barlow was beside himself now that he realized he was always under the surveillance of somebody. Even the lizards!

Chapter 15

MORE GRUNT WORK

Saturday, May 25, 1974

Sheriff Sol was up early on Saturday too. After breakfast he rode over to Archie Willis' small ranch. Archie and Twyla had just finished breakfast. Twyla answered his knock. She lead him back to the kitchen where Archie was smoking a Camel cigarette and nursing a cup of coffee. Sol took an empty seat and accepted a cup from Twyla.

Archie said, "Glad you stopped by. We was told all about the dust-up yesterday back behind the courthouse. That was a wake-up call for everyone around here. Big city crime out in the boonies. How's Dewey doing?"

Sol replied as he lit up a Lucky Strike, "He was doing fine when I left the hospital last night. They expect him to be released tomorrow. He'll be on light duty for a couple of weeks, but that's not why I'm here. Gertrude had to put Ernie in their psychiatric ward. He was still catatonic when I left.

"Archie, I've decided not to let him return to work. Nobody but Chief knows that. Ernie's got 24 years of service including his Army time, but he's only 42 years old. What would be the ramifications if he went out on a medical retirement?"

"Well, he would draw 66-2/3rds percent of the average of his high three years. It's tax-free, but here's the issue. Down the road if he wanted to get another job, he couldn't do so unless he gave up the pension and (a) returned to work at the SO, or (b) froze his regular retirement until he's 65. How bad off his he?"

"Don't know for sure, but it's bad. Even if he makes a full recovery, I couldn't take him back. Nobody would want to work with him, and I couldn't leave him on desk duty ad infinitum. Truth is, at this point I don't see him ever being fully functional again."

"How long are you willing to keep him on medical leave status?"

"Well, at least until they let him out of the hospital unless that drags on for months."

"Understood. Well, that gives you some time to see what Gertrude wants to do. She's never been a wage-earner, but the tax-free benefits plus if Social Security disability insurance kicks in, he would probably net about what he draws now. However, if he needs constant attention they might have to put him in a nursing home. I don't think any insurance benefits would cover that. If that happened, she might be forced to find a job."

"Well, we'll give it a little time and see what happens. In the long term we're down one deputy. Any chance the board would let me hire another one?"

"You know I'm a yes, but I need either Hiram Templeton or Fred Krauthammer to vote yes, too. As long as Ernie's on the books that will never happen. They're both reasonable men, but we're already dipping into the rainy day fund just to pay the bills.

"When the residents voted against the increase in property taxes, that pretty much sealed our fate. The vote was close, so I think we'll try it again soon. If we don't get it passed then, we'll probably have to start laying off some employees. Besides that, our county population is down to 2,654. We're still losing residents like we have the Bubonic Plague. We just don't have many options. The roads are in pretty good shape, but the courthouse is old and we need to make some repairs. I'm sorry, but that's just the way things are right now."

"I understand. I remember what you told me last year. Now it's come to home to roost. I eliminated the midnight shift beginning Tuesday. Afternoon shift will be on call. With only eight of us available, that's the best we can do. We're up 40 percent on response-needed calls since 1972."

"I'm in your court, Sol. Get anything on the shooter yet?"

"We got a vehicle - no plate - and an excellent physical description of the shooter. No name, but we're pretty certain he's a member of a specific Latino gang in El Paso. Chief's hard on that. I'm headed over to Buck Boyd's in just a little bit to help Chief conduct the crime scene as it relates to our marked unit. Also, these bandits were hauling 60 kilos of high grade marijuana that they call OHG. Allegedly it's worth $120,000. I haven't made a press release on that, but I probably will come Tuesday. We still have not reached out to next-of-kin on the dead bandits, but then, it was in all the regional newspapers, plus radio and TV, and no one has contacted us, either. Anyway, that's just how backed up we are. We'll get everything done if we all don't kick the bucket first.

"Well, I better go. Thanks, Twyla, for the hospitality and coffee. Arch, let's try and get together one day for lunch this week."

"Thursday noon at Betty's Diner."

"Betty's it is. See you Thursday at noon. Adiós."

"Adiós. Take care of yourself, Sheriff. Give Joanna my best."

"Will do."

Sheriff Sol didn't have time to get back and forth from the hospital by noon, so he decided to check in at the jail. Deputy Noble "Chunk" Bustamante was holding down the fort. Chief hadn't made an appearance yet, but it was still early.

"Hey Chunk, how's it going?"

"No response-needed calls yet. Gertrude called. No change regarding Ernie. I checked in with Dewey. He's feeling a little better. He still expects to be released sometime tomorrow."

"Good news on Dewey. Not surprised regarding Ernie. He was completely catatonic when Barlow drove him and Gertrude to the hospital. By the way, did you see the next two weeks' roster I posted?"

"Sure did. No mids, huh?"

"Not enough manpower. Everyone except Slick, Randy, and Kirk know about the change. Could you give those fellows a call and let them know?"

"You got it."

Sheriff Sol went back to his desk and began working on a press release related to the marijuana seizure. He was just finishing up when Chief Alex walked in. It was only 10:30, but they decided to go ahead and conduct the crime scene search on the Dodge.

Buck Boyd had already recovered two .45 slugs from the tires when he replaced them with new ones. They also recovered one from the post between the driver and rear passenger door which had passed through Dewey. They recovered a fourth .45 slug from inside the back of the front seat which passed through Pérez. That left two which were probably still in Pérez's body. If they could ever find the .45 caliber pistol the shooter used, it would be the last piece of damning evidence they would need to secure a conviction. Chief had hoped that there might be a partial print on one of the projectiles, but he could not see any through his magnifying glass. He would ask the lab to check anyway.

When they were done, Sheriff Sol went to the hospital to look in on Dewey and Ernie. He called it another day of necessary uncompensated overtime when he arrived back home.

Chief Alex went to Pete Ricketts' mortuary to examine Pérez's body, and to take more photographs. Then he told Pete to take it to the medical examiner's office in Del Rio the first chance he got. Afterwards, he went back to the jail and updated the case file. He was home by 3 o'clock.

Tuesday would begin a new workday assuming the relative calm wasn't shattered by a disaster over the Memorial Day weekend. Chief crossed his fingers. He wasn't the only one.

Chapter 16

SHAKING THE LEAVES ON THE TREES

Tuesday, May 28, 1974

Sheriff Sol was up-and-at-'em at the break of dawn. After a great deal of thought, he decided to shake the trees. Maybe in the Chihuahuan Desert, it would be more appropriate to say poke around the cacti and creosote bushes. Watch for which type of reptile or other predator scatters forth. Take the bull by the horns. Quit pussyfooting around. Seize the day. Cowboy up. Grow some balls. All of the above. Take your choice. He was done sitting on his hands and taking whatever came his way.

Both drug mules were dead ducks. Rotting meat. Sheriff Sol had been concerned about a rescue attempt on the wounded prisoner. He never considered a hit to silence him, especially since he never squealed. Talk about taking care of your loyal foot soldiers! Sol would never make that mistake again.

He had decided to make a press release regarding the drug seizure. Tie it to the deaths of both bandits, and the shooting of Dewey. Highlight the viciousness of the unnamed gang. Toot the QCSO horn to generate a reaction from the shooter when he heard about it, especially since he pulled off the perfect hit. Did the dirty deed in broad daylight at the county courthouse parking lot during normal workday activities and got away without a hitch! Sol would use the press release as a form of psy ops. Get in the shooter's head since he probably believes he's home free. Also give the distributor of all that seized weight, the Texas OHG marijuana kingpin, the middle finger in public without actually doing it. Fry his ass a little bit. Torque him and the shooter both up.

He also decided to begin civil proceedings to seize the truck today. Sol very well understood that the hidden (undisclosed) true owner didn't care one whit about the truck. It was part of the price of doing business. Sol just wanted to rub a little additional salt into the wound. More psy ops. Heck! He just decided to put the truck into inventory! It was in that good of condition. It would come in handy.

He also decided to make a highly visible public effort to locate the next of kin. Normally he would be circumspect. Respect the sorrow of a loving family. Not this time. Besides, no loving family came forward to claim either body, so he would take a different approach. Stir the pot. See what happens - who shows his face. If nobody steps up, get court orders for a couple of burials in a potter's field. He thought it might even be apropos to plant them in Judge Sweeney's very own bandit boot hill. Doubtful Judge Sweeney would allow that, though. Those 13 bandits had all been killed and buried by his patriarch, Ripsnort Sweeney, back in the day when Quayle wasn't a county and each pioneer rancher was the law unto himself on the land he laid claim to. The same land he fought and maybe bled for.

Finally, the most counterintuitive step he decided to make was to make a highly visible effort to locate the shooter in his own neighborhood. Make it obvious they knew who they were hunting for, even if they didn't know him by name. Try to spook him or possibly ferret out a snitch. Apply some heat and see what happens. Maybe someone would bump him off just like Joaquín Pérez to tie up a loose end. Maybe it would force the killer out in the open. Either way, put the game of cat-and-mouse in motion.

This is the exact opposite approach as to how the Feds or a local narcotics unit would pursue this case, and he knew it. They'd try to work someone undercover into the gang. Make some buys. Befriend or squeeze the shooter (once they identified him) to roll on the kingpin. Use the murder charge for leverage. Cut the murderer a sweetheart deal to be a witness for the state, always keeping in mind the "Big Picture" - the greater civic good - where toppling the kingpin takes precedence over sending the murderer of a lowlife criminal to prison for life. Grab some monster headlines. Be a giant-slayer, especially if the kingpin is a prominent person.

Sol knew he couldn't pull off his plan unless El Paso County Sheriff Adrian Brady agreed to it. After all, the bad guys all live, work, and play on his turf. He wants to get reelected same as any other sheriff would. Would Adrian go along with him, putting the conviction of a murderer/cop shooter above the conviction of a civic figure who is also a drug kingpin? What would Sol do if the shoe were on the other foot?

Then he thought of a couple of leads they needed to pursue first which might turn up the shooter's name. That would put QCSO in the driver's seat.

To accomplish one lead would require a helping hand from Adrian - a minor request - which he would probably consent to readily. The other lead would require some tedious research. He'd get Chief to set it up, and task Gillespie with the grunt work. If Sol got lucky, both endeavors would result in the intersection of facts which would reveal the shooter's identity, thus giving them probable cause for an arrest warrant. He would really like to get their hands on the murder weapon too, but most likely that would only be accomplished in concert with making the physical arrest. Even so, identifying the killer should provide all the incentive Adrian would need to pursue a murderer/cop shooter first, hoping it might lead to a solid case against a civic leader/drug kingpin who has friends in high places.

Sol picked up the phone and called Sheriff Brady on his private line. He answered right away. "Sheriff Brady here."

"Adrian. Sol Pratt from Quayle County. Got a few minutes to chat?"

"Of course I do. It's been awhile. Two, maybe three years as I recall, but even so, we read about Quayle County SO pretty regularly in the newspaper here. You all are keeping the rest of us Texas sheriffs on our toes with the number of bad boys you all send to perdition. I don't know how you do it with such a large county and just a few deputies. My hat is off to you."

"Thanks Adrian. That's high praise and I appreciate it. By the same token, I'd be remiss if I didn't say that I can't even imagine doing your job. The county's what - 400,000+ residents? You must have a staff of at least 500. You operate one of the largest jails in the state, and still you keep a tight lid on things. What we do over here is small potatoes compared with what you all deal with every single day. I come to you with hat in hand."

"Sol, put your hat back on. Small or not, you have one of the best-run SOs in all of Texas. Believe me, I know. All I have to do is look one county east of me. They couldn't haul your water. What can we do ya for?"

"Look, I don't know if you heard. Chief Alex has been in close contact with Captain Howard regarding a shootout during a traffic stop here last Monday night. The two drug mules were from your neck of the woods. They were hauling 60 kilos of top grade marijuana called OHG. We killed one perp and wounded the other. He was hospitalized in Del Rio.

"Friday morning, the two deputies on prisoner transport were ambushed right here in our courthouse parking lot when they were taking him out of the cruiser. The prisoner was executed and one deputy was shot in the chest. He's expected to make a full recovery. The gunman made a clean escape, but we do have a good description.

"Information Stan Howard provided indicates that all three of these perps are affiliated with a group known as the Hope Street Boys. Apparently it's just popped to the surface. Nobody knows enough about them to venture a guess as to whom they have on their payroll that's resourceful enough to pull off this well-executed hit.

"This brings me to my ask. We have three strong eyewitnesses who've given us a physical description. We'd like to borrow one of your sketch artists for a couple of days if we could."

"Well, Hell yeah! Want me to send somebody today? I will. Keep him the whole week if that's what it takes. A fucking cop-shooter? We want him as bad as you all, especially if he resides in El Paso County. I'll get Stan Howard to send him on his way.

"Another thing. You need to bring yourself over here the next time you all are working with our guys. The missus and I would love to have you all over for supper."

"I surely will, the very next trip if I can get away. Thanks for everything, Adrian. Adiós amigo."

"Adiós, your own self, amigo."

Sol stepped out of the office to get some coffee. He saw Miss Loretta, Chunk, and Chief Alex. He filled his cup before he made his rounds at each desk. Miss Loretta was over her cold and sore throat. She was hard at it working on the time sheets to take up to the county payroll clerk. Chunk was finishing up on a traffic accident report. Chief Alex was working like The Mad Hatter on the Pérez/Carruthers murder/assault file. Sheriff Sol noticed that Chief had several Tupperware containers on his desk filled with yummy rabbit food for his lunch. April was still monitoring his health like a hawk. He nodded at Chief and asked if he had time to come to his office. Without question, he did.

Chief refilled his coffee cup and entered. He closed the door. He asked, "What can I do for you, Sheriff?"

"I've been brainstorming on your case. I've finally decided to make a press release today on the latest shooting and the drug seizure. I'm going to make a big splash so it will reach the ears of the Hope Street Boys in El Paso. I intend to name both our decedents and see if a family member calls. Also, I want you to do the seizure paperwork on the truck. Once the seizure is perfected, I'll have Buck Boyd service it so we can put it into inventory.

"Also, I just got off the phone with Sheriff Brady. He's

sending one of his sketch artists over today to spend the entire week if necessary, to draw perp sketches from Molly Maloney over at Crabtree's and Aaron Booth over at the Co-Op. Also, Slick and Barlow turned up a witness across the river in Diminuto. His name is Carlos Javier Gonzales. They call him El Pato Extraño - The Odd Duck. I want Slick and Barlow to go fetch him when the sketch artist is ready. Any questions so far?"

"What's the story on The Odd Duck?"

"He saw, and even spoke to the perp on Wednesday evening, while he doing an escape recon to Brewster County. He saw him again on Friday about noon when he was fleeing the scene. His description matches Molly's and Aaron's. He's about 80 years old and sharp as a straight razor. Not only that, he noticed that the blue getaway van with the white stripe had Texas plates on it Wednesday. Friday morning it had a New Mexico plate, which the perp took off and replaced with the Texas plates. Oh yeah. The perp was wearing a bandanna over his face on Friday.

"I'm going to all this effort so Gillespie will have three source references. That's because I have a hunch that besides being from El Paso, he's also a recent parolee or serve-out.

"I want you to call the Texas Department of Corrections and ask for photographs of each parolee and serve-out in the past year who meets these parameters: Latino male, 30-40 years of age, from El Paso and surrounding counties. If you get any guff or foot-dragging let me know. I'll go up and see Judge Sweeney and ask if he'd sic Senator Darnell Sweeney on them. I want these photographs by Friday!

"Soon as we get 'em, you task Gillespie to compare the sketches with the photographs. If I'm right, she'll identify our shooter. Then you do a work-up on him and come see me.

"This is the reason my door's closed now. What I'm about to say is just between us. Adrian doesn't know it yet, but assuming we get an ID and arrest warrant on the perp, I'll send a posse to El Paso. I'll ask for Adrian's assistance. Lieutenant Wendell will probably throw a hissy fit. He'll want to sit on our warrant to make a drug case on Pedro Ibarra. Try to leverage the warrant to roll the shooter into squealing on him. Heck, if I were him, I probably would, too. We'll do all we can to pacify him, but he may be sore forever.

"We need to arrest the shooter so we can search him and wherever he lays his head to recover that .45. With any luck, El Paso may get enough evidence during the search to pop Ibarra. Of course, we may not, in which case El Paso Narcotics may never forgive us. Any questions?"

"Damn, Sheriff! This is brilliant! Makes me think I need to hang up my Sherlock Holmes hat and break my magnifying glass. I'll get right on this."

"Nope. You're still our Sherlock Holmes and Gillespie is still Dr. Watson. Oh yeah. Call Stan Howard. He's making the arrangements for the sketch artist. Get him a room at The Travelers' Rest. Charge it to our account."

"Sheriff, I want on that posse."

"You're already on it."

"Thanks. Let me get to work. I got to see if Pete Ricketts has the bodies back from the Val Verde ME's office. This week is going to be busy."

Sheriff Sol called for a 4 o'clock press conference on the courthouse steps. El Paso and Del Rio were bringing their cameras.

The ball was in play.

Chapter 17

MAN PLANS AND GOD LAUGHS

Tuesday, May 28, 1974

Pedro Ibarra was still seething over the 60-kilo loss of his merchandise. It was possible, even likely, that the Quayle County fuzz had discovered his product after the traffic stop with Armando and Joaquín. In other words, it could have been a lucky break for the cops.

It was equally as possible that a one-horse town police department wouldn't bother to dig through a ton of horse manure. What a shitty job! That being said, it was too risky to send someone over to Mosby to try to recover the truck. Even if they were successful, it would leave a trail straight to his front door. Get over it. The truck was lost forever.

The most perplexing problem was that the seizure had not been reported in the news. The pigs always love to gloat when they knock off a load. Take pictures of themselves in front of the contraband like they had just killed a trophy lion. So what's up with not following past braggadocio rituals? It didn't make sense if they actually got their grubby mitts on it.

Could they have stolen his pot? You know, a few corrupt, hick cowboys get rich beyond their wildest dreams. He didn't think so. This was too much weight. They would need a broker. Otherwise they'd fumble the ball. Get caught. Besides, surely they would have surfaced by now. Word would be on the street that some new guys have Oaxacan Highland Gold. Pedro decided that this was a very low probability scenario.

Maybe Armando and Joaquín were trying to rip him. Where would they run to? They had no connections. Besides, they were both reliable boys. Pedro truly regretted that it was necessary to bump off Joaquín, but he had no choice. Looking at life in prison - and that's exactly what he would've gotten down there in Hickville, USA - he woulda had to rat if he ever wanted to see daylight again. So no, they didn't have any big ideas. Besides, even if they did, they're both croaked now.

Could anyone have fingered this load to the cops as a way of fucking with him? Maybe. He was having a minor turf war with the Tres Deuces. The problem with the Deuces is, his territory and theirs were practically on top of each other - inexact and unagreed upon boundaries - but the big thing was the Deuces did not have the OHG. Only him. Nobody wanted the Deuces shit weed anymore. All the heads wanted the OHG and who wouldn't?

But what if it were the Deuces who ripped them off. He couldn't imagine that they had enough moxie to try to rip him off on their own, absent insider information. It would be open warfare. Now he had Chico as an enforcer. Who did they have? Nobody. Mr. Magoo. That's who. He would win and they would lose and they knew it.

But what if one of them had a cousin on the police force down there in Hickville, Quayle County? What if the cops were tipped? But if that were the case, how did they get the tip in the first place? Did he have a leak?

Pedro quickly ran through his mind everyone on the OHG manpower roster. He couldn't imagine any of those guys doing that. Could it be Geraldo Flores, his cousin's most reliable cross-border courier? Unthinkable!

What should he do to keep the Deuces in line? He had no proof - just a hunch. If it were them who tipped off the fuzz and he didn't retaliate, they would think he was weak. They would try to sandbag him again and again. Maybe next time steal his OHG and sell it.

What to do?

Hell with it! He'd send Chico to bump off one of their guys. That would send a message loud and clear. Fuck with me. I'll fuck right back twice as hard. He'd send Chico out after he met with his parole officer this morning. Just tell him the job had to be quiet with no witnesses.

So that's just what he did. Chico went out alone on foot without so much as a word to anyone. The neighborhood wasn't much more than a mile long by a half-mile wide. Somebody would be more likely to remember a car than a pedestrian. He put on a greasy San Diego Padres baseball cap one of the guys had tossed into the trash bin. He left his jacket behind. He wore dirty jeans and his raggedy boots. He concealed his gun under a dirty white, baggy tee-shirt. He also took his switchblade. He would use it if he could to eliminate the sound of a gunshot. He knew exactly where he'd look first.

He walked over to the river behind Gustavo's Cantina where a lot of illicit deals went down. If one of the Deuces stepped out the back door of the tavern to get a blow job or take a leak, Chico would slice his throat and go merrily on his way. Leave him bleeding in the dirt for the stray mongrels to feast upon.

The coast was clear when he arrived. Not a soul around. Not surprising. Everyone knew this place was hazardous to your health.

He found an empty brown, quart bottle of Blatz beer to use as a prop. He sat down on a log in front of the rusting hulk of a white, 1962 Plymouth Valiant which had been stripped of anything of value long ago, particularly its engine and wheels. Chico held the bottle in his left hand and pretended to be passed out drunk. He didn't wait long. A couple of Deuces nicknamed Reno and Sucio (because he was always grubby), opened the back door of the saloon and stepped outside. Chico recognized them right away. Useless foot soldiers.

Ricardo "Reno" Cisneros was 29 years old. He was 5-feet, 7-inches tall and weighed 140 pounds. Greasy black hair and brown eyes. He had a bad case of acne which left him scarred for life. He had served three years in prison for grand larceny (auto). Before that, he got two years on probation for selling an ounce of weed. He was known on sight by most of the uniformed cops.

Eugenio "Sucio" Estrada was 24 years of age. He stood 5-feet, 6-inches tall and weighed 185 pounds. Also black hair, but buzzed off close like a prison inmate, and brown eyes. He was a Marine Corps veteran of Vietnam and he had a tattoo on his left forearm to prove it. He enlisted when the judge gave him a choice of serving ten years for strong-armed robbery or serving his country in the armed forces. It was a no-brainer. They taught him to be a cook in the Marines, and a very good one at that. He did most of the cooking for the Tres Deuces whenever they had a blow-out. The robbery was the only arrest on his rap sheet. He was largely unknown to the cops.

Today, May 28, 1974, was their unlucky day. You could say they were shit outta luck.

They walked to the woods on the riverbank to smoke some weed. They saw the drunk who was passed out next to the rusty Plymouth but paid him no mind - a fucking oxygen thief. They rolled and fired up their blunts and began waiting for bliss to overtake them. Make all their worries disappear. They were well on their way ten minutes later. They never noticed the drunk until he was within ten feet of them.

Reno looked up and said, "Buzz off, pendejo. We ain't giving you no money even if you blow us in front of your mother." Then he and Sucio began laughing uncontrollably.

Chico continued staggering past them. Then he spun around and sliced Reno's throat from ear to ear. It was such a complete surprise that Reno had little time to contemplate before the Grim Reaper carted him off to Hell.

Chico shoved Reno to the ground and walked over to Sucio, who looked at him in utter horror without comprehension. Chico stabbed him in the heart and twisted its two-edged blade to sever all the arteries. As Sucio began to fall, Chico pulled the knife out, stepping back to avoid the torrent of gushing blood. He bent over and wiped the knife and his hands on Reno's jeans. Then he searched for guns but these worthless pricks had none.

He lifted both their wallets and took the cash. Make it look like a robbery. Reno had $154, and Sucio had $26. Then he threw both wallets in Reno's pool of blood and soaked them good, front and back, to conceal any latent prints if there were any. He wiped his hands again on Reno's jeans to clean off most of the blood. Then he rolled Reno face down into his own blood.

He walked back to Pedro Ibarra's garage at a leisurely pace. Nobody noticed him. It was 12:30. He was back in his cabaña behind the garage, taking a shower in a little over an hour.

Pedro asked if the job were done. Chico nodded his head yes. Pedro asked if there were any complications. He shook his head no. Then Pedro paid him $500 in new, crisp Andrew Jacksons. Easiest money he ever made.

Later that evening, Pedro was smoking a Te-Amo Churchill Robusto in a Maduro wrapper, savoring a crystal glass of José Cuervo Gold tequila. His wife, Ruby, was sipping on a crystal glass of Robert Mondavi's Fumé Blanc. They were watching the news before supper. Pedro wanted to see if his handiwork made the news. Naturally, he did not share the day's events with Ruby. She was, by choice, happily oblivious to all of his crooked dealings.

Sure enough, the lead-in story spoke of the brutal slaughter of two local men whose bodies were discovered in the woods near the river behind a cantina favored by local residents. Both had been stabbed. Robbery was the suspected motive. The names of the victims were being withheld pending notification of next of kin.

Pedro restrained a smug smile.

Ruby was horrified. She began reciting a prayer silently as she fingered her rosary beads. Her lips were moving without audio.

The bloodshed was too close to their home.

Towards the end of the 30-minute program, the newscaster began coverage of the extended El Paso area. The sheriff of Quayle County, who looked like a gigantic Geronimo in a tan uniform without a feather, spoke of a traffic stop a week ago in which the driver and his passenger exited the vehicle and began shooting at the deputies. One assailant was killed on site, but the other was wounded and hospitalized in Del Rio.

Deputies who were transporting the second assailant from the hospital to the jail in Mosby, were ambushed in the parking lot of the Quayle County Courthouse by a lone gunman driving light blue Dodge van with a lateral white stripe. The gunman murdered the second assailant and wounded one of the deputies. The authorities believe the second assailant was murdered to prevent him from exposing the owner of the 60 kilograms of Oaxacan Highland Gold marijuana he and the other man had been transporting on Monday. The decedents have been identified as Armando Cruz, age 24, and Joaquín Pérez, age 19, both of whom were last known as residents of El Paso.

The investigation is ongoing. The Quayle County Sheriff's Office is requesting the assistance of anyone who knows the next of kin for either Mr. Cruz or Mr. Pérez. Please call 905-641-8650, and ask for Chief Alexander Snodgrass.

Ruby choked on her wine. She asked, "Pedro, don't those boys work for you?"

"They did, but not for some time now. The last I heard they were working in a car wash. Nice boys, too."

"Do you know their families?"

"Armando's parents are dead. I think he still has some brothers or sisters in the area. Not sure about Joaquín. I'll ask one of the guys to see if they can locate someone from Armando's family. If they do, maybe that person will know someone in Joaquín's family. It's the least I can do. In fact, I will pay for both of their funerals."

Both Ruby and Pedro were quiet during their meal. Ruby was thinking of those poor boys. What would their mothers think? Pedro was thinking he needed to put on his civic leader clothes and decry the violence. He knew eventually the cops would be coming to him for some answers. He needed to shield himself by being more visible and outspoken. Flex enough to keep the poverty-stricken residents in his good graces, and demonstrate to the cops that they did not want to take him on if they suspected he was complicit in any way. Remind them of his power and standing in the community. At the same time, he needed to prepare for a revenge strike from the Deuces. He wished he had waited one more day for the facts to reveal themselves before he took matters into his own hands. Now he would likely be fighting a war on two fronts.

Chapter 18

WORKING LIKE DEMENTED BEAVERS

Wednesday, May 29, 1974

Chief Alex used hushed drama and his softest touch when he called the Texas Department of Justice yesterday to request photographs of recent Latino male serve-outs and parolees from the El Paso region.

He emphasized the bold, mid-morning timing of Pérez's murder and shooting of a deputy sheriff, in a courthouse parking lot during a workday by a lone gunman, who was believed to be a recently released prisoner. The audacity! Anybody could have been in the killer's crosshairs!

It worked. Maybe someone up there in the puzzle palace at the state capital annex building made the connection: Quayle County, and its favorite son, Senator Darnell "Fireball" Sweeney. He was a strutting peacock about his family's heritage in settling the Trans-Pecos region of Texas during its wild and woolly days. His ancestors killed more rustlers and bandits than Sam Houston killed Mexican soldiers in the Battle of San Jacinto.

Everyone in Austin knew Senator Fireball held the pursestrings for anything related to the Texas justice system. Take your choice. He could be either a strong ally or a ruthless enemy for all things related within the Texas criminal justice system. What's the hurt? Task some anal retentive minion to conduct the research, pull the photos, and get them in express mail by close of business. So what if the larger cop shops had to wait one day longer for a request of this type? What's another day in the greater scheme of things - that is, if the sheriff's office didn't have Senator Fireball's favor?

Is that what happened? Chief Alex didn't know. He would like to think he had mastered the art of persuasion. Either way, they were sending his mugshots in today's express mail.

Also, Forensic Artist Clancy Rush, El Paso County Sheriff's Office, showed up bright and early at the jail to sketch as many renditions of a killer as Quayle County wanted. Chief Alex had already put Molly Maloney and Aaron Booth on standby.

Chief also sent Slick and Barlow over to Diminuto on horseback trailing a saddled horse to pick up the Odd Duck and bring him back. In compensation for his tip and time, Slick had already purchased ten laying hens and one feisty cock, all of which were caged just like he had promised. Cost the QCSO a grand total of $36, not including lunch at Crabtree's.

Slick already had a pack-mule ready to go for the trip back. He wanted to ensure that El Pato Extraño was in possession himself of all his birds once they made delivery. Who knew how many might disappear during his absence while he was across the river?

By the time Slick and Barlow returned with him, Clancy had already completed the sketches from Molly and Aaron. Clancy had a little more difficulty drawing Aaron's description because he hadn't studied the killer's face all that much. Molly on the other hand, had been salivating like a lovesick teenager as soon as she saw him. She had him down pat. Then when El Pato Extraño described him, the SO hit the trifecta. Molly's and the Odd Duck's descriptions were nearly layovers.

Clancy had fulfilled his mission by 3 o'clock. He decided to lay over for the night before heading home. He was enjoying some frosty Dos Equis at the Dry Gulch Saloon with Chunk before Slick and Barlow had even saddled up for the trip back to Diminuto.

When the mail arrived, Miss Loretta sorted it and gave everything addressed to Chief Alex to him. He ripped open the envelope from the Department of Corrections and scanned all 36 photographs. He spotted one with a good likeness to the sketches. Then he bundled up the package and gave it to Gillespie, who poured herself a fresh cuppa joe, and sat down at the junior deputy's desk and began her perusal like she was taking the SAT examination. It took less than three minutes. She jumped up and exclaimed, "Got him! It's Rafael "Chico" Salazar!"

Chief smiled to himself. He had already come to the same conclusion. He said, "Come on, kiddo. We need to take a walk upstairs and see DA Able DeWitt. First, let me run Salazar's rap sheet to get his pedigree.

A few minutes later, he pulled off the printouts from the teletype machine. There were three pages: one from the FBI's NCIC [National Crime Information Center]; one from the combined states' NLETS [National Law Enforcement Telecommunications System]; and one from Texas DMV [Department of Motor Vehicles]. Both NCIC and NLETS had the same information. Both reflected that Salazar had been arrested by the El Paso Police Department for manslaughter in 1956. He received a 20-year sentence. He was incarcerated at the Texas State Penitentiary in Huntsville. He was paroled in 1972. Nothing further. DMV records reflected that he obtained a Texas driver's license in 1972. It was still valid.

"Got him, and it fits!" He picked up his case file and away they went.

Able was free and they got straight down to business. When they were done presenting the case, Able said, "Let me see if I have this right.

"You have several spent bullets from a .45 which were recovered from Dewey, Joaquín Pérez, and the Dodge police cruiser, but no gun or shell casings.

"You have two witnesses who identified the suspect from a police artist's sketch. Both saw him just minutes before the shooting, but didn't actually see the shooting.

"You have a Mexican witness who also identified him and the getaway van the day before the shooting and an hour after the shooting. The first time this witness saw him, the van had Texas plates. After the shooting, he saw the man switch the New Mexico license plate that your first witness saw, back to Texas plates. Nobody copied either license plate number.

"Also, the first time the Mexican witness saw the suspect, he was driving from the U.S. border. He asked for a different route so he could sneak back across the border into the U.S., closer to El Paso. The second time he saw the suspect, he drove towards this same western egress/exit route.

"Neither Dewey nor Ernie have been asked to identify the suspect from this mugshot because he was wearing a bandana mask during the shooting, and because Ernie is still psychologically incapacitated; however, the Mexican witness saw the suspect remove a bandanna from his face before he switched license plates.

"The two deceased marijuana transporters are from El Paso.

"Finally, your suspect is from El Paso, and he has a conviction for manslaughter.

"Is that about right?"

Chief responded, "Correct. That's what we have right now. We can't recover the gun unless we arrest the suspect or get a search warrant for his dwelling or vehicle, and I know for damn sure we don't have enough yet for search warrants."

Able replied, "Let me say that you all have done a masterful job in this investigation. Very insightful and thorough. Problem is, it's all circumstantial. Everything you have is dynamite, but we don't have a smoking gun - yet. People have been convicted on circumstantial evidence alone, but it's risky.

"Tell you what. Go back downstairs and write up a complaint alleging one count of murder and another for aggravated assault. Bring it back to me before 4 o'clock and let me review it. Your affidavit has to have everything in it that you just told me. Type out a warrant form too. If it's all there, we'll try to take it to Judge Sweeney before he leaves for the day. Who's going to be the affiant and how long do you think this will take you?"

Chief Alex responded, "Gillespie's the affiant and we can be back in an hour."

"Very good. I'll call tell Judge Sweeney's office to expect us before 5 o'clock. Don't be late."

At 5:15, Gillespie and Chief were bounding down the stairs to Sheriff Sol's office with the complaint and arrest warrant in hand, the former duly deposed and signed by Gillespie, and the latter signed and sealed by Judge Sweeney. Chief and Gillespie both had a dog-eating-shit grin on their faces.

Sheriff Sol looked up from the mountain of paperwork on his desk and said, "You two look like the cats who ate the canary. You must be bringing me good news."

Chief replied, "We got the warrant for Rafael Salazar, also known as Chico, for murder and aggravated assault. We could leave tonight and serve it tomorrow if we got the go-ahead from Sheriff Brady."

"You all surprise me. I didn't expect we'd have it until tomorrow at the earliest. Get out of here while I try to catch Adrian before he goes home. I'll let you know."

Chapter 19

MEANWHILE IN EL PASO

Wednesday, May 29, 1974

Tuesday night, private citizen and local Latino advocate Pedro Ibarra called the El Paso *Daily Bugle* and KEPT TV, Channel 2 on your dial, to inform them he would be making a public statement outside Saint Boniface Catholic Church at 10:00 o'clock Wednesday morning, assuming they wanted to send a reporter to cover it.

Wednesday morning by 9:30, a crowd of approximately a hundred Latino citizens were already gathered to hear it. It was quite a production, but not the way Pedro had anticipated.

Pedro was 55 years old. He stood 5-feet, 9-inches tall. He weighed 155 pounds. His hair was thick and black and carefully coiffed with pomade like Elvis Presley's. He was attired in his finest black suit which had a Mexican flair. It had yellow and red piping along the collar, lapels, cuffs, and outside seams of the trousers. His beige Stetson had a wide brim which was slightly turned up all around. The crown had a red lizard skin band. Was it a cowboy hat or a sombrero? It was difficult to determine.

To set off his ensemble, he was wearing red, lizard skin Tony Lama cowboy boots with low heels. They set off his hat band perfectly. He wore a white French-cuffed dress shirt with a red bolo tie. The clasp was a sparkling silver crucifix. Finally, he was wearing all three of his World War II medals on his left breast - his Purple Heart with one Bronze Oak Leaf Cluster for combat injuries sustained in Africa and Anzio; his European-Africa-Middle East Campaign Medal with three Campaign Stars; and his World War II Victory Medal. Pedro had been a half-track driver in the Army, but he had seen plenty of combat.

A U.S. flag was on one side of his podium. The Mexican flag was on the other. Basically, Pedro was surrounding himself with images of his church, his nation, and his heritage.

Pedro began by thanking Padre Gabriel for allowing him to speak in the front church courtyard. Then he thanked everyone for taking time out from their busy workday to come.

He began by reminding his audience of his heritage. His esteemed father, Mateo, walked across the river in 1910 to forge a better life with nothing but the clothes on his back and a wooden case with his tools. He was a cobbler by trade. He obtained employment in the Tony Lama Boot Factory. He and his family all worked hard. All six of his children graduated from El Paso High School back in the day when Mexican descendants were hardly welcome. He and his younger brother, Bruno, served their nation in the Army during World War II. His youngest brother, Enrico, served in the Navy during the Korean War.

After the war, Pedro obtained a loan and opened his garage on Hope Street, still located at it's original site. It was only a two-bay garage in 1946. By good fortune and hard work, he was able to expand it to it's current eight bays. He operates with a very small return on investment to keep prices low for his friends and neighbors, and he will always continue to do so.

His wife, Ruby, is the daughter of Diego Martínez. He was a trained mortician in Ciudad Juárez. He, too, crossed the river for a better life. He worked hard and saved his money. In 1943, he purchased an empty building on 15th Street and turned it into Our Mother of God Funeral Home. He passed away several years ago, but now his sons, Alfredo and Emiliano, are morticians and they carry on their family tradition.

Background firmly established and amplified, he got down to business. "Amigos, I love our country and our state and our city and our Latino neighborhood. I love Saint Boniface. I love my family and I love my neighbors. I love all of you, but I am distressed by all the violence which seems to be getting worse day by day.

"Two young boys from this neighborhood, Armando Cruz and Joaquín Pérez, were recently slain by gunfire in a small town 300 miles from here. The news outlets allege that they were transporting illegal drugs, and that they engaged the authorities with violence. Armando was killed by police and Joaquín was injured. After he was treated in the hospital, he was slain by an assassin as he was being transported to jail. Even a deputy was shot!

"This is difficult for me to accept, because I personally knew both of those boys. Good boys. At one time or another, they both worked for me. Then they went their separate ways. I'm devastated. I told Father Gabriel that my family will pay for both their funerals. Alfredo and Emiliano have agreed to render their services for free at Our Mother of God Funeral Home.

"But that's not all! Things got even worse since then! Yesterday two more neighborhood boys were murdered down by the river. Reno Cisneros and Eugenio Estrada are dead. I didn't know Eugenio, but I knew Reno by sight, although we were never formally introduced.

"What is going on? We need to look after our neighbors. Be kind. Extend a helping hand. Do not kill one other. I want to encourage anyone who has information about these recent murders or any other unsolved murders to please contact the local authorities.

"Does anyone have any questions?"

"Yes. I do. Lucas Barrera from KEPT TV. What can you tell us about the drive-by shooting which took place outside your business just moments ago? Do you have any idea who would do that or why?"

"My business? What are you saying? Was anyone injured?"

"My understanding is that the police don't think so. Do you know why you were targeted Mr. Ibarra? Does it have anything to do with this news conference?"

"I'm sorry. I don't know. I must return to my shop immediately. Thanks to everyone for coming out today." Then he ran to his red, 1972 Cadillac Sedan de Ville with the white vinyl roof, and roared off.

Pedro parked as close as he could get to his repair shop. There were cop cars parked willy nilly everywhere! The entire area around his business was seething with cops. A crowd of neighbors was gawking from the sidewalk across the street where they had been cordoned off. Two uniformed police officers prevented them from getting any closer.

Plainclothes officers were quietly conducting inquiries, searching for witnesses. A yellow police off-limits tape stretched all across his property. A uniformed patrolman even tried to shoo him off as he was walking up, but he proclaimed loudly that they were blocking the entrance to his business! The patrolman told him to wait while he contacted the supervisor in charge. Pedro was fuming, but he held his tongue. He was an important man with a civic presence to maintain.

A few moments later a uniformed lieutenant walked over to greet him. He said, "I'm Lieutenant Harry Bartholomew. I'm sorry for the inconvenience, Mr. Ibarra, but we're conducting a crime scene of your property. Your wife and a young man are waiting in your office. They're both fine. Nobody was hurt. Follow me."

Once he was inside the office, his wife came running up to him. They embraced. He rubbed his hand lightly across the back of her head in a soothing manner, like one would pet a cat.

She said, "I am okay. Someone drove by the shop and started shooting. Someone in the garage shot back. That's all I know. I didn't see it. Then all of your employees vanished except for Paco. He was in the office with me. I was afraid somebody would shoot you while you were speaking to our neighbors, but the police said no shots were fired over there."

"No. I was safe.

"Lieutenant, what have you determined?"

"Mr. Ibarra, now you know that nobody was injured, I must ask you a few questions before I answer yours. Do you wish to speak to me alone, or would you rather we interview you and your wife together?"

"Together is fine."

Just then Roland Epperson walked up. Pedro knew him. He was the Captain of Robbery/Homicide. He said, "So sorry for your troubles, Mr. Ibarra. We're thankful no one was injured.

He continued, "Someone driving a black, 1964, four-door, Chevrolet Impala drove by your business very slowly at 10:04 a.m. A young Latino male in the right front seat yelled something at one of your employees. Your employee yelled something back. The car sped off. Then at 10:07, it returned. The passenger fired six shots from a revolver into your open bay area where three or four of your employees were gathered around. No one was hit. Someone in your shop returned two shots from a Remington 12-gauge pump shotgun, which we found on the shelf under the service desk in the garage. We recovered two spent, Western brand, 12-gauge shotgun shells marked number four buck, on the floor of the bay. They match the other shell we found in the chamber and two in the magazine of the shotgun.

"Who owns that shotgun, Mr. Ibarra?"

"I do. I keep it under the counter for protection, and now I am glad that I do. This assault on my business and my employees is outrageous!"

"We agree. We'll hang onto the empty shells but you can keep your shotgun. Hopefully, no one will ever need to use it again.

"Our first unit arrived at 10:09. No one was here but your wife and young Mr. Paco Cano. I have to ask. Is something wrong with him?"

"Yes. He was damaged when he came out of the womb. He's 16 years old, but has the intellectual capacity of a 7-year-old. I let him work for me cleaning up and running simple errands. I pay him minimum wage, but at least it's something. It gives him pride in being useful. His family lives two doors down. His father is a milkman and his mama helps clean Saint Boniface. He's a sweet, innocent boy."

"Sounds like he's lucky to have you."

"No Captain. We are lucky to have him."

"Of course. Well, we need to speak to the rest of your employees - all of them, whether they were here or not. We need to try to figure out if this drive-by was a warning to you, or a private feud with one of them.

"How many do you employ? We need to take a look at your payroll roster for names, social security numbers, dates of birth, addresses, phone numbers, and the like. You don't have any employees who are off-book, do you?"

"I do not! I employ six mechanics, Paco, my wife, Ruby, and of course myself. I cannot imagine anyone angry enough at me to do this awful thing. I would have taken precautions if I thought so. My wife can get you what you need. Anything else?"

"If you had to guess, which of your employees returned fire?"

"I wondered about that, too. Any of them could have, but I cannot single out anyone more likely than another."

"How many of your employees live in the mini-motel you have out back?"

"Right now, just the one. His name is Chico Salazar. He's only been with me a short while. He's a good worker. He was recently released from prison on a raw deal. It was self-defense. He hasn't made much money yet. That's why I let him stay here."

"What sort of a raw deal?"

"He was an up-and-coming local boxer in the Golden Gloves, just like Cassius Clay, except he's Latino and Clay is black. A heavy weight. Just graduated high school, about to turn pro. Had a real future. He went into a bodega down the street here to buy a numbers ticket for his papa. Walked into an empty shop except for a local ginzo from the mob threatening to tune up the owner.

"One thing led to another, and the ginzo tried to kill Chico with a two-by-four. Instead, Chico killed him. No witnesses if you know what I mean. Mob guy was connected. Chico was a young Mexican with no connections. He drew Judge Armand Potter, if you're old enough remember that rat bastard. Crooked as they come. Anyway, Chico got 20 years for manslaughter instead of a pass for self-defense. Just got out on parole a few months ago. He's a great mechanic. Parole officer comes by each month to check on him. In fact, he was just here yesterday. Name is Owen Applewood. Call him. He'll tell you the same thing I did."

"Employ any other cons?"

"Nope. I do a record check on all my employees before I hire 'em."

"Think Chico Salazar was the lone defender?"

"I'd be surprised. He's more than capable, but he knows he can't be around a gun while he's still on parole. Nah. It hadda be one of the other guys."

"Correction. He can't be around a gun forever. He's a convicted felon. The only way he can ever be around a gun legally is to apply to the Bureau of Alcohol, Tobacco, & Firearms [ATF] for a Relief From Disability. Normally they won't even entertain the request unless the guy's sentence has been up for ten years. Even then they're stingy. Better let Chico know that if he doesn't already."

"Well, the topic of firearms has never come up between him and me. Besides, he went to prison even before he ever had a chance to own a gun. I know damn well his papa never had one. Too poor, but I'll tell Chico you mentioned it. Anything else?"

"Yes. Who do you think the shooter was making a move on - you or one of your employees?"

"I honestly don't know. I didn't know I had any enemies. Same for any of my boys, but you can never tell. Could be one of 'em got in a beef over a chica, but if so, I never heard about it. They'd never tell me anyway if they did. Be too worried I'd fire 'em."

"You know anyone who drives a black 1964 Impala?"

"I wish I did. You can bet your sweep bippy I'll be keeping my eye out for it. I'll let you know if I see it. Anything else? I need to get my shop operational again."

Captain Epperson looked around. CSI [Crime Scene Investigations] was done and gone. The crowd had dissipated. The yellow tape was in a trash barrel. All but one marked unit was gone, and that patrolman looked like he was getting ready to depart.

"Just that we still need to interview all your employees tomorrow. You call 'em and get 'em all in headquarters by 10 o'clock. They need to report to Lieutenant Horace Greathouse in Robbery/Homicide. He'll send a detective out right away to bring them into the interview rooms. Agreed?"

"Agreed."

Everyone in El Paso County had heard about the drive-by shooting. Captain Stan Howard called Captain Roland Epperson of City Robbery/Homicide to see what he knew.

Captain Epperson said they were operating under the assumption that the shooting was in retaliation by a local street gang for something it blamed Pedro Ibarra or the so-called Hope Street Boys for doing. He said he supposed that they have to start looking at Ibarra's auto repair shop as the headquarters for the new gang. However, there wasn't one scintilla of evidence that Ibarra's shop was selling weed or doing anything else that was illegal. He was clean as a plucked chicken. That being said, they did have that new double gangland slaying down by the river, back behind Gustavo's Cantina. Whoever did that got away clean - no witnesses, no evidence; however, nothing pointed to Ibarra or his crew.

He told Captain Howard that nobody but Ibarra's wife and a

retarded boy, both of whom had been in the office, were present at the crime scene when police arrived. Since no one present who had standing voiced a complaint, detectives tossed the entire premises, including it's mini-motel out back. They also searched every motor vehicle on site. They went through every cabinet, closet, trash bin, everything. No stolen cars. Nada. They didn't recover so much as a single marijuana seed.

He also reported that Ibarra claims he had six wrenches working for him, even though no one was there. Rafael "Chico" Salazar is one of them. Ibarra's supposed to corral them all up by tomorrow morning for complete interviews. Nevertheless, other than a description of the car involved in the drive-by, they have nothing. By now that car is probably in Juárez, or it's a burned-out hulk somewhere in the desert. They put out a BOLO, but they aren't holding their breath. They are still squeezing snitches, but haven't had any luck so far.

That was everything.

Captain Howard thanked him and said they would put out some feelers, too.

Then he told Chief Deputy Derrick Hornback, who told Sheriff Brady. Then Captain Howard moved onto other pending cases.

Chapter 20

BAD NEWS

Wednesday, May 29, 1974

Sheriff Sol phoned Sheriff Brady at 5:30 p.m. Once again, Sheriff Sol was lucky. Adrian picked up the phone.

It was a short call. Adrian was up to his neck in alligators. Even so, he was cordial and glad to hear from Sol.

Sol said, "First, I want to thank you for loaning your forensic artist, Clancy Rush, to us. He did a masterful job. He obtained three close likenesses of our shooter. We compared them with 36 mugshots of recently released prisoners from DOC, from which we positively identified Rafael "Chico" Salazar of El Paso, as the shooter.

"We ran it by the DA, who concurred that we have enough for a complaint to obtain an arrest warrant for murder and aggravated assault on a police officer. Judge Sweeney just signed it. I was thinking of bringing a few of my best deputies and myself over tomorrow so we could team up and execute the warrant on Friday. We didn't have enough for a search warrant, but we're hoping to find the murder weapon on him or wherever he's laying his head. He's on parole, so I'm betting his PO will be helpful. Whaddaya think?"

"Well, I'm happy to hear that Clancy demonstrated why we're so high on him. I'm also impressed that you all were able to get photos from DOC so fast. How the Hell did you manage that?"

"Let's just say that our local state senator, who's the top dog on the Senate Justice Committee, has some stroke with DOC. They graciously expedited our request."

"Wish I had a friend like him. Out of curiosity, have you seen last night's news or heard today's news on the radio?"

"No. Sounds like I should have. What happened?"

"Yesterday, two local gangbangers got whacked in the city down by the river. No leads yet. That, and perhaps your press release or both, likely prompted Señor Pedro Ibarra the Virtuous to make his own news release this morning. He extolled the character of two perps you know all too well - Armando Cruz and Joaquín Pérez - both of whom expired prematurely, so says he. Pedro also decried the murders of yesterday's stellar citizens who also just happen to be in the retail drug business.

"But it gets worse! While Pedro was busy castigating Anglo cops for all the past sins in El Paso, someone did a drive-by at his business and vamoosed. Got away scot-free. Nobody was hurt. Also somebody from Pedro's shop returned fire with a shotgun. By the time EPPD arrived, which only took three minutes, all of Pedro's employees had flown the coup. Ibarra's solitary defending angel was most likely Chico Salazar but we'll probably never know for sure.

"Anyway, Ibarra's supposed to produce all six of his bonafide employees for interviews tomorrow morning, but you know they'll have their stories straight by then. Of course, he won't bring in any of his spot labor employees like Armando Cruz and Joaquín Pérez because he claims he doesn't employ any. Good news is, the PD tossed the entire premises, including the pad out back where Chico stays. Bad news is, believe it or not, they didn't find anything anywhere which shouldn't have been there.

"So, what I'm saying is, if we pop Chico now, it's highly unlikely we find the gun he used in Mosby. I know you need it to cement your case. Do you really want to do this tomorrow or Friday? Wouldn't it be better if you all kept quiet about that warrant and we sat on this a little bit? Let him think he's still clear? Without that gun, Pedro will make Chico's arrest sound like another vendetta by sinister, evil, Anglo cops. Besides, Pedro may send Chico out to settle the score with whomever did the drive-by if he knows who's behind it. That may flush him out in the open. Maybe not.

"If you're absolutely committed to arresting Chico right away, we'll do it for you when he comes in for his interview. We'll do whatever you want."

"Christ on a crutch! We don't have a choice! Now we gotta wait!

"Would it be helpful if I sent my two best deputies over to augment your guys or the PD? I assume they'll be conducting surveillances or making undercover buys, or whatever magic you all come up with to solidify your case against Pedro."

"Maybe. Problem is, nobody has even the beginnings of a case against Pedro. It's all an educated conjecture. Let me talk with Derrick and Stan. I do know EPPD Captain Roland Epperson from Robbery/Homicide thinks Ibarra is dirty. How about this? If my guys think it would be beneficial, I'll call the Chief of Police, Cedric Pierson, and run it by him. It's a generous offer. However, I know sending your go-to guys would make your office awfully lean while they're over here."

"True enough, but we want Salazar bad, not to mention Ibarra if he's pulling all the strings. You know, contract murder. Makes him even more despicable than Chico. "I'll just wait to see what you all decide. As of now our case against Chico is on ice. Thanks for everything, Adrian."

"Right back atcha. We're all on the same sheet of music, Sol. I'll get back to you, but it may not be until sometime late tomorrow."

"That's fine. As always, we're in your debt. Adiós."

"Adiós, Sol."

Sheriff Sol hung up. He waited several minutes to collect his thoughts. All the deputies present were hooting it up over the arrest warrant. They were all salivating in anticipation of serving it personally, which of course, would never happen. Pie in the sky.

Finally, he stepped out of his office. He stood in the doorway, hands pushing against both sides of the frame. He filled it up like a hungry grizzly bear in a cardboard shipping box for a refrigerator. He asked, "Chief, you get a chance yet to enter that warrant into NCIC and NLETS?"

"Nope. Sorry. I'll get right on it."

"Hold up. Listen everybody! I just got off the phone with Sheriff Brady. He asked us to take a pause and this is why. Yesterday, two piss-ant dope cowboys got murdered by persons unknown down by the river in El Paso.

"Today, Pedro Ibarra held a news conference suggesting that Armando Cruz and Joaquín Pérez should be nominated for sainthood on account of their good works. He also cried crocodile tears over the other two jokers who just got waxed. Notice he made no distinction between an outlaw lawfully shot or killed while engaged in a shootout with police, and murder by an outlaw. Sheriff Brady thinks Ibarra's news release may have been in response to mine. Try to obfuscate. Muddy up the water. Deflect unwanted attention away from himself. Wrap himself in the robes of righteous indignation. Put law enforcement into a defensive posture while he surreptitiously continues his unlawful enterprise. All those things.

"However, while he was making his news release someplace other than his home or business, someone pulled off a drive-by shooting at his auto repair shop. No one was hurt. They think Chico Salazar returned fire with a shotgun, but they'll never prove it. All Pedro's employees took a powder. No one was present when the cops arrived. The good and bad news is, no one with legal standing to object was present, so EPPD conducted a thorough search of the premises and the vehicles, to include Chico's on-site apartment. Problem is, they didn't turn up diddly shit. Nada.

"Pedro's supposed to corral all of his employees and bring

them to EPPD headquarters for witness statements in the morning. Adrian said we all know Chico won't be packing a gun at the police station, so we'd be pissing in the wind arresting him there, expecting to get our hands on it. He's right.

"He suggested we keep the warrant to ourselves for the time being. Let Chico feel like he's home free. See if he retaliates regarding the drive-by.

"I'm in complete agreement with Adrian. We need to sit tight. Sorry, but that's just the way it is.

"Gillespie, that does not preclude you from calling Chico's PO [parole officer]. His name is Owen Applewood. Ask some softball questions, but do not mention the warrant. It's okay if you hint that Chico could be a witness, but nothing more. Let the PO know we're just putting out feelers. That's it. We do not want Chico getting called in by his PO for an interview. Savvy?"

"Got it, Sheriff."

"Okay. If you're end-of-shift, pack it in. Everything else can wait until tomorrow. Thanks for all your hustle these past two days. It will all pay off before you know it. We just have to be patient.

"One last thing. Anyone got an update on Ernie or Dewey?"

Chief responded, "April spoke to Gertrude earlier today. No change. Ernie's still in the hospital detached from reality. Nobody knows how long this will take. However, Gertrude called while you were on the phone with Sheriff Brady. She asked for you to call her right away. She said it's important."

"Okay. Anything else?"

Kirk Shoemaker said, "I stopped by Dewey's on my way to work. He's doing fine. Hopes to come back on limited duty in a week or so. Said to tell everyone hello."

"Well okay, then. Guess I'll call Gertrude and try to stop by and see Dewey on my way home.

"Good night, you all. Give me a call if something important comes up."

Sheriff Sol went back into his office and closed the door. He had a pit in his stomach. He did not want to make this call. He feared it would be necessary to tell Gertrude it was time for Ernie to retire. He took a deep breath and dialed the Atwood residence. Gertrude answered on the first ring.

"Thanks, Sheriff, for calling me back so soon. I really need to talk to you. Could you stop by here on your way home?"

"Of course. Be there in about ten minutes. See you then. Bye bye."

"Thanks. Bye."

He called home and told Joanna where he was going. Then he said, "You don't have to hold supper for me. Just save me a plate. Be home as soon as I can."

When he arrived at Atwater's, he noticed that both kids were gone. Gertrude invited him into the parlor and directed him to the overstuffed easy chair. She said, "I made coffee. Would you like a cup?"

"Yes, please. Black."

She poured their coffees and brought him one. Then she sat in her rocker. She took a sip and set hers down on the end table. She said, "Sol, Ernie will never be able to resume his duties again. He's a broken man. There's no other way to put it. I've spoken to his psychiatrist, Dr. Moody, and he doesn't know if Ernie will ever be right again. Of course, he holds out hope, but said it could be months or maybe years before he returns to any semblance of normalcy.

"I went from there to see Archie Willis. I asked what retirement options were available. He gave me the application to file for retirement benefits. He said the medical retirement would be Ernie's best option, but I'd have to get legal guardian status and power of attorney to act on his behalf. He would receive 66-2/3rds percent of his pay, tax-free, for as long as he's incapable of engaging in gainful employment, even up to age 62, at which point he would transition to his regular retirement of 56 percent, which is taxable; however, he could begin drawing his Social Security old age retirement benefits, so we'd still be okay.

"Then I went to Sam Davis's office to see about getting legal guardianship and power of attorney. He told me to get a letter signed by Dr. Moody spelling out Ernie's medical situation. In the meantime, he would draft petitions for power of attorney and legal guardianship. He said he would also set up an appointment with Judge Sweeney to petition the court.

"So while I was there, I called Dr. Moody. He told me to stop by tomorrow on my way to see Ernie and he'd have it ready. Then Sam said we could probably get everything completed tomorrow so I could file the retirement papers. If we're lucky, Ernie could start drawing his benefits on July 1st, but more likely August 1st. It's not the way we planned it, but "Man plans and God laughs". We're blessed state and county employees have such a good retirement plan."

"My goodness! You have been busy. Hate to see Ernie go, but this is probably for the best. He's more than earned his retirement benefits. Just sorry it came about this way. Besides, if he does get well enough to work again, I'm sure more than a few businessmen around town would offer him a job that's less stressful."

"I hope so, but I ain't holding my breath. Sheriff, it's all I can do not to break down in tears every time I see him. My man is completely shattered. That last ruckus done him in. I haven't even thought about what I'll do when he does comes home, especially if he don't return to reality. It's just too awful to imagine."

"I'm sure it is. Everyone at our church has him in their prayers. Is there anything I can do for you now?"

"No. Just pray for him and me and the kids. I'll let you know if anything comes up."

"Please do. You can call me anytime. Well, I better go. I need to stop by Dewey's and see how he's getting along."

"Thanks, Sol. You're a true friend. Give Dewey and Elsie our regards."

"Will do."

When Sheriff Sol arrived, Dewey was sitting in his rocker, drinking lemonade, and reading an Army Field Manual on some of the finer esoteric points regarding payments to military vendors for equipment which costs over $100,000. He had a yellow highlighter in his hand. Elsie asked if Sol would like some lemonade but he graciously declined. He had his sights set on a tumbler of ice with a large splash of Ezra Brooks seven-year-old just as soon as he got home. He thought Dewey looked really good for a man who had been shot in the chest only five days ago.

Dewey said, "Hey, Sheriff. Thanks for stopping by. I was getting a little bored, so I decided to catch up on some of my Army Reserve homework. I gotta teach a class on this at our next weekend drill. It wouldn't do if some of the mid-level NCOs [non-commissioned officers] knew more about this than their sergeant major."

"I 'spect not. How're you feeling?"

"Actually, I feel pretty good, all things considered. Doc said I can return to limited duty on June 17th, so long as I pass the medical exam on the 14th, which I know I will. Two weeks later I can return to full duty."

"That's the best news I've had all day. We really need your help. You aren't having any feelings of anxiety about this are you?"

"If you mean like Ernie, the answer is Hell no! I wish I hadn't got shot, but I ain't afraid to suit up and do my job. I'm game as a banty rooster. Ask Barlow."

"I don't need to ask Barlow. I already know you're game. Soon as you get back to work and feel up to it, I want you and Barlow to hone up on your shooting skills. Get back in the groove. It'll improve your confidence. The office will spring for the ammo. When Barlow hears he can shoot on the county's dime, he'll pester you non-stop until you all do decide to go."

"Thanks, Sheriff. I can sure use the practice. Barlow can testify to that, too."

"Well, is there anything you need? Anything I can do for you?"

"Nope. Thanks for asking. I feel a little better each day. Appreciate the visit. Give Joanna our best."

"Will do.

"I almost forgot. Gertrude asked me to send her regards. Just so you know, Ernie's still lost in the weeds and the prognosis isn't good. She's expressed an interest in him getting a medical retirement. Archie and Sam Davis are helping her do that. Both she and Ernie have a very long row to hoe, especially if he never returns to reality. I hope you can forgive Ernie. They booth need your prayers in the worst way."

"I do forgive him, Sheriff. Nobody saw this coming. I just need you to know I'm made outta tougher stuff than Ernie. I know he's a good guy and he meant well. It's too bad his mind snapped. We'll all miss the old Ern."

"You're right on all accounts. Well, gotta go. Take care. Call if you need something before you come back to work, okay?"

"Will do. Adiós."

"Adiós."

Chapter 21

THE EBB AND FLOW OF POLICE WORK

Thursday, May 30, 1974

First thing in the morning, Gillespie contacted the Texas State Probation & Parole Office in El Paso. She spoke with Chico Salazar's PO, Owen Applewood. Gillespie said they were contacting acquaintances of Joaquín Pérez, seeking new leads regarding his murder. Salazar was one of the acquaintances they wanted to contact.

PO Applewood thought it was doubtful Chico knew anything useful, even though they lived in the same barrio. Applewood said he conducted his monthly check-up with Chico at his job site on Tuesday. Although the topic of Pérez's murder never came up, Chico didn't appear to have any concerns, especially regarding unsolved crimes.

Applewood slipped in a vouch for Chico, saying he had done well for himself since his release from prison. "He has a good job and an acceptable residence. He's saving his money. His boss is pleased with his performance, and to the best of my knowledge, he's not associating with known criminals." Even so, Applewood thought it was unlikely Chico, being an ex-con, would assist law enforcement even if he did know something.

He finally asked, "Do you want me to call him in a for an interview about this?"

She replied, "No. It was just a long shot. I think you're right. It sounds like I'm spinning my wheels. Chico probably doesn't know anymore about the shooting than I do. Thanks for taking my call and for your insight. I've got some other folks to contact who are more likely to point us in the right direction than Chico.

Good day, sir."

After she hung up, Gillespie thought it had been a mistake contacting the PO. She didn't learn anything they didn't already know, and she might've unintentionally tipped Chico off that they knew his name and were looking at him.

Around lunchtime, Miss Loretta fielded a call from Pete Ricketts. He said a man named Salvador Cruz and another named Juan Pérez were at his mortuary with a hearse from the Mother of God Funeral Home in El Paso. They were there to pick up the bodies of Armando Cruz and Joaquín Pérez. He thought Chief would want to know.

Sheriff Sol sent Deputy Kirk Shoemaker over there to oversee the transfer. Kirk confirmed the identities of both men, and accepted their explanations of their relationships to the decedents. (Truthfully, Kirk was there to confirm familial identities because Sheriff Sol suspected they might be two of Pedro Ibarra's off-book employees, otherwise known as drug mules.)

As they were wrapping up, Salvador asked about taking possession of the pickup truck Armando and Joaquín had been driving, since it belonged to his deceased father's estate. Kirk replied that the truck had been legally seized by the sheriff's office because it had been used to transport illegal drugs.

Salvador kicked up a minor fuss, saying his father's heirs should not be penalized for the unauthorized actions of his brother. Kirk replied that the letter of the law had been adhered to; that the district court judge had signed off on it; and, that Salvador needed to hire an attorney if he wanted to pursue the matter further. Then Kirk said that Salvador shouldn't hold his breath for a favorable resolution because the law was crystal clear regarding a seizure of this type. Law enforcement agencies across the nation have seized many vehicles used to transport contraband regardless of true ownership.

Shortly thereafter, Salvador and company departed

unrequited with the bodies. Mr. Ibarra had told him getting the truck back was a long shot, but he paid Salvador $20 just for asking. Said he would give him $100 if he did manage to get the truck back.

About 4 o'clock, Sheriff Sol received a call from Sheriff Brady. He said, "Sol, things are happening around here a lot faster than I expected. I'm calling to see if you're still willing to send me two of your best men. Understand, they could be here for several weeks."

"If it gets us closer to solidifying our case against Chico Salazar, and hopefully Pedro Ibarra, the answer is still yes."

"I believe it will. Who were you going to send?"

"Slick Oldman and Barlow Adams. You may recall them."

"Hell yes, I do! Slick took out that prick, Leo Potts, who got Deputy Slocum's gun away from him and killed Corporal Orbach. Then last year, Barlow killed Rocky Givens and Bug Eye Tinsley, two of El Paso's worst denizens of the decade. If Texas had a Who's Who of Law Enforcement's Finest, Slick and Barlow would both be on the top of the list.

"Okay. Here's the deal. DEA smells blood in the water as it relates to Pedro Ibarra. The agency is funding a federal drug task force with the primary target being the illustrious Mr. Ibarra. Special Agent Carmine Valenzuela is heading it up. Know him?"

"I don't, but Chief Alex does. Thinks he's a swell guy."

"Alex is right. It'll be seconded by my Narcotics Lieutenant Fred Wendell. I'm also sending Sergeant Julio Elias from our Intelligence Section. He and Chief Alex are old pals.

EPPD is sending Sergeant Elvis Boatwright from Narcotics, Detective Casper Leonard from Robbery/Homicide, Detective Wayne Barnett and Detective Emilio Gómez from Narcotics, and Officer Amanda Romero from Patrol. She's only got a year or so on the job, but she's already done some really good undercover work for both Intelligence and Narcotics. They say she's as savvy as your Deputy Gillespie. Slick and Barlow will complete the ten designated positions.

"DEA is getting Special Deputy U.S. Marshal designation for all members of the task force. Basically, it means they can make arrests outside of their own jurisdictions just like a Fed. The designations are good for a year with extensions possible.

"They'll operate out of a warehouse DEA owns at 226 Leon Street on the south side of the city. No sign on it anywhere. Just the street address. It's not too far from the river. Used to be a bonded warehouse owned by a liquor distributor. The task force is meeting there Monday morning at 0800 hours.

"Tell your guys soft clothes only, but include a suit or sport coat and tie in case they need to go to court. Lodging for anyone needing it, probably only your guys, will be at the Best Western. I'll make sure Carmine notifies the front desk of your guys' names. DEA's picking up the tab, plus they're paying per diem and travel expenses for out-of-towners. In addition, they're picking up overtime up to 20 hours a week, per officer, at his hourly rate, for as long as the task force is operational. Tell your guys to bring a recent payroll stub to verify their hourly rate. I have no idea how long this assignment will be. Any questions?"

"Just one. We don't have any undercover cars."

"Forgot to mention that. DEA has the cars, all with federal and local radio frequencies. Most of 'em were seized elsewhere, so they don't smell like bacon [a slur on cops as in pig]. All different makes and models in good repair, or so I'm told. Won't look like the FBI with all their matching black Ford, four-door sedans with small hubcaps and whip antennas. All the license plates are cold [registered to fictitious persons at fictitious addresses]. Tell your guys to drive their POVs. They can leave them parked overnight for safety in the warehouse if they so choose."

"Will do. If my guys have any questions, I'll tell them to call Agent Valenzuela. I know Chief has his number."

"Good deal. Sol, we've assembled a fucking All-Star cast. We expect big things. We won't keep your guys any longer than necessary, but it could possibly go for a month or so. We truly appreciate Quayle County's contribution in this, Sol. Thanks a lot."

"No. Thank you, Adrian. Adiós."

"Adiós. We'll stay in touch."

Sheriff Sol hung up. He asked Miss Loretta to get ahold of Slick and Barlow and tell them he needed to see them ASAP. He knew Slick was off, but Barlow had just finished his day shift. Then he asked Chief to come into his office and shut the door.

Sheriff Sol briefed Chief Alex as soon as he entered and took a seat.

Chief said, "Wow. I'm jealous. I thought overtime was just a made-up word."

"Me, too. I guess I'll have to call Archie and get the Supervisors' blessing. They've never paid a dime of overtime to anyone in spite of what the recent U.S. Department of Labor regulations say. Of course, they still won't be paying it. DEA's footing the bill."

"Heck, Sol, even without the overtime, this is an opportunity of a lifetime. Think about it. Playing cops and robbers to your heart's content. They'll be spoiled forever and won't wanna come back and return to routine patrol duties. It's like being a cop on television."

Sol replied, "I have no doubt they'll have fun. However, they'll be pulling some long hours. Very little free time. Barlow has a wife and Slick has his ranch. They'll be worn out and happy, but they'll be ready to come home after a couple of 80-hour weeks. Besides, when has patrol duty ever interfered with them hunting down criminals?"

"True. Hope you're right. It's just that this is like being *Starsky & Hutch*. Not only that, everyone here will be pulling a lot of extra hours without overtime while they're gone."

"Who's Starsky & Hutch?"

"New television program. They're plainclothes detectives in

a fancy ride who catch more criminals than Batman and Robin. They're good-looking with cool clothes and have flair."

The small talk continued until both Barlow and Slick arrived. It took less than 15 minutes. Sheriff Sol waited until the Ghost of Wyatt Earp and the Avenger of the Innocents took a seat.

Sheriff Sol said, "Fellas, the Bluebird of Paradise just landed on your windowsill. You're probably getting the best assignment either one of you will ever get while on the job. Chief and I are both green with envy.

"For the next few weeks, actually the timeline is open-ended, you two jaybirds will be assigned to a DEA Task Force in El Paso. The primary target is Pedro Ibarra. The secondary target is Chico Salazar, including his .45 caliber murder weapon. You'll be lodged at the Best Western, meals, lodging, and transportation paid for by DEA. They'll have your names at the front desk. You'll drive DEA's soft cars and use their radios. Wear soft clothes for obvious reasons, but bring a suit or sport coat and a tie. You may wind up in court.

"DEA SA Carmine Valenzuela will be in charge. Chief Alex has his number. He knows Valenzuela and thinks highly of him. EPSO Narcotics Lieutenant Fred Wendell is segundo. There are six other locals from El Paso on this task force. If you want their names, ranks, agencies, and current work assignments, I'll give them to you at the end of this briefing.

"Sheriff Brady says DEA is paying overtime, so that probably means 60 to 80-hour workweeks. I'm sure they'll explain it to you. You need to bring a payroll stub so they can confirm your hourly wages.

"Soon as we're done here, I'll call Archie and see if the Board of Supervisors will let you all keep the OT. I expect they will, but as you both know, Quayle County has never paid a red cent in overtime since it became a county in 1910, not that overtime was even a hypothetical concept back then. Nevertheless, they've gotten away without paying it since it became mandated a few years ago by the U.S. labor laws, so they probably think it's just a suggestion and not a requirement. I can guarantee this will stir up a hornet's nest with the supervisors, but maybe this is just what we need to budge them off the dime.

"Write this down. You report for duty at 0800 hours on Monday, June 2nd. That means you need to get there Sunday evening. Report to 226 Leon Street. It's a covert warehouse owned by DEA. It's on the south side of El Paso near the river. Locate it before you bed down for the night.

"You'll be sworn in as Special Deputy U.S. Marshals. The commission extends for a year. It allows you to make both state and federal misdemeanor and felony arrests outside of your jurisdiction.

"If you have any questions, call Agent Valenzuela. If you can't reach him, call Sergeant Julio Elias from the SO's Intelligence Section. Also, I need to hear from at least one of you everyday. No exceptions! Any questions?"

Slick asked, "How did you manage to pull this off, Sheriff?"

"This is just how important it is to the Feds to bust Pedro Ibarra. It also means we'll be severely strapped while you all are gone, but that's how important busting Chico Salazar is to us. Do your best. Get it done. Have some fun, but be careful. Then get your asses back home. That commission is good anywhere for an entire year. We may have other opportunities here or elsewhere for you all to exercise it."

Barlow said, "I guess that means DEA is paying for our gas to get back and forth."

"Yep, so long as you have your mileage and gas receipts."

Barlow said, "Thanks, Sheriff. You don't know how much this means to me."

Slick said, "Same here. Look, I gotta go. Need to stop by Jake's Pawn Shop before he closes."

Sheriff Sol said, "Both of you jaybirds get outta here. Make us proud."

Slick rushed over to the pawn shop and entered just five minutes before closing.

Jake asked, "What's the big rush, Slick? I'll be open tomorrow."

He replied, "Something's come up. I need a new gun right away. Specifically, a Charter Arms Bulldog, five-shot revolver, in .44 Special. Prefer the three-inch barrel. Got any?"

"Does a hobby horse have a hickory dick? Of course I do. They're all blue steel. Don't make no nickel-plated ones so far as I know. That okay?"

"That's perfect."

Jake escorted him over to the counter where three .44 Special caliber Charter Arms revolvers were on display. They all looked the same. He reached in and got one and handed it to Slick. Slick handled it with intense scrutiny. Tested the tightness of the cylinder when the gun was cocked. Aimed it at the clock on the wall. Dry fired it. Checked the tension and smoothness of the trigger pull. Not as good as his 30-year-old Peacemaker, but not bad. Set it back down on the glass display case. "How much?"

"For you? $95. I'll even throw in a box of 50, Remington .44 Special, 246-grain, lead round-nose cartridges for free."

"How much is ammo?"

"$8 bucks a box. Need anything else?"

"A cleaning kit, and a leather inside-the-waist holster for a righty. Also a second box of cartridges."

$1.50 for the cleaning kit. $6 for a Buckheimer, holster made just for this gun. Anything else?"

"That's it."

Working it all in his head, Jake said, "That'll be $110.50 plus 5% sales tax. Total comes to $116.03. Also, being it's been probably 30 years since you've purchased a firearm, you probably ain't seen this before. You gotta fill out this ATF Form 4473."

Slick snorted, scratched his chin, and completed the form. He signed his name with a flourish, just like John Hancock signed his on the Declaration of Independence. Then he asked, "How's that for a former lance corporal of the United States Marine Corps during World War II? I didn't sign for the last gun I had back then. Just picked it up from a dead Marine and kept on firing. My issued gun was broke. Nobody ever asked me to sign my name back then. They was just glad I kept on killing Japs." Then he counted out the exact amount and placed it on the glass countertop. He picked up the bag with his merchandise and said, "Gracias. Much appreciated."

He started to walk out.

Jake asked, "Much belated thanks for your service, Marine. Anything wrong with your six-inch Peacemaker?"

"Nope. It's just that I've got an assignment which calls for a belly gun. This'n fits the bill to a T. Still taking the Peacemaker with me just in case. It ain't never failed me in all them years. Can't say that about my first M-1."

"You ever fire that Peacemaker rapid-fire a couple hundred rounds, squished down in the dirt and the darkness while you was fighting off crazed kamikaze banzai savages?"

"Point well taken."

"Good luck, amigo. Come back anytime."

"Will do. Adiós."

Barlow returned home fast as he could.

"Sarah asked, "What did Sheriff Sol want? Sounded urgent."

"Yes and no. How much time do we have?"

"We need to be at Mom's in 20 minutes. They'll be ready to eat in a half-hour. Daddy's roasting a lamb on the barbeque pit."

"Did you get a bottle of wine?"

"Yes. Momma's favorite. It's in the fridge. Will you please hush up and tell me now?"

"How can I hush up and tell you at the same time?"

"Smarty pants. Hush up and give it to me."

"That's what I'm fixing to do. It's better for me if you take off all your clothes first."

"You bad boy! Now you're really gonna make us late." Even so, she smiled and peeled off her sandals, dropped her skirt and panties, pulled off her blouse, and took off her bra. She was completely naked in 15 seconds.

Then she helped Barlow out of his drawers and started massaging and licking his libido. She instinctively knew how much arousal he could take. She kept it up until just before he had a gusher. She knew they didn't have enough time to satisfy him twice. She bit the rear of his shaft nearly all the way back to it's origin, hard enough to stop any premature emissions. Then she stopped and bent over the overstuffed chair in the living room. She twerked two or three times to get his mind off of his temporary hurt.

That was all it took. Barlow put his hands on her hips and spread them wide. Even though his Johnson was blind, it knew exactly where to go and what to do. Then he played bury the bone, slide the salami, and heat the meat. They were both consumed by the intensity of the sensations coursing through the nether regions of their bodies. Sweat was pouring off both of them. They were nearly drowning. At the same time, they both were concentrating on increasing the sensations for themselves and for each other.

They gasped for breath. They needed more oxygen, but couldn't take time to breathe. The inner beast wouldn't let them. Still they worked hard to postpone the climax. Just one more minute! Just 30 seconds more! Ten more seconds! It was impossible! They finished the climb to the top of Mount Everest almost simultaneously.

They collapsed for a minute. Then Sarah wrestled her body away from Barlow's. She ran to the bathroom shouting, "Barlow. Hurry up! We're gonna be late!"

Barlow walked to the kitchen and picked up the receiver from the wall phone. He dialed the Bar B. Clarice answered. Barlow said, "Hello, Clarice. It's me, Barlow. I got held over a little bit at work. I'm gonna take a quick shower and change clothes. See you in about 30 minutes."

Clarice smiled. She had a pretty good idea why they were late. All she said was, "Okay. Thanks for calling. Come as soon as you can. That's not a double entendre. I don't want Arthur to burn the meat. Neither is that."

"You got it." Then he asked himself, did she know? Why did she say come as quick as you can?

Both Sarah and Barlow hurried to get dressed. Happy jumped in the car with them and off they went.

On the way, Barlow reported, "Sheriff Sol is sending Slick and me to El Paso to work temporarily on a DEA Task Force. The target is Chico Salazar and his boss, Pedro Ibarra. We'll work out of an old warehouse with seven other cops and a DEA supervisor. We'll drive their undercover vehicles and use their radios. We'll be commissioned as Special Deputy U.S. Marshals. The commissions are good for a year and allow us to make arrests outside of our jurisdiction. We'll be staying at the Best Western Motel in downtown El Paso. Meals, lodging, and gas are all paid for by DEA, but this is the best part. DEA is paying for overtime. Sheriff Sol is checking with Archie just to make sure the supervisors don't balk at it, even though Quayle County isn't footing the bill."

"How long will you be gone?"

"Not sure. Probably a couple of weeks."

"Wow! We could certainly use any overtime you'd make, but it sure will be lonely while you're gone."

"Ditto. Ever since the VA money from the G.I. Bill dried up, we haven't been able to sock much away. Even a hundred bucks extra would be huge. I won't know much more until I get there. Job begins at 8 o'clock Monday morning, which means I'll need to leave Sunday about noon."

"That means we'll have to miss church. We'll be too busy

saying our goodbyes Sunday morning. Let's not stay too late tonight. I've got some loving I need to stoke up on, so hush up and let's go."

Chapter 22

DOES CRIME EVER TAKE A PAUSE?

Friday, May 31, 1974

Pedro's supply of Oaxacan Highland Gold was dwindling. He needed an infusion. At the same time, he was thankful that he had the foresight to store his stash anywhere except at his business or home. Otherwise, he'd be eating a shit sandwich in the bottom of the El Paso County dungeon in a stark, concrete block cell. His saving grace was that two years ago in a stunning stroke of genius, he began to store his stash in an old hearse he bought from his brother-in-laws, Alfredo and Emilio Martínez.

The way that came about, the Mother of God Funeral Home had prospered beyond the brothers' most optimistic projections. Flush with dough, Alfredo and Emilio decided to upgrade to a new hearse and sell their old one. The old hearse was a sparkling, black and chrome, 1956 Cadillac. It only had 32,000 miles on it and ran like a scalded dog. With the tender loving care it had been given it could have performed to specifications with ease for another dozen years, but the Martínez brothers decided it was a relic from the past. The corpses never noticed that the hearse was out-of-date, nor did they care, nor complain, but the grieving family members probably did, or so the pompous brothers decided. It had to go.

Pedro smelled a deal, so he offered $650 and they accepted promptly without a counteroffer. The old hearse ran as smoothly and quietly as the White House Presidential limousine, except for the President's limo being newer with bulletproof glass and perhaps a little more panache. Pedro stored it in an old, six-bay garage he purchased at 604 Amarillo Street, four blocks north of his business.

That was another fire sale bargain. Only a few trusted associates knew today that the building belonged to him. It still bore the faded wooden sign which read, *Carlos' Speedy Taxi Company*. Carlos had been croaked in a knife fight over some pussy and the company faded away into oblivion shortly thereafter. That was over a dozen years ago. Pedro scooped up the garage for $1,300 from a hard-up, pissed-off widow woman. Carlos' puta had all the cock and the jewelry and his widow had all the bills! Asshole deserved what he got! Then the garage sat vacant and forgotten about for years, housing nothing except for dust, spiderwebs, and mouse turds. Those who knew about Pedro's ownership had died or apparently plum forgotten about it.

Then when Pedro decided to up his game in the retail weed business, he remembered the garage. Initially he stored his stash in one, and then two old, broke-down lateral freezers in his shop in a locked tool closet. Then he bought the hearse. He parked it in the garage under a canvas tarp to protect it. Then he discovered it was large enough to store 160 kilos of weed.

He beefed up security at the forsaken taxi garage with heavier metal doors, iron security bars across all points of access, top-of-the line locks which would do the gold vault in Fort Knox proud, security lights, and a local alarm which would, if there were a breech, shatter your eardrums for five agonizingly long minutes before it automatically shut off.

It had happened only once. Pedro's second cousin, Señor Mario Ortez, a scrawny, bald-headed, bow-legged widower aged 76, lived by his lonesome in a tiny adobe cottage two doors down from the old taxi garage. Mario had lived in this same dwelling since 1922. He had been awakened by Pedro's alarm at 3 o'clock on what up until then had been a quiet, peaceful, Tuesday morning slumber. He called Pedro to tell him to come down and turn the fucking thing off, but you know he never did because it shut off by itself after five minutes.

Mario got up all pissed off. He put on his disreputable old Stetson, worn out house slippers, and faded yellow and white, vertically striped bathrobe with tobacco juice stains dribbled all down the front. He stuffed his cheek with a large wad of Mail Pouch loose leaf tobacco. Then he picked up his trusty Remington, 12-gauge, double-barrel shotgun loaded with number 1 buckshot, which he had used greatly to his satisfaction two score and ten years before to terminate two satanic sheep rustlers from this earthly realm, not to mention scores of coyotes who did not believe in God, either.

Nicotine infused, dressed, armed with a pocketful of extra shells, Mario scurried out the door to investigate. He didn't need a flashlight. The perimeter lights on the building provided plenty of light. A thorough external search of the premises revealed that the party unknown who had set off the alarm did not gain entry. He was in the wind - a gone pecan. Lucky for him too, that Pedro never discovered who it was.

Pedro considered all this background information as ancient history, nearly forgotten. Today, Friday, May 31, 1974 in the Year of Our Lord, was a spanking new day in a new, more prosperous era. This is why.

In the wee hours of the morning, Geraldo Flores smuggled 200 kilos of Oaxacan Highland Gold into El Paso County in the back of raggedy milk truck with Elsie the Cow's faded picture painted on the side. For the first time ever, Geraldo did not take the usual route coming up Mexico Highway 45, which becomes US Highway 54 at the border checkpoint in El Paso, Texas. Today he took Mexico Highway 2 to US Highway 90 at Fort Hancock, 50 miles east of El Paso, but still in El Paso County, where they had bribed the guards on the midnight shift on both sides of the border. No more seized loads! Brilliant!

One of the bent Border Patrol agents was Armando Cruz's cousin, Bruno Cruz, age 31, with four years on the job. The other was a burned-out, 45-year-old Anglo needing three more years to retire. He was twice divorced, with five kids and a bad gambling habit. His name was Conrad Turnipseed, originally from Duluth, Minnesota, where it's so cold in the winter the only thing they do in wintertime is fuck and breed like hamsters. The new route took a little longer, but it was well worth it financially, not to mention less hazardous for their mules.

Salvador Cruz and Jenaro Herrera accepted the transfer in an abandoned car wash two miles north of the checkpoint. Today they were driving the blue and white Dodge van that Chico had used in Mosby, except now it was painted a solid mint green. They brought the product back to the Amarillo Street garage, where Pedro himself verified the count while Chico stood guard. Then Salvador and Jenaro departed with 40 kilos to deliver to Luis Romero in Las Cruces, New Mexico. His nickname was the Candy Man.

The Candy Man was making a bundle selling one-ounce baggies to the college crowd at New Mexico State University. He was a prolific salesman with a great product. He was also a former business college student who decided he didn't need the degree in marketing to make his fortune. He was right, too, so long as he didn't get caught or rubbed out by a competitor.

Pedro was pleased to have Luis as a client, but since the fiasco in Mosby, he really needed to acquire a few more clients with deeper pockets who could purchase bigger loads. He had Rodolfo Velásquez and Tomás Jiménez on standby to make a speedy delivery today if he conjured up another buyer. Pedro checked with Pepe Aguilar in Del Rio to see if he was ready for another load, but he was not. Pepe said he would call next week to set up delivery once he had reduced his inventory. All that meant was he didn't have the cash on hand yet.

Therein lay the problem. Since Pedro had changed from retail sales to wholesaler, he didn't generate enough sales yet to keep his mules steadily employed. He understood that a man needing more money would look for supplemental work. Pedro didn't want that. He expected loyalty from his unofficial employees, but loyalty is a quid pro quo. It requires a regular cash flow. Young men at the bottom of the totem pole have a tendency to blow whatever cash they have in their pocket when they're flush. They seldom think ahead. Selling wholesale brought in more revenue for him and for his mules, plus it diminished everyone's risk exponentially. The primary drawback was that any loss was a major hit. He couldn't afford many more losses like the one in Mosby. It looked like nothing more doing today, so he locked up and returned to his shop. Chico returned with him.

Upon his return, he had a note to call Amos Coggins in Alamogordo, New Mexico. Amos had always been a one-to-two kilo client. Today he wanted ten. Pedro ultimately talked him into buying 20, delivery to be made at the usual location at 4 o'clock. Fortunately, Rodolfo and Tomás were still at the garage hoping to make a run. Pedro told them to stand by while he and Chico picked up the product.

Upon their return, Pedro told Rodolfo and Tomás to take the faded blue, 1962 Chevrolet Biscayne, two-door sedan with blackwall tires and small hubcaps. It looked like a poor peasant or clergy mobile. Pedro deliberately left it looking like Sad Sack's pathetic means of transportation to keep it from drawing too much attention; however, the 350 CID, [cubic inch displacement] small block V-8 engine was souped up and designed to outrun anything on wheels, especially the law.

Pedro warned Rodolfo to be alert for a potential rip since he had never sold this much weight to Amos Coggins at one time (but Pedro himself upped the quantity)! He questioned whether Amos could actually come up with cash to cover the purchase. He instructed both mules to examine the currency carefully to make sure none of it was counterfeit. They already knew what was expected if Amos was anything but square with them.

Most important of all, Pedro ordered them to bypass the

Border Patrol checkpoint on US 54 just north of Highway 506. Pedro said for them to turn east at 506 and follow it to Piñon at Highway 24, continuing thence north to Mayhill, where they would pick up US 82 eastbound. That would take them to the north side of Alamogordo, and they should know the rest of the way from there. He said the roads were well marked, but to buy a map if his instructions were too hazy. Rodolfo assured him they would.

Rodolfo and Tomás placed the product in a stout metal footlocker with a massive padlock. They slid it to the farthest recesses of the trunk and covered it up with an Army blanket. Then they packed the rest of the trunk with a small generator, a large toolbox, chainsaw, gardening implements, and a garden hose. Then they double-checked the loads in their Smith & Wesson .38s to make sure they were ready for trouble.

Pedro's final instruction was for them to call him as soon as possible after they completed the deal or waxed Amos if this were a rip. That added an exclamation point to what they originally considered a milk run.

Chapter 23

THE TASK FORCE BEGINS OPERATION

Sunday/Monday, June 2/3, 1974

On Sunday, Slick and Barlow followed one another to El Paso, arriving at 6 o'clock. They checked into the Best Western.

No issues there. Reservations were in order. Then they piled into Slick's old black, 1948 Studebaker pickup truck and drove to a convenience store where they bought two city maps of El Paso. Barlow navigated and Slick drove. They had no problem locating the warehouse at 226 Leon Street. It was a massive two-story, metal structure surrounded by a cracked asphalt parking lot with a chain link fence around the perimeter. The fence had a sign which read NO TRESPASSING, but the doublewide gate was wide open and fastened to poles on either side by a chain. They ventured in.

A white, 1968 Ford Galaxie station wagon was parked outside the pedestrian entrance to the building. Slick knocked on the door. It sounded hollow inside like a rattly base drum. A couple of minutes later it was opened by a 35-ish, white male with shaggy brown hair under a Texas Rangers baseball cap. His eyes were bright blue, brighter than most and very striking. He had a thick Fu Manchu mustache and a USMC bulldog tattooed on his upper left arm. He stood 6-feet tall and weighed in at 180 pounds of taut muscle. He was wearing new, Wrangler bluejeans, an untucked baggy gray tee shirt with TEXAS A&M on the chest, and scuffed brown cowboy boots. He smiled and asked, "Can I help you gents?"

Slick replied, "I'm Slick Oldman and this here is Barlow Adams. Did we come to the right place?"

The man stuck out his right hand for a shake. Slick and Barlow noticed he had an iron grip. The man replied, "You sure did, but you're about a half-day early. Welcome to our office, codenamed the Castle. I'm Carmine Valenzuela. Glad to meet ya. Come on in. I'm setting up for tomorrow morning."

They stepped inside. Carmine shut the door and turned the lock. The light was dim inside, with most of it filtering in from windows about 20 feet high along the top of the walls. The first thing Barlow noticed were ten OD green, Army surplus desks with office chairs on rollers in two rows of five, with the rows spaced about five feet apart and facing each other.

He saw five metal, five-drawer OD green Army surplus file cabinets, one of which had a government calendar taped on the side. There was also a safe, and a long, Army surplus library table with eight ladder-back chairs. In addition, there was a large table with a police radio console, teletype machine, copier, and four telephones. Electric cords were running in a semi-tangled mess every which way, some as far as 30 feet, to a massive conglomeration of floor sockets. There was also a five-gallon water cooler with the proverbial upside down blue plastic water bottle, a trashcan, and a sleeve of cone-shaped, three-ounce paper cups.

Another table was stacked with manuals, statute books, map books, and office supplies including reams of copier paper, wire metal inboxes, staplers, hole punch, clipboards, boxes of pens and pencils, yellow, blue-lined notebooks, rolls of tape, and many other miscellaneous office necessities. Barlow noticed two boxes of tan, cardboard attaché cases with plastic handles. Carmine said the briefcases were cheap but they worked, and were there for anyone who wanted one, so Barlow took one. There was also an improvised, open living room area to the far left of the work space with a refrigerator, three old divans, four easy chairs, a couple of coffee tables, several small end tables, a console-size television, and an AM-FM radio.

Barlow looked deeper into the cavernous building. He was surprised to see three rows with 16 (total) mismatched motor vehicles parked quietly in the shadows on the far side of the building. They were parked near four overhead garage doors.

Slick and Barlow were still standing and gawking, getting their bearings. Carmine was rummaging through a file cabinet. Looking up with a fist full of papers, he said, "Welcome. This will be your office until we wrap up this case. Make yourselves to home. As long as you all are here early, you may as well get some of the admin taken care of. Here are some personnel forms you need to complete, plus your warehouse keys and U.S. Government gasoline credit cards. You can use the cards for gas, oil, wiper blades, flat tires, oil changes and the like, but only on the government cars which you see back there. Make sure you turn in your receipts each time you make a purchase. Otherwise, you'll end up forking over the cost of the purchase.

"Look around and take your choice of whichever undercover units you all want to start with. We'll probably switch around occasionally just to keep the bad guys guessing. Also, since you all are staying at the Best Western, I suggest you leave your POVs parked here in the garage. It's alarmed. There's a keypad on the wall inside the walk-in entrance and another on the post on the way out by the garage doors. We'll change the codes periodically, too. Right now the code is Star-1811. Any questions yet?"

Slick replied, "Not me."

Barlow asked, "Could we get a unit tonight, and leave Slick's truck here? Then I'll switch out tomorrow morning."

"Absolutely. Slick, you get first dibs."

"Thanks. Soon as I fill out my forms I'll go pick one. By the way, you a gyrene, are ya?"

"Yep. Noticed my tattoo, didn't you? 3rd Division. Infantry. Republic of Vietnam. 1965-1966. What about you?"

"Same club. Infantry. 1st and 3rd Divisions. 1942-1945. Guadalcanal, Guam, and Iwo Jima."

"That's a lot more action than I saw. Thanks for your service at a time when our nation was in true peril. What about you, Barlow? You in?"

"Army. 9th Division. Field Artillery. Vietnam. 1968-1969."

Carmine replied, "Then you know, too. It's always comforting to work with men who've crossed the Rubicon and returned better and wiser for it. Nobody knows for sure how they'll react until the lead is flying."

Slick asked, "You get in DEA straight from the Crotch [Marine Corps]?"

"Not quite. I did two years on Dallas PD first, which is where I'm from. The old BNDD [Bureau of Narcotics & Dangerous Drugs] offered me a job as a special agent to move over here at a much lower starting salary than I was making on the PD. I had to pay for my move too, but fortunately at that time I wasn't on the hook buying a house.

"I jumped at the chance. I knew I would make up the money down the road. Later on, Uncle Sam drafted a number of U.S. Customs special agents who were plenty happy in Customs, mostly the ones who worked drug smuggling, into our outfit and reflagged us as DEA. That was a couple of years ago. Actually, it made things better for those of us from BNDD. I really like my job. It fits me to a T.

"We're no longer an agency within the U.S. Treasury Department. Now we're a part of DOJ [Department of Justice], but we're the poor white trash except maybe for the INS [Immigration & Naturalization Service]. They don't get much respect from the FBI, either.

"Slick, you're a Marine. It's just like the Corps. We do more with less. Always have. Always will. Our guys don't have the FBI's budget or clout, but we operate independently with far less micromanagement compared to them, plus our agents don't have a two-by-four stuffed up their asses. We all know we're not bulletproof. We're real cops like you with two distinctions. The first is, all we work is dope. The second is we have jurisdiction anywhere in the U.S., it's territories, military installations overseas, etc. Different than the Bureau [FBI], we don't think we're better than state and local cops. I guarantee you'll see what I mean by the time we've wrapped up this case."

Barlow smiled and replied, "I can see it already."

Slick and Barlow got busy filling out the personnel forms. Same-o, same-o, except for a different bureaucracy. Each made sure to staple a copy of his last pay stub [Leave & Earnings Statement to federal employees] to the second form so he would get paid his hourly rate for overtime. Then they walked over to look at the undercover units.

Slick made up his mind right away. He zeroed in on a metallic blue, 1964 Cadillac Coupe DeVille. It was sun-faded with 130,000 miles on the odometer. It looked like what it was. A formerly fabulous automobile driven by a man whose best years were behind him now. A perfect match.

Barlow selected a faded, dull, white-over-yellow, 1970 GMC Jimmy with a V-6 engine. He picked it because of the white fiberglass topper over the bed. Now he could haul all his stuff without it being exposed to the elements, plus he could lock it. Less exposure to theft, especially in a big city like El Paso. It had 74,000 miles on the odometer. He checked to make sure the spare tire was serviceable and that the jack was intact. Ditto for the service manual and registration in the glovebox. He noticed a copy of the local radio call signs [10-Code] which was rubber-banded to the driver's sun visor. The back of the visor had a list of important locations - places like hospitals, federal, state, and local government offices, cop shops, impound lot, schools and colleges, landmarks, parks, etc., including their addresses and telephone numbers.

Slick and Barlow walked back up front and signed the log book for their respective choices of vehicle. Then Carmine handed them the keys. He said, "Okay. That's all for today folks.

See you all at 8 sharp tomorrow morning. It'll be a big day for everybody, even Mr. Ibarra but he doesn't know it yet.

"Chief Deputy U.S. Marshal Wilbur Enright will escort Western Texas Federal District Court Judge Roland T. Fenwick over here at 9 o'clock. Wilbur will give you all the do-and-don'ts of being a special U.S. deputy marshal, so listen good. Then when you all are duly impressed and a little apprehensive, Judge Fenwick will swear you all in. Wilbur will hand out your badges and ID cards. They will exit stage right and go on their merry way. Lieutenant Fred Wendell, EPSO, will provide an overview of the case. Then I'll hand out assignments and we'll get started. Any other questions before we go?"

Slick and Barlow looked at each other. Then Barlow replied, "Nope. See you tomorrow."

Carmine set the code, locked up, and followed them out the gate, which he also locked before he left.

Slick enjoyed the drive from the warehouse to supper at a Tex-Mex saloon called Humberto's. He said, "I always wanted to drive a Cadillac. Now I know why everyone wants one. It's like riding on a cloud. Surprised you didn't go for the Corvette, being a young feller and all."

"Nah, I always hated the guys driving cars like that. They're impractical. Besides, they say guys who drive sports cars are compensating for having a small winky. Wouldn't want to give someone the wrong impression."

"I guess yours is so big you should be driving a Volkswagen."

"You got that right. I let Sarah drive it everyday."

"Touché."

The next morning lived up to all their expectations. They met the other members of the task force. It didn't take them long to decide Sheriff Brady was right. This was a consortium of Who's Who in West Texas Law Enforcement. From what they observed, it looked like everyone left their egos at home when they showed up for work, too.

They met Chief Deputy Marshal Wilbur Enright and Judge Roland T. Fenwick. They could've been pricks due to their important jobs, but they weren't. They got straight to the point. No frills or hyperbole. Big boy rules all the way. Take note. They were regular joes entrusted by the federal government to perform big jobs. Follow their examples and learn.

Barlow inspected the circumscribed silver star, Special U.S. Deputy Marshal badge closely. It was pinned inside a black leather, vertical folding wallet which included a small copy of his commission signed by the chief deputy. The wallet was designed so it could be folded in reverse with the commission side of the wallet placed inside a shirt pocket so the badge could be displayed on the outside. Barlow took his badge out of the folder to look at the back side. His badge was inventory number 7211.

Lieutenant Fred Wendell passed out information packets to each officer after the judge and chief deputy marshal departed. He said, "People, it is common knowledge within this room that our primary target is a prominent Latino businessman in El Paso named Pedro Ibarra, codenamed Papa, followed by his believed-to-be button man, Rafael "Chico" Salazar, codenamed Sonny. We've got dossiers on both Papa and Sonny and their known associates up here on the console table. They're in the light green files, as are all dossiers, and only dossiers. As we get more information, we add to them. When you get a chance, come up here and give 'em a perusal. Do not remove them from the office area.

"Sonny is well-known to both Quayle County deputies here on the task force. Sonny murdered one of Papa's drug mules last week when he was being transported from a hospital to their jail. The decedent's name is Joaquín Pérez. Papa cried huge crocodile tears over his demise during his recent press conference. It appears to us that Papa sanctioned the hit to prevent Pérez from snitching to save himself. During the hit, Sonny also shot a Quayle County deputy, who is expected to fully recover. When you get an opportunity, you may want to speak to Slick or Barlow one-on-one for additional details. The outcome of these felonious shootings is that Quayle County is sitting on a murder arrest warrant for Sonny, which they're holding in abeyance, mostly at the behest of Sheriff Brady to give us time to make our case against Papa, but also to give them time to recover the murder weapon, which is a Government Model .45, if you happen to come across it.

"Up until this weekend, we didn't have any concrete evidence that Papa is a supplier of any type of illegal substance. What we had was information from several denizens in the local cannabis traffickers' pipeline that Papa is the only American importer of an extra potent variety of cannabis known as Oaxacan Highland Gold, which we've dubbed OHG. Lots of chatter but nothing viable. Not one actionable lead. However, we did some deep-dive checking, which as you detectives out there all know, takes time and usually costs money.

"OHG is grown in the state of Oaxaca in Southern Mexico. The cartel which developed it and claims sole proprietorship (with the resources to back it up, I might add) is controlled by a wealthy plantation owner well-connected in Mexican state and national political circles. His name is Victor Estrada, and his younger brother, Mateo, is his enforcer-in-charge. They trademark their product with an image of a black rooster on each kilo brick.

"I know. All of this is fascinating news, but why should we care?

"We care because we now know the source of OHG is related by blood to Papa, through their maternal grandmother. That's the tiny thread which ties this altogether, and which cost a small fortune to learn and verify. It's helpful, nice to know, but not enough. Then Saturday morning, we developed a strong, actionable lead.

"Friday night, a uniformed deputy named Chester Barnes

arrested a 24-year-old Latino female named Rosa Benítez. Her stage name is The Pink Rose. She's a friendly [informant]. Her codename is Jezebel. She's a pole dancer at a strip joint in Fort Hancock called Ana's Fantasy World, codenamed the Beehive.

"The Beehive is owned by Anastasia Gómez, age 44, codenamed Mama. Mama is an astute businesswoman. She's been the proprietor of the Beehive for the past eight years, after having been a performer there since the early 1960s. She's still a beautiful woman, and after years of hands-on, hard work, she's coming up in the world, both puns intended. Her claim to fame, back in the day when the Beehive was owned by Harry Gonzales, now deceased, and known then as Harry's Harem, was that she could smoke a cigarette with her twat and even pick up quarters with it. As you can imagine, she was in high demand back in the Bad Old Days. Now she owns the joint, yet another pun intended.

"Anyway, Friday night, our patrol deputies were copping license plate numbers at the Beehive up until just before it closed at 2 a.m. We've heard rumors for quite some time that various types of unlawful substances are being peddled there. That should come as no surprise to any experienced lawman when you consider the type of establishment it is, and the clientele it caters to. However, we haven't had any problems there in several years, so it hasn't really been a priority on our radar.

"No doubt drug deals for personal consumption have been transacted there many times, but not necessarily with Mama's collusion. That's yet to be verified, and quite frankly I'd be surprised to learn she is involved. She has way too much to lose. Why risk it when she already peddles the number one commodity most men desire? Besides, consensual sex transactions for financial compensation are only misdemeanor violations, whereas most illegal drug transactions are felonies. Nevertheless, as a result of our interface with the Beehive on this case, the SO is now keeping a watchful eye on it.

"Getting back to point, by closing time, our uniforms had

faded into the shadows to observe Beehive patrons who might be driving under the influence. If a patron was weaving on the roadway or otherwise reckless, the uniforms kept pace long enough to determine if a traffic stop was warranted. If so, they made a stop.

"The Beehive was empty by 2:10, except for a few employees and Mama, herself.

"Deputy Barnes had stayed behind to see if any of the employees departed drunk. He saw a young woman get behind the wheel of a little red Mustang convertible which had been parked behind the tavern. She pulled out and headed west on US 90. She was weaving, so Barnes initiated a traffic stop. Turns out, she was stoned, not intoxicated. She was busy trying to light another blunt (made from OHG as we later learned), at the time she was stopped. She was in felony possession of an unopened one-ounce baggie and another one which was nearly full. Deputy Barnes placed her under arrest. He was almost ready to transport her to the substation in Fabens. In fact, he was filling out a tow request on her car when she offered to identify her supplier if he would let her go.

"Barnes called for his supervisor, Sergeant Dick Bergeron, who had worked previously in Narcotics as a detective. Long story short, Sergeant Bergeron had another deputy drive Jezebel's car to the substation unimpounded. Then he called Detective Morales from Narcotics to interview her. After Morales heard what she had to say, he called me.

"First, let me say Jezebel is an 11 on a scale of 1 to 10. She would probably be a 12 if she were stripping, and a 13 if she were giving you a lap dance, and her score would keep on rising the more she did. She provided us with a great deal of inside information about the Beehive, which I did pass along to Vice, and which Lieutenant Conroy promised to hold in abeyance until after our case is complete.

"Of keen interest to us here on the task force, for the past several months, Jezebel has been consorting with two bent U.S. Border Patrol agents. Let me state emphatically that we are withholding this information from Border Patrol Internal Affairs [IA] until we are ready to make arrests. If they knew what I'm about to tell you now, they'd rush in like Attila the Hun and massacre everyone and demolish everything to include our case. We will make a full disclosure in due time. When we do, both of these rogue agents will be bound up tight like a pair of plucked Thanksgiving turkeys.

"The first bent agent, Bruno Cruz, age 31, codenamed Woody, is a first cousin of Armando Cruz. He was killed by Deputy Adams here, during a so-called routine traffic stop which quickly turned asymmetrical. Armando Cruz and Joaquín Pérez were transporting 60 kilos of OHG through Quayle County . . . ."

You could actually feel the surprise and hear the sudden intake of breath by members of the task force as soon as Barlow's name was mentioned in connection with a shooting, not least of whom was by Barlow, himself. All eyes were focused on him now.

After a long pause, Lieutenant Wilkie continued. "Thought that would get everyone's attention. Both smugglers were armed with .38 Special revolvers and Pérez had a 12-gauge shotgun. They initiated the gunfight.

"Pay attention, people! This is who we're up against. They will shoot first!

"Let's put this together. A bent Border Patrol agent codenamed Woody, with four years on the job, and his deceased cousin were both in possession of OHG. Where did they get it? It had to originate from Papa, because he's the only OHG distributor in Texas so far as we know. At any rate, he's the only one with blood connections to the growers.

"Also, the vehicle Armando Cruz was driving during this incident was registered to his father, Diego Cruz, a recently deceased (natural causes) ex-con on Papa's payroll. Plus, not confirmed yet - still waiting for checks to come back - both Armando Cruz and Joaquín Pérez were previous W-2 employees at Papa's garage, codenamed the Snake Pit, legally known as Pedro's Auto Repair Shop. It's located at the intersection of 900 Hope Street and 16th Avenue. Papa's residence, located at 911 Monarch Street, is codenamed the Taj Mahal. None of this, even collectively, is sufficient convicting evidence against Papa, but each factoid is one more nail in his coffin.

"Continuing, Jezebel said her secondary source for OHG is Woody's partner, another bent Border Patrol agent named Conrad Turnipseed, age 45, codenamed Shorty, because Jezebel says he has a real small dick. He has 16 years on the job. Both Woody and Shorty work the midnight shift at the border entry point in Fort Hancock, codenamed the Swimming Pool. Get this. They're the only two agents there on the midnight shift on Tuesday through Thursday.

"Extrapolating, both Woody and Shorty must be getting paid in OHG with Papa's blessing to let it pass through their checkpoint unmolested.

"Jezebel says she overheard Woody and Shorty whispering, in which Woody said another load was coming in Wednesday night. Assuming this is true, we'd like to follow it discreetly and see where it goes. We DO NOT, I repeat DO NOT want to take this load down unless our hand is forced.

"This is why. We don't know where Papa stores his stash. We'd be remiss not to do all we can to find it and execute a search warrant there the same time we spring our trap. Furthermore, Papa might not be present when the load is stored or disseminated. Also, he has multiple mules we have not as yet identified. Plus, we still want to catch Sonny with his .45. Finally, we want to put some time and distance between the bust and our friendly. Hell, we don't even know who any of Papa's clients are yet!

"Carmine and I have put our heads together coming up with

a plan of action. I'll let him explain it to you."

Carmine stood and faced the troops. He had a clipboard in his hand. He said, "As you all may have heard, the U.S. Attorney's Office here in the Western District of Texas has a general policy not to prosecute marijuana trafficking cases unless the seizure is 100 kilos or more. Quayle County already has 60, which I think we can tie in, so that helps; however, I believe that's just a drop in the bucket compared with the volume Papa has access to, and is importing and peddling. What I'm saying is, more is better.

"We don't have a big enough budget to do an undercover buy of scores of kilos. Depending on the quantity purchased, the street value is anywhere from $1,000 to $2,000 per kilo. Even if we had the budget, we don't have an undercover who Papa knows or who he would trust enough to make a sale.

"We also don't have enough PC [probable cause] to get a wire tap on Papa's phones. If you've ever worked with the FBI, you know that's how they make 90% of their cases. Ergo, we have to do this the old-fashioned way. We have to build our case brick by brick via surveillance and maybe by flipping someone close to him that's in the know. However, we do have a friendly and another way to make our case.

"There's ten of us, so I've divided us into two, five-man teams. Sorry Amanda, man is my generic term for both sexes. We'll work 12-hour shifts, 8 a.m. to 8 p.m., and vice versa beginning tomorrow. Team Charley, for Carmine, will start out on night shift. Team Frank, for Fred, will start out on day shift. We'll flip shifts periodically, assuming we don't morph into another system out of necessity.

"Detective Casper Leonard, Sergeant Julio Elias, Deputy Slick Oldman, and Deputy Barlow Adams are on Team Charley. Patrolwoman Amanda Romero, Sergeant Elvis Boatwright, Detective Wayne Barrett, and Detective Emilio Gomez are on Team Frank. Don't be upset if you get switched. Necessity is the mother of invention.

"Today, I want everyone to make sure he knows where Papa lives and where the Snake Pit is located. Cop license plates and vehicle descriptions when you see one you think is affiliated with Papa. He has a dozen or more vehicles that we have identified already. They're also in his green file. Make sure you memorize the faces of Papa and Sonny so you'll know them on sight.

"We have four 35-millimeter cameras with both color and black-and-white film and long-distance lenses for those who are proficient with cameras. Black-and-white works best after dark. We also have six sets of Navy surplus binoculars if you don't already have your own. These are nearly as big as a sawed-off shotgun and as heavy as a bowling ball, but the clarity is unmatched. The Navy used them for deckhands on watch.

"Team Charley will conduct surveillance tonight on the Fort Hancock Port of Entry, codenamed Swimming Pool, and to a lesser degree on the Beehive. Team Frank, nose around a little this afternoon and see if you can figure out where Papa's stash house, codenamed Jackpot, is located. Fred and I will compare notes at shift change.

"Be flexible. Our operation is lean, but we have an all-star cast. You could say we're operating a run-and-shoot offense in a matter of speaking. Fresh ideas are always welcome. You all know what the objectives are, so keep your eyes on the ball.

"Okay. Get to it soon as you're ready. Also, come see me or Fred if you have questions. Otherwise, Team Charley, I will see you all at midnight at the Petro Truck Stop off I-10 in Fabens.

"One last thing. The radios should already be switched to Channel 5, which is the frequency we will be using. Double check. Report in at the beginning of your shift. Also, please note. Not all police agencies do this. Maybe yours doesn't. Task Force protocol is to say the call sign of the unit you want to talk to first. Then use your own call sign. Then say your message. For example, I'm 700. Fred is 710. I want to speak to Fred. I say, '710 - 700. Meet me at Castle.' Then Fred replies, '700 - 710. Roger that.

See you in 5.'"

"The reason we do this is because your lizard brain will wake up and pay attention whenever your call sign is spoken. It reduces the likelihood that the message will need to be repeated because you weren't listening. Everyone understand?"

Nobody replied.

"Good. I take that as a yes. Call signs are in your packets. Adiós."

Chapter 24

LAW ENFORCEMENT FED STYLE

Monday, June 3, 1974

Phase 1 began today. Before they left Monday afternoon, Slick and Barlow studied the call signs. Carmine Valenzuela was 700, of course. Fred Wendell was 710. After that they were in alphabetical order. Barlow Adams was 720. Wayne Barrett was 730. Elias Boatwright was 740. Julio Elias was 750. Emilio Gomez was 760. Casper Leonard was 770. Slick Oldman was 780, and Amanda Romero was 790. They switched on their radios and called one another for a radio check. Everything was right as rain.

Then they departed the Castle and took a cruise through the Hope Street area of El Paso. They needed to take a gander at Pedro's Auto Repair Shop located at Hope Street and 16th Avenue. Barlow made a quick mental adjustment to correct himself and thought Snake Pit, instead.

He was impressed. It was much nicer than he had supposed. It took up six lots. The garage itself was shaped like a Quonset hut, except it was made out of real stucco painted a pale yellow with light blue trim. The bay doors were open. It was full of cars with several employees that he could see. It seemed to be doing a thriving business. He noted that this would be a difficult location in which to conduct a surveillance even if you were Latino. The street looked like a Mexican bazaar where everyone knew everyone by face and by name. Strangers and strange automobiles would stand out in the crowd like the king who wore no clothes.

Next they made a pass at the Taj Mahal, two blocks away at 911 Monarch Street. Easy place to locate. It was the predominant house on a block in which the houses were modest, no more than 1200 square feet. The Taj Mahal was twice that or more on a double lot, surrounded by a four-foot adobe wall. Perfect for a major-domo. Besides, it was the only two-story house within sight. Just like the Snake Pit, this location would be a difficult location to watch without being noticed.

They tooled around the neighborhood a little more before heading back to the CBD [Central Business District] for an early supper and private time in their rooms. They both called the office and their homes before making an effort to cop a few winks. They agreed to meet in the lobby at 11 o'clock to head out to Fabens and hook up with Team Charley to pull their first midnight shift.

Slick and Barlow had just walked in the Denny's restaurant when the task force radio traffic got frenetic, so they missed it all. It was probably just as well because Barlow would have been all mumped up that he wasn't included.

"Castle or 710 - 730."

"730 - 700."

"700 - 730. I need some back up. I'm following a light green Dodge van. It just popped out of the Snake Pit with two Latino males. The garage doors were down, so I thought it was closed. I think they've got a load. It's headed pretty fast towards the I-10 entrance ramp at Belton Street. If anyone's available I could use some help."

"730 - 710. What are you driving?"

"710 - 730. I'm in the metallic blue, 1973 Ford Maverick with the souped up engine."

"730 - 790. I'm in the area. I should be able to intercept and take the eyeball [lead car in a surveillance with the target in view.]"

"All units - 710. I'm en route. Any other Team Frank units copy?"

"710 - 760. En route."

"710 - 740. En route. What are you all driving?"

"All units - 790. I'm in the black, 1973 Trans Am. They just got on the westbound ramp. I've got the eyeball."

"All units - 760. I'm in a red-over-white 1972 Buick LeSabre."

"All units - 740. I'm in a silver 1966 deuce-and-quarter [Buick Electra 225]. Just entered I-10 westbound."

"All units - 710. I'm en route in a gold 1971 Chevy Nova. Somebody get out ahead of the target. You all know what to do. Eyeball call out the exits as you pass. Don't forget to switch off. It's too early in the game for anyone to get burned."

"710 - 700. I'm going home. Call me later on whenever you get a chance if there's any developments. I'll be back on the air at 2300 if you all are still out. You'll probably lose radio contact with us if you go as far as Van Horn. Good luck."

Chapter 25

MAKING HAY WHILE THE SUN SHINES

Monday/Tuesday, June 3/4, 1974

Pedro could feel the air under his wings. Pepe Aguilar from Del Rio had called. His panties were in a wad. He was in a bind. He needed his standard 60-key load right away. He was willing to pay $5,000 extra if it were delivered today.

Pedro smiled. When he was hurting for revenue last week and needed to make a quick sale to Pepe, he wasn't ready. No can do. Now the tables were reversed, so bad in fact, he was willing to pay an 8.25% premium.

Pedro checked the time. It was 2 o'clock. He could do it, but it would be tight. He said he'd have the delivery there by midnight.

Pedro was a little worried. Was Pepe setting him up for the fuzz by offering a bonus? Surely not. Maybe he was just getting paranoid. Nevertheless, he warned his mules, Rodolfo Velásquez and Tomás Jiménez, to be on the lookout for a rip before he ushered them on their way. That was the same thing he told them the last time he sent them out.

They already knew they were fucked if this were a rip tonight, but they never let on to El Jefe. No two men could escape the clutches of that creepy King Kong fucker - uglier than a sackful of assholes - or all those junkyard dogs, let alone the rest of Pepe's other employees. However, they'd delivered to Pepe's shop before. He had treated them right.

Not only that, El Jefe knew where Pepe lived. He'd be signing his own death warrant if he did them dirty. Jefe had Chico, the ultimate weapon, who wasn't near as big as King Kong, but there was something about him that just reeked of danger and death.

Chico was as deadly as a pit full of vipers and everyone could see it, except Chico never let on. He never showed his emotions or expressed anger but everyone knew it dwelled just beneath the surface. The Anglo law had done him wrong but he had survived. Now he was stronger and deadlier for it. Nobody in his right mind would ever cross Chico. With those comforting thoughts in mind, they went along blissfully at 70 miles per hour, not a worry in the world. This was a cakewalk. It was also another big payday for them.

Rodolfo and Tomás followed the same routine as they had before. They followed I-10 eastbound to Stockton where they stopped briefly to refuel, drink 16-ounce Big Reds, and eat two (each), monstrous, greasy, gas station burritos topped off with crispy, fried pork rinds. Rodolfo emptied his bladder and Tomás voided his bowels after eating. They never noticed Fred Wendell (710) refueling his gold Chevy Nova, or Elvis Boatwright (740) pull up in his silver deuce-and-a-quarter and run to the john.

Sated and eager to be on their way, they never paid attention to Amanda Romero's (790) black Trans Am which passed them as soon as they pulled onto I-10 from the entrance ramp. They were also too busy to notice the headlights from Emilio Gomez' (760) red-over-white Buick LeSabre 200 yards behind them, nor the headlights from Wayne Barrett's (730) blue Maverick when he took over the eyeball from Fred (710). In fact, they didn't have even the tiniest notion that they were surrounded by half a task force of dope agents who wondered where on earth they were headed.

At Sonora, the targets turned southwest onto US 277. They continued all the way to Del Rio at US 90, where they turned east. Fred had been in front of them and he had guessed correctly, turning east first. Boatwright (740) and Romero (790) peeled off at the all night Amoco station to refuel, but neither Rodolfo nor Tomás noticed. They had slowed way down, looking for roadsigns, and specifically their landmark, the Dairy Queen.

Gomez (760) and Barrett (730), bringing up the rear, backed way off.

The targets passed Carpenter Street, Drury Street, Independence Street, and suddenly Liberty Street was right on top of them. They slammed on the breaks and made a wide turn northbound onto Liberty. They had missed the Dairy Queen because it was closed and dark, but corrected quickly and began looking for the junkyard. It was easy to find because it was 11:15 p.m., and the only place on Liberty Street with any lights on. Besides, they had been there before.

The members of the task force each found a place to pull off the highway and hide.

"All units - 710. Everyone check in with your location."

"730 and 760 are at the Dairy Queen.

"790's pulling out of the Amoco. 740 will be leaving momentarily."

"All units except for 730, standby at your current location. 730, get the name of the street where the targets turned. Then take a drive down it. See if you can locate them without getting yourself burned. We've come over 400 miles to get here, so we're bound to be close. After you come back, assuming the target's not moving, everyone who needs fuel, fill 'er up. Everyone copy?"

"730 copies. The name of the street is Liberty.

"760 copies."

"790 copies."

"740 copies."

"730 moving out."

Wayne Barrett (730) put his mike back in his glovebox and flipped the microphone switch to off. Then he turned north and began a slow crawl up the street. He hadn't gone very far when he realized the only lights on the street were coming from a fenced in junkyard/auto repair shop. Then he saw he was on a dead-end street. Damn!

He noticed a guy standing at the end of the junkyard

driveway out by the street watching him. Time to wing it. He pulled into the driveway far enough to back out. Wayne had the driver's window rolled down. His left elbow was hanging out.

The man was huge like the professional wrestler Andre the Giant, except uglier like Abdullah the Butcher. He asked, "What the fuck are you looking for, bud?"

"Is this Independence Street? I'm lost."

"Nope. You done missed it. Next street west of here on the other side of the Dairy Queen. Look, pilgrim. You ain't in the best of neighborhoods here. A feller could get hisself shot as a prowler if somebody took a notion he was up to no good. Cops would just write it off as using bad judgment. Savvy?"

"Savvy. Thanks for the warning. I ain't looking for no trouble. Just pulled down the wrong street is all. Sorry to bother you. Adiós."

The giant watched as Wayne turned around. He looked like he was trying to cop his license plate number, but Wayne had already made it hard for him by taking the license plate bulb out of its socket and putting it in the ashtray. Once he got turned around, he sped up until he got back to US 90. When he cleared it, he got back on the air and said, "710 - 730. I'm headed to the Amoco to refuel. I saw the van in a junkyard on the west side of the street. It was the only place with the lights on. The biggest, ugliest badass I ever saw met me at the front gate. I'm pretty sure he believed my story about looking for Independence Street, which is the next street west, but it would be real bad juju if he saw me again. Liberty Street is a dead-end, so they have to come out past the Dairy Queen when they leave."

"730 - 710. Anyone else who needs gas better get it now. 740, you take the Dairy Queen. 790 you take my position north of there at the IGA. Also, you come up and take the eyeball if they go west. 740, you take it if they head east."

About 20 minutes later the van turned west on US 90. They followed it back to Sonora, where the two men secured lodging at the Desert Rose Inn. There was a Days Inn a quarter-mile down the road. Lieutenant Wendell and Amanda Romero watched until the men checked into Room 207 on the second floor. Amanda got Room 213. Fred requested and got Room 105, directly in front of the parked van. He told the other officers to check in at the Days Inn and be ready to roll at 8 o'clock. It was 2:15 a.m.

Fred used a payphone outside the motel office to call the EPSO Radio Dispatch Room. He identified himself, and asked the dispatcher to call for Unit 700 on Channel 5. If he answered, ask him to call dispatch for a message. Then he listened while the dispatcher called for 700. He answered. The dispatcher told him to stand by for a message. Fred said to tell 700 to call 710 at 905-998-0601, which was the number of the payphone where he was standing by. 700 replied that he would call within the next five minutes. Fred thanked the dispatcher and hung up. He lit a Chesterfield while he was waiting.

Three minutes later the phone rang. Fred answered, "Carmine?"

"One and the same. Got some good news?"

"I believe so."

"Shoot."

"We tailed the van to a junkyard/auto repair shop on the northwest corner of Liberty Street in Del Rio. We codenamed it Compound. Don't know the name, but the junkyard is on a dead-end street at the very end. Liberty runs north from US 90. The drivers of the van were both Latino males, 20 to 25, thin, about 5-feet, 8-inches tall, dark hair, no facial hair or distinguishing features that we could see. The van stayed there for 25 minutes before going to Sonora, where they checked into the Desert Rose Inn, room 207. Amanda and I also have rooms there, and the rest of Team Frank are at the Days Inn down the street. That's about it."

"You think they were delivering a load?"

"What else could it be?"

"Agreed. You think there's any need to tail the van back home?"

"Not really. We might even get burned for nothing."

"Agreed.

"Okay. I'll let the team know they can sleep in. We'll return to Castle in the afternoon."

"Good deal. Get some rest."

Chapter 26

TEAM CHARLEY GOES TO WORK

Tuesday, June 4, 1974

Both Slick (780) and Barlow (720) were up and at 'em at 11 o'clock. They had a 30-mile drive, but they wanted to arrive early so they could refuel and buy some snacks. Sergeant Julio Elias (750) was already there in the olive green, 1972 Corvette with the removable hard top. He was parked in front of the building, standing in front of his unit drinking a hot cuppa joe and smoking a Marlboro. He smiled when he saw Slick and Barlow pull up. He waved and shouted while they were gassing up, "I figured you two hombres would beat everyone else here."

Slick shouted back, "The early bird catches the worm. Guess you're hungry, too."

Elias shouted back, "I suspect there's enough worms for all of us."

After refueling, Slick and Barlow parked in the spaces on either side of Elias. They got out and shook hands all around. Barlow said, "Chief Alex told us all about you. He said you know everybody in town, including a retired professional wrestler who owns a saloon with the most beautiful dancers he's ever seen."

"He's right about the dancers. Chief Alex told me about you all, too. He said Sheriff Sol always sends you two jaspers whenever he has a dangerous predator problem."

Slick replied, "He sends me because after Archie Willis retired, I'm the oldest and orneriest deputy he's got. My last name is Oldman for a reason, you know. I ain't married so if I get croaked, the county doesn't have to pay out no retirement benefits. He sends Barlow because . . . ."

Barlow interrupted and finished the sentence, "Barlow has a wheelchair in the back of his unit so he can roll Deputy Oldman to wherever the gunfight is supposed to take place. Otherwise, I'm just a pretty face to offset Slick's ugly mug. Sheriff Sol doesn't want the rest of the world to think all us Quayle County residents are as ugly as Slick."

While they were jawboning, Casper Leonard (770) pulled up in his black-over-cream, 1971, Mercury Cyclone GT, muscle car. Being a robbery/homicide dick for 11 years, it was virtually impossible for Casper to dress down. He thought he was. He resembled a Texas-style Jack Webb portraying Sergeant Joe Friday in the TV show *Dragnet*. He was wearing khaki trousers, a pale yellow dress shirt, bolo tie, forest green sport coat, brown, Tony Lama round-toed, cowboy boots, and a beige, Open Road Stetson. They couldn't see it, but he was carrying a nickel-plated, Colt Python .357 Magnum in an El Paso Saddlery, cross-draw holster. The thing which seized Barlow's interest, however, was that Casper was smoking a six-inch, 60-gauge, H. Upmann, Maduro torpedo.

Monkey see. Monkey do. Casper inspired Barlow to light up one of his own cigars - a six-inch, 54-gauge, Maduro Churchill handcrafted by Romeo & Juliet. This began an instantaneous male bonding process between Barlow and Casper.

At the stroke of midnight, Carmine Valenzuela (700) pulled up in his white, 1968 Ford station wagon. He got out and greeted his troops. Then he lit up a Mexican cheroot, so Slick followed suit and lit an unfiltered regular Camel cigarette.

Carmine said, "Before we leave the lot, everyone check in by radio. Want to make sure we're all hearing each other.

"Without going through the Border Patrol for obvious reasons, I tried to come up with photographs of Woody and Shorty. Naturally there are no mugshots on file so for the time being, we'll have to make do with the descriptions on their driver's licenses.

"Woody is 31 years old, 5-feet, 8-inches tall, and 180 pounds. He's Mexican, of course, with black hair and brown eyes. Shorty is a white male, age 45, 5-feet, 11-inches tall, 170 pounds, blue eyes and sandy hair. Supposedly he's going bald, according to Fred's CI [confidential informant], codenamed Jezebel, so his hair is probably thinning. They're supposed to be the only two agents on duty tonight so we should be able to make them out, especially if you all brought some binoculars with you.

"We need to get descriptions of any POVs they're driving, including plate numbers. Tonight's a dry run for us. Find yourselves some good hidey-holes where you can see what's going on. Look around for places where you would offload and transfer 60 kilos of weed. Tomorrow, we hope to see the transfer and even film it without getting caught. We want to follow it to Papa's Jackpot. We don't want to make an arrest unless our hands are forced.

"Also check out the Beehive, at least from the outside. Casper, you look so suave and debonair, I oughta send you in to see if you get solicited."

"Carmine, I'm game if they actually perform an illicit act on my body. You know, sacrifice myself for Team Charley. Not up for it if all it's going to be is 'I'll show you mine if you show me yours.'"

"Casper, I'd take you up on that except I'm concerned about your mental wellbeing. What if the girls started calling you Shorty just like our target? We'd have to tag you Shorty Number 2 instead of 770."

The guys all started hooting it up.

Casper replied, "No risk of that, Sir. Pretty sure my nickname would be Magnum Johnson. I'd probably be invited to go on the porn circuit, make some stud films, except I love my job too much. Thanks for thinking of me, though."

Once everyone who needed to refuel or buy snacks was ready, they conducted the radio checks and headed eastbound the 25 miles to Fort Hancock.

The Swimming Pool [Fort Hancock Port of Entry], though small, was lit up like an airport runway. There was only one entry and one exit lane. One marked Border Patrol unit was parked behind the small cop shop. They could also see a light-colored pickup truck, make uncertain, and a dark sedan, which looked like a 1965 or 1966 Ford Galaxie. Two border patrol agents were visible inside the building.

They could also see the Mexican Port of Entry about a quarter-mile further south. It was lit up, too, but not nearly so brightly. There were two marked police sedans parked over there, both of which looked to be in sad shape. Every now and then a uniformed officer stepped out of the building to stretch his legs.

Barlow had a hard time finding a suitable discreet vantage point which hadn't already been taken, so he decided to look for someplace where a 60-kilo load could be offloaded without drawing unwanted attention. Besides the two bent agents, the only other people in sight were the five of them in Team Charley. They could probably offload in the middle of the street and there wouldn't be anyone around to notice in the wee hours of the morning.

It was a slow night. Then about 0300 hours, 700 told all units to meet in the gravel parking lot of the Starlight Drive-In movie theater. That's when he filled them in on Team Frank's unexpected trip to Del Rio to a junkyard codenamed the Compound. Barlow was green with envy.

Slick said, "Carmine, the Val Verde County Sheriff is a personal friend of mine. His name is Will Shive. I did a two-week undercover over there for him several years ago. He's a great sheriff and as honest as a Franciscan monk. I could call him and ask for an assessment of that junkyard owner and his employees if you want. Loop him in. I know he would keep it on the down low, plus his deputies would be available to help us if we wind up raiding the joint."

"Slick, you are a very resourceful man. I need to make the call myself so he will know we're a federal task force and that this is a straightforward invitation for him to join our investigation as a full member. The idea being, that any charges levied against the perps in his bailiwick would be prosecuted in Federal Court. His office would get all the credit for that. This is important, because the more kilos of dope we can tie into our case, the harsher the prison sentences will be.

"At the same time, I will rely heavily upon the relationship you and I have to provide me with a vouch. If he trusts you and you trust me, he will go all out to help us. Also, with him knowing that both you and Barlow are part of our task force, it will be the same as an endorsement from Sheriff Sol, himself. Before we get back to work, give me your best number for Sheriff Shive. I'll call him this morning before I go 10-7 [out of service].

Slick replied, "No problemo. Two last tidbits. Will was in the Marines during Korea. I think he was a lance corporal. He was awarded the Purple Heart. Also he has a boy who is beginning his second year at Texas A&M, for what it's worth."

"Both salient bonding points.

"Anyone else have any comments or questions?"

Barlow replied, "I do. I hope we do observe the drug transfer and successfully follow it to the Jackpot without getting burned, but what next? Just the little bit I've seen of the Hope Street neighborhood, I don't see how we could possibly keep the Jackpot under 24/7 surveillance."

"Very perceptive of you. The answer is we couldn't, but we don't have to. One of the perks of belonging to a well-funded, major metro police or sheriff's department, or a federal law enforcement agency, is that we have access to toys that most agencies do not have.

"All we have to do is locate the Jackpot, and more importantly, its ingress/egress points. DEA has a technical support unit in most major metro cities like El Paso. We'll task them to put up as many pole cameras as we need to cover all access points to and from the Jackpot.

"Basically, our guys borrow a local utility truck and utility company uniforms. Actually, they already did that a few years ago. Then in broad daylight, they pick the best telephone pole(s) for our viewing purposes, set out some orange cones, climb the pole(s), and hook up the cameras. They're concealed in the same type of apparatus as you see scattered about on many utility poles. Nobody's the wiser.

"Then we record and monitor the cameras in real time on closed circuit TVs set up at Castle by our techs. We can do this legally so long as we don't have sound, which as you probably know, would require a wiretap warrant signed by a federal judge, which we could never get because the law enforcement affiant, meaning me, must demonstrate that his agency has already exhausted every other less intrusive way to obtain the information needed to prove the criminal activity, which we haven't. Besides, these affidavits usually number 50 or more pages and are more painful to write, let alone get approved, than a dissertation for a Ph.D. in nuclear physics. This, by the way, is the primary investigative method our brothers in the FBI use to make their cases. It's their stock in trade. They have professional affidavit writers on their staff. It's what they do. Without wiretaps, they couldn't find a Jew in Tel Aviv.

"Once the pole cams are in place, we can watch for deliveries, but more importantly, for outgoing dope runs, because Jezebel should keep us plugged in on incoming deliveries. We'll maintain at least two units on five-minute response times 24/7 to scramble for mobile surveillances with additional units to catch up ASAP [as soon as possible]. This allows us to identify Papa's clients. When we think we've identified just about everyone in his American network, we shut it all down. We'll plan it for a day when Papa receives a load, just to ensure he can't claim ignorance. We'll try to coordinate the client raids at the same time if at all possible.

"Does this help to bring what we're doing all together?"

Barlow replied, "It does for me. I was a lost babe in the woods. I've never worked dope before or anything like this case for sheer magnitude. Now I get it. I'm truly honored to be here."

"Barlow, I'm sincere when I say we are honored to have you. We need your particular skill sets, same as we do for everyone on this task force. None of us are masters of all the law enforcement skill sets. Anyone else?"

There were no other questions or comments. They all went back to work.

The night ended quietly for them, just as it began.

Team Frank's day shift on Wednesday proved to be just as uneventful.

Chapter 27

SOMETIMES THINGS JUST COME UP ROSES

Wednesday, June 5, 1974

Team Charley showed up at the Swimming Pool a little before midnight, quietly optimistic.

Barlow knew what to expect because in addition to last night, he had done his share of midnight surveillances several years ago on a sheep rustling case.

Fun or exciting?

Maybe at first. Then not so much.

Initially, the midnight surveillances pass as quietly as a soft shower in the middle of a spring night. It had been a new experience for Barlow as a deputy, but not as a soldier. Being on watch in a combat zone is a horse of a different color, especially when you know the enemy is out and about. That being said, surveillance in law enforcement has its element of danger too, but it's not quite the same. You think you're poised for combat, but it happens too infrequently to keep a lawman on his toes, different from being a soldier in a foxhole in a war zone. Before too awful long, each uneventful night morphs into something excruciatingly boring, like watching the grass grow on a putting green. You know. Keep watch so the field mice won't drop little turds on the manicured lawn and burn out the grass. At least during all those midnight surveillances as a rookie deputy, Slick had been right there with him showing him the ropes, in many ways just like he was tonight.

One night back in 1970, being a little too eager and possibly a mite too noisy, on top of being silhouetted against a moonlit sky, the stakeout team unintentionally tipped its hand ten seconds too early during the ambush to arrest some rustlers.

What were the consequences of their haste or carelessness? Bright flashes of lightning with projectiles whizzing all around them like supersonic hornets, followed a micro-second later by the percussion sounds of outlaw firearms discharged to terminate their lawful efforts. You know. To kill or maim them. To get away unscathed with all their lucre, which in this case was a herd of sheep. This tiny little segment of the lawman's cosmic universe erupted furiously into a matter of life or death for just a few seconds - a veritable moment in time. Two villains died. One got away. One was arrested.

To be victorious in combat means not to die, especially in vain. During this particular case, the wake-up call of sudden combat happened not once, but twice. The second time they were better prepared. Even so, one of the good guys, a Texas Ranger, was wounded. Three villains bit the dust, never to rise again. C'est la vie. Life marches on, even if the combatants don't.

Would their mission be successful tonight without anyone getting hurt? Barlow certainly hoped so.

Last night they determined that Woody drives a tan, 1973 Ford F-150 pickup truck. He calls 612 Mesa Street in Fabens home. At least that's what his vehicle registration reflected. Slick had done a drive by. It was a small, run down adobe house on a tiny lot with chickens and chihuahuas running to and fro all around the yard, turning it into a minefield of animal shit. Step on a mine. Release a toxic odor.

Woody's partner, Shorty, was living in room 202 of the Fabens Arms Hotel. Guess that's how it goes when you have two ex-wives and God only knows how many kids. Shorty drives a black, 1966 Ford Galaxie 500 registered to him at 813 Arnold Drive, also in Fabens. That's where his second ex-wife, Carlotta Turnipseed, resides with four school-age kids and her new boyfriend named Jody. Are all the kids Shorty's? That's the $64,000 question.

Carmine also reported that Val Verde County Sheriff Will Shive was on board. The junkyard, codenamed the Compound, where Team Frank followed one of Papa's vans is called Pepe's Scrap Metal Shop. It's located at 110 Liberty Street, surrounded by a chain link fence, and protected by six or eight vicious junkyard dogs.

The proprietor is Pepe Aguilar, Latino male, 46 years of age, black hair, brown eyes, Pancho Villa mustache, 5-feet, 9-inches tall, and 150 pounds. He has one old arrest for grand larceny (auto), dating back to 1958, when he stole his pastor's 1955 white-over-brown Packard 400 sedan. Pepe told the court that his only crime was joyriding, not felony theft. He borrowed the car without asking because he had a chica lined up who said she would take him around the world. He said he planned on returning the car as soon as he got his ashes hauled. Supposedly, Judge Wilson Roberts had mercy on Pepe when he learned he had just enlisted in the Navy, or that's the way they tell it. Sheriff Shive had a little different version.

He said it's true that Judge Roberts was an old salt, having graduated from the U.S. Naval Academy in 1937. In fact, he was serving on the battleship USS Nevada (BB-36) when it was torpedoed by the Japanese in Pearl Harbor. Judge Roberts was a lieutenant junior grade back in those days. A month later, he was awarded the Navy Cross for rescuing 16 wounded sailors who were drowning and/or floundering in the burning, oil-soaked harbor during the bombing.

So Judge Roberts, in an act of mercy towards a fellow sailor, reduced Pepe's felony charge to misdemeanor petty larceny. He sentenced Pepe to six months in jail at hard labor, sentence suspended pending Pepe's service in the Navy. If he served his full term of enlistment and received an honorable discharge, the sentence would be vacated. It's doubtful Judge Roberts ever gave Pepe's case another thought.

Pepe returned to Judge Wilson Robert's court in 1962, with

his DD-214 in hand. It reflected that he was given an honorable discharge as a petty officer 3rd class. Judge Roberts made good on his promise, and so ordered that all was to be forgiven. Pepe never had to serve any time. Not one day. He was a free man with no strings attached. Sounds like a Horatio Alger story, huh?

This is the other version.

That follow-up day in court really was Pepe's lucky day. That same night, Judge Roberts had a stroke while he was banging his 22-year-old Playboy Bunny wife and her twin sister both at the same time in his king-size bed. He became disabled and was forced to retire. Then, so the story goes, Judge Roberts attempted a repeat performance several weeks later, dying in the saddle with an erection that never faded away. They said he was hung like John Dillinger. Supposedly there's an autopsy photograph which proves it. Not only that, he was wearing his red argyle socks for good luck when he expired.

So, did Judge Wilson Roberts give Pepe a break because they were both sailors, or was it because they were both horn dogs? Who can say for sure? Either way, Pepe lucked out, and maybe Judge Wilson Roberts did too, passing away while in the performance of the one thing he loved more than anything. He wasn't awarded another Navy Cross, but he did go down in the annals of Val Verde County history.

Getting back to Pepe, codenamed Lucky, he had been on the VVCSO radar for a number of years under suspicion of running a chop shop. They nearly had him once, but the victim of the stolen car in question, which had been reduced to a hulk minus all its valuable parts, recanted his theft report. He said he had been ashamed to admit that he really lost the car to Pepe in a poker game. He was trying to keep it from his wife who was furious and threatened to divorce him. However, the detectives observed that when he came in to withdraw his report, he had a black eye and several abrasions on his face, not to mention a broken arm that he refused to talk about. It was obvious what had happened, but he stuck to his story so the case against Pepe was recorded as nolle prosequi [case dropped] by the district attorney.

Sheriff Shive did not know Lucky was also in the weed business. He said he would put out a few discreet feelers, but other than keeping a watchful eye, he would await further instructions by the task force.

Sheriff Shive also mentioned one of Lucky's more notable employees named Igor Sampson, codenamed Goliath. He's a white male, 39 years of age, 6-feet, 6-inches tall, weighs 270 pounds, brown eyes, brown hair, bushy beard, hairy as a gorilla and twice as strong. He has two priors - one for disorderly conduct in 1970, and the other for aggravated assault, reduced to misdemeanor assault, sentenced to serve nine months in the county jail in 1972. Served in the Army from 1955 to 1958 in the 82nd Airborne Division. Given a BCD [Bad Conduct Discharge] for beating up his squad leader in a drunken barroom brawl, which is the only thing which kept him out of prison at Fort Leavenworth. Believed to be Pepe's enforcer.

After the briefing, all five task force units went back to their respective hidey-holes where they could watch the Swimming Pool.

At 2:47, an old, white, refrigerated milk truck with a faded Elsie the Cow logo painted on the side, subsequently determined to be a 1953 model Dodge, pulled into the northbound lane at the Mexican Port of Entry. A short, portly Mexican male, 50 to 60 years of age, roughly 5-feet, 5-inches tall, 225 pounds, wearing raggedy bluejeans, white tee shirt, mostly concealed by a short-sleeve, green and yellow checked shirt, and a filthy, worn out straw hat, codenamed Fatso, got out of the truck.

The two Mexican Federales walked over and greeted him like he was their favorite uncle.

They had a five-minute chat. Then Fatso opened the driver's door of his cab and pulled out a brown paper grocery sack which appeared to be half-full. He handed it to the taller, thinner Federale, who peered inside. Thereafter, the shorter Federale wrote something on a document fastened to a clipboard, at which time Fatso returned to his truck. Then the taller Federale raised the barrier and Fatso drove to the Swimming Pool.

Both Woody and Shorty approached the milk truck on the driver's side. After a two-minute chat, they opened the gate and let him pass. Then they both got into Shorty's car and followed the truck to Davis Street between 4th and 5th Avenue to an old, ratty, two-bay, coin-operated, self-serve car wash that looked like it could be out of business. There were no lights on in the car wash, but the street lights provided enough light to see what they were up to.

Sergeant Julio Elias (750) was taking black-and-white photographs as fast as he could. Casper Leonard (770) copped the license plate on the truck before it pulled into the car wash. It had an Oaxaca, Mexico plate, number 1433CV.

When Special Agent Carmine Valenzuela (700) passed by the car wash, he saw Shorty and Fatso offloading bricks from the back of the truck and placing them into the trunk of Shorty's Ford. Jezebel's information was correct! There was no way to determine an accurate count of the load, but Slick (780) found a hidey-hole with a partially obscured view and counted 32 passes between Shorty and Fatso.

Soon as they offloaded, both vehicles returned to the Swimming Pool. Fatso continued on back into Mexico, and Woody and Shorty resumed their official duties. They had only been gone for 11 minutes. The task force officers resumed their various surveillance posts. They thought they would be here until end of shift for the two bent Border Patrol agents but they were wrong.

At 4:21, a dark, early 1960s model Chevrolet sedan pulled up to the Border Patrol shack and parked next to Shorty's Ford. Two men got out of the car. Hard to tell for certain, but they both looked like young, thin, Latino males. Both Woodie and Shorty stepped out of their office to greet them. Using a telephoto lens, 750 began snapping photos. The four suspects counted and offloaded bricks, placing them into the trunk on the Chevrolet. 700 counted 54. 780 counted 60. Barlow (720) counted 58. Soon as they were wrapping up, the radio got busy.

"720 - 700. Start heading towards I-10."

"720 copies."

"780 - 700. Be prepared to pick up the eyeball."

"780 copies."

"750 - 700. You'll pick up drag when we head out. Take as many snaps as you can before you leave."

"750 copies."

"770 - 700. Are you ready to roll?"

"700 - 770. That's a big 10-4."

"720 - 700. Soon as I'm certain our target, now codenamed Blueballs, is approaching the westbound entrance ramp, I'll let you know so you will be ahead of us. Copy?"

"720 copies."

Three minutes pass.

"All units - 780. We're rolling north to Highway 90. Standby for direction."

"All units - 780. Blueballs is turning west on Highway 90."

"720 - 700. Go west on I-10 but try to parallel our progress."

"720 rogers that. Getting on I-10 westbound."

"780 has the eyeball now. Blueballs must have the blueballs. He's only driving 45."

"780 - 700. He's checking for a tail. Drop back. I'll pick up the eyeball."

"780 slowing down and pulling off into a Gulf service station."

"700 has the eyeball. Still headed westbound on US 90 about 15 miles east of Fabens."

No chatter for 17 minutes.

"All units - 700. We're picking up I-10 in Fabens. 750 you got the eyeball?"

"750 has the eyeball on I-10 just west of Fabens. That you up there ahead of me 720?"

"720 is 10-4. Does anyone have Blueballs' plate number yet?"

"720 - 700. Standby. The number is R-Rascal, S-Stupid, 4-4-3-9. I'll be on Channel 4 getting a registration."

Two minutes pass.

"All units - 700. The registration comes back to Carlos' Speedy Taxi Company, located at 604 Amarillo Street, El Paso. Registration's clear. Who's got the eyeball and where are we?"

"700 - 720. Just acquiring the eyeball. Blueballs has picked up the pace. 65 miles per hour now. 770 - You in the wings?"

"That's a big 10-4."

"All units - 720. Just passing the Horizon City exit. I'm pulling off. 770 - It's all yours."

"750 - 700. Do you know where Amarillo Street is?"

"Sure do."

"Roger that. See if you can get out ahead of us. Check out 604 Amarillo Street. Last thing we want to do is bring a parade down that street, assuming that's where we're headed."

"Copy that. 750 en route."

"770 - 720. Where we at? I'm trying to catch up."

"Just coming up on the exit at US 54. I think he's headed to Dyer Street. That's the way I'd go if I were going to Amarillo Street."

"Just passed 54. Standby."

"North on Dyer. Can someone pick up the eyeball?"

"700's got it."

"700 - 750. 604 is an old garage it looks like. Carlos' sign is pretty badly faded. However, a late model white over red Cadillac is sitting in the driveway with the engine running. Can't see who's driving or how many are in it. Texas license plate number B-Big, P-Prick, 7-1-1-1. That belong to who I think it does?"

"That's Papa's ride. We might have just located the Jackpot. Can you get a photo?"

"Negative. I kept on rolling."

"All units - 700. Back off. Give Blueballs some space. Think we've found Jackpot. Who's got the eyeball and where are you?"

770. Almost to Amarillo. I'm dropping off."

"780's picking up the eyeball in the old blue Caddy. I'll ease up so I can make a pass after Blueballs' has had a chance to light."

"700 here. Easy does it 780. Just need confirmation Blueballs went to 604. Anything else we might get for free is just lagniappe. Do not get burned."

"780 copies. Blueballs just turned east on Amarillo. Standby for further."

Two agonizing minutes pass.

"All units - 780. Just cleared the site. Two Latino males from Blueballs were in the driveway talking to Papa and Sonny, I'm pretty sure. The garage door was open. Only thing I could see was a large motor vehicle parked in the garage with a canvas tarp over it. Don't think anyone even noticed me pass."

"All units - 700. Great job. Meet back at Castle as soon as you can for a quick debrief. All copy?"

"780 copies."

"750 copies."

"720 copies."

"770 copies. Refueling first."

Chapter 28

The Scent of Blood

Wednesday, June 5, 1974

It was 0630 before all of Team Charley showed up at Castle. By then, Carmine had already brewed two pots of coffee. Everyone was in a celebratory mood. They all believed that they had cracked the nut. They now had the location of Jackpot. Furthermore, as best they could tell, not a one of them had been burned.

Carmine laid out the plan. He said, "Great team effort, you all. I'm impressed. It looked and sounded to me like you all had been working together for years. No glitches. Phase 1 is now officially over.

"For immediate followup before you all disappear and crawl into bed, I need everyone to fill out at a Form 22, and put down whatever salient facts or observations you came up with tonight. Whatever you saw or heard. License plate numbers, descriptions of suspects, vehicles, time specific events occurred. Everyone has something that could prove important if we come to an impasse. Share it with the group. Who knows what little thing might rise to significance?

"Also, you can write it in pencil or ink, or better yet, print it if your cursive is illegible. If you can type, go for it. It doesn't matter. We have several typewriters here. Consider Form 22 your classroom notes in preparation for a big test. When you're done, put them in this big, green, cloth-bound, three-ring binder behind the divider with today's date. If you're not certain what to put down, look at what Team Frank wrote regarding their surveillance to Del Rio.

"Next up, Julio, can you get your pictures developed this morning by your lab?"

"Yep. I'll ask for two sets. They'll probably be done by noon. Ask Fred Wendell to check on them. They'll move mountains for him."

"Good deal. Next. I'll get the DEA EST [Electronic Surveillance Team] busy on the pole cams we need. With luck, they'll be up and running by COB [close of business, meaning normal business hours 8 a.m. to 5 p.m.] today. It means they'll also have to set up monitors here for us to do our job. It's not a big tasking for EST so long as someone else doesn't have them doing something the Big Cheese thinks is more important.

"Also, the first day I told everyone to be flexible. We're changing work hours beginning today. Team Frank will now be working 6 a.m. to 4 p.m. Team Charley is now working 4 p.m. to 2 a.m. Both teams may actually work longer than scheduled depending on circumstances. That's because we're shifting gears to Phase 2.

"Once the pole cams are up, we'll be monitoring for dope coming in or going out of Jackpot. We will maintain two, two-man surveillance teams per shift. The duty team will be on a five-minute response. Mostly, we're looking for loads going out. The back-up team will then move up to five-minute response.

"Folks, we need to find out who and where the retailers are. If it looks like it's going to be a long distance haul, we'll scramble both A and B teams.

"Next. Fred will meet with Jezebel sometime today for more information. Also to pay her for last night's tip. If she gets another delivery date, the midnight shift evolves back to Team Charley.

"Guys, I don't know how long Phase 2 will go on. Phase 1 went faster than we imagined. Hopefully, we'll have everything we need in two weeks or so. Now that we have some solid info instead of just stumbling around in the dark like we did the other night to Del Rio, Phase 2 will likely be super active. Lots of hours.

That's what you all signed up for, right? Catch some high value villains. Make a difference. Make a few bucks in overtime. Have some fun, and maybe a little excitement while you're at it.

"One last thing. Don't be shy about switching out cars. If you need more speed or more concealability to blend in, or the seat's uncomfortable, or if you have even the slightest notion you could've been burned, swap out units. That's why we have extras.

"Any questions?"

Crickets. Nary a word. Everyone got down to business before shoving off. Z-time was fast approaching to replace overtime for them all.

Chapter 29

TIME SITS STILL

Wednesday/Saturday June 5/8, 1974

Phase 2 begins. By the time Team Charley returned to duty at 4 o'clock Wednesday afternoon, EST had performed its magic. They had erected a pole camera almost directly across the street from Jackpot at 604 Amarillo Street. They also set up a second one at the corner of Dyer and Amarillo, because that was the most logical exit route from Jackpot. In addition, they set up a third one at the corner of Hope Street and 16th Avenue to pick up the entrance to the Snake Pit, and a fourth one just down from the Taj Mahal at 911 Monarch Street.

Barlow was surprised at just how crisp the black and white CCTV monitors were. Better than he got on his TV in Mosby. Also, they were all backed up by reel-to-reel tape recorders. Now all they had to do was sit down and watch. Wait for the action to come their way.

Carmine put Julio Elias and Casper Leonard on Wednesday's duty team. They would switch responsibilities with Slick and Barlow on Thursday.

Lieutenant Fred Wendell reported that Jezebel did not have any new information. However, if either Woody or Shorty are flush with OHG, one or the other is certain to hook up with her on a date. She would contact Fred as soon as she got more information.

So both teams sat and watched the CCTVs on their respective shifts.

They watched and watched and watched.

Wednesday passed.

Thursday passed.

Friday passed.

Barlow was bored to distraction. He considered having Sarah come spend Saturday night. She couldn't make it because they had a rodeo on Saturday. Next weekend was free. She'd come then if things weren't too hectic. Problem was, there was no way for Barlow to know.

Carmine was worried that Papa was onto them. He started working on a Plan B. His boss, SSA [Supervisory Special Agent] Reed Morrow, told him to relax. Papa wasn't a dime bag distributor. He was a wholesaler. He made fewer sales, but they were all significant. Be patient. Carmine was allowed to get nervous only if they had no action for two weeks, but Reed was certain that would not be the case.

Carmine did not share his concerns with any of the troops, including Fred. It seemed that everyone was beginning to have doubts, but Carmine was the Rock of Gibraltar. He was a soothing presence to all. Even so, everyone was antsy. Nerves were beginning to fray.

Then Saturday rolled around.

Chapter 30

MY CUP RUNNETH OVER - PS 23:5

Saturday, June 8, 1974

On Saturday morning about 9:15, a passel of folks descended upon the Jackpot all at once. Three motor vehicles and six males for certain. It was as if a new ice cream store had just opened up. The CCTV monitor was in black and white, but Team Frank didn't need color to identify Papa's white-over-red Cadillac. They also recognized the Dodge van that they had followed to Del Rio. They did not recognize the Chevrolet Biscayne sedan, but they had read about it on Team Charley's Form 22s. This was the car Team Charley had codenamed Blueballs after they observed it pick up a load of bricks from Woody and Shorty. They could make out Papa for sure, and Chico too, based upon his height and reserved demeanor. They could not positively identity any of the four younger-looking men, other than to say one of them looked a lot like the driver of the van on Monday night. Nevertheless, it was obvious to all present that something important was afoot.

Fred (710) sent his duty team, Amanda Romero (790), driving a black 1973 Trans Am, and Sergeant Elias Boatwright (740), driving a silver 1966 deuce-and-a-quarter, to get set up where they could keep an eye on the intersection at Amarillo and Dyer Streets. Two minutes later, Fred scrambled his backup team with Wayne Barrett (730), driving a blue 1973 Maverick, and Emilio Gomez (760), driving a red-over-white 1972 LeSabre.

Fred was glued to the monitor which was focused on the front of Jackpot. He watched them pull the garage door up. Papa and Sonny walked inside. It was difficult to see what else was inside other than them. Something big. Perhaps a motor vehicle or a large stack of lumber or bricks under a tarp. It would remain an unknown unless they removed the tarp. A thin young man, presumably a mule, pulled the Chevrolet sedan into the garage. The door came down.

Four minutes later, the door went up. The sedan backed out. Another young man climbed into the right front seat. Then the automobile codenamed Blueballs headed towards Dyer Street.

"790 and 740 - Castle. Loaded Chevy sedan headed your way. Let me know when you've got it in sight. Two males in front seat. Car is most likely blue Chevy, codenamed Blueballs. Copy?"

"740 copies. We've got it. Let you know where we're going once we know."

"Castle copies."

Fred dialed Carmine at home while he continued to watch the monitor covering Jackpot. The garage door went up again. The van pulled in and the door came down.

"Valenzuela residence."

"Carmine! Fred here. We've got two vehicles with loads departing Jackpot. Blueballs has already left. The van is in Jackpot probably getting loaded now. I'm all out of troops."

"I'll get Julio and Casper to roll on Blueballs. I'll send Slick and Barlow to catch up with the van. I'll meet you at Castle in ten minutes."

"See ya then."

The garage door went up. The van backed out. Fred couldn't tell if it had a passenger, but he thought so. Otherwise, there was one man unaccounted for.

"760 and 730 - Castle. Van headed your way. Not sure if it has a passenger but think so. Also 720 and 780 have been scrambled to assist you.

"Break. 740 and 790 - Castle. 750 and 770 will be headed your way to assist in a few. Both teams let me know when you all marry up."

"760 copies. What are 720 and 780 driving?"

"760 - Castle. 720 is in a white-over-yellow GMC Jimmy. 780 is in an old blue Caddy."

"760 copies."

"740 - Castle. Before you ask, 750 is driving an olive green 'Vette. 770's driving a black-over-cream Mercury Cyclone."

"740 copies. Blueballs jumped up on I-10 northbound. Probably going to New Mexico. Let you know when we know. 790, can you pick up the eyeball?"

"740 - 790. Roger that."

"Castle - 760. The green Dodge van that I just codenamed Green Mint, is on eastbound I-10 at Trowbridge. Could be headed back to Del Rio."

"760 - 720. I'm up, also eastbound on I-10 just behind you. What are you driving?"

"Red-over-white Buick LeSabre."

"760 - 780. Copy your last. I'm about five miles behind you but closing fast."

"760 copies."

"What's 730 driving?"

"730 here. I've got the eyeball on Green Mint now. I'm driving a blue Maverick."

"790 has the eyeball on Blueballs northbound on I-25. Maybe headed to Las Cruces."

"790 and 740 - 750. Copied your last. I'm about ten miles behind you but I'll be there in a jiffy. Driving an olive green Corvette."

"790 copies."

"790 - 770. Also headed your way. Driving a black-over-cream Mercury Cyclone. I'll try my best not to blow the doors off your Trans Am."

"All units - 700. Team leaders call out to let Castle know when your teams have merged. Castle can likely monitor as far as Las Cruces. After that, we're probably deaf. Ditto to the eastbound teams. We'll probably lose you if you get as far as Van Horn. Team leaders affirm your copy my last transmission. Team Frank first."

"740 copies."

"730 copies."

"750 copies."

"760 copies."

"700 copies all."

There was constant chatter on the radio for as long as Carmine and Fred could monitor from Castle, with simultaneous surveillances going two different directions. Both supervisors were convinced that the teams would carry on just fine without them. At the same time, both were quietly disappointed that they weren't out there having some fun, too.

Fred opined, "Dollar to a doughnut hole the eastbound group goes back to that junkyard in Del Rio, the Compound."

Carmine replied, "No bet. I think you're right."

An hour and change had passed. Castle received a telephone call from Sergeant Julio Elias (750). He reported that Blueballs met a Latino male driving a new Caddy, white landau top over avocado green, at a bodega in the 1600 block of University Avenue. Then the Caddy led Blueballs to a small park at Miners Lane and Central Avenue. They went behind a row of three dumpsters at the rear end of the pavement all the way to what passed for grass. Call it a xeriscape. Amanda (790) parked and took a stroll. She got a brief look at the transfer of several bricks from the trunk of the Biscayne to the trunk of the Coupe de Ville. She described the customer as about 25 years of age, 5-feet, 8-inches tall, medium build, shaggy black hair, wispy mustache, NMSU tee shirt, bell bottom jeans, flip flops, basically a hippy-looking dude. The license plate number on the Caddy is New Mexico 582-662. Nothing distinguishing regarding either of the mules. Both Latino, 20-25, thin, black hair. One was pockmarked with acne. That's all she got. Blueballs departed and is now headed north on US 70 towards Alamogordo.

Fred ran the license plate. It came back on a 1974 Cadillac registered to Luis A. Romero, of 282 Winston Street, # 23, in Las Cruces. Romero was 23 years old, 5-feet, 9-inches tall, 135 pounds, brown eyes, black hair. Fred also ran NCIC and NLETS for a criminal history and wanted checks. No outstanding warrants. Romero had one prior in Las Cruces back in 1970 for misdemeanor possession of marijuana. Paid a $100 fine.

Another hour and a half passed. Castle received a second call from Julio Elias. Blueballs dropped a second load off at a rundown, single-wide, tan-and-white, 60-foot house trailer on a ten-acre ranch on US 54 on the north side of Alamogordo. Address on the mailbox reads 2527 White Sands Boulevard.

The driveway is about 75 yards long. Julio was able to park on the opposite side of the highway under a billboard sign. He had an unobstructed view. He took two, 36-count rolls of color photographs of the transfer using a telephoto lens. The scrawny-ass mules offloaded 25 bricks from the trunk of their sedan. He was able to count it because all three of the bad guys were counting it as they dropped the bricks one-by-one into the buyer's OD green, Army duffle bag.

Purchaser was a large white guy, maybe Latino but looked more like an Anglo, bushy dark hair, full beard, looked about 35-40 years old, big fucker, maybe 6-feet to 6-2, 220-250 pounds, beer belly, jeans, white tee-shirt way too small, and he was strapped with some kind of handgun in a brown holster.

One of the mules - the driver - received an 8-by-11-inch manilla envelope from the purchaser. You could tell the driver was counting the money before he and his partner got back in their ride. The entire transaction took less than ten minutes.

Julio photographed the license plate on a white Ford pickup truck, probably early '60s model, which was parked up near the trailer, so they could check the registration as soon as he got the film developed. Oh yeah. The pickup had a white aluminum topper.

Now Blueballs was headed southbound on US 54, probably back to El Paso.

Fred told Julio that once Blueballs returned to base, probably at the Snake Pit, for them to come back to Castle and start writing their 22s. If there's no further activity, once they're done, they're off for the rest of the weekend.

In fact, that was exactly what transpired.

Several more hours passed. Sergeant Elias' crew had completed their 22s and had long gone adiós amigo. Fred made a chow run for him and Carmine at Mickey D's [McDonalds]. They were anxiously awaiting a call from the eastbound group.

A little after 2, Castle received a call from Slick. He was calling from a payphone at an old Humble service station in Sonora. No problems so far. Looks like the Green Mint was making a return trip to the junkyard. Did Carmine want to give Sheriff Shive a heads up? Also, unless something popped up, would there be any issue if he and Barlow spent the night in Mosby? They could be back by the time afternoon shift rolls around on Sunday.

Carmine said he would call Sheriff Shive and let him know. See if he wanted to set up a couple of discreet surveillance posts. Also let him know you will meet him in the IGA parking lot on US 90 east of the junkyard after the Green Mint departs Del Rio.

Yes. Barlow and he could spend the night in Mosby. Call him before they leave to come back on Sunday. If nothing was shaking, they could delay their return until midnight.

"Roger that. Thanks!"

An hour later, the Green Mint pulled into the Compound owned by Pepe Aguilar, codenamed Lucky. Knowing it was a dead-end, none of the task force surveillance team members followed it down Liberty Street to actually witness the stop. All they witnessed was the Green Mint departing westbound on US 90 past the Dairy Queen. The dirty deed was done. They knew it but didn't witness it. No need to press their luck now and take a chance of getting burned on the way back home.

Wayne Barrett (730) and Emilio Gomez (760) joined Slick and Barlow in the IGA parking lot, where they met Val Verde County Sheriff Will Shive for the first time. He was accompanied by his Narcotics Squad supervisor, Sergeant Herman Walker.

This was an extremely cordial meeting. Sheriff Shive was glad to see both Slick and Barlow again, and to meet Wayne and Emilio. He was pleased to be intimately involved in this major investigation. After greetings and small talk, he said, "Val Verde County is proud to be involved with this task force. We have a cancer growing down here on Liberty Street that we thought was nothing more than an unsightly, benign wart. Thanks to you all, we now know better. I'm sure that together we can excise it.

"Slick, after Carmine's call, I scrambled my best surveillance guys. We were set up more than an hour before the delivery. I had our photographer set up on the roof of the old vacant hardware store across the street. He and his two backup deputies came in from Freeman Street, which is the next street east of Liberty. Nobody had a clue they were there.

"We also had a set of eyes on the back side of Pepe's little empire inside a friendly's house. He couldn't see a helluva lot, but he was there if a problem developed. We also had a couple of clandestine units out here on 90. We videotaped the suspect van go to and from the Compound.

"My photographer says he got some great shots of them offloading furniture from the van before they ever brought out the bricks, which they carried inside the garage. He said it looked like there were 60. Could have been a few more. Then he got the van driver coming out of the garage with a big fat white envelope. They reloaded the furniture, shook hands all around, and the van cut a chogy. He got face shots of everyone involved. We'll get the film developed and mail you all a copy on Monday. I'll give Carmine a call in a little bit, but I wanted each one of you to know that this was a very successful day for all of us."

Slick responded, "Sheriff, could I ask a big favor?"

"Shoot."

"Would it be possible for your man to make us three sets of photographs? We need two copies at the task force. Also, I'm pretty certain Sheriff Sol would like a copy since we still have our murder investigation open, even though it's on hold until the task force case is over.

"Then, the really big ask is if you could send a courier with the photos to the sheriff's office in Mosby. The reason is, Barlow and I got permission to spend the night at home before going back to El Paso on Sunday. That way we could take the pictures with us, and Carmine will have them first thing Monday morning."

"Easy peasy. Consider it done. Anyone else need anything?"

Nobody did, so after goodbyes, everyone went lickety-split to wherever they needed to be. Wayne and Emilio decided to make the long drive home so they would have Sunday with their families.

Barlow made a beeline for home. He knew Sarah would either be there or over at her folks' ranch.

He was fortunate. Sarah had just returned from the ranch as he pulled into the driveway. He didn't have any luggage and all she had with her was Happy, so Barlow scooped her up and carried her into the front door just like he did the day they were married. It was his non-verbal way of saying, "I missed you and I'm ready to knock the bottom out of it right now." This was no time for conversation. It was a time for action.

Sarah couldn't have agreed more. She giggled and gave him a French kiss while he was fooling around trying to insert his key in the front door lock. Maybe that was an unintended simile of what was to come forthwith. There was no time to waste. It was a photo-finish race to see who could get naked first.

Sarah won. Of course, she was only wearing three garments and a pair of sandals. Then she helped peel off the rest of Barlow's clothes like a monkey peeling a banana. After he was picked clean, she dropped to her knees and gobbled his banana to get to its creamy filling. Barlow was too horny, and Sarah was so good at what she was doing, that she won her prize in a minute-and-a-half in spite of Barlow's best efforts to save himself for marriage with her sweet spot.

Yum, yum. Sarah smiled at Barlow.

Barlow had a glazed look on his face when he regained his wits. He was standing naked in the living room next to the front door he had not locked, with a sticky, wet semi-erection. His boots and clothing and gun belt and all of Sarah's garments, meaning dress, bra, panties, and sandals, were scattered on the floor like a madman had burgled the house. Barlow realized he was still wearing his Stetson.

Sarah was stark-butt naked looking finer than he could ever remember, except perhaps in her wedding dress at the alter, even though he had already undressed her in his mind. He looked again. She was smiling and smacking her lips. She was also gently rubbing the sweet spot between her legs. Then she turned around, bent over, and rotated her hips in a slow rhythmic motion. She stood up, looked over her shoulder, and whispered, "My turn, now cowboy. My engine's purring but I need a tune-up. Are you gonna letch at me all day or are you gonna quench my fire?"

Barlow realized his Johnson was swollen again twice its normal size and pulsating so hard it hurt like he was banging it against the sink countertop. He followed Sarah into the bedroom. She lay on her back, legs open wide, sweet spot fully exposed, and tried to pull him down on her, but he resisted. He scooted down between her legs and gave her some face time. Quid pro quo. She said she was in a hurry and didn't have time for that, but fair was fair. Besides, it was titillating for him too. It didn't take very long before she was panting and gushing. The pump was primed, as it were.

Now he had to wait a little bit for her nerve endings to quit pinging before Roscoe could mount her from behind and take them both to Nirvana. Barlow decided to massage her feet. It seemed to work. After a few minutes she said, "Time to mount up, cowboy. I'm ready to rodeo. Let's see if there's any play left in that monster of yours."

Barlow played a little rough with her. She loved it. He rolled her over onto her knees and scootched her gorgeous fanny to the side of the bed. He spread her cheeks and paused to stare. Then Roscoe took over.

Roscoe found her sweet spot and breeched it ever so slowly. He was driving her wild by going so slow. She wanted all of it now! He moseyed along like he was taking a stroll in the park. She wanted more! Her frantic rhythm put him into a slow trot. Not enough! Faster! He broke into a comfortable canter. Better, but still not enough! Finally, with all her witchy woman tricks consuming him, he increased speed and thrust into a full, all-out sprint. The race was on. He had no idea where the finish line was, so he ran and ran until Barlow was gasping for air, and then he ran some more. Barlow had to hold Sarah firmly by her shoulders as he was power-thrusting or he was going to fall off.

Sarah kept encouraging him. "There. There. That's it. Keep it up. Just like that. Faster. Don't Stop. Please don't stop. I'm almost there. Keep going. Yesssss!" Then she squealed and collapsed.

She was done. Barlow was too. He ran to the bathroom and put out a forest fire until his bladder was dry as a bone. He turned out the lights and climbed into bed next to her. He pulled the sheet up around them. The Sandman had already bagged her. Happy was lying on the floor next to him. Before Barlow fell asleep, he realized that he had never spoken a word to her. She had spoken very little except when she was in the throes of ecstasy. Then he fell fast asleep, happy to be back home next to her. Content.

Chapter 31

APPROACHING THE FINISH LINE

Monday, June 10, 1974

Barlow and Slick reported for duty at 3:45 p.m. They both had a fabulous weekend and now they were ready to slay some more dragons. Slick handed the two sets of photographs taken in Del Rio to Carmine, who was in a fabulous mood. He probably got laid. At 4 o'clock when everyone on Team Charley was present with coffee in hand, he addressed the team.

He said, "Listen up everyone. This case is progressing much faster than I had imagined. We've crossed the threshold. We've documented well over a hundred kilos of OHG, though so far the only ones we've put our mitts on are the 60 kilos Quayle County has in their evidence locker.

"We've identified three major buyers. We still don't know the names of Papa's mules, but we will once we enter into Phase 3. That's when we arrest everyone and execute the search warrants. The payoff may be much closer at hand than you think.

"The first of our two blended teams on Saturday identified two new buyers in New Mexico. The first is Luis A. Romero, also known as The Candy Man, which we're using as his codename. He's 23 years old. It appears that he's a major source of weed for the New Mexico State University students in Las Cruces, of which he once was. At least that's the intel the NMSU PD passed along to the Las Cruces PD.

"The second is a real piece of work named Amos B. Coggins, 36 years old, codenamed Grizzly, who resides in Alamogordo. He's a really bad one. Already served nine years in the New Mexico State Prison for voluntary manslaughter. Otero County

SO said he's a known associate of the local branch of the Bandidos Motorcycle Club.

"Then Sheriff Shive in Val Verde County identified Pepe Aguilar, codenamed Lucky, owner of the scrap yard on Liberty Street in Del Rio, codenamed the Compound, and his hired muscle, Igor Sampson, age 39, codenamed Goliath because he's one big, mean, son of a bitch. He had an aggravated assault reduced down to a misdemeanor, for which he only served nine months. Sheriff Shive believes that's largely due to Pepe Aguilar's lawyer's influence. He said the whole thing smells fishy.

"We've got copies of all their photographs and rap sheets in the green files, so make sure you study them.

"My SAC [Special Agent in Charge], Ralph Eaton, has asked me if we couldn't go ahead and move this investigation along like we have an itch which needs to be scratched. Truth is, DEA has some other cases which are getting bogged down and may need some additional help from some or all of us. Don't think that's a good deal even for a minute. Being auxiliaries to someone else's ongoing investigation means we would most likely draw the least desirable assignments. It's always better to work your own cases than someone else's.

"So, this is what we have on our agenda. Right now, the most important thing is for you all turn in your 22s from Saturday's little escapade. I know. You all didn't see much, but maybe you can add more detail regarding the description of the two mules.

"Next, Fred is meeting with Jezebel today to prod her into getting us some more information. We need the next delivery date unless you all want to work permanent midnights for the next week or so.

"This is why. We want to bust Papa when his crew delivers the next load to him at Jackpot. Chico will most likely be there as his bodyguard. Remember, we want Chico's gun. Also, we'll scoop up at least two mules. Once we have everything locked down, we'll get a search warrant for the garage unless we see bricks stored inside in plain sight.

"That's not all. Once the load leaves the Swimming Pool, we'll have a team standing by with members of the Border Patrol Internal Affairs unit to hook up Woody and Shorty.

"But it gets even better. We'll also have someone from our task force in Del Rio for liaison with Sheriff Shive's men. Soon as we secure Jackpot, we'll phone him so he can round up Lucky and Goliath and that crew.

"Ditto for The Candy Man in Las Cruces and Grizzly in Alamo. We'll have a presence at each of these raids, but we'll give the locals all the credit. Spread the wealth. Kudos for everyone. That means even NMSU PD. Everyone gets recognized. Then next time we need something from any of them, or if they get some useful intel, we'll have some steadfast friends with all these agencies.

"So what all this means is right now, beginning today, we need to begin the rudiments to obtain arrest warrants on everyone we can identify, and generic ones for the mules for whom we cannot identify by name yet. That means we need affidavits with particulars sufficient to get a federal judge to sign the warrant. Fred and I'll do Papa's. Barlow, you and Slick can do the honors on Chico unless you all are happy with the warrant you already have. Then we need the rest of you to pick any of the known buyers. Amanda can do Candy Man because she saw him up close and personal. Need someone for Lucky, Goliath, Grizzly, and someone for any of the mules he can identify from the surveillance photos. I know one of them had an acne-scarred face.

"You begin by writing what you know or what we have on file. Go as far as you can. Then we'll add to it as we get more info. All we need is enough to get an arrest warrant signed by the judge. The AUSA [Assistant U.S. Attorney] will draft additional charges for presentation to the Grand Jury before the first preliminary hearing is held.

"All this is the easy part. We also need affidavits to obtain search warrants. Some of you may never have written one. Those who have will tell you it's much easier to get an affidavit approved for a criminal complaint than it is for a search warrant. Fred and I will work on Jackpot. We need affidavits for the Snake Pit, Taj Mahal, the scrapyard, Pepe's house, Grizzly's house, and the Candy Man's house. We need someone to go up there and find it. Take photographs. Also, to be on the safe side, affidavits for each of the motor vehicles we've identified.

"As it relates to buildings, the starting point is the legal location and a detailed description of it. Motor vehicles need descriptions, VINs, license plates, etc.

"Before you all start committing hara-kiri (or seppuku for the samurais out there), I do have some good news. I have copies of 54 affidavits for search warrants we have obtained in the past here in the Western District of Texas, and 16 criminal complaint affidavits. Find one or two to use as a go-by, which is close in similarity to your particular tasking.

"I know some of these affidavits cannot be completed until we do our raids. However, the more information you put down now, the less you will need to do when the pressure is on. That is especially true for search warrants.

"Consider this. Where do you think Papa or Lucky hide their ill-gotten gains? Think they deposit their cash in a bank, or leave it lying around in an unsecured briefcase? Think they store it at work or at home? If it's at home, what information do we have which would convince a judge to sign off on a search warrant for that? Probably be much easier to find Candy Man's cash than it will be Papa's. I can guarantee his is in a safe hidden somewhere.

"Lastly, we are not done running out our surveillances. We'll scramble if we see a load going out, so be prepared.

"Any questions?"

Casper Leonard said, "I have one. Do you have an AUSA on

board who will approve our affidavits before we dash off into the night and lay siege and wage war against the Philistines, otherwise known as federal magistrates?"

"Yes. Actually there are two. Primary is Edwin Cooper. His backup is a newbie named Phyllis Epps, who is extremely good for a rookie. Let me know when you're ready, but I'd like to see it before you show it to them. I might be able to save you some time making corrections. I have their direct lines for when it's time to call them. Anything else?"

"How soon do you imagine we'll see another load come in?"

"It's anyone's guess, but if not this Tuesday through Thursday, then next. We'll be in a hurt locker if it's tomorrow. I have a whole lot of planning and coordination I need to work out first. If you're on good terms with Our Father Above, ask him if He would push it off 'til next week."

Barlow smiled and replied, "Roger that. See what I can do."

"Anyone else? No? Let's get to it.

"Oh yeah. Team Charley is on days this week beginning tomorrow. Team Frank is on afternoons."

Chapter 32

EXPANDING THE CLIENT BASE

Tuesday June 11, 1974

Chico was replacing the brake pads on his favorite of all the shop vehicles, which was the white over orange, 1960 GMC pickup truck. El Jefe walked over to him scratching his head. He was holding an unopened letter in his hand. He asked, "You know anyone in Tucson?"

"Nope."

"How about a J. Nettles?"

"I did some time with a guy named Jay Roscoe Nettles. Everyone called him Roscoe. Seems like he was from Arizona."

"What was he in for?"

"Murder. Same as me."

"Who'd he kill?"

"Some dude in a poker game. Dude cheated him and Roscoe called his hand. Dude jumped up out of his seat and pulled a sheath knife to slice him, but Roscoe bested his hand with a .38 caliber, double-barrel derringer. Two shots to the chest. Dude was a local and Roscoe was an outsider and that was all she wrote. Cops snatched him up and he got 25 years."

"Where'd this happen?"

"Some little one-horse town up in the panhandle in Deaf Smith County. Can't recall the name of the town. Why?"

"Just wondered. Looks like you got a letter from him today in care of Pedro's Auto Repair Shop."

"That's because I wrote him a letter some while back when he was still in the joint. This is the address I gave him. Never heard back and forgot all about it. Guess he's out now."

Pedro handed him the letter. He said, "Better not let your parole officer see this. No consorting with known felons."

"Don't worry."

Chico pulled out his switchblade and slit the envelope open up at the top with surgical precision. Then he sat down on a stack of used tires and read it. It was dated June 8, 1974. It said:

Chico,

Hope you are doing okay. If you get this letter and are interested in catching up, call me at 602-331-7687. This is my sister's number. I'm living at her place for the time being. I'm usually here until 2 o'clock. I have an afternoon job which keeps me busy until midnight most evenings. Take care.

[Signed] Roscoe

Chico memorized the number, folded the letter up, and put it back in the envelope, which he then folded in half and put in the inside pocket of his jean jacket. He put a five-dollar bill in the till and took out the equivalent in nickels, dimes, and quarters. Then he went to the payphone booth outside and called. Cost him 65 cents for three minutes. It rang three times before Roscoe answered.

"Lucy Anderson residence."

"Roscoe, it's me. Got your letter today."

"Hey, buddy, I was hoping you'd call.

"Look, I ran into Elvis Purvis at a tavern called Little Momma's about a week ago. He pulled a heist on a drugstore in El Paso looking for some pharmaceuticals and cash. Apparently the cops jumped him as he was pulling out of the parking lot, but he shook 'em. He thinks they might have copped his license plate, so he's on the lam. He was passing through here on his way to Nevada when I bumped into him.

"That's not really why I wrote you, though. You know a dude they call Hediondo?"

"Yep. I know of him. Piece of shit. Why?"

"You ever do anything to him?"

"Nope."

"You must have. What's the skinny on him?"

"He's in a gang goes by the name Tres Deuces. Let's just say they're in the same import-export business as my El Jefe, only his product is far superior to theirs. Difference between night and day superior. Nobody wants the Tres Deuces shit anymore. We're putting them out of business. Other problem is, we're plowing the same field. They don't like us. We don't like them. What's the connection?"

"Elvis is friends with Hediondo. He told Elvis you whacked a couple of their guys. Said you nearly cut one guy's fucking head off. They put out a contract. They're laying for you."

"That's crazy. I don't know why they're spreading this shit around, although I do know someone offed a couple of their guys a while back. It was on TV. Guess I better keep my eyes peeled if they think it was me. Thanks for the tip, amigo. By the way, isn't Elvis still on parole?"

"Yep. That's why he took a powder. He said if they hang that heist on him he'll be back inside for life."

"Well, okay then. I owe you one. Give me a holler if you ever come to El Paso."

"Will do, but there's one last thing."

Long distance operator breaking in on the call - "Deposit 65 cents for three more minutes please."

Chico inserted the correct change. Then he asked, "What's the other thing?"

"Elvis says your crew has this new wild shit called OHG. That's what Hediondo's group is really after."

"Right you are. Be a cold day in Hell before that would ever happen."

"What about me? Could I get some?"

"Not sure. Maybe. It's pricey. You got the dough?"

"My employer does. What's the price?"

"Well my boss only deals with wholesalers. Minimum

purchase, and I mean the very minimum, is 20 keys."

"What's the rate?"

"A thousand per key for 20 or more."

"We could do that. How long it take to get it?"

"Assuming my boss agrees, by 8 tomorrow night. You do understand it's COD [cash on delivery]? No credit."

"Of course. You all deliver?"

"We do. Where?"

"Where I work - Little Momma's Tavern - 372 East Buckley Street, downtown Tucson."

"I'll meet you sometime tomorrow before 8 o'clock unless my boss nixes the deal. I will call you right back if that's the case. Otherwise, expect to see me when I get there. It goes without saying you'll be in some bad juju if anything upsets the applecart. No fucking around. My boss is a mediaeval kinda guy. Comprendes?"

"I do. Wouldn't expect anything less. Thanks a lot, pal. See you tomorrow, and hey! Keep a watchful eye out for Hediondo and his pals. I'm not blowing smoke about that. Adiós."

Chico went over to the service counter and waited until El Jefe was free. Once he looked up, Chico whispered, "I called Roscoe. Two things. First he told me that the Tres Deuces have a contract out on me. You know why. Second, he wants to purchase 20 keys. I told him $20K, and that I would deliver it personally by 8 tomorrow eve unless you nixed the deal."

"How does he know about the contract?"

"A guy we both know from the joint is buddies with Hediondo. That's how he knows."

"How do you want to handle that?"

"I'll take care of it later this week. I know where their badass jefe, Dogface Ortega, lays his ugly hound dog head at night. It may come unattached somehow. What about the deal in Tucson?"

"Do it. Take Salvador and Jenaro with you. Drive the blue

Chevy. It's so Plain Jane, it's invisible."

"You got it, Boss."

Chapter 33

MORE FUN FOR TEAM CHARLEY

Wednesday, June 12, 1974

At 10:05 Tuesday morning they picked up activity on the monitor zeroed in on Jackpot. Papa showed up in his Caddy. Chico and two mules were right behind him in the Biscayne (Blueballs).

Carmine said, "All right, guys. Saddle up and get on over to Dyer and Amarillo. I'll let you know when they head out. One of you stick with Papa until you see where he goes. Good luck."

Slick said, "I got Papa."

Carmine said, "Good. Casper, find a spot near the I-10 entrance ramp. Julio, don't forget your camera."

"You got it."

"Ditto."

Pretty much the same drill as it was on Saturday. Chico stepped out of Blueballs and opened up one of Jackpot's garage doors. The Chevy followed Papa and Chico, both of whom walked in. Then the door came down. Five minutes later, the door went up and the Chevy backed out. The door came down. Papa locked up. He looked up and down the street. Then he got in the Caddy by himself and backed out. Both cars headed towards Dyer Street.

"All units - Castle. Everyone's moving towards Dyer."

"780 has Papa."

Five minutes later, "Castle - 780. Papa's at the Snake Pit. I'm en route to the convoy."

"780 - Castle. Copy."

"All units - 750. Blueballs westbound on I-10."

At 10:45, Casper radioed, "Castle - 770. We crossed into New Mexico headed towards Deming."

"770 - Castle copies. You're breaking up. Someone call me once you land."

It was smooth sailing all the way. Blueballs maintained the posted speed limit in the right lane. They cruised past Deming. Barlow was out in front. Casper had the eyeball.

At Lordsburg, Barlow dropped off to refuel. Julio picked up the eyeball.

Blueballs continued onto the exit at Willcox, Arizona. They pulled into a Flying J Truck Stop to refuel and gobble up some groceries. Casper refueled too. Then he drove next door the Arby's to grab a bite. Julio found a dumpster at a small grocery across the street with a good vantage point. He took a half roll of photos using a telephoto lens. Then he refueled at a Sunoco station down the street, where he also bought a hotdog and a 7-Up to hold him over until suppertime. Barlow had been in the lead, so he took the next exit at Cochise and bought a couple of tacos and a Barq's root beer while he waited for the convoy to catch up and pass. Actually the tacos were pretty good.

Twenty minutes later the convoy was back on the highway westbound towards Benson. They sailed past Benson towards Tucson, where they took the second exit, which took them to the CBD [central business district]. They made a right onto Buckley Street and pulled into a tavern called Little Momma's. They all went inside.

Barlow and Casper found hidey-holes across the street where they could watch the front door and Blueballs. Julio squared the block and drove into a parking lot with a half-dozen semi-trailers backed in next to a chainlink fence, which marked the rear boundary between the trailer parking lot and the tavern lot. Julio called in his location and said he would be off the air on foot. He parked, grabbed his camera, and found a spot where he could view the back door of the tavern, the alley between it and the business next door, which as he could recall, was a dry cleaners. He squatted down behind some bushes where he could watch without being seen.

He didn't wait long. The back door of the tavern opened and four subject males stepped out. One was Chico, and another was one of the mules. The first unknown subject was maybe 50 years of age, 5-feet, 10-inches tall, 220 pounds, wearing black dress slacks, a long-sleeve, white dress shirt, and a bright white, straw cowboy hat, meaning it was brand new. The second unknown subject was about the same height, 35 years old, 170 pounds, brown hair, Fu Manchu mustache, wearing bluejeans, a short-sleeve, red plaid shirt, and a blue Texas Rangers baseball cap. He had a tattoo of some sort on his left forearm.

A minute later, the other mule drove Blueballs through the alleyway. He pulled around to the tavern and parked nose in. (Perfect!) He got out and walked around to the back of the car and popped the trunk. The other four men joined him.

Chico leaned into the trunk and brought out one brick. He handed it to Cowboy Hat, who pulled out a pocketknife and slit the package. He pulled out a pinch of marijuana and sniffed it. Then he extended his hand and let Ranger Cap smell it. They both grinned.

Cowboy Hat pulled out a white business envelope and handed it to Chico. He opened it and pulled out two packets of currency. He flipped through both. Satisfied, he put the cash back into the envelope and stuffed it into his right, inside denim jacket pocket. Then the mule driver reached in the trunk and handed Ranger Cap two white pillow cases. Then he and the other mule began removing bricks from the trunk. They filled each pillow case with ten kilo bricks.

When the transaction was complete, Cowboy Hat shook hands with Chico, and followed Ranger Cap back into the tavern. Chico and the mules got into Blueballs and drove back through the alleyway to Buckley Street.

Julio had photographed the entire incident. He ran back to his unit, fired it up, and radioed. "All units - 750. I got the whole thing on film. They just sold 20 bricks."

"750 - 780. They're headed back to the interstate. My recommendation is if they're going back home, we let 'em go and break off."

"All units - 750. Agreed. Let me know. I'm catching up."

They followed Blueballs as far as Cochise before they broke off to refuel and eat a sit-down meal at a steakhouse. While they were waiting for their food, Julio called Castle. He spoke with Carmine, passing along everything which had transpired.

Carmine said, "Great news. When we hang up, I'll call the DEA office in Tucson and see what they can turn up on Cowboy Hat, Ranger Cap, and Momma's Tavern.

"I have some good news, too. Jezebel said she hit up Shorty for some OHG. He claimed he was nearly out, but he thought he could score some next Wednesday. He promised to bring her some Wednesday night before he went to work. She asked for a pound and he said not a problem. That means he's expecting a load in the wee hours Wednesday morning.

"Everybody will probably be gone here before you all get back tonight. Tell the boys I said great job. I'll see you all tomorrow morning."

"Roger that. Will do. See ya tomorrow."

The rest of the evening was uneventful.

Chapter 34

PREPPING FOR THE BIG SHINDIG

Thursday/Tuesday, June 13/18, 1974

To say the next six days were frenetic would be an understatement. In spite of all the pre-raid efforts members of the task force had already completed, they still had a mountain of work to finish before midnight leading into Wednesday. Specifically, there were six raids in three states to plan for; seven or perhaps even more search warrants to obtain (if it became necessary to search some motor vehicles without the owner's consent); and, at least 15 criminal complaints (including the accompanying arrest warrants), a number which could quickly increase. The AUSAs were definitely going to earn their keep this week and on into the coming weeks with court appearances and trials, the latter of which are the essence of the criminal justice system in America.

DEA SAC Ralph Eaton, DEA ASAC Brady Carr, AUSA Edwin Cooper, and his back-up, AUSA Phyllis Epps, all insisted on a sit down with the local supervisor who would be in charge at each of the raid sites. They asserted it would be easier if they met with each supervisor separately. The purpose was to ensure that there would be no misunderstanding regarding everyone's responsibilities during the raids, arrests, prisoner transport, interviews, and searches. To assist with that, one DEA special agent would be attached to each group, not to lead it (with the exception of Jackpot), but for liaison and continuity.

In preparation for this three-state criminal roundup, they needed to:

(A) Identify who would be the team leader for each raid site;

(B) Plan for transportation of arrestees, first to a site where they could be interviewed, and then to jail and/or the nearest magistrate. That meant coordinating with the various courts for initial appearances, especially for those arrests not in El Paso;

(C) Assign someone to be responsible for collection and maintenance of all evidence seized, and especially to follow proper chain-of-custody procedures for each site;

(D) Assign a photographer for each site;

(E) Coordinate the timing of the raids (to lessen the possibility that targeted suspects would be tipped off);

(F) Identify the location of the nearest hospital emergency room for each raid site in the event someone got injured;

(G) Assign team members, and identify which local officers (by name) would be utilized at each site. Everyone participating must be accounted for;

(H) Obtain search warrants signed by a federal judge for those sites which needed to be searched; if all the information necessary to complete the affidavit was currently unavailable, prepare the affidavit with everything which was available so last minute details could be added quickly to obtain a warrant. Ditto for arrest warrants.

(I) Identify wrecker services and tow lots for all motor vehicles which would be seized. This would include all vehicles positively identified as having been utilized in the transportation of contraband;

(J) Identify a local locksmith who could open a locked safe in the event it becomes necessary;

(K) Ensure each agency involved in the investigation and/or raids is identified in a joint press release, which would include a representative from each agency, if possible.

(L) Arrest warrants needed to be obtained for these subjects at the following venues:

(1) Unknown Subject Mexican Smuggler, Codenamed Fatso, Fort Hancock;

(2) Border Patrol Agent Bruno Cruz, codenamed Woody, Fort Hancock; Cousin to Armando Cruz, killed by Quayle County SO transporting drugs; Nephew of Diego R. Cruz, burglar, now deceased, who was formerly employed by Pedro Ibarra;

(3) Border Patrol Agent Conrad Turnipseed, codenamed Shorty, Fort Hancock;

(4) Pedro Ibarra, codenamed Papa, primary target, El Paso;

(5) Raphael "Chico" Salazar, codenamed Sonny, secondary target, El Paso;

(6) Unknown Subject Mule #1, aka Acne, El Paso;

(7) Unknown Subject Mule #2, aka Green Sneakers, El Paso;

(8) Unknown Subject Mule #3, aka Muscles, El Paso;

(9) Unknown Subject Mule #4, aka Salvador, El Paso;

(10) Pepe Aguilar, codenamed Lucky, Del Rio;

(11) Igor Sampson, codenamed Goliath, Del Rio;

(12) Unknown Subject Worker #5, Buckteeth, Del Rio;

(13) Unknown Subject Worker #6, Balls Scratcher, Del Rio;

(14) Unknown Subject Worker #7, Schnoz, Del Rio;

(15) Unknown Subject Worker #8, Gimp, Del Rio;

(16) Luis A. Romero, codenamed Candy Man, Las Cruces, NM;

(17) Amos B. Coggins, codenamed Grizzly, Alamogordo, NM;

(18) Jay Roscoe Nettles, codenamed Ranger Cap, Tucson, AZ;

(19) Clinton R. Teeters, codenamed Cowboy Hat, Tucson, AZ.

The aka monickers were decided by studying surveillance photographs taken by Julio and VVCSO, using the most obvious features or characteristics. They hoped to put names on all of them before game day by showing photographs to select informants, narcotics detectives and beat patrolmen. The targets #18 and #19 were identified by DEA SA Homer Skinner from the Tucson DEA office.

Search warrants needed to be obtained for:

(1) Pedro Ibarra's off-site garage, codenamed Jackpot, El Paso;

(2) Pedro's Auto Repair Shop, codenamed the Snake Pit, El

Paso;

(3) Pedro Ibarra's residence, codenamed the Taj Mahal, El Paso; (Already knew the Snake Pit did not have a safe or any cash stored there, so it was probably stashed in his house. Problem is, not enough PC yet to obtain a search warrant. Hope to obtain consent and not need one.)

(4) Pepe's Scrap Metal, Inc., codenamed the Compound, Del Rio;

(5) Luis Romero's apartment, codenamed Candy Land, Las Cruces, NM;

(6) Amos Coggins' house, codenamed Bear Squat, Alamogordo, NM;

(7) Little Momma's Tavern, codenamed the Oasis, Tucson, AZ.

When Carmine called Sheriff Will Shive, he was pumped. This was monumental! Small agencies seldom have the opportunity to work cases of this magnitude. He and his chief deputy, Neil Chase, arrived first thing Thursday morning, being the first remote supervisors to be briefed. Sheriff Shive said he would be the on-site supervisor.

While they were there, they mapped out their raid plan and assisted the two AUSAs in completing a search warrant for the Compound and rough drafting one for Pepe's house. They did the same regarding the complaints for the arrest warrants, identifying the unknown subject workers, numbers 5, 6, 7, and 8 respectively, as Aaron Potts, Buford Smithfield, Roland Winters, and César Cisneros.

They planned to set up at 0600 hours Wednesday morning, and conduct the raid once the shop was open and all the suspects were there. AUSA Edwin Cooper went with them to the U.S. Courthouse to get the warrants signed by U.S. Magistrate Nicholas Delaney. DEA SA David Troy from El Paso was assigned as their liaison.

Lieutenant Bruce Townsend from the Dona Ana Sheriff's

Office and Sergeant Wilfred Gerard from the Las Cruces Police Department came Thursday afternoon. Lieutenant Townsend said he would be the supervisor on site. He said they planned to invite Sergeant Ernesto Delgado from the NMSU PD to participate, since he had provided the narcotics investigators much of the intelligence they had regarding drug trafficking on campus.

Lieutenant Townsend said he didn't expect any trouble from Luis Romero, nor did he believe a search warrant would be necessary. He worked with AUSA Phyllis Epps to write the complaint and arrest warrant.

He said they would set up on Romero's apartment at 0600 Wednesday morning. They would execute the warrant at 0630. DEA SA Mickey Nelson from El Paso was assigned as their liaison. He also took them before U.S. Magistrate Delaney to get the warrants signed.

Captain Giles Drago from the Otero County Sheriff's Office came Friday morning. He said the Alamogordo Police Department would not be involved since Amos Coggins' house was not in the city limits. He said all the local law enforcement officers knew Coggins and that he was bad news all the way around. Captain Drago opined that Coggins would probably not go down without a fight, so they would have the SWAT Team make the arrest. They would set up at 0500 and make the arrest as soon as they saw movement.

Captain Drago also worked with AUSA Epps to write the affidavits for the search warrant and the complaint. DEA SA Miguel Iglesias from El Paso was assigned as their liaison. He also took him before Magistrate Delaney to get the warrants signed.

DEA SA Homer Skinner and Lieutenant Jamison Rogers from the Tucson Police Department came Friday afternoon. They said they would set up on Little Momma's Tavern at 7 o'clock on Wednesday. Normally, nobody's there until 10 o'clock. They did not expect any trouble; nevertheless, they did want a search warrant in addition to the two arrest warrants. They worked with AUSA Phyllis Epps to complete both. SA Skinner and Lieutenant Rogers appeared before Magistrate Delaney to get the warrants signed.

Also on Friday, Lieutenant Fred Wendell, through his narcotics contacts, identified Pedro Ibarra's unknown subject mules numbers 1, 2, 3, and 4 as Salvador Cruz (brother of Armando Cruz, son of Diego Cruz, cousin of Bruno Cruz), Jenaro Herrera, Rodolfo Velásquez, and Tomás Jiménez respectively. Fred and Carmine worked with AUSA Cooper to complete the complaints for the arrest warrants on the mules and Pedro Ibarra.

Then, in an abundance of caution, they decided to obtain a federal arrest warrant for Chico Salazar for trafficking (transporting) Schedule 1 drugs from El Paso to Tucson, even though the state warrant from Quayle County for murder and aggravated assault took precedence. In addition, they completed the affidavit and the search warrant for Ibarra's stash house. (They didn't think they would need one for Ibarra's business, and they still didn't have enough PC for his residence, but at least they had affidavits partially completed with what they did have.) Fred and Carmine appeared before Magistrate Delaney, swore to the affidavits they had, and got the search and arrest warrants all signed.

At close of business Friday, Carmine told Team Charley to sleep late and come in about 10 o'clock Saturday morning. He said he would track them down if they had any movement before then. Likewise, Fred told Team Frank, who made up the afternoon shift, that they could knock off two hours early.

Saturday at noon, SAC Ralph Eaton, ASAC Brady Carr, AUSA Edwin Cooper, AUSA Phyllis Epps, SA Carmine Valenzuela, and Lieutenant Fred Wendell had a command staff meeting in the DEA District Office conference room. They discussed the planning and coordination which was proceeding well, even better than expected.

The flies in the ointment were Agent Bruno Cruz and Agent Conrad Turnipseed. The Border Patrol had not been notified that the Task Force had these bent agents by the shorthairs for conspiracy to smuggle marijuana, a Schedule I drug. Their concern was that the Border Patrol would go off the rails for investigating their employees without their knowledge and participation. Which law enforcement agency wouldn't be incensed?

They had an extensive and at times a heated discussion. A final decision was reached after Ralph put his foot down and said, "Ed, we've beaten this dead horse long enough. The bottom line is, DEA is not the fucking FBI! We do not operate like we're holier than thou.

"I'm well aware of the risk - premature corrective action taken by Border Patrol IA [Internal Affairs] or maybe even a tip-off by another bent Border Patrol Agent. I get it. We've kept the Border Patrol in the dark way too long after we had Cruz and Turnipseed stitched up. If we don't bring them in now, if we wait until the night before the raids, they won't have anything to do with us for years to come, and I couldn't blame them.

"I know their chief, Colonel Patrick Patton, very well. I consider him one of the most honorable, forthright people I have ever known. You all pour yourselves another cup of coffee and wait right here while I make a call. It shouldn't take long."

SAC Eaton went back to his office and shut the door. He called Colonel Patton's house. He hoped he was at home.

Ralph was lucky. Pat had just come in from the golf course.

After the customary greetings, Pat said, "Ralph, I know you've got bad news or you wouldn't have rung me up until Monday - that is, unless you're asking me if I want to go to the baseball game tonight. You know the Diablos [El Paso AA team in the Texas League] are playing at home tonight. Game starts at 7:05. I've already decided to take Junior to go see it.

After a pregnant pause, he asked, "That's not it, is it?"

"Afraid not. I would love to go with you to the game, but I'm a little tied up. I'll check back with you during their next home stand. I should have some free time by then.

"Unfortunately, I'm afraid it is bad news. We're working a pretty significant, multi-state drug smuggling case. Looks like a couple of your guys might be mixed up in it. At least we have some damning evidence. No smoking gun yet."

"Let me guess. Bruno Cruz and Conrad Turnipseed."

"How did you know?"

"Cruz sold a few ounces of weed to a mutt we're looking at for aiding some illegals to sneak across the border. Not a coyote per se, but close. The snitch is a native-born American citizen, but the money was just too tempting and he thought he could get away with it. Unscrupulous, greedy bastard. He's looking at a few years in the federal can. He's trying to reduce his exposure, so he ratted out Cruz.

"Truthfully, it sounded like sour grapes to us, not to say that we're winking at an agent selling weed. An alien smuggler is a much higher value target than an employee selling a dime bag of weed. We do have plans to address it, as in give him the boot, but I didn't think the situation would rise to the level of significance as to obtain federal prosecution.

"So, since Cruz and Turnipseed work together all by themselves, he has to be involved, too. One shits and the other wipes his ass. They're that close. We've been keeping an eye on both of them, but other, bigger fish to fry have popped up since then, plus we aren't giving the snitch a Get-Out-of-Jail-Free card if this is the best he can do. I know this sounds lame when an integrity issue as at stake. Suffice it to say that this matter is still open.

"By the way, you do know that the Border Patrol does not have it's own Internal Affairs [IA] Unit?"

"What? You don't mean the FBI does your house cleaning for

you?"

"It's not quite that bad but almost. The Border Patrol is like the Marine Corps, of which I am intimately familiar, having donated a few pints of blood for them in the name of freedom and democracy during the Korean War.

"The Marine Corps is a branch under the Navy, through whom we must pass to get to DOD [Department of Defense]. The Border Patrol is an organization under the INS [Immigration & Naturalization Service], through whom we must pass to get to DOJ [Department of Justice]. We all have our masters and unfortunately INS is ours. They have some special agents assigned to IA who are more than happy to come dig through our underwear drawers. That's who this case has to be referred to. I know the guy in charge of INS-IA, name of ASAC Andrew Laughton, and most of the time he's a reasonable sort if you can overcome his imperious attitude. Sometimes it's all I can do not to clock him.

"Look, it would be to my advantage to notify him myself and have him contact someone in authority in your shop. That way if he gets a few kudos for ferreting out a couple of turds, he owes me for the referral. Can you give me any details?"

"Hey, no problem. I get it. We got our crosses to bear, too. That's a great idea. Besides, if ASAC Laughton stubs his toe, he'll have the U.S. Attorney crawling up his rear end so far he'll have to cough to get him out.

"This is the deal. We have photographs of Cruz and Turnipseed letting a known smuggler enter with a truckload of weed, as in dozens of bricks. We think another load is coming in during their midnight shift early Wednesday morning. If it does, once they accept their 30 pieces of silver, in the form of a brick or two, and the load is on it's way, we plan to arrest the Mexican mule after he offloads it to the American mules a few miles away from the border. The plan is to do this very quietly.

"We'll have a team following the load to the stash house.

While that's ongoing, the plan is to follow up immediately with the arrests of Cruz and Turnipseed. You'll need to be prepared to staff their vacancies right away.

"We'll insert INS-IA into our task force, and they will nominally make the arrests of Cruz and Turnipseed. We'll be overall in charge of the busts and the prisoner interviews at a site of our choosing. When that's over, INS-IA can perform their due diligence and transport all three of them to the federal lockup. No fucking immigration shelter for the Mexican mule. That's off the table. He'll help us with information regarding his jefe, or he will never see the light of day again. Even if he does puke up his guts, he's still getting a nice long vacation in one of BOP's [Bureau of Prisons] stellar criminal housing facilities. After his serve-out, INS can send him on his merry way back across the border with our blessing and gratitude.

"Like I said, we plan to follow the load and make several more busts Wednesday during daylight, east from Del Rio to all the way west to Tucson. From that perspective, Cruz and Turnipseed are pissants in the grand scheme of things, except they tarnished their badges and got paid in bricks of marijuana to let some major loads come across the border unhindered.

"If you would, send a couple of the best INS-IA agents over to our task force crib Monday morning about 9 o'clock, and we'll loop them in. They can sign the affidavits for the complaints, and they will be the two agents responsible for making the arrests on Cruz and Turnipseed. We'll assign someone from the task force who's intimately knowledgeable about the case to participate in the off-site interviews before turning them over to the Marshals Service.

"Later in the day, after we've completed all our raids, I will make a press release. The Border Patrol and INS-IA will be included in our list of participating agencies. How does that sound to you?"

"Like you'll be turning lemons into lemonade for the Border

Patrol."

"That's what friends do."

"Who do the INS-IA special agents contact?"

"DEA SA Carmine Valenzuela at 551-3768. That's a back door number at our off-site building, which is an old warehouse we call Castle. It's located at 226 Leon Street. Tell them to be prepared to go to work as soon as they report Monday morning. There's a lot of pre-raid planning we still need to do."

"Will do. Thanks Ralph. Don't forget about going to a ballgame next home stand."

"Copy that. See ya soon. Adiós."

SAC Eaton returned to the conference room and filled everyone in with the agreement between himself and Colonel Patton.

They moved on to naming specific task force and DEA personnel for each assignment. The list was extensive, and even after speaking to the local team leaders, there were still some question marks. At least they had a couple more days to fill in all the names.

At this time, noteworthy assignments included:

(1) Lieutenant Fred Wendell and DEA SA Monica Donaldson would man Castle. (2) Carmine and the rest of Team Charley, minus Sergeant Julio Elias, would conduct the raid on Jackpot, to be timed as soon as the mules arrived with the shipment and both Papa and Sonny were there. Initially, Carmine suggested sending Slick to help out Sheriff Shive in Del Rio, but Slick said he and Barlow were partners and they wanted to be on the same raid team. In that Chico was expected to be at Jackpot and he was Quayle County's primary interest, Slick was granted his wish;

(3) DEA SA David Troy and Detective Wayne Barrett were assigned to the Del Rio raid;

(4) DEA SA Miguel Iglesias and Sergeant Elvis Boatwright were assigned to the Alamogordo raid;

(5) DEA SA Mickey Nelson and Patrolwoman Amanda

Romero were assigned to the Las Cruces raid;

(6) DEA SA Homer Skinner and Emilio Gomez were assigned to the Tucson raid;

(7) DEA SA David Richman and El Paso PD detectives (not identified at this point) were assigned to the raid on Snake Pit;

(8) Sergeant Julio Elias and a TBD Border Patrol supervisor were assigned to arrest Fatso in Fort Hancock in a marked unit to give the Border Patrol a presence in the arrests;

(9) DEA SA Isaac Alexander would be assigned with the INS-IA SAs on the Cruz/Turnipseed interviews. He was specifically given this assignment because he was a muscular, 6-feet, 6-inch, pale-complected Anglo, almost an albino, with pale blond hair and pale blue eyes, who spoke flawless Mexican, and who exuded intimidation without the necessity of speaking. His primary mission was to dissuade the INS-IA SAs from deviating from the agreed-upon plan by his very presence.

At 3:30 the command confabulation broke up. The big cheeses departed. Carmine and Fred went back to work. Carmine called ESU and cut a work order for them to install pole cams Monday morning to cover the U.S. border crossing at Fort Hancock, and at the vacant car wash nearby where the drug transfer took place.

Sunday was spent ironing out more details. Monday was more of the same. Details! Details! Details!

Then Tuesday morning they were alerted regarding a huge fly in the ointment. It could wreck everything.

Chapter 35

UNEXPECTED TURN OF EVENTS

Tuesday, June 18, 1974

Monday night. Chico had waited long enough. Today was Dogface's Day of Reckoning.

Dogface wasn't his real name. That's just what Chico called him because he looked like Augie Doggie or Doggie Daddy [from the 1960s cartoon show *Quick Draw McGraw*].

His real name was Paco Sánchez. He was a 30-year-old piece of shit who was the nominal jefe of the Tres Deuces. Nominal because he was a pussy in a crew of even weaker pussies. They thought they were bad, and they were bad compared to a 4th Grade Sunday School class. Compared to real men though, they were weak - all pussies. Tonight they would find out just how weak they were with a cold, harsh dose of reality. Tonight Chico was the Grim Reaper. It was high time for them to scramble and find sanctuary up under the couch with the other cowardly chihuahuas indigenous to this neighborhood.

Dogface was responsible for the contract on Chico that Hediondo had been flapping his gums about. Dogface put word out on the street because nobody in the Tres Deuces had the balls to try and fulfill it. They all knew they'd die a painful death if Chico found out they even considered it.

Chico knew where to find Dogface without his posse or any witnesses. He lived by himself in his deceased mother's house at 611 Patience Street. He considered himself a major league swordsman. He had a string of six ugly skanks, of which for three of them he was the baby daddy. He screwed each one on the very same night, every Monday through Saturday. It was a rotation, just like starting pitchers for a baseball team. They all lived within a quarter-mile of his house.

It was well-known that Dogface had this phobia about sleeping anywhere except in his own bed, all by himself; therefore, he satisfied himself with each woman in her own pad. When he was sated from screwing or too drunk to get it up again, he walked home alone. He packed a short-barreled Colt .38 Detective Special revolver everywhere he went, and he thought that made him invincible.

On Monday nights he screwed a chubby 20-year-old chica named Rosemarie Leone. She used her mother's maiden name because she didn't know who her own daddy was. Chico knew where Rosemarie lived. So at 11 o'clock Monday night, he put on some raggedy jeans, a navy blue tee shirt, and his worn out sneakers. He stuffed the .45 inside his waistband, pulled his shirttail down over it, and strolled down the street. He avoided areas where people were out and about as best he could. It wasn't very hard because this was bedtime in a poor, residential neighborhood.

He concealed himself underneath a worn-out Chevy Nova, parked in the front yard of a dark house situated across the street from Dogface's digs. (Chico knew the elderly residents, owners of the car, and that they kept early hours. By now, they would already have finished counting sheep, and be snoring up a storm.)

He lay on his stomach and waited patiently. An hour later, his bladder started nagging him that it was about burst. Naturally, this was when Dogface made his appearance from the alleyway down the street, staggering his way home. He entered his house through the front door, obviously locked because he fumbled around with a key (which he dropped twice) to get it open. Took him three minutes. The time was 1:30.

Chico waited another hour, just to be safe. All the while his bladder was screaming bloody murder. Finally, he crawled out from under the car and watered the left front tire until his bladder was bone dry and singing like a canary in ecstasy. Not a drop left. Put a huge divot in the sand. More like an arroyo. It was the most gratifying piss he had ever taken. The relief was instantaneous and almost orgasmic. This ought to drive the stray mutts crazy when they wander along to mark their territory!

On the off-chance someone might be an insomniac and was looking out the window, he walked down the block and squared it. He came up Virtue Street, and cut through an alley until he was one house down from Dogface's. He hopped a short chainlink fence into and then out of the next-door neighbor's backyard. He crept up to an open window in the kitchen of Dogface's house, and listened. Not a sound.

He took the screen out and placed it up against the wall. Then he climbed inside the window, right over the sink. He eased himself down silently and listened some more. Before he even left the kitchen to check down the hallway to the bedrooms, he heard peaceful, rhythmic snoring. He reached in his hip pocket for his switchblade. Then he had better idea. He tiptoed back to the kitchen counter and pulled the biggest knife out of a butcher block of knives. It had a huge triangular blade about ten inches long. The blade was well-sharpened. Perfect!

He crept down the hallway and looked into the bedroom where he heard the snoring. Dogface was lying face up on top of the sheets, stark buck naked. His clothes had been dumped in a stinky pile on the floor. His revolver and wallet were on top of the bureau, next to his keys and a pocketknife.

Chico took one of the pillows and placed it over Dogface's face and pushed down hard. He started to rouse, and then Chico used the kitchen knife to slice his throat from ear to ear. The pillow soaked up the blood, which was gushing like a broken water main. Dogface kicked once and stopped. Chico could hear gurgling noises, and then they stopped, too.

Chico took the knife into the bathroom and washed it off. He dried it and put it on the bed next to the corpse, careful not to leave any fingerprints. Then he retraced his steps down the hallway to the kitchen. He closed the kitchen window and set the latch. He opened the backdoor, which only had a doorknob lock. He reset the lock, used his handkerchief to wipe off any fingerprints, stepped out into the backyard, and quietly pulled the door shut. He replaced the window screen, and took a different route back to his apartment.

Back home, in an abundance of caution, he stripped off naked, putting his clothes and shoes into a plastic trash bag. He showered off, and put on some clean clothes. He took the sack containing his bloodstained clothes and sneakers, and soaked them in gasoline. He placed them in the 55-gallon barrel which they used to burn the combustible trash. It was nearly half full. Then he lit it, using the charred broomstick leaning against the wall to sift through the debris as it burned, making sure nothing was left unconsumed.

Then he placed his weaponry in his black canvas gym bag, along with his extra ammo and cleaning kit, and stashed it in his top secret hidey-hole. It was under the trapdoor in the wooden junk shed on the property next door with the vacant house, all of which was owned by Pedro, but titled to his cousin, the 76-year-old slayer of ovine rustlers, none other than Señor Mario Ortez.

Chico knew the heat would be out in force once Dogface's body was discovered. He also knew the Tres Deuces would blame him, but he didn't think they'd be stupid enough to finger him to the fuzz. That's why he killed Dogface with his own blade. Confuse the cops.

He probably should have stolen something to make it look like a robbery, except he didn't want anything which belonged to that dickwad. However, just in case the Tres Deuces fingered him, he didn't want to be caught holding his switchblade or gun. If he needed a weapon right away, he'd just have to use Pedro's shotgun under the service desk. He'd shot it before, and it worked just fine.

He crawled into bed. It was almost 5 o'clock.

Wait and see. He knew he didn't leave a trace of evidence. He slept like a baby.

Chapter 36

WHAT NOW?

Tuesday, June 18, 1974

Carmine returned to Castle at 0630. Nobody was there. He was bone-tired. Too much work and not enough sleep. One leads from the front. That's one of the tenets of leadership. Everything was coming to a head. Tonight was the big night. He told himself he could sleep late Thursday morning, but he knew that was a fantasy. There would be more fires to put out, more dragons to slay, until this case was finally closed with all the headaches of judicial action completed, as in the legal maneuvering by both prosecution and defense, court hearings, trials, and sentencings.

He went to work, making his day's to-do list. It was lengthy. Then the phone rang. The time was 0735.

"Castle. Carmine speaking."

"Carmine, it's Fred. Just got some news. Could be real bad for us."

"Tell me."

"Just got a call from Captain Roland Epperson, in charge of EPPD Robbery/Homicide. It seems that they found the jefe of the Tres Deuces in his bed with his throat cut ear to ear. Name is Paco Sánchez. A fucking lightweight, but a still nuisance, like a pesky fly. Doesn't appear that anything was stolen.

"You may recall back around the end of May, two gangbangers belonging to the Tres Deuces were found murdered behind Gustavo's Cantina down by the river. One was Sucio Estrada. He was stabbed multiple times in the heart. The other was Reno Cisneros. Had his throat cut ear to ear, same as Paco.

Happened in broad daylight in the middle of the week. No leads. No witnesses. Everyone working narcotics thought this could be the beginning of a drug war over turf, but it really wasn't.

"Then a day or two later someone did a drive-by at Ibarra's business while he was making a press release in front of St. Rita's. No one hurt. No substantial leads. It was believed to be in retaliation by the Tres Deuces for the death of the two gangbangers. If it was, it was lame. Remember, at that time we knew next to nothing about Ibarra and his Hope Street Boys.

"Now this looks like it could possibly be a payback from Pedro Ibarra by Chico Salazar. Of course, it could have been a private vendetta by someone else. No one knows."

"Who found the body?"

"One of the Deuces named Jorge Liberto, 17-years-old. Went to check on Sánchez about 6:30 this morning because he didn't show up at their clubhouse for a meeting, translated to mean he was supposed to give them some weed so they could go to work."

"Any leads in the house?"

"Nope. Both doors locked. Windows all shut and fastened. No fingerprints. Killed with his own knife taken from a butcher block in the kitchen. Real professional job. No contraband in the house except for Paco's revolver. He was a convicted felon. House wasn't tossed. That's also why Captain Epperson wants to go roust Chico. At least he had the courtesy to call me first. He knows we got something going on."

"Does he have any evidence, anything other than his hunch?"

"Nope. Just plans to shake the trees. See what happens."

"Are you friends with Epperson?"

"Oh, Hell yeah. Solid guy."

"Fred, could you read him in on tonight's big summer soirée? Let him know EPPD has guys working on this; that we've already got a murder warrant for Chico. Swear him to secrecy. Tell him we owe him big time?"

"Roger that. I think he'll play ball with us."

"What about Chico? Think he's at work today?"

"Not sure. Probably. You know Ibarra won't make a move tonight without Chico by his side."

"I do. See if Epperson will give us some breathing room. Then meet me back at Castle. I'll start scanning the video footage at the Snake Pit from last night through early this morning to see if I can pick up footage of Chico coming or going. I'd feel a whole lot more comfortable if I knew if Chico was there. You know, as in not having taken a powder."

"Gotcha. See you in a little bit."

By the time Fred arrived, Carmine had located the CCTV footage with Chico coming and going. He documented the times. Once the bust was over, codenamed Operation Snake Pit, he would get a copy of the film footage for Captain Epperson. It would certainly beef up his hunch.

Sergeant Elvis Boatwright, Wayne Barrett, Emilio Gomez, and Amanda Romeros were all excused today to travel to their out-of-town raid sites. Sergeant Julio Elias was meeting with his Border Patrol counterpart. Slick, Barlow, and Casper Leonard were cleaning their guns, calling their loved ones, working crossword puzzles, or otherwise twiddling their thumbs. At lunchtime Carmine bade them adieu. He said he would meet them at the Petro Truck Stop in Fabens at 11 o'clock.

They all departed at peace with the world. Casper went home. Slick and Barlow had a steak dinner at Cowboy Oscar's Texas Emporium & Saloon. They both knew they'd be eating junk food until Operation Snake Pit was over. Then they went back to their rooms and crashed. Neither one of them slept as well as Chico.

Chapter 37

CLEANING OUT THE SNAKE PIT

Wednesday, June 19, 1974

Phase 3. All of Team Charley met at the Petro Truck Stop in Fabens an hour before midnight. While they were there, Captain Alonzo Alvarez, U.S. Border Patrol, driving a marked Border Patrol unit, teamed up with Julio Elias. He would stick like glue to Captain Alvarez until all three border suspects had been thoroughly interviewed and processed. The reason being, nobody on the task force really trusted the INS-IA personnel, nor did Captain Alonzo nor Colonel Patton.

ASAC Andrew Laughton from INS-IA, began the evening riding with Carmine. SA Candace Knopf, also INS-IA, did likewise with Barlow. The INS-IA agents had stashed their unmarked unit, a shiny new, black, 1974 Ford LTD, four-door sedan, in Fort Hancock for use after the transfer of marijuana from Fatso to Papa's mules. (Had they not ridden with task force agents, they would have been clueless with respect to what was going on, especially since they did not have access to the task force radio channel.)

The plan was for Captain Alvarez and Julio to arrest Fatso first, just as soon as Papa's mules were out of sight. That would be the catalyst for the arrests of Woody and Shorty by the INS-IA agents, with an assist by Casper Leonard and Barlow, both of whom would break off after the suspects were cuffed and stuffed. Then they would beat feet to join the mobile surveillance of Papa's transport team.

It's dicey arresting an armed law enforcement officer. If he's dirty and feels trapped, he will likely break bad and do whatever it takes to escape. That's why Barlow was put on this particular assignment by Carmine. He knew Barlow would not hesitate to drop the hammer on Woody or Shorty if it became necessary. Carmine didn't have much faith in the INS-IA agents, both of whom were unknowns. Probably fold like a pair of cheap suits at the first indication of trouble.

Success depended upon coordination and cooperation by all parties. This was the most critical portion of Phase 3 and they were shorthanded. Of course! So what else was new? It seems to be the nature of law enforcement. Alas! So much, done by so few with so little, on behalf of the apathetic and the ungrateful, but primarily intended to benefit the Silent Majority.

They set up in their usual locations by 11:50. Shorty arrived first, followed by Woody. Julio took some extremely long range photographs with his biggest telephoto lens, especially of the two border guards on the Mexican side. Maybe someday they'd come in useful.

Time passed agonizingly slow, just like the flow of the somnolent Rio Grande in summertime.

Barlow's INS-IA partner was much different than he had expected. Quiet. Polite. Asked intelligent questions. Feminine - not a feminazi. No chip on her shoulder. Eager to contribute to the overall objective. Easy on the eyes. She was 27 years old, engaged to a Border Patrol agent whom she met during her initial law enforcement training. Her original posting was to have been in San Diego. She accepted an assignment to Internal Affairs in order to reside in El Paso where he was posted.

Finally! At 2:47, Fatso showed up in his faded, vintage, Elsie the Cow milk truck at the Mexican border checkpoint, dressed as dapper as always. Not! Dressed more like the guy who services your septic tank. Smoking a stale, five-cent, King Edward cigar or something equally as awful. Greetings were exchanged, as well as a brown paper grocery sack which appeared to be about half full. From there, he proceeded a hundred yards to the U.S.

border checkpoint, where the same ritual took place. Woody and Shorty returned to their little office, and Fatso proceeded to the old vacant car wash a couple of miles away. Two of Papa's mules were already standing by for delivery in their mint green Dodge van, codenamed the Green Mint.

All hands were in place, watching from various vantage points, like vultures hovering over a mortally run-over 'possum or some other varmint as it putrefied and blossomed into noxious carrion for fine vulture dining.

Not everyone could see everything. Julio snapped dozens of photographs while 120 bricks were transferred from Fatso's truck to the van. In return, Fatso was handed an overstuffed, white business envelope. He peeked inside. It was bulging with 12 straps of 100, $100 Federal Reserve Notes. He smiled and returned to his truck. El Jefe would be pleased. Fatso turned the truck around to return to the border checkpoint from whence he came. By then, the Green Mint was just an afterthought in his simple mind. It had already vanished, headed lickety-split back towards I-10. Slick picked up the tail all by his lonesome. He was fine with that. Slick knew what he was doing.

When the Green Mint was no longer visible, Captain Alvarez and Julio quietly slipped in behind Elsie the Cow in the marked unit. Captain Alvarez flipped the toggle switch under the dashboard, illuminating the nighttime darkness with the roof-mounted, "gum-ball machine" [oscillating light in a blue glass globe. It featured the brightest aircraft landing lightbulb on the market at that time]. The brilliant blue, flashing strobe light was mesmerizing, especially in the eerie nighttime silence of the desolate desert. Nobody around "in these here parts" to witness this traffic stop, except maybe an insomniac jackrabbit or a pair of copulating lizards.

Fatso made haste to pull the milk truck over on the shoulder of the road. He knew he wasn't speeding, and that his lights and horn and all other accessories were operational. His licensing and insurance papers were all in order, too. Therefore, he assumed this was just a routine stop by a bored Border Patrol Agent with nothing better to do. So be it. He stepped out of the truck, already searching his wallet to retrieve his driver's license. He'd driven back and forth across the border in Elsie the Cow maybe a hundred times. Never a problem. Nothing to worry about. Besides, he was in no hurry. Just a minor aggravation. It was all good. Nevertheless, he still had a nervous smile on his face to demonstrate he was peaceful and eager to please.

Julio beat Captain Alvarez out of the cruiser. He aimed his cocked Government Model Colt .45 at Fatso's huge, round, hairy tummy, peeking out where the bottom button of his shirt was missing. Fatso nearly melted with fright into the sandy, cracked macadam. He surrendered peacefully, eyes as big as dinner plates, but not a second before he soaked his baggy trousers. From the look of things, he had to go really bad. Julio stepped carefully around the colossal man-made puddle surrounding Fatso when he cuffed him behind the back.

Captain Alvarez opened Elsie the Cow's passenger door. The envelope with the $120,000 payout was lying on the front seat next to Fatso's half-eaten, jumbo-size, Milky Way candy bar and the remainder of his sack lunch. No weapons in the cab. Not even a crowbar.

An EPSO wrecker which was on standby, hooked up Elsie the Cow and followed Captain Alvarez' marked unit to the EPSO substation in Fabens. This intensified Fatso's anxiety tenfold. Now he realized he wasn't going to the INS catch-and-release compound.

"Oh, chihuahua!" Now all was revealed. He was seriously screwed! "Mother of God!"

In the interim, Carmine and Barlow dropped off the INS-IA agents at their unmarked Ford sedan. Carmine split as quickly as he could to catch up with Slick, who was still by himself tailing the Green Mint. The INS-IA agents, with Casper and Barlow close behind, made a beeline to the U.S. Border Patrol checkpoint.

Woody and Shorty stepped out of the office to check on the suspiciously unmarked IA car and its occupants. Everything smelled like the FBI to them. No longer bored, Woody took a last draw on his Old Gold cigarette and tossed it away. Shorty stepped out scratching his balls like he had poison ivy and a bad case of the crabs. At the same time, Casper and Barlow stepped out of their vehicles and walked up towards the "INS-IA-mobile" parked up by the guard shack. Shorty unhanded his itchy balls and headed over towards them, scowling and directing them to return to their vehicles. At this moment, ASAC Laughton and SA Knopf decided to exit their vehicle.

Before Shorty got six feet, Barlow and Casper drew their firearms and told him he was under arrest. Shorty had been nipping out of a half-pint bottle of Jim Beam he had in his hip pocket, plus he had already finished his first one, so he wasn't as sharp a tack as he thought he was. Nevertheless, he quickly cogitated what two large caliber handguns pointed in his direction could do to him from this distance, and he came close to voiding his bowels. The weakest, tiniest bit of flatulence would have set forth an eruption like a septic Old Faithful in Yellowstone. Shorty realized the deck was stacked against him, so he quickly thrust his arms high in the air like he was singing Leonard Cohen's *Hallelujah* with the Mormon Tabernacle Choir. Casper cuffed him behind the back and retrieved his service revolver, while Barlow kept a bead on his 10-ring.

Monkey see - monkey do. Pete and Repeat. The two INS-IA agents drew and aimed their service revolvers at Woody, shouting in concert like it had been rehearsed, "INS Internal Affairs! You're under arrest, Cruz!"

Woody took pause, his lizard brain telling him to go for it, but he had waited a tad too long. He had elevated his gun hand up to his waist to draw his holstered revolver, but he saw the intensity of SA Knopf's glare and realized she was a half-second from sending him straight to perdition. He raised both his hands slowly, halfway up, similar to football goal uprights, and capitulated. Then he ripped a gross, raucous, toxic fart. It reverberated like thunder. He had murder in his eyes. ASAC Laughton cuffed him, seized his revolver with his left thumb and forefinger like it was a writhing rattlesnake, and led him by the arm back to the guard shack. He said, "Step inside, you filthy, slimy, double-crossing weasel. I own your worthless ass now."

Casper led Shorty back to the office with Barlow following, and they all went inside. The grocery sack with four kilos of OHG was sitting on the countertop, almost winking at them. SA Knopf replaced Casper's handcuffs with her own and returned Casper's to him. ASAC Laughton looked over at Casper and Barlow with a smug little smirk on his face like his balls were all swole up and he'd been the big cheese in control all along. You know - the icy cold, lord-to-peasant stare. He coughed lightly into his closed fist to clear the frog in his throat and said, "We got it now, June Bug. You all are free go about on your merry way. Toodle-oo, boys."

Just then, two marked Border Patrol units with absolutely perfect timing pulled up and parked. Lieutenant Colonel Maxwell Grimes and three patrolmen stepped out. They marched straight into the office like an honor guard. Lieutenant Colonel Grimes had the appearance of a high-ranking Marine Corps drill instructor. He fixed a hairy eyeball on both of the busted, corrupt agents like they were a pair of broke-dick dogs. Shorty had a hang-dog look to match, but Woody more closely resembled a rabid pit bull. Either way, each perp was experiencing his worst fucking nightmare, and it wasn't going to fade away when he woke up. If Woody's look could kill, Lieutenant Colonel Grimes would have been fried like a man-size pork rind at a rodeo barbeque.

Lieutenant Colonel Grimes growled, "You two assholes really disgust me." He ripped the badges off their shirts and laid them on the desk next to the dope. Then he took out a pocketknife and cut the threads stitched around their shoulder patches. He ripped them off, too. He placed them in the ashtray on the desk. He pulled a can of lighter fluid out of his pocket and soaked both patches. Then he lit 'em up and watched until they were completely consumed. He followed up by spitting on the residue, nominally to ensure the fire was out, but mainly to express his contempt even further. All eyes were focused on him in disbelief, except for Barlow, who smiled. He thought, "Well done!"

Afterwards, a border patrolman relieved the shamed agents of their gun belts. The other two patrolmen gave Woody and Shorty a thorough search, minus the body cavity examination. At least there was that minor accommodation extended to their vanity, although the patrolmen might've thought they'd get farted or shit upon by this pair of assholes.

Casper said, "Boys . . . and girl, it's been a real slice of life. The Lone Ranger and I got somewhere else we need to be. Dragons to slay. Damsels to save. Kudos to you all. Adiós."

Barlow followed up. He said, "Candace, it was nice working with you. Good luck. You too, AN-DREW," drawing out his given name to demonstrate contempt for his pompous attitude and close resemblance to a supercilious shoe clerk in a pricey department store. "Maybe we'll see you all around someday. Bye."

Then Barlow and Casper skedaddled to catch up with Carmine and Slick.

So far, so good.

Casper got on the horn. "Castle and 700 - 770. Come in. All is well regarding Woody and Shorty. No problems. 720 and I are scrambling to catch up with the motorcade."

"Castle copies."

"700 copies. We're on I-10 three or four miles west of the Fort Hancock entrance ramp. 720, you take the eyeball once you catch up. 770, see if you can get out ahead of us about a half-mile."

"720 copies."

"770 copies."

"Castle - 700. Any activity at Jackpot yet?"

"Negative, 700. Will let you know as soon as we see something."

"10-4, Castle. 710, could you take that beater you're driving and take up a position on the far side of Jackpot in the event Papa and Sonny open up before we get there? If that happens, we'll follow the load right in behind it before they can close the garage door. We need that door open. If it comes down to that, the shit will hit the fan the moment we arrive, so be prepared."

"710 copies, and en route to Jackpot. Monica is assuming command in Castle now."

"700 copies. 720 - 700. Before we get to the Dyer Street exit ramp, I need you to get out ahead with that jalopy you're driving, and set up down the street past Jackpot somewhere near 710. Be ready, but try to be invisible. Copy?"

"720 copies."

The next 30 minutes were uneventful.

Barlow goosed it a mile before the Dyer Street exit. He shagged ass to Amarillo Street. En route, he called, "Castle - 720. Any activity at Jackpot yet?"

"Negative, 720."

"720 -710."

"Go ahead, 710."

"Go towards the end of the street to the next intersection at Haycroft and make a U-B [U-turn]. You'll pass me on your way. I'm parked behind a light-colored, 50s model Chevy pickup with a load of used tires. I've got a clear line-of-site [aided significantly by a streetlight which illuminated the front of the garage. The garage security lights had not been turned on tonight for some unknown reason.] Pull in behind me and cut your engine. Copy?"

"720 copies."

"Castle and all units - 700. We're exiting I-10 at Dyer. We

should be at Amarillo in two more minutes."

"All units - Castle. Still no activity at Jackpot."

"All units - 700. Green Mint turning onto Amarillo now. 770, 780, and I will not follow. Repeat. We will not follow. We'll take up positions here on Dyer."

"Castle copies."

"All units - 710. I've got the eyeball. Green Mint just arrived at Jackpot. So far the suspects have not exited the vehicle."

"Castle copies."

"700, 770, and 780 copy."

Ten minutes passed. It was 4:15. The pre-dawn was just starting to break.

"All units - Castle. Papa pulled out of the Taj Mahal. Stand by."

"All units - Castle. Papa arrived at the Snake Pit. Stand by."

"All units - Castle. Sonny just got in the car with Papa. They're backing out."

"All units - 700. Hold your positions. 710, as soon as Papa arrives and someone gets out to unlock the garage door, sing out. We'll be on our way Code 2. [Full speed with lights and siren optional.] You and 720 wait for us unless they get the door open before we arrive. Then proceed with all caution."

"710 copies."

"720 copies."

"All units - 700. Papa just pulled down Amarillo."

"All units - 710. They just arrived at Jackpot. Stand by. Sonny got out of the car. Looks like he's going to unlock the door. 720 and I are moving in on foot. We'll be off the air. We'll try to wait for you."

Fred and Barlow opened and closed their car doors softly, hardly making a sound. None of the perps seemed to be paying attention. They were engaged in mindless pursuits to include sitting in a vehicle, standing around, stretching, smoking, chatting, or essentially just waiting, all typical activities, while

Sonny fiddled around trying to unlock the door. They all seemed to be at ease. No rush. No worries. Just another day at the office. Nothing to see here, Boss.

Mule #1, the one in the passenger seat wearing a cowboy hat, got out of the Green Mint and stepped over to speak with Papa, who was still behind the wheel of the Caddy. He had rolled down the driver's window while he smoked, and waited impatiently. He was a little irritated. It seemed to him like it was taking an awful long time to open the fucking lock. He wanted to get this over with so he and Chico could go over to Toby's Diner on 21st Street and have some breakfast. For some reason, he was especially hungry this morning.

Shortly after Mule #1 got out of the Green Mint, the driver, Mule #2, who was bare-headed, followed suit. He stretched, trying to work out the kinks. Then he lit up a Mexican cheroot and took a long, satisfying drag. He blew out a smoke ring.

Maybe another minute passed. Sonny finally unlocked the massive padlock on the industrial grade, galvanized steel hasp securing the garage door. It had been a long and painful episode of fumbling around, searching for the right key from a ring too full of keys in the dim light. The keyhole was acting up, too. Had a hard time inserting the key. That pussy could have benefitted from a little lubrication first.

He bent over and grabbed one of the handles on the door to start pulling it up. Fred and Barlow observed all of this. They continued to creep as quietly as they could up towards the garage, crouched down, taking advantage of whatever was available for concealment, to include the Green Mint itself and some extra dark shadows. They had drawn their revolvers as soon as they unassed their vehicles. Fred was carrying a Smith & Wesson Model 36, Chief Special, which was a 5-shot, .38 caliber, snub-nose revolver. Barlow was carrying his Smith & Wesson, Military & Police Model 58, .41 Magnum revolver with a 4-inch bull barrel.

Suddenly the peace and tranquility of the night was shattered by the raucous noise of motor vehicles with souped-up engines accelerating rapidly to red-line RPMs.

Carmine and Casper came screaming up the street, one-two in that order, sounding like a pair of teen-age drag racers on a Saturday night. The very best thing which had been going well for the arresting officers had been the element of surprise. Now it was prematurely lost before they could get the drop on the perps, the idea being to preempt a gunfight. Now all suspect faces except for Papa were staring in the direction of the approaching, racing vehicles, wondering "What's with these two assholes? Don't they know people are trying to sleep?"

Then they noticed the flashing blue lights concealed in the grills of both offending automobiles. Mule #1 yelled, "Cops!"

Concealed handguns were quickly drawn by all concerned except for Papa, who, besides being annoyed at the racket, was just too cool to be bothered. This is why he hired Chico, his sociopathic problem-solver. Papa left his fancy, nickel-plated, Smith & Wesson Model 19 Combat Magnum, .357 caliber revolver with a 4-inch barrel, rosewood target grips, and adjustable white outline rear target sight blade and red ramp front sight, laying inert in his glove box. Even now, when he should have prepared for combat or taken a powder, as in fight or flight, his muddled thinking was to let Chico and the boys deal with the problem, assuming they actually had one. Just because these were speeding, unmarked cop cars headed in his direction, didn't mean they were coming here specifically to bug him.

Except that it did! Everyone but Papa could see that.

Carmine and Casper screeched to a skidding halt in front of Jackpot's two-lane, gravel driveway where all the criminal activity was unobtrusively afoot. The dramatic entrances by Carmine and Casper were noble from the perspective of police back-up responding quickly to another cop's life-threatening emergency; however, it was an extremely bad idea tactically. Too late now. The damage was done. Besides losing the element of surprise, they put themselves directly in harm's way. Carmine and Casper bailed out of their units, using them for cover, both rolling out the driver's door on the far side of the garage, away from the armed dope suspects.

About 20 seconds later, while the suspects were still busy gawking at the unwanted new arrivals, Slick cruised by ever so slow, a distant third in his old Caddy. He rolled past Carmine and Casper very sedately, and parked three car-lengths away, up the street in a tow away zone in front of a fire hydrant. The bad guys didn't pay him any mind because he was quiet, and he didn't have flashing blue lights. Duh! Slick eased out of the Caddy, straightened his Stetson, and took his old sweet time, sauntering back towards the imminent gunfight. His .45 Long Colt Peacemaker with its 6-inch barrel was firmly in hand. Wyatt Earp would have been proud of Slick's panache.

Chico and the two mules reacted quickly and decisively to the screeching cop cars. Both mules swept the area with their Smith & Wesson, Military & Police Model 10, .38 caliber revolvers with 4-inch barrels, loaded with six rounds of hot, Super Vel hollow-point ammo. Their necks were on a swivel, looking to acquire a despicable cop target. Show off. Flex a little. Impress El Jefe, Señor Ibarra, with their magnificent combat prowess, if only a contemptible law dog would pop up and show his ugly mug. How come they haven't started shooting yet? The mules thought they had it all covered. Stitched up tight. They convinced themselves that they were badass gunslingers, and that they were in absolute control, masters of their neighborhood.

Chico was far more competent than these two wannabes and much more reserved. He knew if he waxed a cop he'd have to flee to Mexico, at least until the heat cooled off. Maybe forever. He hoped that fleeing would not be necessary. El Paso was his home. He pulled the Colt .45 caliber, Government Model, semi-automatic pistol out from his waistband. He released the safety and pulled the hammer from half-cock to full cock. He had seven rounds in the magazine, plus one in the pipe. All were ready to reap death and destruction if need be on whomever he selected. He was deadly and he knew it from past experience. Not like these arrogant pups with him.

Up until this time, nobody had noticed Fred or Barlow, hidden in the shadows behind the Green Mint, and now Slick was on the scene. Everyone present on each side was hardwired for a lethal fight except for Papa, who believed his employees had everything under control, and all he had to do was lay back and reap the benefits. Besides, he could disavow all of them if he had to. After all, who would deign to point an accusing finger at an upstanding, Latino businessman, one who contributes thousands of dollars to the church and other charities every year, a stellar benefactor of the community, not to mention an extremely handsome icon such as himself?

Exasperated, and in the absence of cowering police targets Chico had yet to see, Carmine's car caught his interest. Tired of waiting and ready to get the ball rolling, he fired three times in rapid succession through the front passenger window, all of which passed through the driver's window, shattering both, and spraying glass shards everywhere. Chico did not consider this an effort at a kill-shot. Just a wake up call.

Fortunately, Carmine had rolled out of his ride a couple of seconds before. He could not see his adversary from his current position, lying on his side and looking out from under the chassis of his car. His Browning Hi-Power, 9-millimeter, semi-automatic pistol was of no use to him until he could lay eyes on the assailant. Damn!

Casper was using his car for cover just like Carmine, except he was kneeling and popping his head up over the hood ever so often to see if he could acquire a target. He was carrying a nickel-plated Colt Python, .357 Magnum with a 4-inch barrel. It really pissed him off that he scuffed the toe on one of his highly-polished, Tony Lama boots, and got both knees of his dress slacks dirty. Probably ruined them. Bastards!

Barlow was laser-focused on Chico. As soon as he popped three caps in Carmine's direction, he became fair game. Barlow put two rounds rapid-fire into his chest, before pivoting right and putting two rounds into the chest of Mule #1, whom he caught in the corner of his eye, aiming his revolver straight at him for what reason? To invite him to come to his birthday party? Doubtful. Nevertheless, Mule #1 was a shade too late in pulling the trigger and it cost him his life. Both he and Chico lay bleeding out in the gravel driveway, deader than brothers Frank and Tom McLaury [shot dead in the gunfight outside C.S. Fly's photography studio near the OK Corral in Tombstone, Arizona in 1881, by Wyatt Earp and Doc Holliday, respectively].

Almost simultaneously, Mule #2, the driver of the Green Mint, sent three Super Vel hollow-points whizzing past Barlow, but he missed two feet wide right, nearly hitting Fred instead. Barlow fired his last two rounds into Mule #2's chest, but it turned out to be unnecessary. Slick shot him twice in the chest too, a split-second before Barlow, and Fred added three more rounds in concert with Barlow. Mule #2 had more holes in him than a round of Swiss cheese. He fell to the ground, almost on top of Mule #1.

Papa was an evil man, but not a get-your-hands-dirty type of fighter, at least not anymore. He spazzed in place today. He completely misread the situation. He hadn't killed anyone since World War II, and they were all kraut soldiers trying to kill him. He had the Purple Hearts to prove it. Those kills were all sanctioned by the international rules of combat in war. Nowadays, he told his employees to kill someone and they did the killing for him. Of course, that was illegal - murder, in fact - but way cleaner for him. Harder to prove.

He had been invincible with Chico by his side, but now his junkyard mastiff was dead. Tits up. No longer of any use. Ditto for Rodolfo and Tomás, all three killed before his eyes in a matter of seconds. How could that possibly be? Papa's mind froze up, not knowing what to do. Belatedly, he retrieved his Smith & Wesson revolver from the glovebox. It was up to him now if he wanted to live and avoid a lifetime in prison. He decided to flee.

Papa revved up the engine, and backed his Caddy into Carmine's car as hard as he could, nearly shoving it on top of Carmine, who just did manage find shelter behind the Green Mint. The collision was necessary for Papa to move the car out of his way. Nobody got hurt. He cut his wheels sharp to turn right to escape, clipping Casper as he went and knocking him down. It bruised his left hip substantially, also injuring his pride significantly, but otherwise did no permanent damage. It did render him momentarily out of commission as he was getting up and feeling his injured parts. He limped away from the Caddy as quickly as a gimp can go. To Papa, this was nothing more than collateral damage. Casper shouldn't have gotten in his way. So what? No big deal.

Then Fate played its hand. The Caddy stalled out. Wouldn't start. Who knows why? It had never failed him in the past. Papa bailed out in a blind rage, shiny nickel-plated revolver in hand. He was livid about this turn of events. He had over a half-million in OHG in the back of the van, and these pigs were trying to take it away from him and throw him in a fucking dungeon! Fuck them! They would pay dearly!

Papa zeroed in on, and charged at the nearest, most exposed target, who just happened to be Casper, currently in gimp mode, and feeling some serious pain. He had already re-holstered his revolver. Right now he was focused on finding some cover. Then he would fight, soon as he could lean up against a stable platform.

Papa fully extended his shooting (right) arm. He aimed at Casper to finish him off, stepping closer and closer so as not to miss.

Fred was kneeling down, using the Green Mint for cover. Having dumped his three empties, he was trying to reload his revolver with three fresh rounds, but his hands were shaking and he kept dropping them. His fingers would not fully cooperate in this time of intense stress.

Barlow had quickly reloaded six more cartridges from his speed-loader. [A speed-loader is a hard plastic, half-inch tall cylinder, the same diameter as the revolver's cylinder, with charge holes spaced exactly the same as the revolver's. It secures six unfired, rimmed cartridges, which are inserted bottom down, nose up, and locked in place by twisting the little aluminum knob on the bottom. The user reloads an empty revolver by inserting the secured cartridges in the speed-loader, nose first into the cylinder. He twists the little aluminum knob on the base of the speed-loader to release the cartridges into the charge holes. He slams the cylinder shut, now fully loaded, and ready to commence firing. It only takes a second or two to reload using a speed-loader.]

Barlow and Slick both walked out to face Papa, hoping to grab his attention before he shot Casper. Slick yelled, "Look at me you shithead! You're under arrest."

That enraged Papa even more. He spun around to see his antagonist. He had two. They looked almost alike, as in wild west sheriffs with Wyatt Earp mustaches. One was younger and taller. The other was older and shorter. Both were holding unholstered revolvers down by their sides. They were only ten yards away, standing two yards apart.

Papa forgot all about Casper and refocused on them. He didn't like two-to-one odds, but the pup was probably too young to have much experience. Papa had had all he was gonna take. He wasn't thinking clearly. If he had to kill them to keep his OHG and drive away, so be it. If they got him first, that's the way the cookie crumbles. Either way he was not going to jail.

He squared up like the gunfighters on TV and tried to stare

them down. Neither one flinched. Then the pig he almost ran down with his Caddy stepped out from behind the van holding his gun down by his leg. At least he wasn't close enough to be a serious threat.

Carmine continued walking closer. He yelled, "Put it down, Ibarra. This is a lose-lose situation for you. You can't win."

That was the final tipping point. It was now or never. Papa raised and fired all six rounds at Slick as fast as he could pull the trigger. He turned out to be the world's shittiest shot. He missed each time, although the first round did come close. Slick reciprocated by firing his last three rounds rapid fire into Papa's torso. At the very same time, Barlow finished Papa off with one round right between the eyes. He fell two feet backwards, face up, with a loud thud.

Pedro Ibarra was no more. Now he was a footnote in the history of El Paso criminals. Besides that, he was so disfigured even his mother wouldn't recognize him. His brothers-in-law would have to insist on a closed casket wake.

The Gunfight at the Old Carlos Speedy Taxi Garage in El Paso was over. It lasted less than 90 seconds with 27 total shots fired. All four villains were dead, but there was no time to pause for reflection.

Carmine took charge. He gathered the task force agents and said, "Guys, I apologize to every one of you. I didn't expect this level of ferocity from Papa or his cohorts, perhaps with the exception of Chico. What an incredible display of derring-do you all put on! I haven't seen anything like this since I returned home from Vietnam. Then looking over at Slick and Barlow, he added, "Okay. I admit it. You all did warn me.

"I need to call Castle pretty quick to get EPPD Homicide and EPSO Internal Affairs out here. Ditto for SAC Eaton, but first we need to search the van and the garage for contraband. We gotta find the dope or surely we'll be tarred and feathered. Soon as we do find it, make a count but leave everything intact. It's all got to be photographed, but that won't be done by us. CSI [Crime Scene Investigations] will do that.

"Casper, how are you feeling? Want me to call EMS?"

"No. I'm pretty sure I don't have any broken bones. I can hobble around. I'll stop by the ER later on for some X-rays. Since I'm on City Homicide, I think I can be of greater assistance here than at the ER."

"You know IA won't let you participate."

"Yeah, but I can watch and make sure my guys don't miss something important."

"Okay. Look, we all know each one of these shootings was righteous, but Fred, you, Slick, and Barlow are on ice until IA clears you. Wouldn't surprise me if DEA put me on ice, too, being it was my fandango. Soon as we find the dope, you three head on back to Castle. Your cars are not part of the crime scene. Start on your statements, but get the identities of the two mules before you do go.

"Anybody want FOP [Fraternal Order of Police] or PBA [Police Benevolent Association] counsel before talking to IA?"

Slick asked, "You're kidding, right? We don't have any such animal in Quayle County. Too small. Even if we did, our stories would still be the same. Barlow and I done been through this Monday morning quarterbacking more than once. All law enforcement shootings are presented to the Grand Jury over there, and yet here we are. Still on the job getting paid to enforce the law."

Fred interjected, "I know these IA guys personally. I'd be real surprised if any of them would be looking for a scalp in this case."

Carmine said, "Very well, but if any of you smell a rat, shut the fuck up. Tell them you want to speak to an attorney first. Then come see me. Slick, you and Barlow would be wise to tell Sheriff Sol what happened before you answer any questions or put anything on paper. Capice?"

Barlow replied, "Roger that."

"Okay. Let's find the dope and get the names of the two unnamed perps. Then I'll make the call to Castle. Then you three get the flock out of here. Casper and I will stay behind and protect the crime scene."

It didn't take long. They confirmed 120 kilos in the Green Mint and 82 in the hearse parked in the garage. The two mules were Rodolfo Velásquez and Tomás Jiménez. Velásquez had been the passenger. Jiménez had been the driver.

Fred, Slick, and Barlow returned to Castle.

Their excitement was over. The adrenaline was subsiding, but the satisfaction of taking out Rafael "Chico" Salazar and Pedro Ibarra would linger for a long time.

Carmine's grueling work and extensive planning had just shifted into overdrive. It's the price one pays for assuming the mantle of leadership.

Chapter 38

RESULTS OF THE OTHER RAIDS

Wednesday, June 19, 1974

Carmine radioed Castle. He said, "Castle - 700. Prepare to copy."

"Go ahead, 700."

"Jackpot is secure. We found the stash. We have four dead suspects. All task force officers assigned to this raid are okay. Need you to call EPPD and request uniform assistance to secure the scene sooner rather than later. It could get ugly here in this neighborhood if they don't arrive soon. Also ask them to send Homicide and CSI.

"Then call EPSO and request they send their IA team. Call SAC Eaton and ask him to respond, too. This will probably be on the morning news, and I'm sure he will want to be here.

"Call the County Coroner's Office and ask them to come out. We could also use an EMS unit, Code 1.

"Just you know, 710, 720, and 780 are returning to Castle to write some reports. They are sidelined as of now. 700 and 770 will remain here on site.

"Oh yeah. Tell SA David Richman and his crew to report here ASAP before they go to the Snake Pit. That's very important. Also, are any other DEA personnel free to take on an assignment?"

"I can call ASAC Brady Carr at the main office. He's the only gun-toter left without a specific assignment."

"Would you contact him and see if he could come out here? We need at least one more body for a delicate, but critical assignment."

"Stand by while I call him at home."

"Roger that."

Five minutes later, "700 - Castle. ASAC Carr will meet you at Jackpot in 20 minutes."

"Roger that, Castle. I will be off the air attending to some other, urgent matters."

"Castle copies, 700."

Fred, Slick, and Barlow all rolled in to Castle at the same time a few minutes later. It was a little after 5 o'clock. Once they were in, Slick called Sheriff Sol at home and woke him up.

"Pratt residence."

"Sheriff, it's Slick. Barlow's listening in on a second line."

"This is early. Are both you all okay?"

"Barlow, Sheriff. We're both fine."

"Your raid already over?"

Slick replied, "Yep, for close to an hour now. Barlow and I done shot and killed Chico, Pedro Ibarra, and two mules named Rodolfo Velásquez and Tomás Jiménez. We had some assistance on Tomás Jiménez by Lieutenant Fred Wendell, EPSO. All them jaybirds opened up on us first, or tried to. Barlow and me was just a little faster on the draw than the other guys we was working with, which is why we smoked 'em all. We also recovered 202 kilos of OHG.

"Right now the three of us are on ice. We're at the task force building to write our statements and presumably to be interviewed by EPSO Internal Affairs. So far as we know, the other raids in Del Rio, Las Cruces, Alamogordo, and Tucson have not taken place yet."

Sheriff Sol asked. "Agent Valenzuela or anyone else who was there have any doubts about the shoot?"

Barlow replied, "No. Carmine called 'em all righteous. Can't say for sure but I think he's glad Chico and Pedro are both buzzard food now."

Slick jumped in, "Carmine's good with it, Sheriff. We're just waiting to see what the higher-ups think."

"Either of you expecting any blowback?"

"Nope."

"Okay then. If you encounter any fact-finder who acts like he doesn't see these as clean shoots, clam up and give me a call. In the meantime, I'll call Sheriff Brady at home."

Slick replied, "Good deal. If Sheriff Brady's line is busy it's probably because Lieutenant Wendell is bending his ear."

"Good to know that. Look. I'm glad you're both okay. One of you jaspers call me before you knock off for the day."

Barlow responded, "You got it, Sheriff. Thanks. Adiós."

"Adiós, fellas."

* * * * * * * *

It was a hectic, busy day.

At 7:15, Castle received a call from SA Mickey Nelson regarding the Luis A. Romero raid in Las Cruces. He surrendered peacefully. They recovered 14 bricks and 46 dime bags [one-ounce each] of OHG.

Five minutes later, SA Isaac Alexander called. He said Fatso's real name was Geraldo T. Flores, age 50, originally from Oaxaca, Mexico. Started out as a field hand and driver for a warlord named Mateo Estrada on his 2,000-acre marijuana plantation. Mateo is the younger brother of the powerful drug kingpin Victor Estrada. Estrada is a very prominent family name in Mexico. Apparently the Estradas are well-connected with all the right public officials in Oaxaca as well as in Mexico City.

Four years ago, Flores was an intrastate transporter, moving product from Oaxaca to Juárez. The jefe in Juárez, a wholesale distributor named Rico Castillo, also happens to be a first cousin to Victor and Mateo Estrada. Flores showed some skill smuggling weed across the border into the U.S., so now he's assigned to work for Rico. Flores coughed up his background information because he's a scared rabbit. He's terrified that he could already be marked for execution because he hasn't returned to Rico with the $120,000 payment from Pedro Ibarra. He's refused to testify because that would be a death sentence for certain. He begged for solitary confinement, and that's where he is right now in the El Paso County lockup.

SA Alexander also reported that Bruno Cruz was not cooperating. Conrad Turnipseed was, but he doesn't know much. He knows Bruno and Flores, and he knows of Pedro Ibarra. He knows Bruno is connected to Pedro Ibarra through his uncle, Diego Cruz (deceased), cousin Armando Cruz (deceased), and Salvador Cruz, Armando's brother, who is also one of Ibarra's mules. Both Bruno Cruz and Conrad Turnipseed were placed in solitary confinement because they were law enforcement.

Sergeant Julio Elias and he (SA Alexander) would return to Castle shortly. One last thing: ASAC Laughton is one treacherous son of a bitch in case the rest of the DEA agents didn't know it.

At 7:45, SA Miguel Iglesias reported in from Alamogordo, much earlier than the command had expected. He said Amos B. Coggins spotted the SWAT team moving in on him just before dawn. He broke out a glass panel next to his front door by firing through it with a Marlin lever-action .30-30 carbine. The SWAT team lit him up through the wooden front door and glass. They counted 19 bullet holes in his body.

Coggins was wearing a belt holster with a Smith & Wesson Model 28 Highway Patrolman .357 Magnum revolver. They also found a partial box of .357 ammo and a full box of .30-30s on a table next to his body, which is one reason why they believe he was prepared to go down shooting. Also, the Otero County Sheriff's Office was investigating a drug-related shooting from the night before, and Coggins was their number one suspect. Ergo, they believe that's ultimately what precipitated the gunfight. They searched his property and found five bricks of OHG and 225 dime bags.

At 8:15, SA David Richman and three EPPD detectives

brought in Salvador Cruz and Jenaro Herrera in from the Snake Pit. They were Ibarra's final two surviving mules. They were arrested unarmed without a fight, unwitting that El Jefe and the rest of their gang were dead. They also weren't talking. SA Richman and the detectives departed shortly thereafter with their catch to lodge them in the county jail.

About 9 o'clock, Sheriff Will Shive phoned in. They had been expecting a call from SA David Troy, but Sheriff Shive said he wanted to do the honors. First, he reported that there were no law enforcement injuries from the raid; however, their roof-mounted sniper shot Igor Sampson between the eyes as soon as the task force team started to move in. Igor fired on one of the deputies, but met his demise before he could do any real damage. He's a mess now, but no uglier than he was before. He was armed with a Winchester 12-gauge pump shotgun. The shot he let go with went through the side of one of their marked units as the deputy was driving up. Fortunately, he was unscathed.

The primary reason Sheriff Shive wanted to make the call is that he's the one who shot Pepe Aguilar. Pepe stepped out of the garage firing two shots from that fancy nickel-plated revolver with the turquoise grips that he always wore. He shot one of the deputies in the chest, and he would have been a goner; however, using his own money, he bought a 2nd Chance bulletproof vest two weeks ago and it saved his life today. He definitely got a 2nd chance. Now Sheriff Shive is going to try to get the county to buy a vest for each of his men.

Sheriff Shive was armed with one of the SO's Remington Model 870, 12-gauge pump shotguns. As soon as he saw his deputy go down, he fired a load of double-aught buck at Pepe from ten feet away, hitting him the groin. It tore him up really bad, but they had an EMS unit standing by, and the medics saved him from bleeding out. The good news for him was that the femoral artery wasn't ruptured; however, his manhood and reproductive organs were eviscerated, unable to be salvaged.

He's at the hospital under heavy sedation. He may wish he were dead once he comes to. Sheriff Shive didn't know what the doctors could do to fix it so Aguilar could urinate. Probably have to pee through a tube. His sex life was certainly over unless he becomes a hind catcher for a perv. Will said it was the first time he ever shot somebody in his 14 years on the job.

They also arrested four of Aguilar's workers, including Aaron Potts, Buford Smithfield, Roland Winters, and César Cisneros. Winters was the only one who went for a gun but he dropped it as soon as he saw Sampson bite the dust. They recovered 13 OHG bricks and 31 dime bags.

It was almost noon when they heard from SA Homer Skinner in Tucson. They arrested Jay Roscoe Nettles and Clinton R. Teeters without incident. They recovered 17 bricks and 12 dime bags of OHG.

Altogether, including the four bricks seized from Cruz and Turnipseed, the raids netted 254 kilos in bricks and 8.9 kilos in dime bags. Including Quayle County's seizure of 60 kilos, the total seizure was a little over 320 kilos.

In addition SAC Eaton and ASAC Carr interviewed Pedro Ibarra's wife, Ruby, at home. They had recovered the written combination to Pedro's safe from his wallet. Typical numbers for a lady's man. They were 36-24-36. How could he ever forget that? Maybe he wrote them down for her in the event of his demise.

They knocked on her front door. She answered it in a dressing gown, robe, and slippers. They identified themselves, and said they had a warrant to arrest Pedro for trafficking in drugs. She choked, cleared her throat, and replied that was crazy because he didn't have anything to do with drugs. He ran an auto repair shop for a living. She said he was not at home at present.

SAC Eaton asked, and she responded that they could come in to see for themselves that he was not there, so they entered into the front parlor. They made a cursory search looking for other bad actors and confirmed there were none.

ASAC Carr asked Ruby if they had a safe. Ruby replied that yes, they had a safe in their bedroom, but she didn't have the combination. Pedro handled all of their business concerns.

SAC Eaton asked if she would show them the safe. She said of course, and led them into the bedroom. The safe was located on the floor in their joint bedroom closet on his side. It was fairly small and not bolted into the floor.

ASAC Carr asked if she would sign a waiver for them to search it.

She did. Then she watched while they unlocked it. In addition to documents which did not pertain to the case, they found a ledger which itemized all drug related transactions. They also found three zippered bank deposit pouches. They were filled with $100 Federal Reserve Notes - $370,000 in all.

She almost fainted in disbelief! She said she had no idea. She asked, "Where did all that money come from?" Neither agent responded.

Then she said she needed to call him. He was probably at work. He left really early this morning. He does that sometimes. That's when they told her that he had been killed in a shootout with law enforcement officers at a garage on Amarillo Street earlier this morning. Then she collapsed.

After she gained her composure, they waited while she called her older brother, Alfredo Martínez. She was sobbing uncontrollably. Between waves of near nausea, she told Alfredo what she had been told. He said he would be right over. He told her to ask the officers to wait for him. They agreed.

In the interim, ASAC Carr gave Ruby a receipt for the ledger and the money they seized. When Alfredo Martínez and his wife, Anna, arrived, SAC Eaton explained the nature of the warrant for Pedro, and what they had seized from the safe. Then he and ASAC Carr departed for Castle.

* * * * * * * *

The rest of the day was just as busy as the wee hours of the morning. Fred, Slick, and Barlow were all interviewed by EPSO-IA Sergeant Ronald Atkins and Detective Einar Humboldt. The interviews were straightforward with no curveballs or gotcha questions. Sergeant Atkins said he would present his findings to the Grand Jury Friday morning. He didn't expect any glitches, but he needed Slick and Barlow to remain in town until after the Grand Jury rendered its verdict. He said he would call them at Castle as soon as he received it.

Carmine took time out from all his harried aftermath headaches to tell Slick and Barlow how much he appreciated everything they had done while they were here. He cut them loose at 2 o'clock, right after they turned in their Form 22s regarding the surveillance and their formal statements regarding the shooting incident. Carmine said he knew they were anxious to return back to their homes and he fully understood. He told them to come back at 10 o'clock tomorrow morning to help wrap up.

Barlow said, "Slick and I talked about it. We're going to stop by the Gulf service station on Hancock tomorrow morning to get both of your vehicles topped off, serviced, and washed. We want to return them in as good of shape as they were in when we picked them up. If we're a few minutes late, that's why."

Carmine responded, "I wish we had an entire office like you two. By the way, tomorrow at COB we're all going to eat supper and have an adult beverage or two at Pancho Villa's Cantina. Beers are on me. Put it on your schedule. See you all tomorrow."

SAC Eaton made his press release live on the 5 o'clock news. He did what he said he would do. He gave all the participating agencies full credit for the arrests and seizures. He commended without naming, all the brave officers who were involved in the arrests, and he praised the valor of those who were compelled to use deadly force when their lives or the lives of others were in peril. He said they were a credit to American law enforcement officers everywhere.

Thousands watched it on television, including Sarah and her family, Sheriff Sol, and everyone associated with the Quayle County Sheriff's Office. It was bittersweet for Sheriff Sol. Everyone in Quayle County who watched it swelled up with pride. Slick and Barlow were a credit to everyone in Quayle County, even though they weren't specifically named as members of the task force.

Chapter 39

WHEN THE WHEELS FALL OFF

Friday, June 21, 1974

At 10:10, Sergeant Atkins popped into Castle to shake the hands of Slick and Barlow. He said the Grand Jury voted unanimously that "the untimely deaths of Pedro Ibarra, Rafael "Chico" Salazar, Rodolfo Velásquez, and Tomás Jiménez were brought on by their own felonious deeds when they attempted to slay law enforcement officers in the pursuit of their official duty." Sergeant Atkins said he was proud to have made their acquaintances, and he hoped to see them again someday.

SAC Eaton, ASAC Carr, SA Valenzuela, and the other members of the task force gathered around to wish the Quayle County contingent well and to bid them adieu. As they were leaving, SAC Eaton pulled Barlow aside for a private tête-à-tête. He said, "Barlow, I got a call from Chief Deputy U.S. Marshal Wilbur Enright just a few minutes ago. He asked me to tell you he wants you to stop by his office this morning before you return to Mosby. He's on the first floor of the U.S. Court House. It's located at 511 East San Antonio Avenue, downtown. You know where it is?"

"I do. Am I in trouble?"

"No. I can't see why. The Grand Jury just cleared you and Slick. He didn't give me a reason, but were I you, I wouldn't keep the man waiting. Besides being a swell guy, he's a good man to know if you're in law enforcement in West Texas. He's close with all the federal judges."

"Gotcha. I'm on my way. Just wanted to say once again, I really enjoyed my time here on the task force. I learned so much.

It truly opened my eyes."

"Barlow, we were fortunate to have you and Slick both. Look me up if there's ever anything I can do for either of you."

"Thanks very much. Adiós."

"Happy trails."

Barlow caught up with Slick and told him he had one last assignment to do before he headed home. He said he would see him on Monday.

Slick replied, "You better hurry up Avenger of the Innocents or you'll be late for supper."

Barlow made a beeline for the U.S. Court House. He found a row of parking spaces reserved for law enforcement officers. He pulled Jade into the empty slot at the end of the row. He stepped inside the building and hurried to the Marshal's office. The receptionist did not keep him waiting. She escorted him to a large office with an external brass nameplate which read, *Wilbur A. Enright - Chief Deputy U.S. Marshal*. The door was open, but out of courtesy, the receptionist knocked anyway. She said, "Mr. Adams is here to see you, Chief." Then she smiled and drifted away.

"Come in, Mr. Adams. Come in, and close the door. Have a seat." (He pointed at the left overstuffed, brown leather chair in front of his desk. Its twin was on the right.)

Barlow sat, Stetson in hand wondering what this was about.

"I remember meeting you the day Judge Fenwick swore in the latest DEA Task Force. Actually, I noticed your partner, Slick Oldman - That's his name isn't it? - too. I thought to myself that you both look exactly like what you are - Texas lawmen from yesteryear. Cut out from the same bolt of cloth. Same sweeping mustaches, western garb, confident demeanor, icy cold blue eyes. At ease in your environment. Refreshing. There's too many lawmen these days who're all hat and no cattle. Now I know for certain I was right on the money after that little fracas 0-Dark-30 Wednesday morning.

"I read the after action report in its entirety. You and your partner killed all four suspects. In fact, all seven of your shots were fatal. Slick's were, too. We haven't seen anything like that here in El Paso for 50 years I bet.

"Pardon me. Would you like a cup of coffee? I failed to ask."

"No, thank you, Sir. I'm fine."

"Do you mind if I call you Barlow? Feel free to call me Chief. Everyone else does."

"I don't mind at all. Everyone else does to me, too." [Making a little joke about it. Barlow was beginning to relax.]

The chief smiled at Barlow's chutzpah.

He continued. "I read the short bios DEA had on all nine of you task force fellows (and woman), being that we were going to give you all special deputy commissions, good for an entire year. Everyone on the list looked more than worthy. Then yesterday, I did a deep dive on you. I called Sheriff Pratt and asked him to tell me as much as he could about you. He didn't even have to open a file. He rattled everything off from the top of his head. He even knew your birthday and that of your wife, Sarah, too. I could hear it in his voice. That man loves you like a son. That's a relationship I'm sure you cherish.

"He told me every little detail about you. It's impressive for a feller as young as you.

"Let me get straight to the point. Barlow, I have a vacancy for a new-hire deputy. I'm looking for someone who can track down fugitives without getting hisself killed. I think that could be you.

"Just so you know, a deputy marshal in the U.S. Marshals Service is a Civil Service employee.

"Contrast that with THE U.S. Marshal in each federal district, who's appointed by the President of the United States upon the recommendation of the two U.S. Senators from the state in which the district is located. As a rule of thumb, if the President is a Democrat, the Marshal is a Democrat.

"Once appointed, the Marshal serves at the pleasure of the

President. That usually means when the President leaves office, the Marshal leaves office. The new President appoints the new Marshal. Essentially, the U.S. Marshal is a figurehead, just like the King of England. He doesn't rule his empire, but you'd have to have rocks in your head not to respect him or to piss him off. For goodness sakes, the Marshal is a powerful person! He's got clout. However, most of the time he's a businessman, not a lawman. He seldom knows shit from shinola as it relates to law enforcement, although generally speaking he is an advocate, a big fan, so to speak. Understand?"

"I do."

"Now that's a fucked up way to run a railroad and the government knows it. So the way they fixed it, is by putting everyone in the Marshals Service who is not a Presidential appointee under the purview of the Civil Service Commission. That means job security. They can't run you off because a new President was just elected. That's huge. The only way you can get fired is for cause. That's the way it should be, too.

"Each federal district has a Chief Deputy Marshal, and he runs the outfit in that district. He keeps the Marshal apprised of things. Doesn't try to run roughshod over him. Just the opposite. In the U.S. District of Western Texas, right where you're sitting, that person is me. We have 19 sworn personnel in the Western District with a vacancy for one more.

"It's a merit job. You get hired and promoted through the various ranks, via the Civil Service regulations. You work your way up the ladder. Not everyone wants to be a chief deputy because it's like being a chief of police. You're a fucking administrator, a bean counter. A reader and writer. Not a fucker and fighter. The only real perk as I see it, is you make more money. If you like arresting assholes, I suggest you stay in the non-supervisory ranks. Sometimes I wish I would have. More fun. Understand?"

"I do."

"Deputy marshals do not make as much money as special agents in the FBI or ATF or DEA or any of the other alphabet agencies. Special agents are criminal investigators. Marshals are criminal catchers. Sometimes special agents think they're better than us because they make more money. They aren't, so do not get wrapped around the axle over it.

"Just ask yourself. Which is more fun - what Special Agent Carmine Valenzuela did on the task force these past few weeks and still ongoing, or what you did?

"I'm pretty sure I know the answer to that. Your talent is in tracking down criminals and arresting them - not doing all the tedious and grinding research to prove a violation of law. A lot of conducting a criminal investigation is pure grunt work. It's not all glamorous. Some of it is. You can make yourself blind poring through documents looking for incriminating information. Think about examining bank statements, or LD [long distance] toll records, or drafting affidavits for search warrants to look into your subject's underwear drawer for contraband.

"As a deputy marshal, you don't care about whether the case is strong enough to support a conviction. Maybe lose the case in trial. You've been in law enforcement long enough to know that a not guilty verdict doesn't mean the perp didn't do it or vice versa. Our judicial system is not perfect. All you care about is that an arrest warrant exists, either state or federal. It matters not a whit because you have jurisdiction over both.

"Usually we get called because a crook with an outstanding warrant cannot be located. He took a powder or flew the coup. He's an escapee, or a fugitive from justice, as it were. Get it? You get to do the fun part of the job. Find him and hook him up. Bring him in. Seldom does a deputy marshal have to testify in court, unless in the performance of his duty he had to tune up or shoot the fugitive. Everyone, no exceptions, has to account for himself when he's compelled to use physical force.

"The U.S. Marshals Service is the oldest law enforcement

agency in America. We have jurisdiction over all criminal laws in the United States and its territories, not just federal law. That's why we appointed you and the others on the task force as special deputies for one year. Boundaries don't matter to us unless it's international.

"Regarding pay and benefits, deputies start out as a GS-5, Step 1 on the Civil Service earnings scale. There are 18 grades (ranks), 1 through 18. The higher the grade, the higher your salary. Each grade level has 10 steps, or in-grades. It takes 16 years to go from Step 1 to Step 10 in the same GS level. The higher the step, the more you make, so seniority counts.

"There's overlap in earnings. A GS-5, Step 10, will make more money than a GS-6, Step 1. Also most years, Congress will award us a Cost of Living Allowance, otherwise known as a COLA. Usually it's only one or two percent. It's designed to maintain our wages level with inflation. It usually doesn't, but it beats a sharp stick in the eye.

"For 1974, a GS-5, Step 1 earns about $9,700 per annum. Earnings are paid in 26 equal biweekly installments; however, federal law enforcement officers qualify for what they call AUO. It stands for Administratively Uncontrollable Overtime. What that means is, you get a 25% bump in your salary, up to a GS-10, for working an average of 9 hours overtime each week. You verify this on the last day of each month on an AUO form. It's not hard to do.

"This means law enforcement officers earn 125% of the pay listed for their grade and step. Ergo, a GS-5, Step 1, deputy marshal earns about $12,000 per annum, instead of $9,700.

"Successfully complete your one-year probation (a requirement if you don't want to be terminated), and you get a two-grade bump to GS-7, Step 1. The following year you automatically get another two-grade bump to GS-9, Step 1. After that, it's all based on merit promotions. Nevertheless, if you never get promoted beyond a journeyman GS-9, you will still advance from Step 1 through Step 10 over the course of 16 years, receiving an increase in pay for each step, plus whatever COLAs Congress authorizes.

"We get paid by check every other Friday. We call it Federal Friday. We have great health insurance plans to choose from, and very affordable term life insurance benefits, of which the premiums for both are remitted via automatic payroll deductions. You don't even notice it. It works just like your deductions for federal income taxes, and state income taxes, where the state has an income tax. Thank goodness Texas doesn't.

"You are also highly encouraged to purchase U.S. Savings Bonds via payroll deduction. It benefits you while benefitting your nation. We kind of look at it here in this office as doing something patriotic. Right now all our employees are enrolled.

"If money is tight, just buy the $25 Series E Bonds. They cost $18.75, and fully mature to $25 in 5 years. They continue to earn even more interest if you decide to keep them longer.

"The way it works, they deduct $3.75 out of each paycheck for 5 pay periods until you've paid in $18.75. Then they mail you the bond. You can accrue five $25 bonds a year that way. Put them in your kids names if you like as sort of a college savings plan. Also, the bonds can be cashed six months after the purchase date (listed on the bond) if you really need the money; however, they don't accrue much in interest if you decide to do that.

"Another enormous perk is retirement benefits. Retirement as a federal law enforcement officer requires a minimum of 20 years of service and age 50 to be eligible. That'll get you 50% of the average of your top three years' salary. That includes your AUO! You get 2% additional for each year after 20, maxing out at 70%, which in essence, is 30 years of service. Your military service counts after you get the first 20 years. If you had two years of honorable military service, you'd get 54% instead of 50% at 20 years.

"You earn 13 days of sick leave per year throughout your career. Use it whenever you're sick. You also earn 13 days of annual leave per year for the first three years of employment. It goes up to 20 days a year from 3 to 15 years, and up to 26 days a year after 15 years of service.

"Before I forget to mention it, for those who are so inclined, we encourage service in either the National Guard or Reserves. Uncle Sam doesn't even dock your pay or annual leave while you're away those 15 days each year on annual training! In other words, you double dip during those two weeks. Understand, being in the reserves is not expected. It just isn't penalized if you choose to do it.

"About the job itself. Our duties in the USMS include courtroom security when federal court is in session. It also includes protection of the federal judges and magistrates as needed. For example, we get involved whenever someone threatens to kill the judge who sentenced him, or in fact, for any other reason. Believe it or not, that doesn't come up very often.

"Also, we transport federal prisoners to and from prisons, jails, court, and sometimes hospitals. We arrest fugitives, quell riots as ordered by the President, and we protect victims of civil rights violations, like that guy James Meredith at Ole Miss back in 1962. The latter two duties seldom ever arise. We do a bunch of other things I can't remember right now, simply because they hardly ever come up.

"Suffice it to say, the big three are courtroom security, transporting prisoners, and arresting fugitives, and you will do all three. I really want you for the fugitive work because we have so many in our district, but you will have to take your turn in the barrel on everything else just like we all do.

"The job is here in El Paso. You'd have to move at your own expense, but we have a few contacts, and can help you out. The main thing is, the Government does not pay for the initial move. If you got transferred in the future, say to accept a promotion, the

Government will help to defray most of your moving expenses. It doesn't cover everything. Know this, though. You would never have to move from El Paso unless you accepted a promotion to go somewhere else.

"I want you to go home and talk to your wife about it. I've got a packet here for you to take. It includes a Standard Form 171, which is the federal job application; a Standard Form 86 to get a Security Clearance; a sample of the employment examination questions, which the Civil Service will administer for us here in the building; a form for your physician to complete when he gives you a medical examination (at your own expense); a list of personal documents you'll need, including birth certificate, high school (and college diplomas) with transcripts; marriage licenses and divorce decrees if applicable; DD-214 for veterans; driver's license; waiver for the IRS to audit your last three years' income taxes; and God knows what all else - passport if you have one; brochures on the medical and life insurance policies available to you and your family; copy of the Civil Service Commission GS pay scale for 1974; History of the USMS; and most likely some other miscellaneous documents I failed to mention, like signing up for bonds.

"If you do come on board, you'll need to attend our training academy, which is eight weeks of general law enforcement training in Washington, DC, plus one week of training specific to the USMS. However, they're almost done building a new training facility in Brunswick, Georgia, someplace on the coast near Savannah, and that's where I think you'd be sent. The Marshals Service pays for all expenses, just like the Army.

"Any questions?"

"Gosh, my head's spinning. I didn't see this coming. I'm flabbergasted, and honored, and I don't know what to think. Also, I owe Sheriff Sol so much for hiring me in my current job. I don't want to be disloyal to him or let him down.

"My wife's never lived anywhere but Mosby, where her

family is. I'm not sure what she would think.

"At the same time, I do believe this would be right up my alley, like this is my big chance - a blessing from God that I didn't ask for. I'd definitely like to do it, but I need to talk to Sarah and Sheriff Sol first."

"That reminds me. Sheriff Sol said for you to go straight to the jail from here to meet him. He will wait, even if it's after normal COB [close of business]. Do not go home first. There's something very important to tell you, and he wants to do it in person. I told him I'd call him once you left, so he could anticipate your ETA [estimated time of arrival].

"Talk to your wife and in-laws about this. If you're interested, call me Sunday between noon and four. This is my home number. If you want to go for it, and I hope you do, come see me Monday and bring Sarah. We'll get you started. You'll need to spend one or two nights here. If you decide not, also let me know Sunday and I'll call my 2nd place candidate."

"Chief, if I got hired, when do you think I would start?"

"The process normally takes two or three months, but I'll push this through quick as I can. I'm pretty sure we could accomplish it before the end of July."

"Wow! That's fast."

"It is, but I need to get this ball rolling. You'll understand why if you decide to go for it. Whatever you decide, don't forget to call me Sunday."

"Oh, I won't. You can count on that. Once again, I'm honored you would even consider me. I'll call you Sunday. Adiós."

"Adiós."

Barlow made a quick stop at a Pure filling station on the way out of town to pee and refuel. Then he went to the McDonalds restaurant down the street. He bought a sack with a couple of burgers, fries, and a medium Coke. Then he boogied eastbound on US 90. He put the pedal to the metal, and didn't stop again until he arrived at the Quayle County Courthouse.

It was 5:30. He had driven 300 miles in 4-1/2 hours. The jail was empty except for Chunk, who was headed out the door on a call. Sheriff Sol was sitting in his office. He stood and walked over to Barlow and said, "Barlow, it's really good to see you again." He gave Barlow a brief hug, something he had never done before. Then he closed the door and sat down at his desk. Barlow sat in front of him in one of the wooden courtroom chairs on rollers, handed down to the SO when Judge Sweeney got some new ones.

Sheriff Sol asked, "How are you? You're looking pretty good for a guy who's just driven 300 miles, spent three weeks away from home, worked untold hours of overtime, and shot four scumbags in the performance of his duty. SAC Eaton called here to thank me for sending you and Slick. Sheriff Brady did, too. You made us all proud here."

"Well, I feel pretty good. Just a little tired and hot and sweaty. I'm glad to be back. I heard you needed to see me right away, so I came as fast as I could. Then I have something I need to run by you."

Sheriff Sol unlocked the bottom right door of his desk. He pulled out a fifth of Ezra Brooks 7-year-old Kentucky bourbon and a pair of whiskey sour glasses. He popped the cork and gave them both a generous pour. He held up his glass for a toast. Barlow clinked his glass, and Sheriff Sol said, "Here's to dear friends. May the sun always shine on them." He slammed his drink and poured another one, so Barlow slammed his and held his glass up for a refill.

Sheriff Sol said, "Barlow, I have some really awful news. I've known for three days now. The only soul I've told so far is Joanna. I'll swear you to secrecy until I tell everyone else on Monday. You can tell Sarah and her folks, but no one else, and only then if they agree to keep this to themselves. Promise?"

"Promise." Barlow had a sinking feeling in the pit of his stomach. Did Sol have cancer? What?

"I got called up to a locked-door Board of Supervisors

meeting. The county is on the verge of bankruptcy. As you probably know, the vote for a property tax increase failed again. Substantially more money is going out each month than is coming in. At the rate it's going, very soon the county will be unable to meet its obligations. Even if the tax increase passed today, as things stand right now, they still could not meet all their obligations.

"Part of the problem is we're losing taxpayers like never before. The sheep ranchers like your in-laws, Arthur and Clarice, two of my most precious and lifelong friends, can't make ends meet. Nobody's buying the wool, and mutton is not a highly sought-after meat in the U.S. You know that. Five years ago, Arthur ran over 3,000 head of sheep. Now he's down to 1,600. He said next year he'll be down to 1,000. Arthur is concerned that Cordell will need to find another occupation soon.

Judge Sweeney's reducing also. All of the ranchers are. Many have already packed it in, and sold out or defaulted on their loans. The cattle business isn't faring a whole lot better. The result is that Quayle County is currently down to 2,100 residents, of which only 950 are taxpayers, and they expect to lose another 250 by the end of the year.

"So this is what the Board decided to do. The Works Department is being reduced to two employees. If that old fart Sarah is working for at the rodeo grounds doesn't die or retire, she'll be let go, too. Here at the Sheriff's Office, I have to reduce our staffing down to four deputies, Miss Loretta, and me. Not much hope it will ever return to what it has been, either.

"Ernie's already gone. I happen to know Chief is planning to retire next month. He could go out on a medical, but he has 31 years including his military service, so he's going out under the standard retirement. That means I have to cut three others, all by August 1st, and it has to go by last in, first out. That's Gillespie, you, and Kirk. Gillespie was not a problem. I knew her uncle would take her in a New York second. Kirk is from Alpine too, so I called Sheriff Waters and he's agreed to take them both. They just don't know it yet.

"That leaves you. Chief Enright over in El Paso called to ask me about you. Seems like he has an opening for you . . ."

Sheriff Sol's eyes watered up and a solitary tear lost its fight with gravity. He got choked up and said, "I had a feeling the cutbacks were coming. I prayed and prayed for a solution. This is God's answer regarding you. Take the appointment and go with my blessing. You're the first Quayle County lawman to ever get a federal officer's job."

Sol and Barlow finished off their second bourbons. Sol poured them a third. They sat back in their chairs looking at each other, compassion in their eyes. Both were overwhelmed with emotion. Barlow felt the same way as when he left for Vietnam. He never saw Grandma Bea again. He hoped it would be different with Sheriff Sol.

Finally they finished their drinks. They stood up at the same time.

Sol said, "As far as I'm concerned, you can have as many days off as you need until it's time to go, one way or the other. Just keep me in the loop. Give Sarah and her folks my best regards. Remember what I told you about secrecy."

"I will, Sheriff. Just one question. What about the three part-time deputies?"

"They don't know it yet, but now they're all full-time. It was a difference without distinction anyway. They all averaged well over 40 hours a week.

"Go home. Hug Sarah. Adiós."

"Adiós, Father." Barlow turned away quickly so Sheriff Sol would not see his tears, and walked out of the office.

"Adiós, Son. I'm really proud of you."

Barlow cut a chogie home. Sarah was waiting for him at the door. She asked. "What was so important that you had to go see Sheriff Sol? Momma has a big meal prepared for us. Do you want to change clothes and get cleaned up? You been drinking?"

"Not tonight, Sweetie. Get Happy and lock up. Yes, Sheriff Sol and I had a taste. I'm fine. I'll tell you everything after supper tonight."

Clarice had prepared a beef roast with roasted red potatoes, onions, carrots, and celery. They had tossed salads and biscuits with butter and plum jam. They all drank ice water. Dessert was a pecan pie and coffee. Barlow was famished. It all hit the spot. During supper, the conversation was cordial, with everyone talking about what they had been doing the past couple of weeks. The mundane conversation was mostly for Barlow's benefit.

After supper, Arthur asked if Barlow would like to join him out under the copse of live oaks in the backyard for a smoke and a little Old Grandad. Barlow said he would. The ladies cleaned up and put the dishes in the dishwasher. Then Clarice picked up a chilled bottle of Mondavi cabernet. Sarah brought the stemware.

When they were all gathered, enjoying their adult beverages, and Arthur had lit up a Chesterfield and Barlow was puffing away on his Maduro Punch cigar, he told them why Sheriff Sol called him in. Barlow said he was sworn to secrecy until Monday, but he was permitted to tell the three of them if they agreed to remain mum as well. They all had worried looks, but they readily assented.

Barlow said Sheriff Sol called him in because of a bad turn of events in Quayle County. He mentioned the ranchers having several tough years in a row with no relief in sight. He talked about the significant numbers of residents moving elsewhere, leaving a seriously depleted tax revenue base. He said the county would be bankrupt before the end of the year if they didn't make some serious cuts. He mentioned Chief Alex retiring, and Kirk, Gillespie, and him all losing their jobs by August 1st. He said Sarah would lose hers, too, unless her boss retired.

They all had looks of disbelief on their faces.

Before they began to comment, Barlow continued. He said that Sheriff Sol managed to get Gillespie and Kirk jobs on Brewster SO. Then he said, "I had something to tell Sheriff Sol also, but he already knew about it. He said it was a prayer answered that he had asked of God."

"I was summoned before the Chief Deputy U.S. Marshal in El Paso today, just before I left for home. His name is Wilbur Enright. He offered me a position as a deputy marshal in the Western District of Texas in El Paso, starting at $9,700 per annum, plus a 25% premium for unexpected overtime. It comes to about $12,000 a year. He has one opening and he wants me. The district is enormous, going from El Paso to Waco, and it includes Quayle County.

"Mostly the deputy marshals are responsible for federal courtroom security, transportation of federal prisoners from state-to-state, and capturing fugitives. He said he wanted me mostly for capturing fugitives, but I would still perform all the other duties too, just like everyone else.

"He gave me a packet of forms to fill out by Monday if I'm interested. I told him I had to talk to Sarah and Sheriff Sol first. I have until Sunday afternoon to tell him yes or no. As it turns out, Sheriff Sol already knew because Chief Enright called him.

"I'd have to attend nine weeks of training. Currently that's in Washington, DC, but they have almost finished building a new facility in Brunswick, Georgia, and that's where he thinks they would send me. He also said he thinks they can have me on board before the end of July.

"If I decide to take the job, he wants Sarah and me to come to his office on Monday. He said we'd probably need to stay over one night for sure, but probably two.

"That's it. What do you all think?"

Sarah jumped up and hugged him. She exclaimed, "Yes! Yes! Yes!"

Clarice had tears in her eyes. She said, "I'm already missing you two and the grandbabies you all haven't given me yet."

Arthur said, "I've been expecting the cutbacks in the county now for a long time. It's true. Clarice and I are barely making ends meet. You need to take the job, Barlow. I don't know what Cordell and Darla will do if things don't improve. Ditto for our three hands. We may have to sell out and move someplace else too, if the local economy doesn't turn around. I expect El Paso is as good as anywhere to live in West Texas."

Barlow said, "It's settled then. Can I use your phone? I need to make an LD call to El Paso."

He made the call. The arrangements were made for Sarah and him to meet the Chief at 0900 hours on Monday. Sarah and he would drive up Sunday afternoon and lodge at the Best Western at the government rate.

Barlow and Sarah had just turned the page to a new chapter in their life together.

Epilogue

GRANDMA'S PROPHETIC COUNSELING FOR THE FUTURE

May 27, 1965

It was 3:30 on a beautiful Thursday afternoon. School was finally over until autumn. Barlow ran to the house as soon as the school bus dropped him off. He opened the screen door to the kitchen and rushed inside, allowing the door to slam behind him. He tossed the spiral school notebook he used for homework on the kitchen table. Outta school, outta mind. He saw that Grandma Bea was leaning over the sink peeling potatoes for tonight's supper.

She exclaimed, "What's got over you, Barlow? You know better than to let the screen door make all that racket! Then she turned around and lay the peeler on the countertop. She dried her hands on a towel and saw the ear-to-ear smile on his face. She tried to suppress her own smile when she noticed that he was holding his report card in his hand, offering it to her. "Well don't just stand there. Let me see it. Hurry up!"

He handed her the card. She opened it and studied, like it was her prepared income tax statement she had to sign before she mailed it in.

"Hmmm. As in English II and Social Studies. Bs in Biology and Latin II. C in Geometry! A in Deportment. Even though it doesn't help your GPA, it's what I expect from an Adams.

"Well, well! Barlow, I knew you could do it! 3.2 GPA for the year AND overall for both years. Very good! We'll have to celebrate after supper tonight with the cherry pie I just baked, topped off with chocolate chip ice cream for dessert.

"What courses are you you taking next year?"

"English III, Chemistry, American History, Algebra II, and Automotive Science for my Industrial Arts requirement. They used to call it Shop."

"I see. Nothing too difficult for you, I imagine."

"Nope."

She poured herself a cup of coffee in the WTSU Buffaloes mug Chloe, Barlow's older sister, gave her for Christmas years ago, and sat down at her place at the small, wooden, kitchen table. Today it had a yellow and white checked tablecloth. She said, "Get yourself a Pepsi and sit down. Let's talk."

Soft drinks were usually only consumed one a day max, and only then after mowing the grass, or chopping wood, digging a garden, or some other physical, sweat-producing labor. Exercising your brain like studying geometry did not count. He pulled a 10-ounce Pepsi from the fridge, popped the cap, and plopped down in his chair, wondering what she had on her mind.

She said, "Barlow, you only have two more years before you graduate. What do you plan to do then? You'll be a full-grown man, making all your own decisions."

"Not sure yet."

"Well tell me what you want to do with your life. What kind of job would you like to have? What kind of employment would make you happiest? If you love your job it won't be work. It'll be fun. Give me your top three choices, honey."

"Well, I've always wanted to be a cowboy. Maybe be an engineer on a train. Or . . . if I got really lucky, be a U.S. Marshal like Matt Dillon [protagonist in the *Gunsmoke* television series]. Ride horses. Catch bad guys. Enforce the law."

"Okay. Very good. Shows some imagination. Let's examine these three career fields carefully.

"A cowboy makes very little money. You should know that. Lives in a bunkhouse with the other cowboys, which is provided by the rancher he works for. Usually doesn't own anything except his saddle and tack, and maybe a six-shooter or rifle.

Probably fit all his extra clothes in his saddlebags. Couldn't afford to feed himself. Eats grub provided to him by his boss and prepared by the chuck wagon cook, who makes more money than he does. Can never get married or have any kids because he couldn't support them. Heck! He can barely support himself! Body usually all wore out by the time he's 40. Wind up in his old age mopping floors for the schoolhouse to make a little change, or shoveling manure out of some rich man's barn. Body be so stoved up he can hardly walk. Sit in a broke-down kitchen chair out on the verandah of some old folks home drooling tobacco juice down his overalls, thinking about the young lass he never married because he was a broke cowboy and couldn't afford to. Wonder if he made the right career choice.

"What I think you really mean is, you'd like to be a rancher. Own the cattle and employ the cowboys. Ride the best stallion. The only problem is, you have to have the acreage to feed enough cattle to make a living at it. Land is expensive. You gotta have the land first. Our family doesn't own even ten acres. Where would you get the money to buy the land? I just don't see this as a viable option unless you marry a rich woman who owns a lot of land. Then she would be your master and that would never work.

"So let's look at option two, being a railroad engineer. That's definitely feasible. The Santa Fe Railway, used to be called the Atchison, Topeka, and Santa Fe, is a big operation. Employs a lotta folks here in Texas. Pays well, too. You could probably get on. Have to start out as a brakeman first. Work your way up. Possibly even make engineer or conductor. You could do that.

"Railroad men are gone a lot. Wives usually prefer for their man to be home a little more than railroad men are, but the money's good and nearly everyone who works for the railroad loves his job. So, if the wife really loves her man and can take care of herself and the kids while her man is away, it's a very comfortable lifestyle. You could probably do that so long as you marry the right woman.

"I realize you ain't thinking about getting married now, but one day you will. Pick a good woman no matter what line of work you do, or you'll have sorrow your entire married life, and maybe even after if you wind up in divorce court and some sorry deadbeat is shacked up with your ex-wife in the house you paid for, and mistreats your kids and kicks your dog every time he walks in the front door, all while you're paying alimony and support.

"Next, we have U.S. Marshal, like Matt Dillon. That's a very noble calling to be a lawman, like being a preacher, or a schoolteacher, or a doctor. Notice I didn't say lawyer or banker. Your daddy was a military policeman when he was in the Army. You know that. He talked about it all the time. That's a little like being a deputy U.S. Marshal, except for in the Army, not in the civilian world. I'm pretty sure the real deal makes a whole lot more money than your daddy did in the Army.

"No doubt, it's a pretty hard job to get. Probably have to start out as a local cop or deputy sheriff somewhere. Not a thing wrong with that. The pay is usually not as good as a federal marshal, but you can always work yourself up the ladder if you try hard. Maybe make detective if you'd rather solve crimes than chase criminals. I think you'd be real good at either one. I'd recommend you keep this dream tucked away in your mind for further consideration, but with this one caveat. The Matt Dillons of today don't ride a horse when they're at work. They drive a car . . . ."

"I know that, Grandma! I'm not a kid anymore. I just think it would be cool."

"Don't interrupt, Barlow. That's rude. You been taught better than that! I was just saying that being a marshal or any other type of lawman today doesn't mean you couldn't buy a horse and ride it as a hobby. That would be entirely up to you. Some people would prefer to play golf in their spare time, but only heaven knows why.

"There's one other option you didn't mention, but right now it doesn't look very viable. You could go from high school straight to college like your sister did, except I don't have the money to send you, and your Uncle Clive and Aunt Marilyn got their own kids to consider.

"I'm real proud of Chloe, but I don't understand what she's thinking. She selected English as her major. Fine. We all need to know how to read and write and speak English properly.

"What do you do with a degree in English besides hang your diploma on the wall? Write books? Conjure up TV advertisements? Work at a book store?

"How about teaching English in a schoolhouse? Wouldn't that be an easier job to find? The problem is, to teach you must have a teaching certificate. Chloe's not pursuing that route. She said teaching is the last thing she would ever want to do.

"Guess what else. Now she's got a beau she wants to marry. I'm sure he's a great guy. His name is Bert Kilgore. He's from Abilene. Just like Chloe, he also just completed his sophomore year. Maybe one day she'll bring him home so we can meet him. He's getting a degree in commerce. Someday he wants to be an insurance agent just like his daddy. Laudable goal, but there's a hitch.

"He's in Air Force ROTC. When he graduates, he'll get a commission as a 2nd Lieutenant. No telling where he'll be assigned. It could be anywhere. If they get married, she'll go where he goes unless it's Vietnam. Either way, it doesn't look like we'll see any more of her than we do already. I guess I'm just being selfish. I really miss her.

"The last thing I have to say is, do not borrow money to go to college. Listen hard to what I'm saying. You'll be paying it off, degree or no degree, for the next ten years soon as you're out of school. You do NOT want to start your adult life owing money to the government or some bank. Promise me now you won't ever do that."

"I promise, Grandma."

"Good. Now it's your turn to say your piece."

"The only thing I can say is I love you, Grandma. You've always been there for me. Once I get on my own and get a job, I'm gonna help take care of you. I may start out small, on the bottom rung of the ladder like you said, but I'll work hard and make something of myself. You'll see. I might wind up as an auto mechanic like Daddy and Uncle Clive. I know I could do that. Heck, I already do that and I'm good at it, plus I like working on cars. You'll be proud of me."

"Barlow, I love you too, and I'm as proud of you as I can be. If you want to be a mechanic, that's fine with me; however, don't do it because someone tells you to or because it's the easy way out. If you want to be a railroader or a lawman, then set your mind and get to it. Make yourself happy. That will make your old grandma happy, and if you choose well, it will make the future Mrs. Barlow Adams happy, too. Understood?"

"Understood."

Thus endeth the lesson.

Author's Other Titles

01-Making Mountains Out Of Molehills

It was 1969. Barlow Adams, age 20, was a recently discharged veteran. He was driving late at night on a lonely stretch of highway in the Trans-Pecos region of Texas. He stopped to render assistance to a motorist with a flat tire. What he stepped into was a vicious attempted rape. He rescued the victim, which catapulted him into a deputy sheriffs job.

02-When Dreams Come ~ True Sort of

The year is 1970. Barlow Adams is a young deputy sheriff in a rural county in the Trans-Pecos region of Texas. He's a rookie still learning the ropes. Up until now, his experience has been limited to working in the jail and performing routine patrol work that is anything but routine when bad men decide to exert themselves in furtherance of their wicked ways.

03-A Lethal Odyssey of Cat and Mouse

The year is 1971. Deputy Sheriff Barlow Adams and his fiancé, Sarah Baker, have just married. They've embarked on a motor trip through Texas to New Orleans for their honeymoon. An outlaw motorcycle biker that Barlow arrested and his cellmate have escaped from prison. They have the honeymoon agenda, and they're on a vendetta to murder both Barlow and Sarah, who are unaware of their imminent danger. Deputy Sheriff Archie Willis has been tasked with locating them to ensure their safety. It's a race against time.

04-Evil Lurks In The Darkness, Even When Strong Men Stand Watch

The year is 1972. Quayle County, located in the Trans-Pecos region of Texas, has seen an uptick of illegal alien smuggling from across the Rio Grande. The alien smugglers are determined and violent. The Border Patrol is overwhelmed with greater numbers of human trafficking cases in other areas, and therefore is unable to assist. So it is left up to the tiny Quayle County Sheriff's Office to protect the local citizenry and the illegal aliens by arresting the predatory alien smugglers.

05-Thicker Than Blood Murder, Hide & Go Seek Texas Style

The year is 1973. A four-man crew of stick-up artists has been on a rampage in South Texas along the Rio Grande corridor from El Paso to Laredo. One day they stick up the bank and liquor store in Mosby in Quayle County, killing one person and severely wounding another. Mosby is a small town in a large county, with only 3,000 souls and very little crime. Deputies Slick Oldman and Barlow Adams are tasked to locate and arrest the murderers.

06-Cleaning Out A Snake Pit, Before the Wheels Fall Off

It's 1974. Deputy Barlow Adams is on patrol in Quayle County, Texas, late at night. He initiates a traffic stop on a speeding truck. It screeches to a halt, and both occupants bail out, flourishing firearms. A gunfight ensues. One is killed and the other is wounded. A search of the truck reveals 60 kilograms of high-quality marijuana known as Oaxacan Highland Gold, or OHG for short. This leads to Deputy Slick Oldman and Barlow Adams being temporarily assigned to a DEA Task Force in El Paso. The stakes are high and the drug smugglers are deadly.

07-The Lawrence County Moonshine War - A Jack Rabbit Novel

This is a tale of a changeling shortly after these powers were bestowed upon him. Jack, who began life as a rabbit, fell asleep in arid West Texas shortly after wishing he had a home someplace else in a more temperate climate. When he awoke, he was a young man in a forest glen in such a place. He got exactly what he wished for! The problem was, he was wearing an Army uniform and he did not know his location. He didn't even know which century it was! Jack was suffering from a serious case of amnesia.

About The Author

Earl Snort is the nom de plumé of a retired law enforcement officer with 42 years' experience toting a badge and a gun. Before that he served in the armed forces. He and his wife have been married 52 years. They reside in the South. They have one son, also a law enforcement officer, and two grandchildren.

This is the author's seventh foray into writing fiction. After a lifetime of writing non-fiction to document investigations of true crime, he decided to try his hand at make believe. He hopes you enjoy the yarn.

May 2024